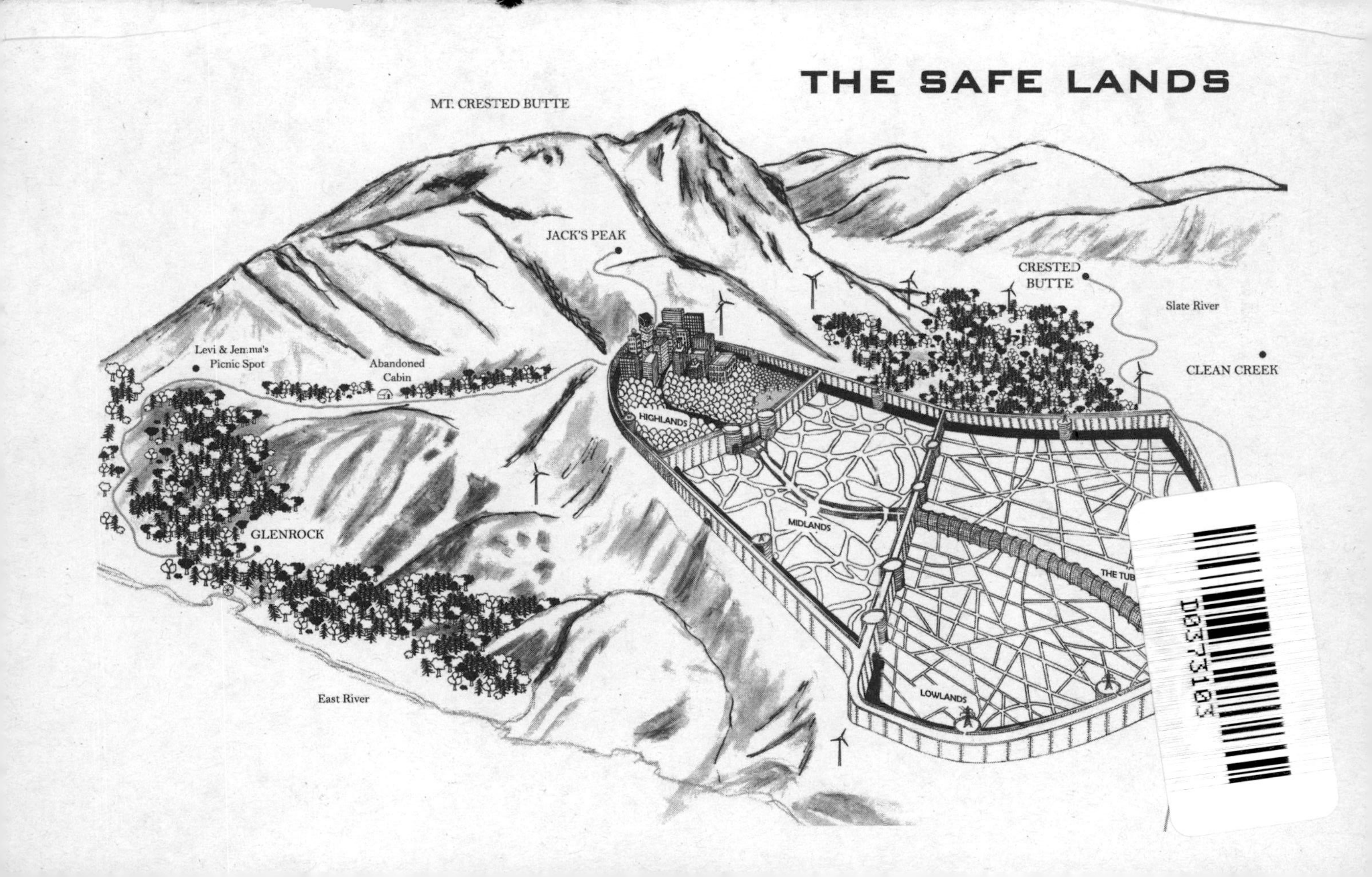
THE SAFE LANDS
MT. CRESTED BUTTE
JACK'S PEAK
CRESTED
BUTTE
Slate River
CLEAN CREEK
Levi & Jemma's
Picnic Spot
Abandoned
Cabin
HIGHLANDS
MIDLANDS
GLENROCK
THE TUB
LOWLANDS
East River

Other books by Jill Williamson

Replication

The Blood of Kings series

By Darkness Hid

To Darkness Fled

From Darkness Won

The Mission League series

The New Recruit

Chokepoint

CAPTIVES

BOOK ONE OF THE
SAFE LANDS SERIES

JILL WILLIAMSON

ZONDERVAN.com/
AUTHORTRACKER
follow your favorite authors

ZONDERVAN

Captives

This title is also available as a Zondervan ebook.
Visit www.zondervan.com/ebooks.

Requests for information should be addressed to:

Zondervan, *Grand Rapids, Michigan 49530*

ISBN 978-0-310-72422-3

The author is represented by MacGregor Literary, Inc. of Hillsboro, OR.

Cover design: Sammy Yuen
Cover photos: Building © Getty Images; Model photo © Sammy Yuen
Interior design and composition: Greg Johnson/Textbook Perfect

Printed in the United States of America

13 14 15 16 17 18 19 /DCI/ 20 19 18 17 16 15 14 13 12 11 10 9 8 7 6 5 4 3 2 1

King Nebuchadnezzar of Babylon declared war on Jerusalem and besieged the city. The king told Ashpenaz, head of the palace staff, to get some Israelites from the royal family and nobility — young men who were healthy and handsome, intelligent and well-educated, good prospects for leadership positions in the government, perfect specimens!

— Daniel 1:1, 3 – 5, *The Message*

PROLOGUE

MAY 2088

They're ready for you, Miss Rourke."

Ciddah looked up at the enforcer and took a deep breath. She hugged her CompuChart and stood from her seat on the bench, wobbling on her stilettos. The enforcer pulled open the door, a yawning maw that expelled a breath of frigid air into the warm hallway.

She tottered toward the entrance but stopped on the threshold.

The auditorium loomed before her, a vast and silent cube. She'd seen it on the ColorCast before: a purple concrete floor; a field of orange velvet bucket seats; walls painted in gradient: lime green at the bottom to black at the top. A spider's web of pin lights hung under the vast ceiling. Though the room had seemed vibrant and cheerful when she'd seen it on her Wyndo, in person everything seemed almost dull and cold.

Three tables on raised platforms stretched along the front and side walls and were covered in lime-green tablecloths. The hooded Ancients of the Safe Lands Guild sat behind each the tables, six to each wall — their eyes fixed on her like predatory creatures.

"Miss Rourke?"

Ciddah spun to face the enforcer, who was holding the door

partially open. No; he was trying to close it, and she was standing in the way.

She stumbled forward, and the enforcer shut her inside. Another deep breath, and she started down the center aisle, each step a sharp crack that echoed through the vast chamber as she made her way toward the witness podium in front.

"The Director of Medical Care's Public Health Report has changed little since our discussion six months ago when this guild approved the requisition of Miss Kendall Collin from Wyoming. We still face a lack of healthy children born within our walls."

Lawten's familiar voice was somewhat comforting, and Ciddah searched for him on the platform. He sat in the center of the front table. His face — the only one uncovered — looked small among the hooded Ancients.

"Then present your case, Mr. Task Director," a grizzled voice said from the left wall, "and we will determine a course of action."

"I call Ciddah Rourke to the witness podium to give her report on the status of Miss Collin's pregnancy." Lawten turned his calculating gaze down to Ciddah as if to remind her, *Just like we practiced.*

Ciddah reached the "podium," a short platform that sat in front of the head table. She climbed three steps to the top and sat in the chair facing Lawten, relieved not to have fallen on her face.

The air-conditioning being pumped in was meant to compensate for several hundred bodies, not the nineteen now present, and Ciddah shivered. It didn't help that her blouse had a low back and capped sleeves, or that she was about to testify before so many faceless Ancients.

"Miss Rourke," Lawten said, "please inform the Guild how Miss Collin is doing. Take your time."

Ciddah didn't need long. There was little to say. Still, she took a deep breath to calm her sparking nerves. "Kendall and her unborn baby are both infected."

Everyone seemed to speak at once. "What do you mean?" "Surely not!" "How could this have happened?" "Where did we go wrong?"

Lawten struck the gavel against the sound block. "Please hold your questions until Miss Rourke is able to complete her report." He looked down to Ciddah. "Continue, Miss Rourke."

She focused on Lawten's face, as if speaking to him alone. "The goal with this transfer was to discover whether we could match an infected donor male with an uninfected female. As you know, it seemed successful at first. But the virus appeared in Miss Collin in the twenty-first week of her pregnancy. We still held out hope for the baby, but in week thirty-five, just last week, tests showed the fetus is now carrying the virus as well."

"Is there any chance that once the child is born ...?" a hooded Ancient asked her.

"I cannot imagine that the virus will disappear, sir."

"What's to be done, then?" the Ancient asked. "Is there no way to irradicate this virus from our populace?"

"I cannot speak to cures, sir, as that is not my area of expertise," Ciddah said. "But if you want to produce a healthy child, it seems you must have two healthy donors."

A stunned pause. "But there are none!"

"There are the Naturals," another said.

"A myth!"

"Naturals are no myth."

"If they are real, how do they continually hide from enforcers?"

"They're no use to us if we cannot find them."

Ciddah sat back and waited as the faceless men argued.

"Forget the Naturals. We should trade for more people from Wyoming. How much will that cost us?"

"Kendall Collin was worth more credits than we all make in a year."

"What a waste."

"We might be able to afford a half dozen more uninfected trades from Wyoming, but will six to eighteen children a year, if Fortune favors us, be enough to save our land? And what after that? How will we ensure these people remain uninfected? That they serve more than one successful term as conscripted surrogates?"

"Kendall Collin received status as a national, a citizen of our land. In the future, we shouldn't allow outsiders to fully integrate into our world."

"We cannot imprison innocent people. And Fortune would not favor us if we did. We are not barbarians."

"Hang Fortune! She has not favored us either way."

"We *must* provide national status to outsider women. The public will be watching."

"Agreed. The publicity of our 'queens' through the ColorCast is too important to morale in the Safe Lands."

"No one need know what happen to the queens postpartum."

"Too dangerous. We need our past queens long after a successful delivery. They are the faces of the future."

"Some future."

"I have another suggestion, gentlemen," Lawten said.

All heads turned to the task director general. Good. Lawten would add some reason to this senseless debate.

"One of our enforcer patrols happened upon an outsider a few weeks back." Lawten's clear voice echoed around the room. "A young male, clearly uninfected. After some discussions, we learned it had always been this outsider's desire to come inside our fair city, and so the enforcers brought him to Otley, who brought him to me."

"Now we have a male donor and no females?" an Ancient asked. "So we attempt another trade with Wyoming and hope that the next girl remains healthy?"

"Hear me out, sir," Lawten said. "I am suggesting something on a grander scale. Enticement. Recruitment. Enrollment."

"I'm not following you, Mr. Task Director."

"We visit this young man's village and encourage his people to relocate."

The Ancient's brow lowered. "A large number of outsiders in the Safe Lands?"

"If they haven't wanted to live here for the past eighty-some years, why would they now?" another added.

"Why give them a choice?" Lawten said, as if just coming up with the idea.

Ciddah's breath caught. How could Lawten suggest such a thing?

"This Guild will not lock innocent people in cages, Mr. Task Director," an Ancient said.

"Please, hear me out," Lawten said. "This young man had been told lies about our people and our way of life. Once he saw our city with his own eyes, he wanted to live here more than anything. And he believes that, once his people visit, they will too."

A thoughtful pause. "So you propose bringing people here, possibly against their will, in order to show them what they really desire?"

"In a way. And I truly believe the outsiders will enjoy living here in time. We only need to require the men to donate for a month or two," Lawten said. "That would give us enough uninfected samples to last for years. With the procedure, of course, the women will have to make greater sacrifices."

"Spoken like a man." This was the first female voice to come from the Ancients.

"I cannot help the facts of biology, madam," Lawten said. "But this sacrifice also means the women will become queens, with the adoration of the Safe Lands heaped upon them. Their surrogacy terms will be filled with luxury."

Ciddah had heard Lawten's ambition before and never cared for it, but here, now, she found his words terrifying. How could she have trusted such a man? How could anyone?

"There are at least three villages in the surrounding area — Jack's Peak, Glenrock, and Clean Creek," an Ancient said. "Maybe more. In the very shadow of our city. That could provide hundreds of surrogates. An entire new generation of uninfected."

Ciddah's hopes flared at the very idea. If they could convince the people to come willingly...

"And what's to ensure they remain uninfected?" an Ancient asked.

"Fortune's numbers. We add a zero, then create a law that only zero can match with zero."

"We can't add a zero, and you know it."

"Yet we can't allow the uninfected the freedom to become infected," another Ancient said. "And we'd still have to number the outsiders to avoid consanguinity."

This train of dialogue confused Ciddah. Were Fortune's numbers based on something other than which life a person was currently living? On DNA? She'd have to investigate this possibility.

"If we would simply remove the stimulant from the ACT treatment each person receives, we would go a long way toward managing this virus and living longer lives."

Another shock. There was stimulant in the treatment? Ciddah's mind grew dizzy with this new information.

"That is not a real option, and you know it. The virus would still exist. And no one wants to grow old," a very Ancient voice said. "Our people want youth, to enjoy this life as much as possible before going on to the next."

No one spoke for a moment. Ciddah was sure they could all hear her heart pounding.

Then the Ancient on Lawten's left spoke. "We will try it your way, Mr. Task Director. Take your troops to one village. *One.* Present the benefits of relocation. And should these people take arms against us, or simply refuse to come, you are to leave. Arm your enforcers with sleepers only. These people are not Safe Landers and, until they are inside our walls, owe no allegiance to our enforcers. Bring back those willing to consider relocation and no one else. If this mission is a success, then perhaps we can approach the other villages in the area."

The group seemed to consider the proposal.

"May I speak?" a familiar voice asked.

Ciddah spun to her right. At the very end of the table, sitting in the back corner, was General Otley. Ciddah had forgotten that there were two guild members under age forty who were allowed to show their faces: the task director general and the enforcer general.

Lawten nodded. "Go ahead, General Otley."

"Outsiders are aggressive," Otley said. "Permission to take dual-action pistols as well? I hope to avoid such force and bring the outsiders in quietly, but sleeper downtime can take as long as two and a half minutes between shots. One outsider can take out a lot of enforcers in that time. I need a way to protect my men in case the worst happens."

Lawten pursed his lips. "Very well. As long as your men understand the goal, General Otley. Uninfected people do us no good if they're dead."

"Understood, sir."

"Thank you for your time, Miss Rourke," Lawten said, looking down on Ciddah. "You are directed to keep this meeting to yourself. If we learn that this discussion has leaked, the consequence will be premature liberation. Is that understood?"

This time the dizziness overwhelmed Ciddah, and she clutched the sides of her chair to keep from falling out. Now Lawten was threatening her? "Yes, Mr. Task Director."

"We look forward to a time when you bring us good news," Lawten said.

"As do I."

"You are dismissed."

Ciddah left the podium and walked across the auditorium, feeling as though all eighteen Guild members were watching her go. Her legs felt rubbery, and she fought to contain her composure at least until she exited the auditorium.

Once the doors shut behind her, she found the nearby bench and collapsed, puzzling over all she'd heard from the leaders of her nation … and Lawten's coldness.

Stimulant in the ACT treatments? Fortune's numbers assigned for genetic purposes? She couldn't fathom any motivation behind such measures, but she'd look into the matter as soon as she was able. And this new attempt to find uninfected donors … only Fortune knew if the Safe Lands had a future. Ciddah could only hope the people of the outsider village would be open to change.

CHAPTER 1

June 2088

Father invaded Mason's bedroom like a hornet. He yanked the psychology textbook from Mason's hands and tossed it on the floor. "You hear me calling for Omar, boy? Stop wasting time, and go find your brother. And don't take all day doing it."

"Yes, sir." Avoiding eye contact, Mason jumped off his bed and darted into the dark hallway, heading for the front of the house. He had indeed heard his father bellowing Omar's name. But since it was Omar's name and not his own, Mason had made the logical assumption that the solicitation was not for him. But such logic had never been Father's companion.

Father's footsteps clomped behind him, and Mason walked faster, not wanting to become the focus of Father's anger. Three more steps to the door...

"Now that Levi's getting married, it's your turn."

That announcement stopped Mason completely. He turned around in the living room, glanced at his mother, who stood at the kitchen table, drying jars for canning, then looked at his father. "Me marry? Now? I'm only seventeen."

"Why wait?"

"Because there's no one I feel particularly drawn to in Glenrock *or* Jack's Peak."

"No matter," Father said. "I've made arrangements with Mia's mother."

Mason felt as if his father had slammed him into a brick wall. He glanced at his mother, but she turned her head back to the jars before he could make eye contact. "Father, there's no sense in my marrying Mia. I'd be more compatible with any other girl, in fact. We should exhaust all options before making such a rash pairing."

"Everyone else is too young."

"I can wait."

"Mia needs a husband. Her mother needs a son." Father shrugged. "No reason to wait."

"But she and I would be terrible together. We're not even friends."

"Focus on her pretty face." Father slapped Mason on the back and stepped toward the front door. "Now stop arguing, and go find your brother. I may have managed to marry him off as well, but it's no good if I can't find him. And I don't want to keep Elsu waiting. Need to leave now if I want to get to Jack's Peak in time."

Mason stared at the open door, listening to Father's footsteps pound across the porch, down the steps, and crunch across the rocky path that led to the village square. His cheeks burned with fury over the nonsense of Mia becoming his wife. "I don't want to marry Mia. I won't."

"Mason," his mother said, "you're smart enough to find a way to make this work."

"But she despises me. And from what I gather from the books Levi brought me, and from my observations here in Glenrock, marriage is difficult enough when the pair have strong affections for one another. I don't want a future of misery for myself or for Mia."

“It’s been two years since Mia’s mother lost her husband. This marriage will mend the hole in their family. They’ll have a man in their home again.”

He stared at her. “But Mother, I will never love Mia.” He couldn’t even force himself to like her.

“Since when has love ever been important to your father? He values strength. Show your strength by making this work.” Mother went back to drying the jars. “You’d best go find your brother before your father catches you dawdling.”

Mason pushed out the front door into the afternoon heat and crossed the porch in three steps. He jumped off the side and kept moving, the wild grass and flowers tickling his bare feet. Grazer’s claws scraped over the plank porch as the dog chased after him and was soon bounding alongside.

Mason leaned over to scratch behind Grazer’s ears. “Where’s Omar, huh, boy? Go fetch Omar.”

The dog panted and squinted his eyes, in no apparent hurry to lend assistance. Mason swallowed the tightness in his throat.

Mia? Really?

Glenrock consisted of a dozen log homes scattered in a forest of pine around the village square’s clearing. Their house faced the entrance road that ended at a roundabout in front of the square and meeting hall. On the distant road, Father was a mere puff of dust as he headed up the mountain trail to meet Elsu.

Mason strode toward the hall, his gaze sweeping over the village, searching for the Old Colorado State Patrol hat his little brother, Omar, always wore. The sun lit the square and illuminated billions of dust motes. This was the time of day when everyone tried to remain indoors to keep cool, and Mason saw no one else besides his older brother Levi and Levi’s friend Jordan.

Both were sitting on their ATVs, which were parked in front of an elevated plank stage. Levi and Jemma's engagement celebration would happen tonight on this stage, and members of the village would sit on the long, split log benches that surrounded the area and cheer the future union. All hail perfect Levi and his perfect fiancée, the future elders of Glenrock.

Mason had no desire for perfection. *But ... Mia?*

He walked toward the stone fire pit at the center of the square and soon was close enough that he could hear Levi and Jordan mumbling. Mason wasn't surprised they didn't acknowledge him. Typical behavior for the heir to the patriarchy of Glenrock and his loyal adherent.

With a long breath, Mason entered the meeting hall, which was easily ten degrees cooler than outside. Jemma, Jordan's sister and Levi's intended, was decorating tables with wildflowers. Some of the younger boys were playing a scavenged Old video game on the television in the far corner. No sign of Omar.

"Hi, Mason." Jemma looked up from the flowers and smiled. "How are you today?"

"Fine. Looking for Omar." Unlike most people, when Jemma asked, "How are you?" she truly wanted to know. But if Mason had answered truthfully, Jemma would insist on more information. And Mason had no time for Jemma's compassion today. "Have you seen him?"

"Not since the harvest field this morning," she said. "I hope you find him. Levi says your father might have made him a match."

"Yes, well, my father and Levi's enthusiasm in this matter only enforces my skepticism."

"*Mason.*" After staring at the centerpiece for a moment, Jemma pulled a mule's ear from her hand and threaded the flower into the arrangement. "You should be happy for Omar. Getting married would be wonderful for him."

"I'm not unhappy. I simply see no point in celebrating that which has not yet taken place."

Jemma practically sang her reply. "'You can nearly always enjoy things if you make up your mind firmly that you will.'"

Mason frowned, pondering her words. "That's not yours, is it?"

"*Anne of Green Gables*, one of my favorite Old books. And Anne is right. So go find Omar so you can celebrate."

Mason left without offering a reply and made his way back across the square to the stage. He suspected his brother would have many baffling encounters with his new bride. How women could find joy in the marriage of complete strangers, Mason would never understand.

The ATVs now sat empty. Levi and Jordan stood on opposite sides of the stage, throwing a little ball to one another so fast it passed through the air as a blur of red.

"Find Omar yet?" Levi asked, walking toward Mason and pitching the ball at Jordan.

Mason stopped in front of Levi. "I thought I'd check the square again, but the only ones out here are you two not helping me."

Jordan flung the ball, and it bounced off the side of Levi's head.

"Ow, you maggot!" Levi chased after the ball and tossed it back at Jordan, who was laughing so hard he barely managed to catch it before it hit the ground.

"Forget Omar. Let's take Mason instead." Jordan threw the ball over the stage.

Levi ducked, letting it fly past the side of the meeting hall. He slouched and sighed, hands on his hips the way Father did when he was disappointed. "Mason's not a good trade."

"I'm standing right here," Mason said.

Jordan ran around the stage. "No, listen. They're all about nature and healing up in Jack's Peak. They'd love Mason. Then I wouldn't have to worry about him messing with my wife."

"Jordan," Levi said. "I meant that Mason is too valuable to trade."

"I never imposed upon anyone's wife," Mason said. "And what happened last week had nothing to do with yours. Cody gave Mother, *a doctor*, permission to allow me, *her assistant*, to observe his wife's labor process for educational purposes."

"For edu — Well, you're never going to educate *my* wife, let alone observe her."

"Your comment is backward," Mason said. "And it was for *my* education, not — "

"*You're* backward."

"I won't belabor my point." Mason started to walk away. He might have to take his Father's abuse, but he didn't have to take it from Jordan.

"I don't even know what that means," Jordan yelled.

"Not surprising," Mason said.

As he stretched the distance between him and the square, Mason heard Jordan ask Levi, "Did he just insult me?"

Mason chuckled and whistled for Grazer, wondering where the dog had gone off to. Jordan wasn't the only man in Glenrock who disliked Mason training to be a doctor. The village doctor had always been a woman. Mason found their fears ridiculous and insulting. Some of the women went hunting, and no one treated them any differently.

He passed by Mia's house. The house that would become his if Father got his way. Women's clothing hung on the line in back. A flower garden ran along the side of the house, and bees buzzed softly as they drank nectar. Mason walked a little faster, entered the forest, and continued down the river path, scanning for his brother. Grazer returned to Mason's side, head down, sniffing the ground.

Mason and Grazer traversed all of Glenrock in their search for Omar, the dog nibbling grass at each stop. They passed by the waterwheel and the generator as it purred along. They searched the garden and greenhouse, doubled back to the smokehouses where Omar sometimes sketched from the rooftops, checked the kissing trees and the outhouses, cut through the woods and the graveyard, crossed the cattle field, and finally walked out of the village.

No Omar. And no clue to his whereabouts.

Instead of returning to the village, Mason headed west through the forest toward the compound. Grazer ran ahead, abandoning Mason to the aspens and pines. It was a two-mile hike to the field that separated the compound from the forest. Birdsong and the rustle of leaves encouraged Mason to take his time under the shaded trees.

Papa Eli, the patriarch of Glenrock and Mason's great grandfather, had forbidden the people to go near the compound that proclaimed itself the Safe Lands, telling everyone it was populated with people who would lead them astray. Despite the warnings, Mason and Omar had stood near the perimeter many times — Mason to forage plants for his mother's medicinal stock, Omar to sketch the compound's walls with his art tools.

Branches cracked to Mason's right. He froze until he spotted Grazer, a brown blur winding between the trees. He hoped the dog stayed clear of the medusaheads today. Mason had spent hours picking awns from Grazer's coat yesterday.

He thought back to what he'd been reading in the Old psychology book before Father had interrupted. According to the writer, the definition of family had been changing even in the year of 2006. The age of *first* marriage — as they called it, since divorce had been commonplace then — had been at an all-time high of 27.5 for men and 25.5 for women. Mason could not fathom how people could have waited so long. Didn't they need to marry young in order to keep their society running?

He was now about ten yards from the tree line. Beyond the shadowed branches, he could see the colorful expanse of wildflowers in the field.

Marriage and procreation were vital to the people of Glenrock, and while Mason saw no logic in waiting to marry until he reached 27.5 years, reaching at least twenty would offer him so much more knowledge and life experience. Why not wait another three years for that?

Waiting was a win-win situation. In three years, one or more of the younger girls would come of age. Why couldn't his father see the logic in —

A chorus of female screams broke the peace of the forest. Grazer sped away like a superhero from one of Omar's prized comic books. Mason's heart lurched. Was someone in trouble? Bear or cougar, perhaps? Mason followed the dog, praying whatever he was running toward was relatively harmless.

The moment he left the forest, the sun's heat struck him. He slowed to a stop and squinted across the clearing, following the ripple in the waist-high grass that marked Grazer's path. The dog was headed toward three girls who were running from ... some strange vehicle. It looked like a giant beetle made of black and blue glass, and it rocked and bounced over the waves of the field like a boat. What in all the lands?

The girls ran toward Mason. They were close enough now that he recognized the threesome as his cousins Nell and Penelope and their friend Shaylinn, Jordan and Jemma's little sister. The vehicle veered after the girls; it could have only come from the Safe Lands.

Mason sprinted, the thin flower stalks whipping his legs. Just as he reached the girls, they darted past, leaving Mason and the invader on a collision course if one of them didn't turn aside. Mason came to a jarring stop, took one long breath, then turned back toward the trees. He looked back to study the vehicle in hopes it would give the girls time to reach the forest.

Grazer bounced around the vehicle, barking as he circled in front of Mason and back to his adversary. The vehicle continued to plow forward, producing no sound beyond a soft whirr and the crunch of tires over the ground.

The girls stood off to the side of the trail's head, watching from behind a grove of aspen trees.

"Hurry, Mason!" Penelope yelled.

Again, Mason glanced behind him. The vehicle had stopped, and a uniformed man was climbing out the passenger side. Mason paused, but when he saw the man was wearing a gun belt, he sped up and ran into Grazer, who'd been threading around him again.

Mason lifted his knees, trying not to step on the dog. His legs tangled in the wildflowers, and he went down like a felled tree. The thick vegetation caught him like a blanket.

He took a few deep breaths, contemplating whether he should get up and run or remain in the grass. Was he hidden? His heartbeat slowed. Movement in the grasses to his left and Grazer's growl on his right made him tense. Mason squeezed his eyes shut, waiting, hoping, praying that the man did not see him.

"You Omar?" a voice asked from above.

Omar? Mason rolled over and looked up into the man's face. He was wearing a navy blue uniform, like the law enforcement officers of Old. A gray helmet covered his head, only exposing the features of his face. Mason noted the man's pale, cracked skin. *The plague!*

Mason held his breath, then remembered Papa Eli's warning that the plague was a bloodborne virus, not airborne, which made him suddenly aware of a scratch on his arm.

"I'm talking to you, shell! Are you Omar?"

The man's voice brought Mason back to his senses. His brother knew this man? He was about to say, "Yes," that he was Omar, to see what the man would say, or even ask what "shell" was supposed to mean, but someone else spoke first.

"That's not Omar. He's Mason," Shaylinn said.

Mason scrambled to his feet. Shaylinn and Penelope were standing a few yards away, clutching each other's hands. Nell still hid behind the aspen trees. He could hear her sobbing.

"Why are you looking for Omar?" Mason asked.

"Not your interest." The man walked back toward the vehicle.

Mason searched for something to say that might gain him more information. "He's my brother. Can I take him a message?"

The man grabbed the top of the vehicle and pulled himself up, standing on the side. "Nice effort, shell." He slid inside, and a black window whooshed down over the door opening, blocking any chance for further questions.

Mason stood with the girls, watching as the strange vehicle turned around and glided away. Grazer chased after it, but Mason whistled him back.

Omar had always loved sketching the compound walls, but apparently his fascination with the Safe Lands went deeper than Mason had realized. When had Omar connected with this person — or these people? What had their talks entailed? Mason found himself oddly jealous, wondering if Omar had been inside the walls and, if so, what he might have seen.

"I thought he was going to kill you!" Penelope said.

"We wanted to come back to you sooner," Shaylinn said, "but Nell tried to stop us."

"Penelope hit me!" Nell yelled from the tree line.

"Mason was trying to help us!" Penelope hollered back. "I wasn't going to let those guys shoot him."

"Like we could have stopped a gun," Shaylinn said.

"They're little guns," Penelope said. "They look like toys."

Shaylinn folded her arms. "My papa says all guns are for killing."

"Nobody was shooting at me," Mason said, hoping to end the argument.

"Why did he ask for Omar?" Shaylinn asked.

"I don't know," Mason said. "What were you all doing out here, anyway?"

"Following Omar," Penelope said. "He promised to draw us yesterday, then he changed his mind. When we asked again this morning and he said no, we followed him."

"And he was speaking with Safe Lands soldiers?" Mason asked. "Do you think that man was an enforcer?"

Penelope shrugged. "We lost Omar in the woods and were trying to find him in the field when that truck came out of nowhere and chased us."

"Why are you guys so mean to me?" Nell yelled, drawing Mason's gaze back to the trees.

Penelope rolled her eyes. "She can be so dramatic. We'd better go before she pretends to faint." She ran to Nell, who hugged her tightly.

Mason and Shaylinn followed. They reached the trailhead where Penelope and Nell were still locked in an embrace, Nell sobbing and gasping in hitches of air.

"Your cousins are strange sometimes," Shaylinn said to Mason.

"Are they?" Mason looked at Shaylinn. She was tall and thick, her torso like a tree trunk. She had the same dark brown eyes as Jordan and Jemma. "Don't all girls cry a lot?"

"Not me," Shaylinn said. "And I've even got a cut on my arm from when I fell."

An injury! Mason might be useless in an enforcer encounter, but at least he could use his medical training to help someone. "May I see?"

Shaylinn turned her back and pointed over her shoulder to her left tricep, where a piece of wood was imbedded in her skin.

"It's not a cut. You've got a sliver. Hold still."

It was a big one, so Mason pinched her arm to make the wood stand up, then used his thumbnail to scrape it free. "All done."

"That was fast," Shaylinn said, rubbing her arm. "Thanks."

"You're welcome."

Once Nell calmed down, the foursome started back toward the village. The girls, all in their early teens, were rarely seen apart and were often sillier than toddlers. Penelope led their pack, brave and careless, while Shaylinn followed in silent wonder and Nell in deplorable protest. The girls all wore loose, sleeveless dresses pieced together from rabbit skins and Old print fabrics — whatever the men had scavenged from the Old dilapidated cities or the women had made in the village. Mason wore the same cattail vest he wore every day with his summer deerskin pants that were shredded below the knee. No one wore shoes in the summer unless they were riding an ATV, which meant Mason didn't wear shoes often. The ethanol used for the scavenged ATVs took a great deal of effort to create, so riding privileges were only given to those who went out to hunt or gather supplies.

Mason's, Penelope's, and Nell's fathers were Justin, Colton, and Ethan, the three brothers of tribe Elias, the ruling family in the village. Like most of Elias, the three cousins looked alike with light brown hair, blue eyes, and pale skin that burned in the sun.

Mason studied Shaylinn as they walked. She had darker features and skin like her older sister, Jemma, but she was thick where Jemma was thin, flat where Jemma curved, and frizzy where Jemma had curls. Shaylinn was not unpleasant to look upon, though his father had already said he couldn't wait for another girl to grow up. Plus, Mason doubted Jordan would approve of Mason marrying his kid sister. Still, the idea lingered.

Mason jogged to catch up with Shaylinn. "Slivers can sometimes become infected, you know. If your arm is bothering you, I can take another look."

"It's fine."

Of course it was; Mason had gotten it all. He groped for something else to say. "So, your sister and my brother ... How's it going to feel to get Jemma out of your house?"

Shaylinn folded her arms. "I don't want things to change."

"Oh. I guess I'm not really looking forward to it either. With Levi gone, Omar and I will receive all of my father's attention."

"Is it hard to live with him?"

Mason shrugged. "I've learned ways to avoid his temper."

"He told me I was fat," Shaylinn said.

Mason didn't doubt it. "Father is rarely positive."

"Do *you* think I'm fat?"

Mason considered her question. "The word *fat* is relative. Compared to Penelope, some might consider you overweight. But if you stand beside my grandma Marian, you'd look quite thin."

Shaylinn's eyebrows — eyebrows that were thicker than Father's — sank low over her eyes, giving Mason the impression that he had said the wrong thing.

Penelope suddenly ran off the trail and into the forest. Grazer took off after her.

"Be careful of the berberis thorns!" Mason yelled. "She's going to hurt herself."

"She doesn't care," Shaylinn replied.

Nell stopped in the middle of the road. When Mason and Shaylinn reached her, she stepped between them and took Shaylinn's hand. "Penelope dared me, but I'm not racing."

They were almost back to the village now. Mason caught sight of Mia weaving a cattail hide on the table in back of her house. She was barefoot and wore an Old flower print dress that cinched at the waist, her body the definition of the hourglass shape. She *was* very pretty. Perhaps he should consider his knowledge of Mia's personality as tentative and maintain an open mind.

Considering the circumstances, it was only fair.

CHAPTER 2

That night, Mason again got lost in his Old psychology book. This time his mother found him.

"You're not even dressed?" she said, peeking into his room. "Everyone else is already in the meeting hall."

Mason shut his book and stood, hoping she didn't notice the reluctance he felt inside. "Sorry, Mother. I'll be right there."

He changed into what his mother considered his formal outfit — an Old black suit jacket over a woven cattail and red nylon shirt with his long deerskin pants — and left the house. He could hear the sound of chanting as he crossed the square.

"Elder Eli, bless my face.
Elder Eli, give me grace.
Elder Eli, teach me more.
Elder Eli gets the floor!"

Mason entered the hall. The smell of fresh bread filled the air. He stopped just inside the door and leaned against the wall, hoping he'd be allowed to remain outside the proceedings for at least a few more minutes.

The hall was warm and bright. The entire population of Glenrock — some four dozen people — sat at four long tables that were filled with platters of food and drink and Jemma's wildflowers. The head table stretched across the center of the longest wall, right in front of the hearth. The other three tables ran perpendicular to it.

Omar sat at the end of the head table, his State Patrol hat making him stand out. Mason never had found him earlier. Though he'd heard Father yelling once he'd returned from the trade with Elsu, furious that Omar had missed his chance to meet a girl from Jack's Peak. Mason had stayed in his room, as far from the conflict as possible.

The thought of conflict pulled Mason's gaze to Mia. She sat with her mother at the table on the far right. Mia was now wearing an Old red-and-black-print dress. Mia liked Old clothing, and Mason often wondered how the other women felt about Mia claiming so many that could be used for fabric.

Papa Eli stood, front and center, at the head table, wearing his cattail cape over his formal deerskins. A fire in the hearth behind him rimmed his body in orange fire glow. At ninety-two, he was still tall and spry. Wrinkles and age spots covered his face, and his hair was thick and white, but his gaze — green and sharp — flitted around the room like a bird seeking its next meal.

"My question is for my grandson Justin. Stand up, boy," Papa Eli said.

Since Grandpa Seth had died a few years back, Mason's father was next in line for patriarch of the village. As such, he sat to Papa Eli's right. Father pushed back his chair and stood. "Ask your question, Elder, and I will answer true."

Mason smiled at how Papa Eli could get Father to play along with the puzzles and songs of celebration festivities. He doubted Father would carry on such traditions once he was the patriarch.

"Riddle me this," Papa Eli said. "The more you take, the more you leave behind. What are they?"

"Pictures?" Father guessed immediately.

Papa Eli shook his head, a wide grin stretching the wrinkles across his cheeks.

Father took longer to come up with his second answer. "Smiles?"

"No, Justin, my boy," Papa Eli said. "When you *take* smiles, you keep them."

The people laughed, and Nell's squeal rose above the others. Father's face darkened a shade at his grandfather's chide, but he quickly said, "Omar's blunders?" and smiled at the words that poked fun at his youngest son.

The laughter dwindled into groans of pity for Omar, who sat staring at his plate. Mother's lips squeezed into a thin line. Father would no doubt hear her thoughts on that "joke" later.

"Three false answers must take his seat, and I will ask another." Papa Eli glanced around the room as Father sat down. His gaze settled on Mason. "Let's see if my great-grandson can fare better. Mason?"

Mason pushed off the wall and straightened his posture. "Ask your question, Elder, and I will answer true."

"The more you take, the more you leave behind. What are they?"

"Footsteps," Mason said, trying not to smile, which would only aggravate his father.

A handful of people responded with an "Ahh!" and the crowd applauded.

As the clapping died down, Mason overheard his father say, "Sissy word games won't put food on the table."

Papa Eli gripped Father's shoulder but smiled at Mason. "Right you are, Mason. And since you answered correctly, *you* have the floor."

Mason took that moment to walk to the head table and sit between Levi and Omar. He nudged his little brother. "You okay?"

Omar shrugged one shoulder. "Why wouldn't I be?" He picked up a roll from a basket and ripped it in half.

"Mason, we're waiting. The floor is now yours," Papa Eli said.

Why had he answered correctly? Mason quickly stood and spat out the simplest riddle he could think of. "Wisdom of the aged, with the length of days. Elder of the line, what youngest is thine? Uhh ..." He searched the faces until he made eye contact with Jemma's father. "Harvey."

All heads turned to the far left table as Harvey stood. "The youngest in my line is Shaylinn," he said, setting his hand on Shaylinn's head.

"No!" Shaylinn, who was sitting beside her father, pointed across the table to where Jordan and his wife, Naomi, sat, their hands interlocked and resting on her belly, which was very large so late in her pregnancy. "Your youngest heir is there, Papa."

The crowd laughed.

"True as that may be, Shay, my youngest heir cannot yet speak for himself — "

"It's a girl!" Shanna, Shaylinn's mother, said.

" — or herself," Harvey added with a nod to his wife. "So the floor goes to you, my daughter."

Shaylinn stood and smoothed out her dress. "A wise old owl lived in an oak. The more he saw, the less he spoke. The less he spoke, the more he heard ... Omar, finish it." Shaylinn fell back into her chair and grinned at Omar.

An owl rhyme for the moody boy who was obsessed with owls. Mason admired Shaylinn for wanting to cheer Omar, and for the clever way she'd done it.

Omar set down his mutilated roll and said, his voice raspy as always, "Why can't we all be like that wise old bird?"

The crowd clapped.

Omar pushed off the tabletop as he stood. "My question is for my father."

And just like that, Omar threw away Shaylinn's gift. The room went silent. Mason lowered his gaze and held his breath.

"I already went," Father said. "Pick someone else."

Papa Eli slapped the tabletop. "Stand up, Justin. Your son has a question for you."

"Fine." Father pushed back his chair and stood, staring at Omar with raised brows. "Ask your question, boy." He didn't bother with the traditional reply.

Omar's neck and ears flushed pink. "Will you take me with you to Denver City?"

"No."

"But you promised I could go."

"Someday, yes. This time, no."

"But Levi went when he was only fourteen. I'm sixteen."

"As everyone in Glenrock knows, *you're* not Levi. My answer is final."

Omar sat down, leaving Father as the focus of everyone's attention. He cleared his throat. "Well, now that everyone is here, uh ... Before we start the engagement proceedings, I do have an announcement. Jennifer of James and I have made a match. My son Mason and her daughter Mia will marry."

Mason's heart slid into his stomach. He stared at the empty plate before him, unable to look at the table on the far right, unable to bear seeing Mia's face. A deep, silent breath, which Mason blew out in a short puff, helped him hold his tongue. How typical of Father to announce this publicly before Mason had even a chance to get used to the idea.

The crowd applauded politely; Nell didn't even squeal. Mason noted how different the reaction was compared to when Father had announced Levi and Jemma's engagement. This was what happened to the leftovers after the people who actually loved each other paired off.

"Will you serve as elder to this young couple?" Papa Eli asked Father.

"Jennifer will serve as their elder as I'm already mentoring Levi and Jemma."

A blessing, in Mason's opinion. He could only imagine what advice Father would give a soon-to-be husband who didn't hunt.

Jennifer added a chair between hers and Mia's. "Come, then, my son, and sit at my table."

Mason got up. Moved across the room. Offered those around him a tight smile in return for their warm ones. He would keep an open mind, focus on Mia's positive attributes, her looks. The chair beside Jennifer was only six yards away, but the journey felt like miles. He sat down. Again, everyone applauded. Polite. Obligatory.

Mia whispered in his ear. "Don't look so excited." And again she spoiled her beauty by speaking.

"I don't see you beaming with delight," Mason said.

"Because *I* had to settle. *I* wanted a hunter for a husband."

Mason ran his tongue along his bottom row of teeth to keep from saying something cruel. He settled on, "It's not too late to marry Omar."

"Omar is *not* a hunter. And he's always sniffling or rubbing his eyes like some dumb toddler."

"He's allergic to pollen."

Papa Eli's raised voice silenced any rebuttal from Mia. "And now let's focus on tonight's festivities. Levi of Elias, you have a request of the elders of Glenrock?"

"I do," Levi said.

"Then stand and make your request known."

Levi stood. "It is my wish to marry Jemma of Zachary two weeks from today."

Jordan wolf-whistled, which set off an infectious round of laughter and applause.

See? How could I do that? How could I stand before all of Glenrock and declare my intentions to marry Mia when I want no part of it?

"Jemma of Zachary, your favor has been petitioned," Papa Eli said. "Stand and tell this community how you respond."

Jemma pushed up from her seat and faced Papa Eli. "I accept the offer."

Nell squealed. More applause.

"Does anyone have reason to speak against this union?"

Levi glanced at Omar, and Mason prayed Omar would not say anything rude. But no one spoke. No one ever said anything during this part.

"What elder will speak for this couple?" Papa Eli asked. "Who has seen their commitment and helped to mold it by offering guidance and mentoring?"

Father stood up, shoulders back, proud. "I have."

Papa Eli looked around the room. "People of Glenrock, you have witnessed an offer of marriage, an acceptance, and an endorsement by a village elder. I hereby declare Levi of Elias and Jemma of Zachary engaged to be married in two weeks time. You are all invited to the celebration. Levi and Jemma, come before me to receive your blessing."

Levi stepped out from behind the high table and waited for Jemma. He took her hand, and they walked to stand before Papa Eli.

Papa Eli placed his hands on their heads. "May God be with you and bless you. May you see your children's children. May you be poor in misfortunes, rich in blessings. And may you know nothing but happiness from this day forward."

Yet another round of applause filled the meeting hall, but Mason's silent scream was a roar between his ears that drowned all other noise. He was happy for Levi and Jemma, sure. But he couldn't imagine that Papa Eli's beautiful words would come true in his own situation.

"Father God, we thank you for the fine company of family and friends and for the blessing of this feast. Amen," Papa Eli said then took his seat.

Jennifer passed Mason a platter of chicken. "I'm thankful to have a man in the family again. James has been gone two years. It's a comfort to know his line won't die with Mia."

Mason nodded, unable to manage a verbal response. He passed the platter to Mia without taking any meat.

"There's no way I'm becoming a vegetarian like you just because you can't stomach being a man," Mia said. "I don't suppose you'll even butcher a chicken."

Would every word from her lips be poison? It hadn't been a question, really, so Mason didn't answer. This might be the first day of his new life of self-imposed silence.

As people talked around them, the volume of his father's raised voice was a welcome distraction for the first time in his life. "I'm *not* taking him, Grandfather," Father said to Papa Eli. "He's a useless extra mouth to feed."

"No one is useless in this world if they lighten the burden of another," Papa Eli said.

"That's just it. Omar *is* the burden on a trip like this. He can't shoot. He can't follow simple instructions. He eats more than the rest of us combined and is too much of a weakling to help carry the haul. The boy only wants to come so he can look for owls or find more art materials for his sissy drawings."

"You'll have many days on the journey to teach him what you feel he lacks."

"Then you teach him. I'm *not* taking him anywhere until he proves he has a brain in that round head of his."

Omar jumped up and ran out of the hall.

"See! Off he runs to cry. Denver City is a trip for men of strength. And Omar has a long way to go."

Mason pushed back his chair and stood.

Mia grabbed his wrist. "Where do you think you're going?"

"To talk to Omar."

"You better come back. You're my dance partner."

"Mia, I don't dance."

"Of course you don't. Mason, everything about you embarrasses me." Her eyes were cold and angry.

"You may as well get used to it." Mason pulled free from Mia's grip and left.

He found Omar in his room, kneeling on the floor before one of his notepads, blackening the eyes of an owl with a charcoal pencil. He'd removed his Colorado State Patrol hat, and his hair was sticking up. Omar's artwork wallpapered his room. Mostly close-ups of animals or people. They made Mason feel like he was being stared at by a million eyes.

Omar ripped away the owl drawing and scraped the charcoal pencil over a fresh sheet again and again, creating the soft lines of a wing. "Go away, Mase. I'm fine."

"*I* wouldn't be."

Another owl materialized on the paper under Omar's skilled strokes, this one soaring. "He's said the same about you before."

"Naw. About me, he says, 'If it weren't for Mason's brain, he'd have no muscles in his body.' Or my personal favorite, 'Don't mind you talking so much, sissy boy, so long as you don't mind me not listening.' "

Omar tossed his shard of charcoal into a tray of pencils, ripped the page from the notebook, and crumpled it. "He never calls Levi a sissy."

"That's because Levi came out of the womb holding a rifle. In regards to Father, I refuse to engage in a battle of wits with an unarmed man. I suggest you do the same."

Omar snorted a laugh. "That's mad good, Mase."

Mason leaned against the doorframe and crossed his arms. "I met an enforcer today."

Omar's hand jerked, drawing a dark line across his sketch. "Oh?"

"Why would an enforcer be asking for you by name?"

Omar went back to shading in the owl's wings. "None of your business."

"So, when I inform Father, it will be none of his business either?" Mason asked.

Omar sighed. "I met them in Crested Butte when I was scavenging. It's not a big deal."

That only raised more questions. "Papa Eli might disagree."

Omar sat back and stared at the wall. "I bet I could find a girl in the Safe Lands."

The words brought a chill over Mason. "Don't say that, Omar. Don't even joke about it. You shouldn't be talking to those people at all."

"Have you really looked at what's inside those walls? From the mountain with my binoculars, I can see women. Lots of them. And lots of color. I bet they have fresh paints."

Was Omar seriously thinking about going into the Safe Lands? The place Papa Eli had almost died trying to get away from? "You know what Papa Eli says about that place. Why he left and came here. They're immoral there. They withhold water as punishment."

"Papa Eli is older than dirt."

"Hey, now. Papa Eli just stuck up for you in there."

Omar rubbed the scar on the bridge of his nose. "A lot of good it did. His *help* only made Father insult me in front of the whole village. They're probably all laughing."

"No one's laughing," Mason said. "Why do you want to go to Denver City, anyway?"

"I want to see what Levi describes. To draw the ruins. It doesn't matter though. Father hates me. Levi hates me. Jemma is marrying Levi. Mia is marrying *you*. Shaylinn is fat. Everyone else is my cousin or lives in Jack's Peak."

"Omar ..."

Omar pitched his wadded-up owl at Mason. "It's true! I should just move to Jack's Peak. Then everyone would be happy. Except I blew that too, because I missed meeting the girl Father found for me, and now she doesn't want me either. Even if she did, it would be worse up there. Jack's Peak men are all about killing animals with their bare hands. I'm no good at any of that."

"What do you want?"

"I don't know. To feel strong. Like I matter. Like someone cares."

Omar looked so small sitting on the floor with Mason standing over him. A child wanting to be loved. "*I* care."

Omar rolled his eyes. "I can't marry *you*."

"You really want a wife?"

Omar moved to his bed, lying on his back and staring at the drawing of a woman's face — a face that looked suspiciously like Jemma's. "If I don't find a wife, Father says I'll starve, since I'm such a bad shot. He wanted me to marry the Jack's Peak girl so *she* could hunt for the both of us. Plus, he's trying to get rid of me."

"Ignore him. And stop feeling sorry for yourself. I'd trade you Shaylinn for Mia if I could."

"Really?" Omar pushed himself to one elbow. "Why?"

"Because Shaylinn is kind. I'd take kind over thin or pretty any day. Haven't you noticed? Mia is just a female version of Father."

Omar sniffed in a long breath and rubbed his nose. "She's prettier than Father."

"Beauty only exists in perception."

Omar raised his eyebrows at Mason. "You don't think Mia is prettier than Shaylinn?"

Mason did, but he couldn't imagine living with Mia's cruelty. "Jemma once said, 'It's beauty that captures your attention, but it's personality that captures your heart.' She likely read it somewhere, but I think it validates my point."

Omar heaved a sigh. "Jemma."

"Don't start. Jemma belongs to Levi now, and you'd be wise to take down that drawing before he sees it."

"Just go away, Mase."

"Fine." Mason walked to the doorway and took one last glance at Omar, who'd closed his eyes as if he might go to sleep.

Mason left the cabin and sat on the porch, gazing out toward the square. People had left the hall and were now dancing to music being played by Elder Harvey and Uncle Ethan. A handful of older women stood in a circle around the dancers, laughing and singing.

"Do the twist, do the twirl,
every boy, grab your girl.
Twist and twirl, boy and girl,
whirl and whirl and whirl!"

Levi and Jemma were dancing on the stage. He didn't see Mia, but she was likely still cross about her first glimpse of what it would be like to marry Mason. Her husband would never dance and would often go into hiding.

Mason prayed Omar wouldn't do anything foolish, like run away to the Safe Lands or follow Father's group when they left for Denver City. Papa Eli might think that Omar and Father would be forced to bond if Omar went on the trip, yet Mason didn't think there could be anything worse than Omar and their father together for two whole weeks.

He was wrong.

CHAPTER 3

The view of the valley from where Levi had spread the picnic blanket at the bottom of the eastern bluffs of Mt. Crested Butte was one of the best in the valley near Glenrock, but Levi couldn't stop staring at Jemma. He'd gone to Denver City for only ten days, but being apart from her had felt like months.

"I don't like leaving you," he said.

The wind made strands of her hair dance around her face, and she brushed them aside. "I don't like you leaving."

"I brought you something." He reached over his rifle and under the edge of the blanket where he'd stashed the little box, and he handed it to Jemma.

She gave him a curious smile. He leaned forward as she opened it, eager to see her reaction.

She gasped and fingered the necklace of pink pearls. "I've never seen anything like it." She handed the necklace back to Levi and twisted her hair to one side.

Levi drew the strand of pearls around her neck and clasped them together, then he kissed the back of her neck and breathed her in.

"Levi." She giggled and dropped her hair back into place. "Where did you find it?"

He leaned his head over her right shoulder and spoke softly in her ear. "Denver City. I found wedding rings too, but you can't see those yet." He settled back beside her on the blanket and offered a coy smile.

"Oh, Levi! Wedding rings too?"

"I know few people wear them these days since we all know who is married to whom and rings are hard to come by, but I thought you'd like to."

"I'd love to." She reached her arms around his neck and hugged him. "I can't wait to marry you. Are you excited?"

He pulled her close. "You have no idea."

The sun hung low in the sky. From where they sat on their picnic blanket on the lower hills of Mt. Crested Butte, the whole valley lay before them. Green and brown mountains stood guard on all sides, the Slate River glimmered in the distance, but the bell-shaped walls that traced the outline of the Safe Lands scarred the beauty of this place. A concrete and barbed-wire reminder that all was not right in the world.

Jemma leaned against Levi, head tucked under his chin. "Tell me about Denver City."

"It's huge, Jem. Buildings sit side by side for miles, and in the center, they're five times as tall as the ones in the Safe Lands." He pointed to the cluster of buildings at the top of the bell in the distance. "When you stand in the middle of Denver City, you can see nothing but towering buildings, Old vehicles, streetlamps, traffic signals ... There are a few trees on each street, and patches of grass and saplings grow in cracks in the asphalt, but the ground is pretty much concrete for miles."

"*Traffic* and *asphalt* ... those words sound so odd. And I find it impressive that those tall buildings are still standing."

"They have deep foundations. And they're built of steel, not wood. Someday I'll lead my own scavenging expedition to Denver City, and I'll stay longer. So many houses have never been scavenged. The things we could use! Toys for the children. More gifts for you."

Jemma fingered the pink pearl necklace and beamed again.

Levi bumped his shoulder against hers. "I knew you'd like it. Found it in a store filled with jewelry. Father has enough treasure to trade for years."

"I can't begin to think how people made such things."

"Gold and silver are just metals people melted down and reshaped. And Mother once told me pearls came from the oceans. They grew inside the mouths of sea creatures."

"And people captured the creatures to steal the pearls from their lips?" Jemma bumped her shoulder back against Levi's. "It sounds like a children's story. Like the one with the tiny world that lived on a flower."

"*Horton Hears a Who!* I love that one. Oh, Jem! We found a bookstore too. Father only let me stop a few minutes, but I was able to grab some of the books with the horses on the— " A plume of dust rose like chimney smoke on the road, and Levi straightened. "Someone's coming." Jemma drew in a sharp breath as Levi grabbed the rifle and looked through the scope. "An ATV." He lowered the weapon and the tone of his voice. "Omar. And he's driving my rig."

Omar was supposed to be the village's lookout all morning. He better not have left the perch empty. When Levi needed Omar, the boy couldn't be found. But when Levi wanted to be alone, Omar was always the first to find him.

"I wondered what was taking him so long." Jemma smiled. "Our picnic is almost over."

Levi set down his rifle and groaned. "Why must he follow me everywhere?"

"I'm sure it's important if he's driving your cart."

"Omar invents trouble."

"He admires you. Perhaps you should encourage him in some way."

Levi looked to Jemma. "You think I'm cruel?"

She cocked one eyebrow. "I know you don't intend to be, but a sharp word from you sends Omar sulking like a chastened puppy."

"I just don't think he should look up to me the way he does."

"Why wouldn't he look up to you? You're his brother. And you're perfect."

If she only knew.

Jemma snuggled against Levi's side and took hold of his hand. "I feel badly about what happened with the Jack's Peak girl. Do you think she'll reconsider?"

"No." And if Levi had known which girl Elsu had been trying to marry off, he never would have gone along. The whole thing had been terribly awkward.

Jemma frowned and sent Levi a pleading look, as if he could force some girl to marry Omar. "But if she can find no husband among her own people, why refuse ours?"

Levi coughed on his own breath. *Because this girl only wants me.* "I don't know, love." He squinted down the valley. The trail of dust from the ATV was larger now. Omar was rounding the final switchback that led up to the ridge.

"Poor Omar," Jemma said. "He's not *that* awful, you know. I considered him once."

Levi's gaze jerked to meet hers. "Did you? When?"

"The day my mother said, 'You chose the best of the brothers, Jemma.' I thought it over, and I had to agree."

Levi chuckled. "And what about Mason? Did you consider him too?"

Jemma took Levi's other hand so that she was holding both. "I love your brothers well enough — as brothers. But I'm worried for Mason. Mia will rule him like an evil queen. They're a poor match, and his agreeing to marry her makes me question his sanity."

"And how was he to refuse after Father announced it to all of Glenrock? Mason will find a way to make it work. He's smart."

"Book smart. Have you seen him try and talk to girls? Information about poisonous mushrooms and rashes doesn't exactly warm a girl's heart."

Levi smirked at the idea of Mason showing Mia which mushrooms to avoid. "You're full of opinions on my brothers today, Jemma of Zachary. I'm not sure how to feel about this."

"Feel blessed to have found true love in a world with so little of it, *farm boy*."

"As you wish." He kissed her hand, and Jemma giggled.

Omar arrived then, stopping Levi's ATV with its attached cart three feet from the picnic blanket and sending a cloud of dust over Levi, Jemma, and what remained of their food. He was wearing Old jeans, his blue and yellow striped shirt, and his Old policeman hat. Without the hat, he didn't look all that different from Levi and Mason. Just younger.

Omar dismounted and walked toward their picnic blanket. "Hello, Jemma," he said, his voice airy as usual whenever he was in her presence.

Jemma offered him a sympathetic smile. "Hello."

Levi didn't budge from Jemma's side. "What are you doing here, Omar? Who's at the lookout?"

Omar wiped a hand under his nose, which never ceased to water. "Penelope took my place. A message came in from Beshup over in Jack's Peak. He has some ammo he thinks you'll want to see."

Ammo. How had Beshup come into such a trade, and why did he want to share it? Levi mumbled, "We *are* low on ammo. The Old stuff is more accurate than any we make ourselves." He glanced at Jemma. "Do you mind if I go?"

"Nonsense!" She reached up and ran her finger down his forehead. "Come see me when you get back?"

"Of course." He jumped up and helped Jemma stand. "But I don't want you going back alone. We'll drop you at the village, then Omar and I will go meet Beshup."

"That'll take too long," Omar said, sniffling.

"And we're closer to the cabin now," Jemma said.

"I can take her back on the motorcycle," Omar said. "You don't need me there to trade with Beshup. I'll just be in the way."

"A ride would be nice," Jemma said, nudging Levi's side. He could tell by the look on her face that she wanted him to be nice to Omar.

Levi sighed. "Give us a moment, Omar." He took Jemma's hand

and pulled her a few steps away from his brother. "I don't like sending you off with him. If by some chance you encounter a mountain lion or a bear, he's not the best shot and tends to panic in a crisis."

Jemma brushed Levi's hair out if his eyes with her free hand. "Our village needs ammunition. I'll be fine."

"Still ..." He threaded his fingers with hers and frowned. "I have a bad feeling."

She squeezed his hand. "You always have a bad feeling. Don't worry so much. I'll see you tonight at dinner."

He slid his hands around her waist and pulled her close. "Two more days."

Her gaze sank into his.

"This is true love, Jemma of Zachary," Levi said. "You think this happens every day?"

She smiled. "You're like a fairy-tale prince. We shall live happily ever after."

"Yes. Just like the prince. But I dress better."

She stepped back and took in his appearance. "I don't know. You might look nice in a doublet and tights." Before he could respond, Jemma stretched on her tiptoes and gave him a quick kiss. If Omar hadn't been staring, she would've been more generous.

Jemma quickly packed their picnic. Levi helped her fold the blanket, then roped it and the basket to the rack on the back of the motorcycle.

Levi walked to where Omar stood beside his ATV and they traded keys. "Drive *slowly.* And watch out for mountain lions."

"Don't worry, brother. I won't let anything happen to your precious Jem."

Jemma climbed on the back of the motorcycle behind Omar and wrapped her arms around his waist. Levi scowled at the smile that spread across his brother's face. Jemma gave him one last wave before Omar started the motorcycle and drove away.

Levi shook off his annoyance with his little brother and climbed onto his ATV. It was time to trade.

CHAPTER 4

Mason and his mother sat at the table, shucking the peas they'd picked that morning. Father sat in the living room, oiling his gun. It was early afternoon, the hottest time of the day, and a blessing to be indoors.

"It's been a good year for peas," Mother said. "I'd like to can at least one hundred pounds this year."

"You should have more than enough." Confident with his declaration, Mason hulled the next pod right into his mouth.

"Don't eat the harvest," Father said.

Because without that one pea pod, all of Glenrock would surely starve.

"Papa Eli!" Penelope's voice came from outside, distant and shrill.

Mason cocked his head at the sound then made eye contact with his mother as she stood and walked toward the door.

Her eyes were wide. "Something's wrong."

"Papa Eli!" Penelope's voice was nearer now.

"Sit. I'll get it." Father shooed Mother back and opened the door just as Penelope bounded up the steps.

Her cheeks were flushed, and the hair around her face was sweaty and sticking to her face. "Safe Landers are coming, Uncle Justin." She panted. "Three big trucks."

Father walked back to the sofa and picked up his gun. "Where's Omar? Why didn't he bring this news?"

"He asked me to watch the perch while he got a fresh sketch pad," Penelope said. "About a half hour ago."

"Mason, get your gun." Father walked back to the door.

"I'm not going to shoot any— "

"Now!"

"Yes, sir." Mason pushed back his chair and walked to the gun rack.

As he reached out to grab his rifle—the one that had accidently taken Joel's life—Father stepped in Mason's way and grabbed his shoulder, looking him in the eye. "I need you, son. Just stand beside me and look tough. You don't have to shoot."

Mason's deep breath filled his chest. He nodded and lifted the weapon down from the wall.

"Should I wake Papa Eli?" Mother asked.

"Let him sleep, Tamera. I can handle this," Father said as he loaded his and Mason's guns. "But round up the women and children and get them into the meeting hall just in case. If there is a threat, it might be easier to defend one location rather than the whole village. Penelope, fetch Harvey and Jordan. They should be down at the river. And if you see your dad or your uncle Ethan—any men you see—tell them to get their rifles and come to the square."

Penelope turned and fled. Mason followed his father out of the house and toward the village square. His heart was beating so hard he could hear it throbbing between his ears. His mother closed the door behind them and followed behind Mason.

"Omar never came for paper, did he?" Father asked.

"No, sir." Mason had no idea what his brother was up to, but it didn't look good.

"He'd better not be in the hall playing video games. I always said that thing was a waste on our generator."

Mason jogged to keep up with his father. A cluster of Glenrock men stood before the stage, guns in hand. There were maybe a dozen — about half the men in the village. Women and children scurried around the rest of the square, most headed to the hall.

"Where's Sophie?" Aunt Susan ran up to Mason. "Have you seen Sophie?"

"No, ma'am."

"Sophie!" Aunt Susan ran toward the outhouses.

"We got a man in the perch?" Father asked when they reached the square. "How far out are they?"

"Richard's up there." Uncle Colton lifted a handheld two-way radio to his mouth. "Colt to Rich Man, what's the ETA?"

The two-way radio emitted a string of static, then Elder Richard's voice. "Well, they're just getting to the forest now. My guess is you've got maybe five to ten minutes."

"Where's Levi?" Uncle Ethan asked as he walked toward the group.

"Went off to have lunch with Jemma somewhere," Father said.

"And Papa Eli?"

Father aimed his gun at the road and looked through the scope. "Taking a nap."

"I'll go wake him," Uncle Colton said.

Father lowered his gun and grabbed his brother's arm. "We can handle this without Grandpa, Colt. The worry will do him more harm. Let him sleep."

Mason disagreed. No one was calmer in the face of conflict that Papa Eli. And no one knew more about the Safe Lands either. Should he speak up? Run and fetch Papa Eli on his own? But he simply stood there, frozen, gun trembling in his hand.

Jordan sprinted into the square just ahead of his father and Penelope. "Enforcers?"

"Looks like," Uncle Colton said.

Jordan spun around. "Pen, go get my mother and Shay."

"I want to fight!" Penelope said.

"No one is fighting," Uncle Ethan said.

Mason adjusted the gun against his shoulder and hoped that was true.

"The house is right there, crowbait!" Jordan said, pointing to his family's cabin.

Penelope scowled at Jordan. "You don't have to call names!"

"Penelope!" Uncle Colton raised one eyebrow, and his daughter stomped toward the Zachary home.

Harvey came to stand beside Father. "How many men you think they've got?"

"Can't say," Uncle Colton said. "Richard said three trucks."

"Could be they're not coming to fight," Naomi's father, Sam, said.

"Seeing as we haven't seen them this close in years, we have no way of knowing. But they must want something," Uncle Ethan said.

Jordan looked off down the road. "Whatever they want, we can handle it."

"Two dozen against an army? How do you figure we'll handle that?" Uncle Ethan asked.

"One less than that," Sam said, eyeing Mason. "He ain't going to shoot."

Mason felt sick. *Please, God, protect us. Let there be peace.*

"Let's not jump to the worst-case scenario here," Uncle Colton said.

"We have to prepare for the worst," Father said. "Here's what we're going to do. Sam, take ten men and spread out on the east side. Ethan, you take ten west. Be my snipers. Harvey, you and Jordan get on the roofs and cover the square. Colton and Mason, stay with me. Go, go!"

As the men ran off, Shaylinn and her mother fled the Zachary home and ran toward the outhouses.

"Where you going?" Harvey called.

"Susan can't find Sophie," his wife said. "We're going to help look for her daughter."

"Well, be quick about it," Harvey said.

Penelope came out of the house and walked straight to her father's side. "I know how to shoot. Levi taught me."

"I don't care if Levi taught you to build a bomb." Uncle Colton pointed to the water spout where Uncle Ethan's young boys were getting a drink. "Your job is to get those boys into the hall, now!"

Penelope stomped her way toward Jake and Joey.

Movement in the trees above turned out to be Jordan creeping down the incline of his family's roof, gun clutched in one hand.

"There they come," Uncle Colton said, nodding at the road.

Mason looked past his father, expecting to see Levi and Jemma returning. Instead, he saw a convoy of strange trucks entering the village.

The first truck was smaller, like an Old ambulance. The other two were as big as Old semitrucks but in one long piece. All three were yellow and silver with metal grids on the sides instead of windows and doors. Like the vehicle Mason had seen a few weeks ago, these were almost silent but for the crunch of their tires over the gravel.

The trucks drove into the roundabout, one behind the other, and the ambulance-like vehicle rolled to a stop near the meeting hall. Mason backed against the fire pit, trying to get into a position where he could see all three vehicles at once, but they were too close.

The metal grids of the ambulance vehicle slid up into the roof, and the driver and passenger climbed out. The back grid slid away as well, and enforcers trickled into the square one by one. There was no movement from the other two vehicles.

Father lifted his gun. Uncle Colton followed suit, so Mason lifted his, keeping his finger away from the trigger. His body throbbed with adrenaline and heat. *I can't do this.*

There were a dozen enforcers total. They wore navy blue uniforms, gray helmets, and boots. All were emblazoned with the golden bell crest of the Safe Lands and a small name patch. The helmets had eye shades that hid the men's faces from view. Holsters held handguns strapped to their hips.

One man stood out from the rest, towering over the others like a monstrous bat. His eye shade had been pushed to the top of his helmet, though a pair of sunglasses and a thick beard covered most of his face. The skin that did show was pale and flaky. He had the thin plague, a disease that, according to Papa Eli, killed a person's immune system over time.

His name patch proclaimed his name was Otley, and despite the illness, the man appeared formidable. Gold rings looped through each eyebrow and the center of his bottom lip, and a gold spike curled out of each nostril like a section of the barbed wire that topped the Safe Lands walls. He also had a white number eight tattooed to his cheek.

"Help you boys?" Father asked.

Otley ambled around the stage. "We're having a membership drive. Wondering if your people are ready for a life with a little more ... fun."

"Not interested," Father said.

"Not surprised, but I'm afraid I can't take that answer. See, we need people to join us in the Safe Lands. Need them to join now. But since I'm a nice guy, I'm going to give you a choice." Otley reached toward his holster.

"Hey, hey, hey!" Uncle Colton said.

He and Father both aimed at Otley, which caused half of the enforcers to draw their weapons as well. All those guns made Mason's nerves so jittery he about wet his pants. *But that would be normal*, he told himself. *A neurobiological response to a life-threatening situation.*

Otley raised his hands and chuckled. "Cool off, shells! Just trying to show you that our pistols hold sleepers *and* killers. The guns have a switch. Blue for sleep, red for kill. Question is, which way do you want us to flick the switch?"

"Can't imagine the dead would make good members for your commune, Safe Lander," Father said. "We only shoot one way in Glenrock, and it ain't for sleeping."

"And you refuse to come take a look at our fine city?" Otley asked.

"That's right," Father said.

Otley sighed. "Remember what I said, men." He turned in a circle, pointing and panning his finger over the enforcers. "One kill each. Sleep the rest of the village."

Otley spun and fired twice. The discharge was like the pop of an electric nail gun. Father crumpled. As did Uncle Colton.

Mason screamed and raised his rifle, but gunfire rained over the enforcers from above. Jordan and Harvey! Mason hit the ground and crawled under the stage, dragging his rifle into darkness. Sharp rocks stabbed his knee caps and palms. Gunfire spat into the dirt behind him, and he crawled faster. All around him men were crying out. Glenrock rifle fire exploded against the airy pops of Safe Lands handguns.

Mason stopped once he reached the middle of the stage. His arms were shaking badly, but he pushed to a kneeling position and looked back. Sunlight lit the edge of the stage. He could see the toe of his father's boot and the top of Uncle Colton's head as both lay on the ground. He threw up without realizing it was coming. The first of it landed in his lap. He leaned over and heaved and heaved, his mind a blur of questions.

One kill each, Otley had said. How had he drawn so quickly? Had he fired sleepers or killers? What did a sleeper do? Should Mason go back? Try to help? He didn't see any movement from his father or uncle, but he had to know. He crept toward them, got close enough to look...

A girl's scream pulled him out of his daze. He forced himself to look away from his father. Suddenly, he was crawling to the back of the stage. He had to help her. Needed to.

"Get away from me!" the girl screamed.

Mason peeked out from under the stairs. Shaylinn, running from an enforcer toward the tree line. The enforcer shot his gun. Shaylinn fell. The enforcer continued toward her. She pushed up to her hands and knees. Fell. Writhed and tried again to rise. Screamed for help.

Mason could only stare from his safe haven. Accusations assaulted his mind in time with the gunfire. *Coward. Sissy. Gutless. Weakling.*

The crack of a gun brought the enforcer to his knees, then to his face, prostrate in the grass a few yards from Shaylinn. Jordan. But Mason could still help.

He pushed out from under the stage and sprinted toward her, his muscles tense, knowing he could be shot at any moment.

"Shaylinn." He knelt beside her. "Can you move?"

She panted in a few long breaths. "I think ... so." She got to her feet.

Mason pulled her arm around his shoulders and helped her stand. "Behind the sick house," he said.

They started for it, but after a few steps, Shaylinn sagged against him. Mason held her up and dragged her along.

"My legs won't work," she said. "I can't make them move."

Mason squatted and lifted her the way men did in Old movies. A groan escaped him at how heavy she was. He sucked in a deep breath and staggered to the sick house, certain he'd drop her, but somehow he managed to reach the far side of the structure before collapsing.

"Shaylinn? Talk to me. Where does it hurt?"

Her eyes were glassy, liquid with unshed tears. "My back."

Mason knelt beside her and rolled her body against his knees. He patted her back to look for a wound and found a small hole in the back of her dress, just to the right of her spine. "There's no blood." A sleeper?

"What's that mean, no blood?" Shaylinn asked, her voice slow.

Best guess? "I assume it means you're going to go to sleep."

"What if I don't wake up?"

"You'll certainly wake," Mason said, struggling for something uplifting as he rolled her onto her back. "Whether you wake on earth or in heaven, I can't say. Either would be good, though, right?"

Her eyes flew wide. "But I don't want to die! I've ... never been in love." Her eyelids fluttered. "Never kissed ... a boy. Always dreamed I'd be beautiful when I ... grew up. Everyone here thinks I'm ... I'm ugly. Omar said ..."

But Mason didn't discover what Omar had said, because Shaylinn's eyes drifted shut.

Mason sank back against the wall of the sick house, listening to the sounds around him. It was quieter now. He could hear men talking but couldn't tell what they were saying or whether they were friend or foe.

Mason looked out onto the square just as the front door to his house swung in. Papa Eli stepped onto the porch, clutching his rifle in one hand. He wore a plain white T-shirt and a pair of black shorts that bared his knobby knees.

Mason scrambled to his feet and sprinted toward his great-grandfather. The old man started to lift his gun in Mason's direction then seemed to recognize him.

"What's going on out here?" Papa Eli asked.

"Safe Lands enforcers asked us to move into the compound. Father refused and they shot him and Uncle Colton. The men fought back, but I don't know who won." Mason sucked in a quick breath. "Some are dead, but some are only sleeping. The enforcers had two kinds of ammo, and I . . . I don't know which kind they used on each person."

Papa Eli looked over Mason's shoulder. "Why didn't someone come get me?"

A sob stole its way out Mason's throat. "Father said to let you sleep."

Papa Eli pursed his lips and sighed out his nose. "Get your gun, and let's go take a look."

Mason ran back to where he'd left Shaylinn and picked up his rifle. Papa Eli met him there, and they peeked around the edge of the sick house. Enforcers milled around the square. Two lifted Jordan's body off the ground and carried it toward the back of the second transport.

Did that mean Jordan was alive? "What are we going to do?" Mason asked.

"Where is everyone?"

"Father sent the women into the meeting hall, thinking that was enough to keep them safe. He split up the men and told them to shoot from the forest and the roofs." Mason took a deep breath, feeling a hint better with Papa Eli by his side.

"So the women are all trapped and no one's shooting." Papa Eli stepped out from behind the sick house. "Cover me."

Mason grappled with his rifle until he was holding it correctly, though the barrel quivered like a branch in the wind. Behind him, footsteps rustled through the ferns. Mason glanced over his shoulder, hoping to see one of the village men or even Grazer. But it was Otley and an enforcer whose name badge read *Lemuel*.

"Papa Eli!" Mason yelled.

Papa Eli spun around, gun ready, and he and Otley held each other in their sights.

Otley frowned. "You're an abomination, old man! How long have they let you live?"

"I was there when they built your Safe Lands, boy," Papa Eli said to Otley. "I didn't want any part of it then, and I still don't."

"Men like you disgust me," Otley said. "To take resources from the young and refuse liberation ..."

Papa Eli chuckled — a gun pointed at his head and he laughed! "You'll think differently someday."

"Not likely, you stimming Ancient," Otley said.

Otley and Papa Eli fired at the same time. The bullet's impact sent Otley flying, and he landed on his back a few yards away. Papa Eli crashed against the sick house wall and slid down it. Blood swelled red and bright against his white shirt.

"No!" Mason pointed his rifle at Lemuel, the barrel a blur from his shaking or from his tears, possibly both.

Lemuel raised his pistol to Mason's head. He too had a number tattooed to his cheek. A number three. "I don't think you've got the juice to pull the trigger, shell."

"Don't kill him!" Otley whispered. "We need the young ones alive." He was still lying on the ground, and though his hand clutched his stomach, he seemed relatively fine.

How could the man still be alive?

"Don't worry, general. My gun's on sleep," Lemuel said, squinting one eye.

Mason pulled his trigger, but it didn't budge. *The safety.* He fumbled with the switch, certain he was about to feel a bullet enter his skull; instead, a gun went off, the report cracking through the air. Mason cowered, and his ears rang. The enforcer Lemuel fell, a hole between his eyes.

Mason whipped around. Papa Eli's arm fell, his pistol clutched in his hand. Mason lunged to his great-grandfather's side and helped him lie down. The bullet had entered just below Papa Eli's right shoulder and looked to have pierced his pectoral muscle and possibly his right lung. He lifted Papa Eli until he spotted the exit wound in his center back.

Control the bleeding, staunch if possible. It didn't matter if his hands were dirty. An infection could be treated later. There was no pressure point for the shoulders, so all he could do was apply direct compression and pray God sent a miracle. He tried to pull Papa Eli's shirt up. No good. He shrugged off his own cattail vest, folded it up, and pressed it over the entrance wound.

Papa Eli gasped. "Careful, boy!"

Good. He was talking, which meant his airway was clear. But that didn't mean Papa would survive. There could still be issues with his lungs and his breathing, and the exit wound was extremely close to the spine. "Turn your head to the side, Papa, so you can breathe better."

"I can breathe fine."

The blood quickly soaked through Mason's vest and coated his hands in a glossy sheen of red. He needed something else for the exit wound, and fast. All the blood was likely draining out the back. He tucked his vest under the exit wound on Papa Eli's back and pressed his hands over the shoulder wound. "Can you move your hands and feet?"

"You're worse than my Hannah." A dreamy smile claimed Papa Eli's face. "You would have liked your great-grandmother, Mason—tenacious in her ministrations, she was. And I'll tell you the same thing I'd tell her; if it's my time to go, your efforts won't matter."

Tears flooded Mason's eyes. He didn't want anyone else to die. *Get it together, Mason—focus!* What else could he do? His body suddenly felt heavy with the realization that until the bleeding stopped or until another pair of hands came along, there wasn't anything else he could do.

His great-grandfather shivered and sucked in a series of weak breaths—he was going into shock. Mason needed to get a blanket, something, but he didn't dare leave Papa's side.

A sting between his shoulder blades knocked him forward, and he barely kept himself from collapsing on Papa Eli. A burning tingle throbbed out from his center back. He looked over his shoulder and felt his head swim.

Otley was watching him. Smiling. Pistol in hand. "Nightie-night, shell."

Mason turned back to Papa Eli, bloody, blurry ... two Papas, three.

The sky was bright blue above him. Fat white clouds. How had he gotten on his back? He needed to help Papa Eli. Stop the bleeding.

But Papa Eli's face appeared above him, dark, backlit by the light of day. He grabbed Mason's hand and squeezed. "Don't let them change you, boy. No matter what. Stay true to ..."

Mason's eyelids slid closed.

CHAPTER 5

The motorcycle jerked over the ruts of the mountain trail. Omar tried to steer carefully, but his efforts only seemed to make the ride bumpier. He liked the feel of Jemma's arms around his waist though, and how they tightened whenever he hit a bump. He hoped it wouldn't be long until he found a fiancée of his own.

Omar slowed to turn onto the valley road, and the ride became much smoother. He sped over the thick treads the Safe Lands vehicles had dug into the dirt and wondered if the tracks were one-way or two. Were the enforcers still in the village? He hoped so.

He also hoped Jemma hadn't noticed the treads as they passed.

Once they entered the forest, the shade cooled him, which made him shiver despite the heat from the muffler warming his leg. The question of what was happening in Glenrock overwhelmed his mind. What would the people say when the enforcers made their offer?

It was a mad good idea, relocating. He'd been inside the Safe Lands only at night, but that had been enough to see that the city was amazing. So modern. To have to work only a few hours each day? To not have to hunt or grow your own food? The ability to do whatever you wanted? And the conveniences! Surely the people of Glenrock would at least want to go inside to see for themselves. Omar couldn't be the only one who'd wondered about the place.

The task director had said the enforcers would come right away. But then three weeks had passed, and Omar had begun to think they weren't coming at all. He'd spent every moment he could watching from the perch, even volunteering for more shifts. He'd almost thought he'd been imagining those trucks when he saw them coming.

Thankfully Penelope, Shay, and Nell had followed him today, begging him to draw their portraits. He'd tricked Penelope into watching the perch, promising her an extra drawing for her trouble, then had gone to fetch Jemma and send Levi away. Something told him Levi wouldn't like the Safe Lands, but if Jemma visited first ... well, she could talk Levi into anything.

Plus, she was worth a million credits to Omar. The task director had promised him a referral fee for every new citizen he brought into the compound. Men were worth only ten thousand credits, so if Levi never came, Omar wasn't out much. Things would move smoother without his interference anyway.

Omar downshifted as he steered the motorcycle into the village square. The three Safe Lands trucks he'd seen from the perch were parked in the roundabout. Pairs of enforcers were carrying bodies to the trucks.

Omar's stomach seemed to turn inside out. No one was supposed to get hurt! The task director had promised a peaceful offer and negotiation. He'd promised.

Several enforcers aimed guns at Omar as he approached. He let the motorcycle coast to a stop. He lifted his hands above his head, but his gaze fell on two motionless bodies on the ground in front of the stage.

With a sick cry, Jemma climbed off and sprinted to the stage. The enforcers tracked her with their guns but didn't fire. She knelt beside the bodies. "Oh! Omar, come quick!"

Omar must have followed, because he suddenly found himself at her side, looking down on the face of his own father.

Dead.

His skin prickled, and he felt lightheaded. He shuffled back a few steps. Father couldn't be dead. He couldn't be. Father was supposed to move into the Safe Lands and be proud of Omar for coming up with the brilliant idea of relocating the people of Glenrock. How could Father be proud if he were dead? And Uncle Colton too? Why?

This couldn't be real. Yes, that was it. He must have fallen asleep in the perch. Once he woke, Penelope would be begging him to draw her, and he'd laugh about all of this. Voices muttered nearby. That had to be Penelope and Shay and Nell. He rubbed his forefinger along the scar on the bridge of his nose until it was sore.

"Omar."

His head snapped back. Jemma was shaking him by his shoulders.

"They want us to go into the hall." Her voice was weepy.

Why was she crying? He ran the back of his hand under his nose. His gaze again fell to the bodies. "Is that ... my father?" His voice came out in a hoarse whisper.

"Omar, I'm so sorry." Jemma sniffed in a deep breath and hugged him. The warmth of her body confused him. Felt real.

Suddenly she was gone. "No! Let go," Jemma yelled. "Omar, please ... Stay with me!"

With her? Stay? He shook his head. "What?" He looked up in time to see an enforcer drag Jemma into the meeting hall.

"Okay, shell, let's go inside." Another enforcer took Omar's arm and led him away from his father. Omar glanced back to make sure his father was ... Yes. There he was. On the ground with Uncle Colton. This was the worst nightmare he'd ever had.

Inside, the air felt cool. The lull of men's voices and the high-pitched wail of a girl crying met his ears.

When his eyes adjusted to the darkness, Omar saw at least three dozen people occupied the meeting hall. The banquet tables had been taken down, leaving the floor bare. His female friends, neighbors, and their children sat along the wall, wrists bound in their laps, half of them weeping, half of them asleep or dead. A sea of navy blue uniforms stood before them: Safe Lands enforcers, armed with black pistols. The enforcer holding Jemma pushed her toward the women.

"No!" Mother yelled. "Omar, get Jemma out of here!"

"Jemma! Run!" Naomi screamed from her place along the wall.

Jemma wheeled around and ran back to the doors, where Omar was standing. "Back outside, Omar. Hurry!"

Then came a pop, followed by a metallic ping on the floor. Jemma gasped and stumbled. Someone screamed. Omar lunged forward and caught her under her arms. Behind her, an enforcer stood, his gun pointed at her back.

"Why'd you shoot her?" Omar yelled, fire searing his chest.

Jemma's eyes filled with liquid. "Getting shot doesn't hurt as much as I thought it would."

"It's just a sleeper, shell," the enforcer said to Omar. "She'll be fine."

Two other enforcers dragged Jemma away from Omar and sat her against the wall by the door. Omar felt somewhat relieved that she'd live but still didn't know what to do.

Kruse, who Omar remembered was the task director general's assistant, glided to Omar's side. He was thin, bald, had a pinkish hue to his skin, and he smelled like flowers. The man held a flat piece of glass in his black-gloved hands and tapped his finger against words that were displayed on the surface. "What took you so long?"

Blood tingled inside Omar's head, making him dizzy. He hoped no one had heard—

"What!" The word came out like a scream torn from Mother's throat. "Omar? You knew about this?"

Omar swallowed and lowered his voice. "Mother, it's okay. I had to go and— "

"What's that femme's name?" Kruse asked.

Femme? Oh, right—their term for girl. "Jemma," Omar said, staring at the strange tattoo on the side of Kruse's head. It looked like a black arm that reached out of his collar, ran up the side of his neck, and splayed its hand over the side of the man's shiny scalp.

"G-e-m-m-a?"

Omar focused on Kruse's face, on the white number five on his cheek. "Um … J-e-m-m-a."

"*Omar*," Jemma said, her voice slurred. "Don't help them."

Kruse tapped the glass and spoke softly. "Jemma. Done."

Omar could feel the women staring at him.

"See anyone missing?" Kruse asked. "General Otley wants to get as many of you outsiders as he can. We've already loaded the males and given you the referrals. And we've credited you for each femme here. You're rich, shell. Anyone else we need to get?"

"Just my brother, Levi. But I have a feeling he'll come on his own." Omar glanced at Jemma.

"That's right," Jemma whispered, her eyes glistening. "Levi *will* come, Omar. And you'll forever regret this betrayal."

"It's not like that," Omar said. "It wasn't supposed to happen this way. We were supposed to be able to choose … to get a chance for a better life." He looked to Kruse. "Why did you kill people?"

"*That* is an excellent question, shellie," Kruse said. "And I can promise you there will be an inquiry."

An inquiry. His father was *dead*. "Is that supposed to make me feel better?"

"What's he saying, Jemma?" Mother yelled from across the room. "Omar?"

Kruse removed a gold paper envelope from his front pocket. "Take this to the Registration Department to get your task station and post. They'll also assign your home." He pointed to a short, muscled enforcer with longish, frizzy brown hair and a tiny mustache. "You can ride back with Skottie. See you around, shellie." Kruse exited the meeting hall.

"No!" Mother yelled. "Omar, don't listen to them!"

The enforcers got the women and girls to their feet and led them out the door in a line. One picked up Shay and tossed her over his shoulder like she was a ragdoll. Another carried Jemma with about as much care.

When Mother neared the door, she tried to approach Omar, but an enforcer held her back. "Omar, why?" she asked. "You plan to work for them? And *live* with them?"

Tears pooled in the corners of Omar's eyes. He sniffed in a short breath and stepped back. "You'll like it there, Mother. You'll see. It's *amazing* inside the Safe Lands."

"What about the thin plague?" Mother asked, her voice laced with tears. "The slavery Papa Eli told us about?"

"Papa Eli was wrong about the Safe Lands," Omar said. "Things are different there now. Better than here. No drafty cabins."

Naomi, who was in line in front of Mother, yelled, "Maybe if you built one, you'd appreciate them more, you lazy slug!"

Omar flinched and focused on Naomi. Like her husband, Jordan, she'd always had a way with quick insults. "They have better electricity in the Safe Lands. Better health care for you and your baby. TVs in every home. Indoor showers with hot water. Air conditioning. And they have so many more people our age. Once you see it, you'll see I did this to make everything better for our people. Once all this is sorted out, it's going to be mad good."

Naomi slipped past an enforcer and trotted up to Omar, her pregnant belly no hindrance to her speed. She cuffed her bound hands against his ear. Omar put his hands over his head and ducked out of reach, but Naomi managed to knock off his hat and grab hold of his hair. Two enforcers dragged her back to the line. "Our fathers are dead, Omar!" Naomi screamed. "You think that's good?"

Omar looked away as an enforcer led Naomi and his mother out the door. He picked up his hat, and his gaze landed on Jemma as she was carried past. His chin quivered. "Don't look at me like that." He put his hat back on. "Levi will come — we both know he will. Once he sees how g-good ..."

The enforcer shifted Jemma in his arms, and her head lolled to face Omar. "You're wrong. You won't get away with this." As the enforcer took her outside, she yelled, "Levi will save us!"

Omar stood by the wall across from the door until all the women had been taken outside.

Skottie approached. His frizzy brown hair looked like a helmet, but unlike the other enforcers, this guy didn't have one. He did have a white number seven on his cheek. Omar realized he'd never asked about the numbers during his visit. All Safe Landers seemed to have them on their faces and right hands, and they must mean something.

"Some crazy flames, huh?" Skottie said. "I mean, we were told these people *wanted* to relocate, but then they showed up with guns and everything went crazy."

"Why'd you shoot them?" Omar practically yelled.

"Walls!" Skottie lifted his hands. "Not me, shell. I just drive the truck. But between you and me, Otley thinks he runs the Safe Lands. He got hit, you know, by some ancient. Maybe that will humble him a bit. We can hope." He walked toward the door. "Let's get out of here. It's dead hot, and my truck has air."

Omar followed Skottie to the third truck in the line. He tried to see his father's body once more, but the stage blocked it from view. Swallowing a lump, he turned to open the door to the truck but found no door handle. Before he could decide what to do, the metal grid that covered the door slid up onto the roof.

Inside the cab, Skottie sat on the driver's side, his door grid already sliding down. "Sorry, shell. I forgot you don't have your SimTag yet. Jump in."

Omar climbed up into the cab. Skottie tapped his right fist on the dashboard, and Omar's door closed.

The dashboard was black with a grid of square indentations, some vent slots, and the imprint of a steering wheel. The push of a button started the vehicle, the other button made the steering wheel rise from the dash. Electric green gauge lights lit up in a line across the top of the windshield: RPM, MPH, Gas, Time.

"Dashboard-air-eight," Skottie said, and cool air shot out from the vents. "Let me know if that gets too cold."

Omar turned to look out the grid. It was clear glass, though — tinted — but there was no sign of the metal crosshatch. "I thought the doors were metal."

"Yeah, that's one-way ballistic SimGlass. Only looks like metal from the outside."

The truck ahead of Skottie's started to move, and Skottie steered after it. Omar watched out his window, craning to get one last glimpse of Father's body.

He straightened, facing the back of the truck before them, wishing he could see through the grid on the back to know who was inside. Naomi had said her father was dead. How many others had died? He hoped Mason was okay. His brother wouldn't have fired a gun. But he could have gotten hit trying to help someone. *Please let Mason be alive.*

CHAPTER 6

Levi steered his ATV and cart up the mountain. The image of Jemma with her arms around Omar's waist kept a scowl on his face, despite his attempts to focus on the coming trade. Omar had been right to arrange this meeting, though. The people of Glenrock were dangerously low on ammunition and gunpowder. If anyone should attack the village ... Well, Levi didn't want to think about such a scenario.

Instead, he imagined how pleased his dad would be when he returned with enough ammunition to last the winter. Such a prize might soften the man enough to allow Levi to travel to Denver City alone next time. The delight on Jemma's face when Levi had given her the pearls filled his thoughts. He liked giving her things, seeing her eyes light up, being the cause of her beautiful smile. And there were thousands more treasures for her in Denver City.

Enough to last a lifetime.

When Levi reached the trading cabin, Beshup hadn't arrived yet. So Levi checked over his ATV, organized his trader cart, and visited the outhouse behind the cabin. When he returned to the yard, he was disappointed not to see Beshup waiting or even approaching. His impatience increased his agitation. The abandoned cabin stood closer to Jack's Peak than to Glenrock. Where was the man?

Hurry up, Beshup. I've got stuff to do. I could be with Jemma right—

The sound of distant gunfire straightened Levi's posture. Several single-shot rifles firing at once. Levi jogged down the driveway to an outcropping of rock that enabled him to see much of the valley.

Another few rounds of gunfire rang out from the northeast, far from where the walls of the Safe Lands split the countryside. His stomach tightened.

The gunfire was coming from home. Who or what were they shooting at?

He paced back to the cabin, then returned to the rocky ledge as more gunfire pattered in the valley below. He walked back and forth a few more times, squeezing his fists and frowning.

Where was Beshup?

As Levi reached the rocky viewpoint for the fourth time, he picked up his two-way radio to call the perch in Glenrock. "Jackrabbit to Rich Man, come in."

He waited ... listened to the static ... and hammered a fist against the side of his rig. He called again, then called his dad's two-way radio, his uncle's, Harvey's. No answer.

Maybe Beshup would answer. "Jackrabbit to Thunder Cry. Come in, Thunder Cry. Over."

Only a moment passed before the two-way radio clicked. "Ten four, Jackrabbit. This is Thunder Cry. How are you this fine afternoon? Over?"

"Where you been, Thunder Cry? I've been waiting at the bird's nest for a while now. Over."

"Why you waiting?"

That was a strange question. "Omar said you have fire to trade."

"Who told you that? We've barely got enough for ourselves."

Levi gritted his teeth. "Omar said you called him."

Static. "I haven't talked to your brother in over a month."

Levi closed his eyes. *What are you up to, Omar?*

"You still there, Jackrabbit?"

"I'm hearing gunfire over in Glenrock," Levi said. "Going to go take a look."

"Let me know what you find."

"Will do. Over and out." Levi tossed his two-way radio into his cart and started the ATV. The mile-and-a-half trek down the mountain had never seemed so far. He wanted to take the shortcut past the Safe Lands, but he'd do his village no good if he were captured. Every minute was agony to him. The men couldn't be target shooting. There wasn't enough ammo for sport.

He steered onto the village road, and the fresh dual-axle tracks in the dirt made him push the ATV even faster. Levi veered onto the waterwheel trail so he could come around the back of the village.

He parked at the river. The only sound was the hydro-generator puttering away. He grabbed his rifle and ran up the hill through the forest, darting past trees and over moss and mushrooms, cutting across the trail's switchbacks. As the hill carried him higher, his legs grew weak, forcing him to slow down.

Something lay across the path before him. A body. He sprinted toward it and knelt beside the form of a man. Elder Sam, Naomi's father, dead, a pistol still clutched in his hand. His body was matted with grass and dirt and looked to have rolled down the incline. Levi's mind screamed, knowing this was real, yet at the same time certain only nightmares contained such horror. His pulse thudded in his head like drums.

As if someone else were controlling him, his hands tugged the gun from Elder Sam's hand and checked it for ammunition. Empty. He tucked it into the back of his pants anyway.

"I'll come back for you, Elder Sam." Levi crept further up the hill. As he neared the village square, he found three more bodies, fallen in the woods: Elder Mark, Elder Devin, and Elder Michael. All had been shot. All were out of ammo. At least it appeared they had died fighting.

Levi also found Grazer, Mason's dog, lifeless near a tree. The mutt had been incredibly friendly — why would someone have shot him?

He left the dog and took off through the forest toward his house. Levi's family home stood on the far side of the square. He went in through the back door and made his way to the front of the house, checked all the bedrooms. No one home.

He ran out the front door and scanned the area. A body lay on the ground halfway between him and the sick house.

Papa Eli.

Levi sprinted across the grass and fell to his knees beside his great-grandfather. Papa Eli, founder of Glenrock and the oldest living member of the Elias tribe, lay on his stomach in the grass. The back of his white T-shirt was coated in blood. Levi set down his rifle. "Papa Eli?" He tucked in the old man's arm and rolled him over. The grass that had been underneath him was red and wet. So much blood. The bullet had passed through at an angle, leaving a hole in Papa Eli's shoulder. Or maybe the bullet had entered from the front and passed out the back. Mother would know.

Mother!

Levi wanted to find his mother, his father, his brothers. Help Papa Eli. Find out who'd done this and—

Papa Eli wheezed in a deep breath. His eyes flashed open, wide and bloodshot, then rolled around in their sockets before fixing on Levi. Recognition softened the look of pain on the old man's face. His voice came out in a raspy whisper. "Didn't get you?"

"No, sir." Levi fought to keep his voice steady. "Who shot you?"

"Enforcers." Papa Eli grimaced. "Killed our men … Took our women and young ones."

Ice pooled in Levi's heart, sending chills down every vein. "To the compound?"

"Afraid so." He reached out and patted Levi's thigh. "Thought we'd be safe … Thought they'd leave us alone … We were wrong. *I* was wrong. You have to … get them back."

"Yes, sir."

Papa Eli slapped Levi's thigh the way he slapped the tabletop to get everyone's attention at mealtimes.

"I hear you loud and clear, sir. I won't let you down."

"Good. Good." He closed his eyes and took a few deep breaths.

"What can I do?" Levi asked. "Mason and Mother are the doctors. I don't know how to help — "

"Don't fret." Papa Eli opened his eyes and focused on Levi. "My Hannah's … gone … twenty years now."

Levi swallowed hard. "That's a long time to be missing someone."

Papa Eli nodded slightly. "I was … looking forward … your wedding. That Jemma … a pretty girl. Kind too. You're smart to grab … her."

Rage filled Levi's chest at the idea of Jemma in the Safe Lands. "I'll get her back, sir."

"I know." He took a ragged breath. "And I'm going … leave you to it. Head to eternity … with my God and … my Hannah."

Tears flooded Levi's eyes.

Papa Eli patted Levi's thigh again, this time much softer. "Good man. Lord knows best." He closed his eyes. "Been with me all these …"

Levi watched his great-grandfather's face as the life left it. Levi fell back onto the grass, staring up at the hazy pine trees, wondering if Papa Eli's soul were floating to heaven this very moment. His throat burned. His eyes burned too.

No one had earned a proper burial more than Papa Eli. The man had outlived his wife and son. Survived the Great Pandemic and escaped the Safe Lands. Founded Glenrock as an answer to the Safe Land's tyranny and governed the village thereafter with wisdom and grace, following the teachings found in the Bible he loved. Trained up three generations to follow in his footsteps.

Was Levi truly the only one left? Papa Eli had said they'd taken the women and young ones — which meant Mason, Jordan, and Omar likely lay dead on the grass somewhere too.

A fat drop of water struck Levi's cheek. Summer storms were common, but as distant thunder crackled, Levi wondered if God had looked down on Glenrock and shed tears for the death of its people.

Levi lay on the grass, letting the rain soak him, giving in to the tears, praying for help, for guidance, for sanity. The storm cloud passed quickly, and Levi decided he too should get moving. He pushed himself up and went looking for survivors, his mind racing, trying to piece together the truth. Omar had lied to him about Beshup's trade, and he couldn't fathom why.

Just when Levi thought he'd finished his tears, he found his father's body. Elder Justin had been shot once in the forehead. Likely, he hadn't suffered, which was some consolation.

He found no survivors in the village. There were eighteen dead—thirteen elder men, four elder women, and little Sophie, who'd been only six. No sign of Jordan, Mason, or Omar.

Levi couldn't dig eighteen graves himself. But he couldn't leave the bodies to the wolves, either. Over the next two hours, he moved the dead, including Grazer, to the square where he could keep an eye on them. He piled the weapons in the back of his cart. Then he decided to dig three graves in the cemetery: one for his father, one for Papa Eli, and one for Sophie.

The digging took him well into the afternoon.

Several times, the horror gripped him, and Levi lost himself in a fit of tears and rage, beating the shovel against a tree or the ground until finally the spade separated from the shaft.

Once he'd buried the three and said a prayer, he sat down against a tree. His palms stung with blisters, and his arms ached. He nodded off once, told himself to get up and do something about the other bodies, then nodded off again into full slumber.

CHAPTER 7

Omar was shaking now. How had everything gone so wrong? His whole body felt numb and tingly like he was going to throw up. As much as he tried not to think about it, Father's face was burned on Omar's brain. Closing his eyes didn't help. Relocation was supposed to gain him acceptance with his people, not cast him out even more. He fought to steady his breath, crossed his arms to fight the shaking.

"You juicing, shell?" Skottie asked.

Skottie's mustache looked like two strokes of paint going out from each nostril. "What?"

"Stims, joy juice, hard candy, vapes. Uh ... narcots?

"Narcotics?" Omar asked, recalling the word from Old movies.

Skottie bobbed his head. "That's what I said."

The guy thought Omar was on drugs? "Someone killed my father! And it was because of me."

"Ahh, premie lib," Skottie said.

Omar looked over at Skottie. "Premie what?"

"Going on to the next life before reaching your age limit. I hear having someone go through that can be tough. How old was your friend?"

Omar rubbed his scar. "My father was forty-six."

Skottie shrugged. "Past his time then. Safe Lands used to liberate at fifty, but they changed it to forty back in seventy-two. It's for the best. No one wants to get old."

The best? "But I just left him there. I should go back. Bury him maybe. And the others. Can we turn around?"

"Walls, no, shell." The truck bounced over a hole in the dirt road. "Ask the Tasker G when you take in your fancy gold ticket. No way I'm putting my skin under fire for an ancient."

Would Omar ever understand what these people were saying? "You keep calling me a shell — what does that mean?"

"It's a name we use for someone who's so sick with the plague that their mind is gone. They do weird things like eat dirt or forget to get dressed. But we also use the word to describe clueless outsiders. Hopefully you won't be a shell for much longer."

As they drove through the forest, it was silent but for the air conditioning and Omar's raspy breathing.

"So." Skottie tapped his fingers on the steering wheel. "You tasked a deal. What did they promise?"

"Uh ... I'm supposed to get a position with the enforcers." A position that would have shown his father he wasn't worthless. A position that didn't seem to matter as much anymore.

"Ah, we'll be seeing each other then. You'll have to take basic. I'm in there now. Then you'll be assigned a task internship somewhere. They made me a driver. But they let me carry a gun, which about liberated my friend Charlz when he found out. Charlz collects guns, but he's interning in patrol and only gets to carry a stunner. Charlz already has ten different stunners."

The task director had promised Omar an officer's rank within the enforcers. He hoped Skottie wouldn't be offended when he found out that Omar was jumping ahead of him in rank. Now that he'd alienated his entire village, he needed any friends he could get.

"What else? Got to get your mind off your friend. What do you like to do for fun?"

Omar forced the image of Father's face away. "I draw and paint."

"Ooh, artist, eh? You'll have to check out this store called Task for Art in the Highlands. They've got all kinds of real paint in there. I'm assuming you meant Old art and not SimArt."

"What's SimArt?"

"It's like the window of my truck. SimTech illusion." Skottie tapped the iridescent number seven on his cheek. "Same way this does. Same way that black hand on Kruse's head works."

They left the forest, and sunlight brightened the cab. "I don't understand."

"I'll show you." Skottie unbuttoned his jacket and shrugged it off his shoulders. He held out his right arm. "Pull my sleeve."

Omar did. Once Skottie's arm was free from his jacket, he held it out again. It was solid with bright tattoos. Green, red, yellow, blue, silver images melded together in a combination of abstract art: a cat's face, a dagger, a pair of dice, a skull, a net stocking, a thorny rose.

"Did it hurt?" Omar asked, still studying the colors. "The needle?"

"No needles. SimTags itch a little when you get them, but that's it. No one wants to be tagged for life. It's all simulation. Electronic ink."

Omar studied Skottie's arm again. "How does electronic ink work?"

"I'll do my best, peer, but there's a reason I don't task in tech." Skottie turned the wheel, following the truck in front. The Safe Lands walls rose in front of them. "Every national gets two SimTags for identification. One here" — he tapped his cheek — "and one here." He held up his fist, and Omar could see another number seven on the back of his right hand. "Each SimTag covers a three-inch diameter. You can get more, then they 'talk' to each other to create bigger images."

Like tiny computers? "How many did it take to do your arm?"

"Twenty-five. I also got ten on my chest and twelve on my back."

"How do you choose the pictures?"

"In any SimArt store, or, if you like art and get the right adds, you can change them yourself. Some people even design their own."

Omar already had ideas for what he could do with SimTags.

The truck slowed to a stop before a massive gate. On either side of the road a concrete pillar rose into the sky like a grain silo. Enforcers stood on the tops, weapons pointed down toward the truck. A concrete wall stretched from each pillar into the distance.

A huge boom of metal made Omar jump. The noise was followed by metallic clicking. When the sound ceased, the truck rolled forward again. They passed under a gate. All went dark, and then the bright sky appeared overhead again, separated by a tunnel of mesh wire the truck was driving through. The Safe Lands in the daytime was all new to Omar.

He peered out his window at blurred figures that were wading in a vast field of green that reached their knees, stooping to pick from the plants. The scent of livestock was thick on the air. Every so often they passed a mishmash of buildings and intersections before returning to endless fields spread out on either side of the tunnel.

"Some people work in the fields?"

"Sure. Not everyone can get tasked to the enforcers, right?"

The truck passed under another gate and tunnel, this time without stopping. On the other side, they drove through a grid of streets similar to the Old neighborhoods in Crested Butte, just in much better condition.

A massive TV screen, bigger than the truck, loomed on the side of the road. It showed a man and woman in matching outfits. The woman had chin-length, smooth black hair and was wearing a pale yellow dress with black dots. The man wore a black suit with a ruffly yellow bow tie. Words scrolled beneath their image: *Finley and Flynn discuss Lonn liberation.*

"They show movies on the road?" Omar asked.

"Expos," Skottie said. "That's a DigiBoard."

"What's a Lonn liberation?" Omar asked.

"Ooh, Richark Lonn the rebel. He Xed out years ago, but they finally caught him. He's way overage, so he's due to get liberated and move on to the next life."

"They're going to execute him?"

"Death is life, peer."

Omar had no response for that. He wished Mason were here. His brother was smart and always knew what to say.

They were traveling uphill now and soon stopped before a third gate. This one had pillars like the main gate and a dividing wall that ran across the land.

"Why so many gates?"

"The people in the three areas keep mostly to themselves. A lot of Midlanders task in the Highlands, since no one who lives in the ritzy Highlands ever manages to test for service positions — nothing suspicious there, ha ha. But there's only so much room up here, so lots have to live in the Midlands and commute in. The gates keep everyone where they belong at the end of the day."

The truck lurched forward again. It passed between two massive steel doors that were as tall as the concrete pillars, then they entered a thick forest.

They approached another DigiBoard, but this one flashed still images. One showed a woman with pale blue, sparkling skin. Text flashed across the screen that said, "Veins showing through your makeup? Try Roller Paint. Available in over two hundred colors, textures, and prints. Smoothes all flakes and completely covers varicose and spider veins."

The truck departed the forest and made its way toward the buildings clustered at the top of the bell — buildings taller than the concrete pillars at the last gate. The city rose against the bright sky; the sight stole the breath from Omar's lungs.

The truck carried them into the middle of the towers, joining more vehicles on the road. People walked along the sidewalks, many wearing black and pale yellow like the people from the DigiBoard. Omar swore he saw someone with green skin, then realized that with SimTags and Roller Paint, he probably had.

Electric signs displayed words in lighted, moving letters: *Savoy. Westwall. Golden Lily. Monogram Room*. Omar could only assume they were the clubs he'd been told about on his first visit. Skottie turned into a bright, covered loading zone — the ceiling solid with round lights the size of apples — and stopped before a wall of dark glass doors that reflected the massive vehicle. Omar could see his own eyes looking out through the grid illusion. Two men dressed in gold and blue uniforms with shiny gold buttons stood on either side of the glass doors, staring ahead as if they were statues.

"If you wait, I'll drop you by City Hall," Skottie said. "It might be a while, though. Or you could walk. It's just two blocks to the right from the end of this driveway."

Omar didn't want to stand around and watch the enforcers carry his kin into the building. Or to be seen by anyone from the village. "I'll walk. Thanks." He turned to the door and realized again that he had no means of opening it.

Skottie laughed and tapped his fist on a square on the dashboard. Omar's door started to rise. "You want me to show you around tonight? I can take you to a glossy dance club."

"Really?" Had Omar made a friend? "Sure. Thanks."

"You'll have to tap my number. If they don't give you a Wyndo, ask your doorman to tap me. The number's 7 – 67 – 18."

"7 – 67 – 18."

"That's right. Talk to you later, peer, and stay out of trouble."

Omar walked to where the driveway met the main road. Cars sped past in blurs of color and glass. He felt as if he were standing in a movie. He turned right and started walking but soon forgot his plan to enjoy the sights, lost in the memory of how he'd left his father dead on the ground. He should have spoken up. He should've done something. His father had been right: Omar *was* a sissy coward.

The next time he noticed his surroundings, he'd nearly passed City Hall. He craned his neck all the way back to look up the side of the building. It was made of ten silvery glass cubes, one stacked on top of the other like giant building blocks. Each block was turned slightly so that the corners jutted out at different angles — an impressive example of cubist architecture. The light hit it in ways that Omar thought would be interesting to sketch in charcoal.

The elevator to the tenth floor didn't thrill Omar as much today as it had a few weeks ago. The task director general's receptionist sent him right in. Omar took a deep breath and pushed in the door.

The rectangular room had a shiny wooden floor, sparse chrome and red suede furniture, and floor-to-ceiling windows on three walls. Clean, sharp, simple — minimalist design. This was another reason the Safe Lands intrigued him. So much beauty and architecture. There was none of this in Glenrock. Until Omar had visited the Safe Lands, he'd never seen anything from the Old art books Levi had given him.

Lawten Renzor, the Task Director General of the Safe Lands, sat at his desk. Kruse, the pink-skinned, bald assistant, stood beside him. The task director looked no different than the first time Omar had met him. He was tall and hunched with a tiny head, a glowing yellow nine on his cheek, a large nose, and almost no muscle on his bones. He had ink-black hair and eyebrows that looked even darker against his papery, white skin.

If Omar were to draw a caricature of the task director, he'd make him look like a vulture. But the man's lips were so full, he could also pass for an ugly woman. A vulture in a dress, perhaps.

"Ah, it's our outsider friend," the task director said. "Come sit. We have much to discuss."

That's right, they did. Omar just needed to work up the courage to say so. He needed to be strong and brave like his father and brothers. The enforcers had broken their promise, and it was up to Omar to make sure the task director understood how unacceptable that was. He sat on a red suede chair on the other side of the task director's desk.

The man's tiny, shrewd eyes searched Omar's face, omniscient eyes that seemed to know more than they should. Omar avoided looking at them now; instead, he focused on a mobile sculpture hanging above the task director's desk. It had nine black leaves and one red one, and shifted hypnotically.

"We have a problem, Omar of Glenrock," the task director said.

His words captured Omar's full attention, and he dared to meet those black pupils with his own. "We do?"

"Kruse informed me that several were killed in the attempt to relocate your village, including two women of childbearing age and one female child."

One blow after another. Who? Who else had died in his quest for a better life? A child?

"Nine fertile males were also killed," the task director said, drawing Omar's focus to the number nine on the man's cheek. "And one of the two we have in custody is being difficult."

Nine males killed. Omar pinched his leg, trying not to think about the deaths he was responsible for. His curiosity won out, however. He had to know. "Who lives? Of the men?"

The task director glanced at Kruse, who picked up his glass computer, which had been sitting on the edge of the task director's desk. "The outsiders named Jordan and Mason."

A chill gripped Omar, causing his arm hair to stand on end. Mason lived. Praise God. Then he flinched — *could* he praise God after what he'd done? Would God welcome his prayers at all?

"This loss changes things," the task director said, pulling Omar back to the present.

Omar crossed his arms, trying to look like his father — tough and intolerant. "How so? It was the, uh, enforcers who killed my people. And after you had promised a peaceful visit."

The task director sighed. "Yes, I confess: things got out of hand. But Kruse tells me you were not present when the enforcers arrived. How were they to explain their offer to the people without your help? From what I was told, our men were met with a militia that refused to listen. This was your idea, Omar of Glenrock. And you let your people down."

The words melted Omar's spine, and he slouched in the plush chair. So much for being tough. "But you said women were the most important. And I had to fetch one who wasn't in the village. I was trying to help."

"I understand. But there are consequences to your actions. First, because of the lack of males harvested and the refusals to cooperate from the one we're dealing with now, you'll be required to make donations twice a week."

Omar cringed. He didn't fully understand the Safe Lands' way of procreating, but knew it was vastly different from how things worked in Glenrock. "For how long?"

"As long as I deem necessary. And you must not pair up with any women."

Pair up meant romance. "That wasn't part of our deal! I want a wife."

The task director's brow furrowed over his large nose. "And I don't want you infecting yourself with the thin plague. You'd be useless to me then."

Omar stared at the task director, unable to utter a sound for several moments. "So you never intended to let me marry? Even though you knew that's what I wanted above all else?" His heart slammed inside his chest. "There must be *some* women who aren't infected."

"Why, yes, there are. Eight of pairing age, in fact," the task director said. "I believe you know them already as they're from your village."

"What? No!" Omar fumed. "You promised me a wife!"

"I told you there were many women here, not that I would assist you in finding a lifer. But the fact that you are the only male able or willing to donate at this time — as I've said already — has changed our original agreement. Our mission is top priority. You're welcome to any of the uninfected women, though."

"The females from Glenrock — they all detest me! And none of them are my age." A thought struck him. "Where do you come up with eight?"

"I pre-registered eight women between the ages of fourteen and thirty-six for the surrogacy pool we quaintly refer to as the harem," Kruse said. "Those too young for the harem were placed in the boarding school or nursery, and the other women were too old."

"Half those women are already married!"

"Were," the task director said. "And that's not my problem."

"It is! Your men killed their husbands. You think their wives would want to marry the guy who made all this happen? This is your fault, not mine. My being there wouldn't have kept your men from shooting people."

"You imply that our people fired first?"

"I don't know!" Omar was losing control of the situation, but he couldn't have betrayed his village for nothing. There had to be some way to save this. "What about that other place? Wyoming. Can I visit Wyoming to find a wife?"

The task director rubbed the loose skin on his neck. "If you report to the Donation Center when summoned, avoid liaisons with our women, and keep the Safe Lands' laws ... I'll consider it."

Omar swallowed his anxiety. "I can do that." *I've got to look tough, like Father. Strong.*

"Now, for the loss of the women who died, you'll be demoted one rank."

That wasn't so bad. Omar didn't understand the ranks anyway. "Will I still get to live in the Highlands? Will I still get the credits I was promised?"

"Yes, but I'm watching you, Omar of Glenrock." And those eyes seemed to say, *Now and wherever you go.* "See that you sever all ties to the ways of your people. Their insistence on clinging to outdated beliefs will get in the way of our mission, and it's likely some will try to hold you to them."

"I want nothing to do with Glenrock's ways." Ways that had always left him behind, alone, and the source of his father's scorn.

His dead father.

"Good. Your uniform is waiting with my receptionist, *Captain.* Report to the Registration Department on the second floor to receive your residence and schedule. You'll also need a physical and your SimTag implants. General Otley is your task director, so, if he's mended, he'll assign you to a task tomorrow morning."

"You have an appointment at ten o'clock in the Enforcers' Office," Kruse said.

"Well, there you go," the task director said.

"Okay, thanks. Sir." Omar stood and walked toward the door, feeling foolish for not knowing how to properly address the task director. He reached the door and turned the knob, but the task director general's voice stopped him.

"Thank you for seeking us out and putting this opportunity before us. I hope you find pleasure in life here, Omar. You're one of us now."

CHAPTER 8

Shaylinn opened her eyes to a bright white ceiling. She must be in heaven, because in Old movies, heaven was always white and glowing like this. But Papa Eli had said there would be no mourning or pain in heaven, and the ache in Shaylinn's chest hinted at recent pain.

"Hello?" she called, her voice barely a croak.

She lay on a stiff and narrow bed. When she tried to sit, she found her arms were bound to the bed. Her heart tumbled within her. "Help! Someone help me!" The words resulted in nothing but a break in the silence around her.

She lifted her head in hopes of getting some sort of bearings. A tall cupboard hung on the wall on her right. Down past her feet, a door stood without a handle or knob. To her left, a glowing blue sheet of glass covered the wall. The surface seemed to ripple with low light.

Her cheek itched, and she turned her head to scratch it with her shoulder. That was when she realized she was wearing a thin white dress. Who would take her clothes? What was going on? "Hello? Is someone there? Please, help me!"

This time, the door swung inward. Shaylinn stared at it. *Please be a woman. Please be a woman. God, please make it be a woman!*

A short, blonde woman entered, and Shaylinn almost cried in relief. She was wearing a baggy shirt and pants that were pink with tiny red hearts all over them. In her hand, she carried a little red box the size of an Old paperback book.

"Hello," the woman said. "My name is Ciddah. I'm glad to see you awake."

"Why am I here? Where are my clothes? Why am I tied to this bed?"

"Try to remain calm," Ciddah said. "Can you tell me your name and age?"

"Shaylinn of Zachary. I'm fourteen."

"It's nice to meet you, Shaylinn." Ciddah walked all the way to Shaylinn's bed and looked down on her. Up close, Shaylinn noticed the woman was quite pretty, with a nice figure, and her hair looked like long, shiny corn silk. She wondered if it was as soft as it appeared.

Ciddah smiled, and it seemed genuinely kind. "You're here because you were struck with a sleeper. It's protocol to monitor sleeper victims, as we never know how long they'll remain unconscious. We took your clothes so we could examine you fully. You can have them back. The restraints were to keep you from thrashing about and hurting yourself or one of our medics. I'll remove them, if you'd like."

"Yes, please."

Ciddah touched the side of Shaylinn's bed, and the restraints retracted. Shaylinn slid off the end of the table and backed into the corner by the door.

"There's no need to be frightened, Shaylinn. That's a lovely name, by the way."

Ciddah's friendliness confused her, and Shaylinn could barely think. She needed to get away. How did that door open without a handle?

"I need to explain some things before you get dressed," Ciddah said. "Of all the new female nationals, there were two who were ready for egg retrieval. You're one of them. Fortune blessed us, and we were able to collect two eggs from you without any fertility stims — drugs that we normally use to speed the process along. So we're going to have you come back in a few days for an embryo transfer."

Shaylinn's mind raced to understand what this woman was talking about. "I'm pregnant? But I've never ..."

Ciddah seemed to be fighting a smile. "You're not pregnant, Shaylinn. Not yet, at least. We're hoping to change that in a few days' time."

Shaylinn fought to fill her lungs with air. She hugged herself, squeezed. "Pick somebody else."

"Fortune has chosen you," Ciddah said. "You'll receive a summons when we're ready to do the procedure."

Shaylinn shivered. "But I don't want the procedure. I don't want to be pregnant."

"Don't be silly. It's the greatest honor to be had in the Safe Lands, and you'll be given privileges beyond your imagination. Now, let me show you how to take your meds."

Tears filled Shaylinn's eyes. She blinked them away. "I don't want any."

"It's absolutely necessary. You can learn to take them yourself with a personal vaporizer, or I can inject them into your arm with a needle. Your choice."

Shaylinn sniffled, swallowed, glanced at the door again. "What will they do to me?"

"They won't harm you. It's simply a combination of hormones to help your body become receptive for the embryo."

Shaylinn began to squirm. Tamera, Omar's mother, had taken Shaylinn, Penelope, and Nell aside two years ago and told them how babies were created, and nothing Ciddah was telling her felt right. Especially since she didn't appear to have any choice in what was happening.

"Why are you doing this to me?" Shaylinn asked. "Where's my mama? My sister?"

Ciddah moved closer to Shaylinn. Her skin was creamy white, perfect, like it had been painted. Not one blemish. "I understand this is a lot to take in. That's why we've assigned Kendall Collin as your suite mentor. She's gone through this already. She'll help you understand how it all works." She held out the little red box. "Can I show you this, please?"

Shaylinn shrugged one shoulder. Maybe if she listened, Ciddah would go away.

Ciddah opened the box and turned it so Shaylinn could see the contents. Inside was a thick black cylinder, like an Old lipstick, and three clear tubes filled with yellowish liquid.

"Here are your hormone meds." She lifted the black cylinder out of the box. "This is a personal vaporizer — some call it a PV. PVs are so much nicer than swallowing pills or getting injections. You open it like this." She twisted it at the middle and pulled it apart. "Then you insert one of the vials." She set one of the clear tubes inside the PV with the pointed side down. "And when you put the PV back together and twist, it punctures the vial, and you're ready to go. Take one long breath from the PV three times a day. With each meal is fine. When it runs out, this little light will turn red. That means you need to put in a new vial. Think you can do that?"

Shaylinn shook her head. "I'd rather swallow a pill."

Ciddah frowned. Her lips were perfect too. "Are you sure? PVs are very easy to use."

"I don't want it." It looked like the pipes the men from Jack's Peak smoked. And her mother had told her smoking was a nasty thing to do.

Ciddah nodded and stood. "All right. Why don't you get dressed and meet me out front? Your clothes are in the cupboard. I'll get some pills ready for you. Would you like help?"

Shaylinn shook her head. "I'm okay."

"I'll see you in a few minutes, Shaylinn. Just come out the door and walk to the right."

Shaylinn stayed perfectly still as she watched Ciddah tap her fist against a black square beside the door to open it.

The door whooshed closed behind Ciddah, and Shaylinn jumped

up and opened the cupboard. Her dress was hanging on a hook inside. She grabbed it and went to stand in front of the door, changing with one foot pressed against it in case anyone tried to enter. Once she was dressed, she set her left fist against the pad by the door like Ciddah had. Nothing happened. She lifted her right fist and gasped. It had a white number four on it. *When did I get that?* She rubbed the number, but it didn't come off. She set her right fist against the pad, and the door popped open.

A bright hallway stretched in both directions, lined with doors spaced evenly along each side. She could hear voices coming from the right, the way Ciddah had told her to go. At the end of the hallway to the left, a glowing green exit sign hung from the ceiling. Shaylinn slipped out into the hall and ran to the left until she reached the exit sign. There was no door, but the hallway took a turn to the right, and Shaylinn could see another exit sign at the end of a shorter hall.

She ran to it and slammed her fist against the pad in hopes this door worked like the others. Slowly, it opened into a cool cement stairwell with steps going up and down. She ran down, winding around and around. She tired quickly, certain her heart was going to give out altogether.

And suddenly there were no more stairs. Shaylinn paused to catch her breath and listen for footsteps behind her. Silence. Satisfied that she'd evaded her captor, Shaylinn used her fist to open the final door.

She exited into the night and let the door close behind her. Buildings towered overhead, higher than any tree, so tall they blurred against the dark sky and made Shaylinn feel dizzy. She wandered forward, staring up at the structures, feeling like she was floating in outer space.

She was in the city. She'd always dreamed of coming inside. Now … where should she go? Which way was home?

A siren howled and faded in a breath, like some kind of electric bird call. Then lights flooded the area, blinding her. She raised her arm to block the glare and stumbled back toward the exit door.

"Shaylinn Zachary?" a man's voice called. It sounded tinny and seemed to come from above her head.

She spun, pressed against the exit door, and looked to see who was out there. It was no use. The lights were too bright. She inched to the right, sliding along the door, then the wall of the building. *Please, God! Keep me safe.*

"Don't move," the voice warned.

But she couldn't stay there and let them impregnate her. On the count of three, she'd run. Once she got away from the lights, she'd be able to see. Then she could make a better decision of where to go. Anywhere had to be better than this building.

One ... two ... three!

Shaylinn ran blindly. Before her, the shape of a road materialized. But just as she sped toward it, she heard a buzz like the sound of a rattlesnake. Something pinched her hand, cramping every muscle, and she felt her face strike the ground. She told the rattlesnake to let go, but the words never came out. She couldn't move or speak or even breathe.

Then the attack ended.

"Why you shells won't listen ..." the voice said.

It was some time before Shaylinn came back to consciousness. When she awoke, a man was pulling her out of the back of a car. Her limbs trembled when she stood, and her hands and face burned. Thick scrapes dotted with spots of blood covered both palms.

Tears stung her eyes, but she blinked them back. Shaylinn didn't cry. She was tough like her dad and Jordan, not girly like Jemma. She could get through whatever this was.

"Come on, femme. Let's get you back where you belong." The man was one of those enforcers, dressed in the dark blue uniform. He had pale, papery skin and a rounded frizz of carrot-red hair. He wore no helmet. It probably wouldn't fit even if he tried. The patch on his uniform said *Ewan*.

She followed Ewan through a revolving glass door of a building. Was this the same building she'd escaped from? He led her through a lobby. The ceiling was so low she was sure it would fall down and crush her. The place was filled with dark wood furniture cushioned in forest green brocade, and potted plants that were arranged into sitting areas. Stiff carpet in a pattern of gold, blue, and orange covered the floor. Lights made of crystals dripped from the ceiling.

It was simultaneously ugly and beautiful.

There were people too, dressed in clothing that looked new and clean and strange. Quite a few people wore combinations of black and pale yellow, making Shaylinn think of a room filled with swallowtail butterflies. A frail woman looked Shaylinn up and down with a gaze of surprise and disapproval. She wore a black fitted dress with a thick yellow belt, and her skin looked yellower than normal. The woman lifted a slender, black cylinder to her lips and blew out a plume of black smoke.

Smoking black things? No wonder the poor woman looked so unhealthy. Shaylinn was glad she'd refused Ciddah's pipe.

Ewan led her to where three sets of polished wooden doors stood evenly spaced along one wall. He pressed a button on the wall. A soft bell chimed, and one of the doors slid open.

"An elevator," Shaylinn whispered to herself.

Ewan raised his eyebrows and motioned her inside. She obeyed. Ewan followed her in and pressed the button with a number five on it, and soon the door glided closed. The floor hardly seemed to move, though her body felt like it was being stretched upward. She set her hand on the wall.

Moments later, the elevator appeared to stop, and the stretching feeling was replaced by a queasy flutter in her stomach. The doors slid open, accompanied by the soft ding of the bell. Shaylinn followed Ewan out into another wide hallway; this one had red and black swirly carpeting with gold accents. The ceiling was three times as high as the one downstairs and had fancy crystal lights dripping from it. The hallway led to a set of wide golden doors that had a strange image carved into them, a creature with hooves that was a woman and a cat and a bird all at once.

Shaylinn didn't like her.

Ewan touched his fist to the wall, and when he pulled back his hand, Shaylinn saw the little black square on the wall beside the door.

Moments later, the door opened, and a tall, very shapely woman looked down her nose like Shaylinn was rotten apples. She wore a silky purple jacket and skirt and black high-heeled shoes that made Shaylinn smile and blurt out, "I didn't know anyone still wore those kinds of shoes."

The woman gripped the open door with one hand and held her other hand out to the side, a gold pipe as long and thin as one of Omar's paintbrushes tucked between her fingers.

"This the one you lost?" she asked Ewan.

"I didn't lose her, Matron. She ran off from the Surrogacy Center."

Matron frowned and looked Shaylinn over. "Praise Fortune they all don't look like this one." She sucked on her paintbrush pipe and exhaled purple smoke in Shaylinn's face.

Shaylinn held her breath, expecting to choke, but there was no smokiness or smell at all to the purple cloud — simply moisture.

"Well, don't just stand there, outsider girl. Come in!"

Shaylinn stepped through the door and into a fairytale palace. The carpet was white and plush. It was clean and so very soft on her feet, nothing like the old, dirty, and mildewed carpets in Glenrock's homes. The room was also humongous: a big rectangle with a ceiling as high as the one in the hallway. It had all kinds of fancy chairs and couches, topped with red and gold cushions, and little round tables of dark wood. The ceiling was painted gold and dripped with gold and crystal lights. Two doors took up the left wall. A stairway with a banister made of curling, polished wood stretched along the right wall with a landing halfway up and another one at the top. Straight ahead, a wall made of windows scooped out in a half circle as tall as the ceiling and looked out over a green field.

Matron walked past Shaylinn with little steps, and held her arms bent at the elbows so that her hands dangled as if they were wet and she didn't want to drip on her clothing.

"I've done the spiel already for all your ungrateful friends, so I'll be brief with you. If you have questions, ask your suitemates. Understood?"

What a grouch. "Yes, ma'am."

Matron rolled her eyes. "I'm twenty-seven years old. Do *not* call me ma'am. In fact, don't call anyone in the Safe Lands ma'am, *understood*?"

"Sorry," Shaylinn said.

Matron tossed her head and exhaled. "This is the harem, otherwise known as the home for women with a ticket to paradise. While you're conscripted here, you do not leave the harem unaccompanied. If you need anything, call Sona. She's the harem's housekeeper." Matron inhaled from her pipe and blew it out quickly. "You're very fortunate to be here. Minors are rarely admitted to the harem, but the task director general has made an exception for reasons he has not made known to me. Should you conceive, like your darling friend Naomi, you'll become an icon in the Safe Lands. Royalty among women."

She leveled an unfriendly glance at Shaylinn. "I understand you're one of the first to undergo the procedure. But from where I'm standing, it looks like we'll have to get you more than a makeover. More like a renovation." She chuckled, and it ended in a singsong sigh. "Never fear, though. Our Tyra is a miracle worker. Believe it or not, I've seen her transform women much worse off than you."

This should have felt like a slap to the face, but the idea of a makeover thrilled Shaylinn more than she cared to admit even to herself.

"I'm Matron Dlorah, by the way. The administrator of this establishment." She took a long puff from her pipe and blew it into the air, looking at the far wall. "I'm not climbing those stairs again today, so you're on your own to find your room. I'd ask Sona to help, but she's run to the G.I.N. — an everything store of sorts — to buy blueberries. Naomi said they were her favorite. You're in the Blue Diamond Suite. It's on the second floor. Just take the stairs halfway and go down that hallway. Kendall Collin is your suite mentor, so Fortune's blessed you there if nowhere else. Off you go, then."

Shaylinn followed Matron's instructions and found her way to a door that had a plaque proclaiming the room to be the Blue Diamond Suite. She was tired, and her hands and face hurt. If she could just find a bathroom and some water, she'd feel better. She pressed her fist to the black square beside the door, and it swung inward, revealing a very pregnant teenage girl. Stunningly pretty, really, with golden brown hair, a peaches and cream complexion, and bright green eyes.

"Hello," the girl said. "You must be Shaylinn, yes?"

"I am."

"Shay!" The door jerked open wider, and Jemma pushed past the pregnant girl and gabbed Shaylinn in a fierce hug. "Oh, Shay! Thank God. I was so worried! Where have you been? What happened to your face?" Jemma let go and pulled Shaylinn inside. "Come in and sit. I'll get something to help you clean it up."

Jemma dragged Shaylinn inside what seemed like a home. Everything was bright blue or white or polished wood. The carpet was the same soft white. There was a gleaming wood table and chairs, a small kitchen that flowed from one side of the room, and a sheet of glass that took up most of one wall and was so thin it looked to be painted onto the surface. There were also two couches. Mia and Naomi were each sitting on a different one. Shaylinn was so relieved to see their familiar faces.

Jemma sat Shaylinn on the sofa beside their sister-in-law Naomi, who turned Shaylinn's chin from side to side. A pearly number eight on Naomi's cheek caught Shaylinn's gaze. Shaylinn looked to Jemma, who had the number four. Mia, a number eight. The pregnant teen who'd welcomed her had a number one.

"They put numbers on our faces and hands?" Shaylinn asked. "Like the enforcers?"

"Everyone who lives here has them," Mia said.

Shaylinn looked at her hand. "There's a four on my face?"

"Just like me," Jemma said, sitting down and gently rubbing a wet cloth over Shaylinn's scraped cheek. It stung a little.

"Because we're related?" Shaylinn asked. Naomi and Mia were cousins.

"Maybe," Jemma said.

Shaylinn touched her other cheek. It felt a little swollen, but maybe that side was just scraped up too. "What do you think they mean?" she asked her sister.

"I don't know," Jemma said, starting to wipe Shaylinn's right palm. "We didn't ask for the number, and if the Safe Landers have them, I worry they have some terrible meaning. Hopefully everything will be revealed soon."

"Shay, this is Kendall," Naomi said, referring to the pregnant girl. "She's very nice and has been trying to help us understand what goes on in this crazy place."

"Hi," Shaylinn said. "You're so pretty."

Kendall blushed. "They've done a lot of work on me."

"Really?" Shaylinn couldn't believe it. "You weren't so pretty before?"

"Well, I don't know." Kendall sat on a chair at the table. "They're very good at enhancing what you've got."

Mama used to say that. Use what you've got. "Where's Mama?" Shaylinn asked Jemma.

"We figured they'd be in a different suite, but the only other people from Glenrock that are here in the harem are Aunt Mary, Chipeta, Jennifer, and Eliza. They're in the Fire Opal suite, if you want to go talk to them."

"What about Penelope and Nell?"

Jemma started to clean Shaylinn's other hand. "What happened to you, Shay? Where have you been?"

The way her sister changed the subject made Shaylinn wonder what she wasn't saying. Shaylinn told them about waking in the medical room and how Ciddah said she'd get pregnant. And about running away and getting caught.

"That explains who was number one in their lineup," Mia said.

Shaylinn held up her hand. "No, I'm number four."

"Not that number," Mia said. "The number you are in line to have a baby. Matron told each of us our surrogacy number. Chipeta is six. I'm five. My mom is four. Jemma's three. Eliza is two."

"And I'm one," Shaylinn said. "Of course."

Jemma clapped her hand over her chest. "They mean to force my baby sister to bear a child? That's not acceptable. You're not old enough!"

"When I first heard the word *harem*, I panicked. All I could think of was the harem in the book *Anna and the King of Siam*. You know, Jemma, the one you read to me a few years ago. That's one reason I ran. But when Matron explained it, it didn't seem like that at all. I don't understand."

"The people in the Safe Lands have trouble conceiving," Kendall said. "Living in the harem is meant to be an incentive; giving women a posh environment, not to mention fame, so they'll produce babies for the government. But lately every woman inside the walls has failed to bring an uninfected child to term. Even me."

"What does that mean — failed?" Shaylinn asked. "Your baby is going to die?"

"No. Just that both my baby and I have the thin plague."

Shaylinn looked to Jemma, suddenly chilled. "What Papa Eli warned us about."

"They were hoping that, since I was uninfected, my baby would be healthy too. But the plague infected both of us instead," Kendall said.

"I will *not* let this happen to you, Shay!" Jemma stood and paced between the couches. "We'll find a way out before this happens. And of course Levi will come for us."

"Who's Levi?" Kendall asked.

"My fiancé." Jemma fingered a necklace of small pink beads she was wearing around her neck, and her eyes filled with tears. "He's the Westley to my Princess Buttercup. We're to be married in two days." She sniffed and smiled.

"They're perfect for each other," Naomi said, grinning.

Mia rolled her eyes.

"Marriage doesn't exist in the Safe Lands," Kendall said. "Lifers pair up exclusively, which is sort of the same." She sighed. "There was a boy back home ... Roger had golden hair that always hung down to his nose. I used to imagine we got married and that I kept his hair cut short enough so I could see his eyes."

"You're not from the Safe Lands?" Shaylinn asked.

"I'm from Casper," Kendall said. "That's in Wyoming."

"How can anyone live so far from the safe water source?" Naomi asked. "Elder Eli — he was our village leader. He always told us the only safe water was near Mount Crested Butte."

"There was a water bottling plant in Casper before the Great Pandemic," Kendall said. "The survivors lived off that for years until they invented a water purifier that filtered the virus."

Shaylinn hadn't known that any other settlements existed. How many more might there be across the globe? "But if you can live there, why come to the Safe Lands?"

"My uncle traded me to drug lords, who traded me here."

"Betrayed by family," Jemma mumbled. "Just like us and Omar."

Shaylinn's heart tightened at the mention of Omar's name. "What do you mean?"

"Only that Omar is responsible for everything that happened today," Naomi said.

Shaylinn couldn't breathe, but managed to ask, "How?"

Jemma shook her head. "I don't know. But when he and I arrived at the meeting hall, the enforcers knew him. And they gave him some fancy gold paper."

"A golden ticket," Kendall said. "That's what they call a special provision from the task director general himself. Still, I doubt this Omar is wholly responsible. They would have come for you at some point anyway. Most of the people who live inside these walls don't know how bad off things are. Since the government raises the children elsewhere, people tend to forget the kids even exist."

Wait. "They raise the children where?" Shaylinn asked.

"There are no families in the Safe Lands," Kendall said. "Children are raised by those tasked to caregiving. And the older children live in the Safe Lands Boarding School."

"That's where they took Glenrock's children," Jemma said, meeting Shaylinn's gaze. "Penelope, Nell, the boys and girls — all of them. Even the babies went to a nursery."

"We about had a riot when we figured it out," Naomi said. "And half of us got shot with those electrical guns. We tried to start our own war, clawing and lashing out at the guards with whatever we could get our hands on, but we lost."

"This battle only," Jemma said.

"Yeah, Eliza and Chipeta and Jennifer are probably plotting their next attack," Naomi said. "Mary just cries and cries."

Shaylinn wished she could cry. It was all too horrible to be real. Children taken from their parents? Forced pregnancies? She prayed for God's deliverance and protection, that Levi would come, along with her father and brother, and rescue them before she received Ciddah's summons. And she begged God that Jemma was wrong about Omar, that he'd had nothing to do with any of this.

CHAPTER 9

"You sure he's awake?" a man's voice asked. "We're practically carrying him."

Mason was cold. He opened his eyes, and a dim hallway came into focus. The walls were gray. Halos of yellow light gleamed from the ceiling. Black doors lined the hallway. Where was he going? He was thirsty. He blinked and fought the nausea in his gut. His feet were moving across the floor as though they were disconnected from his body. He tried to stop his forward momentum, but someone jerked his arm.

"Keep moving, shell."

He blinked. Two enforcers were pulling him along. "Where are you taking me?" Mason asked, his voice raspy.

The enforcer on his right chuckled. "He speaks!"

"We're having some trouble with your peer, shell," the enforcer on his left said, "and we want you to talk to him."

"My peer?"

The enforcers stopped in front of a black door that had a silver number seven on it.

"We've had to stun him. Twice." The enforcer on Mason's right was thick with muscle. His face was thick too, with a wrinkled forehead, thick brows, and curly black hair. The name on his uniform claimed he was named Hale. "The task director general wants you and your peer in there to become nationals. When you agree, we'll take you to the Registration Department. Until then, welcome home."

The slender guy on Mason's left nudged him slightly. "Just calm him down enough that we can explain things." His name tag read Bentzon. Mason looked at the man's face and saw he had gray camouflage skin.

He blinked and squinted at the man again. Still camouflage. As his vision cleared further, he also noticed both men had iridescent numbers on their right cheeks. Mason looked down the hall to the right, then left. Both directions looked identical: black doors, halo lights, gray walls.

Where was he? The Safe Lands? Was he actually inside the compound?

"E72 to Highland Gatekeeper, requesting entry to holding cell seven," Hale said.

"Please verify identification," a muted woman's voice replied.

Mason looked both ways again. No woman. Where had the voice come from?

Hale set his fist against a black square on the wall next to the door marked seven. Bentzon lifted the side of Mason's hand against the square, then dropped it and held up his own.

"Identifications verified," the woman said. The door clicked and swung inward.

"Here we go," Hale said.

"Let me out of here, you maggots!" Jordan's voice called.

What was Jordan doing here? If Jordan was the man they thought would listen to Mason's words, the guards were in for a surprise.

"We'll be back in ten, shell." Bentzon pushed Mason inside. The door clicked shut.

Mason reached for the handle but found none. He stood in a gray icebox with a hard, concrete floor. He blinked again and discovered he was wearing a thin gray jumpsuit and black canvas slip-on shoes. Who'd dressed him? There were two metal chairs in the room. Jordan was bound to one. Shackles held his wrists to the sides of the chair, and a chain belt encircled his waist.

"Mason! Unhook me, quick!"

Mason stumbled to the chair and studied the shackles. "They're locked."

Jordan screamed and pulled against the bindings until his face flushed red and veins popped out on his neck.

Mason noticed a pale number four on Jordan's right cheek. The milky color seemed to move, as if the number were made of liquid that had been imbedded under transparent skin. "You have a number four on your face. How did that happen?"

Jordan stopped struggling and looked at Mason. "You have a number nine. And you tell me. What's with these people?" He yanked at his shackles again.

Finally, Mason's brain began recalling what had happened in the village. Gunfire. His father was dead. Uncle Colton was dead. Shaylinn was hurt. Then Otley had shot a sleeper into Mason's back.

Mason sat on the other chair. "We're in the compound?"

"How'd you guess, genius?"

"What happened?"

"I woke up tied to a table in some hospital. I screamed and yelled until the doctor came and untied me. Then I ran. They didn't like that, though. Some enforcers chased me and shot me with some kind of electrifying gun. They brought me here, told me I was being given the great honor of becoming a national, and that my cooperation would save their pitiful world. And when I tried to get away, they shot me again and hooked me to this chair. End of story. Why's it so cold?"

Mason looked up at the ceiling and located a vent. "Must be air-conditioning. Papa Eli told me about it once. It used to be everywhere before the Pandemic." He also noticed a bright yellow camera looking down from the corner of the ceiling. "I wonder if they implanted these numbers while we were in the hospital."

"Pull me to the door," Jordan said.

"What?"

"Come on! Get me close."

Mason got up and dragged Jordan's chair over to face the door, cringing as the metal legs scraped over the floor. When Mason got him close enough, Jordan lifted his leg and kicked the door.

"Jordan."

Jordan kicked the door again. "Open this door, you bowels of a dead skunk!"

"Jordan, stop," Mason said.

But Jordan kicked again, growling this time.

Mason sat back down and watched Jordan kick the door a few more times. Even though Jordan was nineteen years old, he had a tendency to act like he was five. "The enforcers are well aware of your displeasure."

"Good." Jordan lifted his feet and kicked the door so hard that his chair tipped back. It paused on two legs for one second before gravity won out. Mason winced as the chair slammed against the floor. Jordan kept his chin against his chest and managed to keep his head from hitting anything.

"Feel better?" Mason asked.

Jordan eased down his head. "No." He slammed his feet against the door, one at a time, like he was running.

What was he trying to accomplish? "You do realize the door swings inward?"

"Shut up, dog face."

So Mason did. He could think of nothing helpful to say anyhow. His pulse was still throbbing in his ears; it had been since the first gun had fired. Shock, no doubt. His body trying to compensate for the horror of seeing so many killed. He thought over the stages of grief that he'd read about in his psychology book. How could shock not be one of them? And when would he start denying that any of this had taken place? "Why are we alive? Why kill some of us, but not all? I don't understand."

Jordan let his legs fall limp and turned his head, craning his neck and rolling his eyes up so he could see Mason. "Think she's okay?" he asked, his voice a low croak.

Mason didn't know if Jordan meant one of his sisters, his mother, or his wife.

"I mean, she's already pregnant. So they wouldn't hurt her, right?"

Ah, Naomi, his wife. "You saw them take the women?" Mason asked.

"The enforcer said the women were going to bear children for the Safe Lands. Do you think *all* of the women? And *whose* children, huh, Mason?"

Mason cringed. Surely, they didn't intend to force the women ... Only monsters would do such a thing. Almost as unsettling: the Safe Lands enforcers, though violent with their gunfire today, hadn't bothered Glenrock in seventy years. Why now? And why were he and Jordan so important?

Mason thought through what had happened. "The last thing I remember ... Papa Eli!" *Please, Lord, let someone have helped him.* Mason looked at his hands. They were clean. No blood. "Someone washed my hands." He held one out to Jordan. "I was trying to stop Papa Eli's bleeding when I got shot." His eyes stung, his vision clouded. He coughed and sucked in a breath.

"Hey!" Jordan said. "None of that. We have to keep it together. My dad's dead too, but do you see me crying? Huh? We've got to get out of this place, find the others. As hard as it is ... buck up."

Jordan's dad? Elder Harvey dead too? "What if there are no others? And why didn't they kill us?"

"I saw them loading the women and kids into one of those trucks. And I heard an enforcer say they wanted the young people."

"But why?" All Mason truly knew of Safe Landers was that they were inflicted with a terminal disease that stemmed from the original virus that had entered the world's water supply and caused the Great Pandemic. According to the stories Papa Eli had told, the Safe Lands had started as a haven for the uninfected because of the clean water coming from the mountain. But when the waterborne strain mutated into a bloodborne one and Safe Lands leaders neglected the warnings from doctors and continued to engage in wild living, many people left, which was how the outlying villages had come to exist, keeping close to the clean water, but far from Safe Lands' dangers. Papa Eli had warned the people of Glenrock never to marry a Safe Lands national or they'd become infected.

"If they hurt Naomi," Jordan said. "If they hurt my boy …"

"What makes you so sure it's a boy?"

Jordan flubbed his lips. "It's a boy."

Mason smiled. It was a bit forced, but even a half-hearted smile felt good at this point. "If you say so."

Reality suddenly hung heavily on Mason's heart, and his eyes stung. He needed to think. The enforcers would be coming back any minute. And one had told Jordan that the women would bear children for the Safe Lands. Why? And what were the men to do?

"Think Levi's dead?" Jordan asked.

The very idea brought another smile to Mason's lips. "No way. Not Levi."

Jordan straightened his neck and gazed at the ceiling. "He'll come for us, then. And when he does, we're going to kill them all."

Mason had no doubt his big brother would bring fire and brimstone upon this place, but he searched for the right words to curb talk of more death. "That won't change anything. It'll only make you just like them."

"Don't turn into Papa Eli on me right now, Mason. Just leave me to my murderous daydreams, will you?"

The door opened then, whacking against the side of Jordan's chair. Two people entered: Hale and Otley, the giant pierced bat who'd killed Mason's father and uncle and Papa Eli.

"How?" Mason stood, fists clenched. His heart throbbed within his chest. This man should be dead. "Papa Eli shot you."

"Takes more than one round to take me out, rat," Otley said.

Jordan kicked Otley's leg. "Where is my wife, you son of a cockroach's vomit?"

Hale drew his gun, and Jordan stopped kicking.

Otley bent over Jordan. "Your woman's in the harem, rat. I intend to visit her myself."

Jordan's face went red in the space of a breath. "If you *touch* her … If you even *breathe* on her …"

"You'll chase after me, and I'll stomp on you." Otley smacked Jordan's face softly — slap, slap, slap — then walked to the door and turned. "Last chance for compliance, little rats. Become Safe Lands nationals. Give us what we need to create healthy children here. Refuse, and you'll be sent to the rehabilitation center. You have ten minutes to decide." He ducked out the open doorway, and Hale followed, closing the door behind him.

Jordan screamed and pulled against his restraints, cursing and kicking until he ran out of breath.

Mason sank down on the other chair. "I think we should comply."

Jordan turned his head to glare at Mason. "Are you crazy?"

"Our best chance is to play along and see what they want."

"I will *not* become one of them," Jordan said.

Mason took a deep breath. "We're not one of them — ever. But we can pretend to be. We can't do anything from in here."

"If I can get that enforcer's gun, I might be able to get us free."

"You're secured to a chair, lying on the floor, Jordan. You can't get anyone's gun."

"I could get it."

And Mason's father had always admired such foolish brawn over thoughtful logic. Mason glanced quickly at the camera then lowered himself to the ground and whispered in Jordan's ear. "Listen to me. Violence against these people will only lead us to our graves. We have to think." Mason inched a little closer. "Playing along will give us a chance at freedom inside these walls. Then we can find out where the women and children are being held, where to get weapons, and how we might get away."

"You're a coward!" Jordan yelled. "You've always been a coward, ever since Joel died."

The words sent fire through Mason's chest. "I sat by your brother's side until his last breath. But all of you ran off to kill something. So who was the coward, Jordan?"

Jordan's voice came softly. "You used to hunt with us. You used to eat meat."

Mason clenched his teeth, then finally said, "*Don't* start this. I never liked to hunt. I'm not a killer. Of anything. It was that way long before Joel's accident."

Jordan turned his head so he could see Mason. "Naomi would've married him. You know that? She and Joel were close."

Mason huffed a silent laugh. "They both liked to climb trees."

"The kissing trees."

"Jordan, stop." But Mason closed his eyes, thinking of the one time he'd climbed those trees with a girl. Eliza. He'd been so young. He still felt bad about how things had ended between them. He shuddered at the memory.

Jordan's voice softened. "Sometimes I think, what if he'd lived? If he'd lived, then I wouldn't have her. So I'm glad he'd dead, right, Mason? My own brother. I'm glad."

Mason squeezed his eyes tight before opening them. "You're *not* glad he's gone. You're thankful to be blessed with a good wife. That's different."

"I'd die without her. I can't live without her." Jordan broke down this time. No kicking the door. Just sobbing. "What if these maggots do something to her?"

"Hey," Mason stood and heaved Jordan's chair up, grunting with the effort. Once the chair was on all fours, he walked around front. "You said no crying. You told me to buck up."

The door opened. Otley and Hale entered the room. Mason backed against the wall, fighting the urge to run at Otley. *Anger won't help. Anger won't help.*

But Jordan kicked at Otley with renewed vigor. "Why don't you untie me, fight me man to man, you doe-kissing, dog-licking pile of fish guts — you coward!"

Hale drew his gun and fired. Jordan uttered a short cry, then his body went rigid. No bullets. No wires or rays. But Jordan lay silent and limp. How could that be? Hale unhooked him, kicked the metal chair aside, grabbed Jordan's ankles, and dragged him toward the door. The last Mason saw of his brother's best friend was his fingertips trailing around the doorframe.

Bentzon stepped into the doorway, stunning gun drawn and pointed at Mason.

"And you, little rat?" Otley asked, looking down on Mason. "Going to the rehabilitation center as well?"

"No." Mason had to do what he felt was right. And he couldn't help anyone if he followed Jordan's method. "I'll cooperate."

Otley motioned to Bentzon in the doorway. "Take him to Registration."

Bentzon waved his gun at Mason. "Let's go, shell."

Mason walked into the hallway. No sign of Jordan. He wanted to ask where they'd taken him but thought better of it. His words and actions needed to look compliant.

CHAPTER 10

Bentzon transported Mason to a building the guard referred to as City Hall. On the third floor, they entered the Men's Health and Wellness Department and went straight to the Donation Center. A guard gave him a plastic cup, then sent him into a small room with a shower-like stall and sink. Mason paced the floor as he tried to figure out why he'd been brought here. Bentzon hadn't given any hint as to what happened at the Donation Center, almost like he assumed Mason knew. Based on what Jordan had said about the Glenrock women needing to bear children, Mason reasoned the Donation Center was the male's version of the harem.

Mason remembered something his mother once said: that, in the Old Days, doctors had been able to use different scientific methods to impregnate a woman. Those procedures had been lost over time, but he'd read about things such as surrogacy, artificial insemination, and in vitro fertilization in one of Mother's medical textbooks. Based on the amount of technology inside the compound, the Safe Lands had likely regained that lost knowledge.

Mason looked again at the cup in his hands. He couldn't do it.

The cup was opaque, so he put a little water and spit into it, snapped on the lid, and hoped it would at least be enough to get him out of the center. He carried the cup to the enforcer, who motioned for Mason to hand it to a man sitting at the front desk.

Mason held his breath as he and the enforcer waited for the elevator, sure the man would discover his cheat at any moment. To his relief, the elevator arrived, and Bentzon pushed him inside.

Mason was escorted down to the second floor and into the Registration Department, an open room with a counter at one end and a dozen desks to the left of it.

The man at the counter had yellow and black striped hair. "I'm Dallin. I need to take your picture before we start. Can you back up against that wall and stand on those black footprints?"

Mason saw no reason to refuse. Dallin used a rectangle of glass to snap a picture, then returned to his desk. "Have a seat."

Mason sat and tried to relax. If someone was coming to capture him for his faulty sample, they likely would have arrived by now. And acting like a nervous wreck wouldn't gain him much acceptance amidst these strange people. "Um, Dallin, how did your hair get that way?"

"The To Dye For salon," Dallin said. "He comes up with the best mimic looks. Now, I'm going to work up your identification, then you'll take the task test, which will determine your schedule. Since you're new to all this, let me explain. Each national must perform a task to help our city operate — a basic job we assign based on your test performance. We understand some tasks are desired over others, but all must be done to ensure the pleasure and survival of each national. Your test will generate a list of several tasks you're suited for, and you'll work each task for a six-month shift before rotating to the next on your list. After three years, you can retest and see if your list changes. If you find you love a certain task, you can apply to prolong your assignment in that area. But there's no guarantee your request will be approved. Do you understand?"

"Yes, sir," Mason said.

Dallin set a little black pad on the counter. "Press your right fist on the pad." When Mason did, Dallin took away the pad and asked, "Do you have a last name?"

"Our people identify with tribes. I'm from the Elias tribe."

"How about we make Elias your last name? Unless there's another name you'd prefer."

"Elias is fine."

"Okay." Dallin tapped on his computer screen, which was nothing more than a sheet of glass on an elevated base. He sat back in his chair and turned the glass so that Mason could see the surface. Mason's picture, name, and number appeared like on TV screen. The words *task*, *task director*, *task start date*, *region*, and *residence* were displayed below.

"This will all get filled in after you task test," Dallin said. "I'm all done here, so you can sit at any station to test. Go ahead."

Mason moved to the nearest desk. The surface was black glass. Mason looked back to Dallin, not sure what he was supposed to do.

"It's a GlassTop touchscreen," Dallin said, coming over beside Mason. He tapped the screen with his finger. A picture slowly faded from black into a bright blue. The words *TaskTest 6.0* hovered in a white rectangle in the center of the screen. Dallin touched it with his finger, and the screen changed to a series of blanks.

"Tap the screen to type in your name and number and to answer each question."

"Thank you," Mason said, marveling at the machine. Clearly, the Safe Landers had managed to hold on to a lot of technology from the Old Days.

The test was multiple choice, with questions about cooking, drawing, architecture, machines, cleaning, and teaching. Some questions Mason needed Dallin to explain before he could answer.

Around question thirty, the test became more specific, as if the computer were starting to learn Mason's interests. Most questions were now medical or mathematical in nature. Mason didn't understand most of the math questions.

When he expected question sixty-eight to appear, the screen displayed *TaskTest complete. Please report to your test director.*

Mason walked back to Dallin's desk.

"All done?"

"Yes, sir."

Dallin tapped around on his glass screen. "Huh," he said. "You're a smart guy. Got a list of high-level tasks. But the system flagged you since you're an outsider, which means the task director general will have to approve your task list. That doesn't happen very often. Let's see ..." He looked at Mason, then spoke to the enforcers, who were practically dozing in the waiting area. "Why don't you take him to the cafeteria while I figure out what to do?"

Mason followed the enforcers to a vast room packed with people and noise. Rich smells filled his nose. The enforcers took him through a line where he had to press his fist against another black pad before someone operating a glass screen would let him pass. Mason examined the side of his fist and found a small puncture, bloodless. Some sort of implant?

The food was set out in long metal trays. There were so many choices, even for a vegetarian. Mason ate foods he recognized: green salad, peas, biscuits, sweet potatoes, rice, and two slices of pie—apple and one made of gooey nuts. When he finished, the enforcers took him to the tenth floor, then sent him in to meet the task director general.

Mason pushed open the door and entered what felt like a modern palace. The room was furnished in black and red, with hardwood floors and windows that wrapped around three walls, exposing a vast view of the valley below. Mason felt like he was walking among the clouds.

A large desk sat in front of the only true wall. A bald man stood beside it, blocking Mason's view of the man sitting there. Mason closed the door behind him, drawing the bald man's attention.

"Well, Hay-o, Mr. Elias," the man said, walking toward him. "My name is Kruse." He extended his hand, and Mason shook it. "Come meet the task director general, Lawten Renzor."

The man behind the desk was slender, with a hunched posture and a large nose that was flaking badly. His dark and protruding eyes instantly unsettled Mason. They seemed too eager, too knowing.

"This is Mason Elias, the smart one." Kruse winked at Mason.

Kruse's behavior startled Mason, but he forced himself to stay focused on the task director. This man ruled the Safe Lands. That murderer Otley answered to him. If his people were to have any chance, Mason needed to find some way of negotiating with this man. "It's nice to meet you, sir."

The task director nodded his head in greeting, then motioned for Mason to sit. Mason sank onto a red leather chair.

"Your test results show you to be a clever young man, Mr. Elias," the task director said.

"Thank you, sir."

"He's so polite!" Kruse said. "Let him task for me. I could use an assistant who doesn't complain."

With no reaction to Kruse at all, the task director said, "I'd like to place you as a medic."

"I don't know enough to be a full doctor." Working with the medical staff, though, might give him access to something valuable.

"Which is why you'll task as an assistant to a lower-level lead medic. In six months, when you rotate, we could also place you in low-level research. Would you like that?"

Mason had no plans to be within the compound by the time the next rotation came around. "What kind of research?"

"Medical, of course."

The word sent a thrill through Mason. Of course he'd love to study medical research. But he reminded himself his priority was helping the people of Glenrock.

"That said, while your test results were impressive, I have two concerns," the task director said. "First, your education. You learned from outsiders and may not understand our medical procedures. This, however, can be taught. My second concern is honesty. You're smart enough to know what the donation cup was for and either pretended not to know when you filled it or thought you could lie to us. Now, *I'd* be the fool if I placed a dishonest man in a sensitive position, don't you agree?"

Well, Mason had figured he'd be caught at some point. "You would, sir."

"Then why should I allow you to task as a medic and not send you to sweep the streets?"

Mason took a deep breath — if the task director wanted honesty, he would have it. "Because I'm not a violent man. I've only ever wanted to save lives. I'm also a cautious man. And you asked me to do something I didn't fully understand, and fulfill a role I hadn't agreed to take on. I learned many things while I was in my village, and have plenty of common sense, but the culture of Glenrock is very different. Until I grasp an adequate understanding of your ways, don't expect me to conform. I'm willing to learn, but not willing to be forced."

Lawten's dark eyes stared back. "It's quite simple. Male nationals are required to leave a donation once a month. What will it take for you to comply?"

All male nationals? "Explain why I must do this, why it's so important." The answer had a deeper meaning for Mason as well; he couldn't very well come up with an alternative solution unless he understood the problem.

The task director chuckled, a wheezing sound that made the folds of skin on his neck twitch. "You want full disclosure, is that it?"

"I think it's only fair."

The task director turned to Kruse. "Place him in his fifth option, as a level two medic under Ciddah Rourke. And schedule a meeting with Ciddah so I can explain." He turned to Mason. "Ms. Rourke is a Level Nine Medic in the Surrogacy Center. They deal mostly with reproductive appointments, so you'll have access to our process, which should answer most of your questions. And since they're located in City Hall, they also arrange private medical appointments for people in my office, so you will also get to do regular first aid, see how simple procedures differ from those in your village. Ask whatever questions you like, though I suggest you watch your tone. And I'll make sure Ciddah knows you've been given permission to look into how things operate in the facility."

Having that much free rein in the Surrogacy Center was more than Mason had dared hope for, though he wished the task director would have answered his questions outright. But the fact that he had not been taken to the Rehabilitation Center — whatever that was — with Jordan told him that he had value here — value he could use.

"Thank you," Mason said. "I appreciate your giving me this chance to learn."

"I'll be watching you, Mr. Elias. Don't give me reason to doubt your sincerity."

Mason entered the Surrogacy Center's reception area and, as he had been doing all day, approached a desk. Unlike the other buildings he'd seen, the floors, walls, and ceiling here were sterile white.

An full-figured woman with pale yellow skin and spiky black hair sat behind the desk. She was tapping on her GlassTop while talking to herself. "Will Friday the second work?"

Mason stopped before the desk. Unable to stop himself, he asked, "Excuse me. How do you make your skin yellow?"

The woman looked up, and her eyes bulged. She held up a finger. "Great. You're all set then." She tapped on the image of a keypad on her desk, made it disappear, then looked up at Mason. "*Hay-o, Valentine.* How can I help you?"

"Um, you could answer my question about your skin." Mason could feel himself getting warm. Of all the things to ask her, and he had to ask twice. He should instead ask who she'd been speaking to.

"Oh, it's Roller Paint. I've been doing yellow along with Luella Flynn. Kind of getting tired of it, though. She's coming in here today, you know. Filming another check-up with Kendall Collin. It's getting close to Kendall's delivery." She looked him up and down.

Mason frowned, understanding little of her answer. "I'm here to task with Ciddah Rourke. The task director general sent me. Are you Miss Rourke?"

The woman cackled, her mouth so wide Mason could see the back of her throat. "I'm Rimola. I task in reception. I'm *so* glad you're here. Not only are you yummy to look at, now I won't have to rotate to a task where I need to take vitals or stock the rooms with—You're going to be here every week for six months, right?"

Mason fumbled for the sheet of paper Dallin had given him. "I suspect that is the Registration Department's intention for me." Though Mason planned to be back in Glenrock long before then.

Rimola gasped. "Are you an outsider?"

"I'm not from the Safe Lands, no."

She reached out. "Can I shake your hand?"

Mason extended his arm, and Rimola pulled him toward her, rubbing her thumb over the back of his hand. "Fortune be praised, you're soft! I heard all outsiders were rough and leathery."

Mason pulled free and stepped back from the desk. "Miss Rimola, I ... well ... Please let Ciddah Rourke know that I've arrived." He walked to the farthest chair from the desk and sat down.

Rimola tapped and rubbed her fingers over her GlassTop and hummed and sighed and spoke to someone through what must be an ear device, though Mason could see none.

He tried to ignore her. He spent the time focusing on ways he could use this opportunity to help his people, even praying at one point that God would show him what to do. This position could bring him closer to the information he sought.

"Mason Elias?"

Halfway between Rimola's desk and where Mason sat stood an angel. This girl was achingly pretty, more so than even Mia. She had long, golden hair, creamy skin, rosy cheeks, and huge, electric-blue eyes. Once Mason was able to take his eyes from her face, he noticed she was wearing scrubs, like nurses and doctors of Old. They were solid purple, and while most people likely drowned in such baggy clothes, this woman made them look like a fancy dress.

He stood to greet her. She was short and curvy and perfect. He shook the thought away.

"I'm Ciddah Rourke. You can call me Ciddah." She stuck out her hand, and he took it, pleased for an invitation to touch such a lovely woman. Suddenly he wasn't quite as offended with Rimola for her actions—he was now tempted to do the same. "Why don't you come on back, Mason, and I'll give you a tour. Luella Flynn is coming in today, so we won't have much time." She pulled her hand free and walked back toward the reception desk.

Mason followed, kicking himself for having held on to her hand for so long. He needed to focus. He didn't have time to be drooling over any woman, especially a Safe Lands national.

Ciddah showed him the exam rooms, the supply room, and the restrooms. Everything was white and gray and spotless, with the exception of the yellow security cameras in the hallway and reception area. Next, Ciddah led him to her office. It too was white and gray, though portraits of bright flowers hung on the walls, the images changing every few seconds to different flowers. But the place looked like a dog had chased a squirrel through it. Mason could barely see a desk and three chairs under a mess of scattered papers and stacks of handheld computer screens. Wads of paper lay on the floor around the trashcan. The only thing he didn't see within the office was a security camera.

Ciddah whisked a stack of papers off one of the chairs in front of her desk. "Take a seat."

Mason sat on the edge of the chair, and resisted the urge to straighten the stack of handheld computers on the glass desk in front of him.

Ciddah lifted one of the computers off the stack and handed it to Mason. It was about six by eight inches and quite light. She stood beside him and looked down as he held it. "This is a CompuChart," she said. "Any data you input under a national's ID goes straight to his or her file on the grid. That way, you have each patient's history at your fingertips."

Mason studied the screen. "Convenient."

"Yes, well, you start by inputting a national's ID. I'll use mine as an example." Ciddah set her hand on his shoulder and reached over him with her other arm; he was extremely aware of her side brushing against his. She smelled like vanilla and cinnamon. She set her fist against the glass, and the screen flashed to a new page.

Across the top, the screen said *Name: Ciddah Rourke; DOB: 5-2-2069; AGE: 19*

"The ID will bring up the national's information and histories:

medical, obstetrical, gynecological, genetic, social, allergies, medications and — "

"Luella Flynn is here." Rimola's voice called from somewhere on Ciddah's desk.

Ciddah sighed and moved a pile of papers, revealing a small black speaker. She pressed a button. "Show them to exam room three. I'll be right there." She took the CompuChart from Mason. "Thank Fortune there won't be many more of these silly visits. Luella — she's famous, in case you don't already know — has been coming in almost constantly to film the ColorCast specials on Kendall's pregnancy. The nationals have a fascination with our queens. Once Kendall delivers, they'll start focusing on Naomi, since she'll deliver next, but I've arranged it so you'll replace me as the medical consultant for those little spectacles."

"Replace you? But I don't know how to — "

"Don't worry. I'll make sure you know what to say. I just abhor being on the ColorCast. And Safe Landers will love that our new queen wants her friend as her medic."

Mason could not be Naomi's medic. Jordan would never approve. And Mason didn't understand what Ciddah had meant about ColorCast until they reached exam room four.

Bright lights spilled out the door, and he shielded his eyes when he followed Ciddah into the sweltering room. Powerful bulbs and a camera were focused on the exam table where a young pregnant girl lay, looking bored and hot.

A woman stood by the exam table. She had short, spiral burgundy curls clipped with a sparkly flower, and she wore a burgundy pants suit.

"How's the lighting, Byran?" the cameraman asked, though Mason saw no other men.

"Luella?" Ciddah called from the doorway. "We're here."

"Hay-o!" Luella sang. "Make way for the medics!"

The cameraman stepped aside so that Ciddah and Mason could squeeze into the end of the room, which felt more like an oven than the doorway had.

"We're live in sixty!" the cameraman said.

"You're Mason, is that right?" Luella asked.

Mason nodded, captivated by the thickness of the makeup on Luella's face.

"Well, speak, Valentine, so we can get your voice on the boom. Have you met Kendall?"

"No," Mason said.

Luella fixed Mason with a glare. "Speak more than that!"

"Sorry. No, I have not met Kendall. Hello, Kendall," Mason said.

Kendall giggled. "Hello, Mason."

"Marvelous! Byran? We'll need to do makeup and wardrobe on Mason in the future. He's looking a little drab." She turned to Mason. "But you've got a face viewers will love, trigger. Kendall's shows bring in seventy-two percent female viewers."

Luella touched her ear and said, "Will do." She took hold of Mason's arm and pulled him around the end of the exam table. "Byran wants you on Ciddah's left, just behind the foot of the table … that's right. How we sound, Byran?"

"Do I have to speak?" Mason asked.

"No, trigger," Luella said. "In fact, don't speak unless you're spoken to. This is just a facial for you. We want the audience to get used to seeing you on screen."

"Ten seconds!" the cameraman said.

Mason wanted to ask if Kendall was in labor, but didn't dare speak after Luella's instructions. He caught Kendall looking his way, and her friendly smile eased his nervousness somewhat. No wonder Ciddah didn't want to do this anymore. He already wanted to run out of the room.

"In five, four, three, two …" The cameraman pointed at Luella.

Luella came to life, talking directly into the camera. "I'm live at the Surrogacy Center with Kendall Collin for her very last routine check-up." She turned and set her hand on Kendall's belly. "Tell us, Kendall, are you in labor?"

Kendall laughed a little. "I don't think so. But Ciddah says I'll know if it happens, so … I guess not."

"Are you excited or scared or nervous, or all three?"

"Kind of all three," Kendall said, her smile now looking a bit forced.

Luella turned back to the camera. "Medic Ciddah Rourke is training Mason Elias today in how to listen to the baby's heartbeat. We've heard our boy's heart dozens of times, but, Ciddah, tell us how this miracle machine works."

Ciddah's face flushed a bit, but she lifted what looked like a thick blanket off a table behind her. "This is a mimeo imager, Mason," Ciddah said, laying it over Kendall's belly. "We use it to take pictures of the baby and to find the heartbeat. It's programmed into this exam room's Wyndo." She turned to a blue screen of glass that covered half the wall and tapped the word *audio*. "Hear that?" Whirring came from a speaker in the ceiling. "That's the placenta's blood flow. That's good." A pattering, like a distant, galloping horse, replaced the whir. "There's our boy."

Several seconds passed as they listened to the baby's heartbeat.

"That's fascinating," Mason said, smiling.

"Simply magical!" Luella exclaimed, turning back to look into the camera. "Stay tuned for our continuing coverage of Kendall Collins' delivery week. We'll be shopping for new clothes, helping her pack her hospital bag, meeting her surgeon, and talking more with Ciddah Rourke about the entire process. Until then, Safe Lands, find pleasure in life."

"Clear," the cameraman said.

Luella sighed. "Don't speak means don't speak, Mason. I know this is your first day and all, but we're going to have to work on that mouth of yours if you're going to be our new medic." Luella raised her eyebrow at Mason, then strode out the door. "Bye-o, peers!"

Mason's cheeks burned. He didn't want to be their new medic. He had work to do, and this, though intriguing, had been a waste of time. The lights, blessedly, went out, which instantly cooled the air. The cameraman started to pack up his gear.

"Now that *that's* over," Ciddah said. "How's our queen?"

Kendall wiped the corner of her eye. "Just a little emotional."

"I can give you something for that." Ciddah picked up a CompuChart from the counter and tapped on it. "Be sure and tap me right away if you feel any contractions, Kendall."

"What will the delivery be like?" Kendall asked.

"The surgeon and I will meet you at the Treatment Center next Monday morning. Luella will be there with her cameraman, as there's no way they'll miss the birth. I'll be the one to put you under; you won't feel a thing. Before you know it, you'll wake up in the Recovery Center. And that's that. Nothing to worry about."

They were going to film the delivery? "How can the mother be unconscious during labor?" Mason asked.

"She won't go into labor if we can help it," Ciddah said. "We scheduled a C-section."

Mason had read about that procedure. "Is the baby breech? Or is this because of the plague?"

Both women looked at him as if he had twelve eyes.

"All births are C-section in the Safe Lands, Mason," Ciddah said. "It makes everything easier."

"But I get to see him, right? After recovery?" Kendall asked.

Ciddah's forehead wrinkled. "What? Of course not, Kendall. You should know that."

"The task director promised, when I agreed to do all the shots with the cameras," Kendall said, her voice growing soft.

Ciddah frowned and shook her head. "I wasn't informed of this, Kendall. I'll have to check with his office."

Tears ran down Kendall's face, and soon she was outright sobbing.

Mason just stood there, shocked. "Why can't she see her baby?"

Ciddah narrowed her eyes at Mason, and in a harsh voice whispered, "It's not Kendall's baby. It belongs to all of us. And don't you say another thing that might encourage her to think otherwise." She tapped on her CompuChart again, and her tone returned to its former pleasantness. "I'll prescribe you some more meds, Kendall."

"I don't want more meds!" Kendall yelled. "I want my sorrow. I need it!"

Ciddah's face paled. "You *want* to hurt?"

"Better the pain than numbing myself. And I don't want meds for the procedure. If I stay awake through the delivery, I'll get to see my baby before you take him away."

"Now, Kendall, many surrogates experience depression at some level. In fact, what I think would be best is for you to — "

"What *you* think is best?" Kendall sat up and swung her legs off the table. "You've never given birth, have you? Have you ever even been pregnant?"

Ciddah inched back a step, her eyes getting misty. "I — My body rejects the process."

"When I got here, they told me I would be happy, that pregnancy would be a wonderful experience. Well, they were wrong," Kendall screamed. "I should get to *keep* my baby!"

Ciddah rubbed her eyes. "But it's not your baby, Kendall. He belongs to — "

"He's part me. He's half mine!"

Ciddah chuckled and tipped her head to the side. "You can't own a human being."

"He needs me!" Kendall's bottom lip trembled. "And I need him."

"That's ridiculous." Ciddah walked to Kendall's side and touched her shoulder. "What good would you do him? Your tasks have primarily been messaging. You've had no training in raising — "

"I could manage."

"If you have an interest in working with children, why not file a task interest form with the Registration Department and retest?"

"Just check with the task director, okay, Ciddah? He *promised* I could hold my baby."

Ciddah sighed, as if Kendall's request was a terrible inconvenience. "Okay, I'll check with him." She walked to the door, reached for the pad, missed, then turned and opened it. "I'll leave that prescription with Rimola." And she left, the door closing softly behind her.

Mason had stayed perfectly still throughout the outburst, and wasn't sure he dared move even now.

Kendall eased off the exam table, a hand pressed against her swollen belly. She glanced at Mason, her face streaked with tears. "What they do is wrong," she said, her voice a whisper.

Mason nodded. He could hardly believe what he'd just witnessed.

Ciddah had said, *Once Kendall delivers, they'll start in with Naomi.* The Safe Lands intended to remove Naomi's child too — a baby that was definitely not theirs to take. He had to find a way to help her — as well as the women of Glenrock, whether they were pregnant or not.

Maybe he was meant to be in this position. He might be the only chance any of them had.

When Ciddah dismissed Mason for the day, he followed the instructions he'd been given at registration and found his assigned apartment on the fifth floor of a building named Westwall. As much as he hated to admit, the place was incredibly nice, and the idea of living there even for a while excited him. The open room was divided by a partial wall that Mason could walk around either side of. The front half held the entry, living, dining, and kitchen areas. A counter ran along the center wall and had a parallel island. After some initial poking around he discovered the bedroom and bath were on the other side of the wall, and a low, king-sized bed sat against it.

The place had light blue walls, a white marble floor, and black cupboards, black appliances, and black trim. Pictures of black and white trees in black frames hung on the walls throughout the apartment, changing every few seconds like the flowers had in Ciddah's office. The tables and furniture were light sandy-colored wood. A wall of windows in the living room looked out into the city. Best of all, there were no security cameras.

As much as he wanted to linger inside his temporary home, he went back out and wandered the area the doorman of his building referred to as the Highlands. It didn't take him long to find the harem, which had been built in the center of town like some kind of fortress.

Getting out of the Safe Lands was going to be a lot harder than getting in.

CHAPTER 11

Omar found the Registration Department on the second floor of City Hall, but was told he first needed to visit the Men's Health and Wellness Department on the third floor. There, Omar received a humiliating physical examination and two SimTag implants, one on his right cheek and one on the back of his right fist, which were injected with a gun-like medical device. Both tags showed a number nine, and both itched fiercely. The medic also noticed Omar's sniffling and gave him an injection he said would clear it right up. Then the medic sent Omar to the Donation Center. Omar had known this part was coming — the requirement had been reiterated to him several times since he'd arrived.

But that knowledge didn't mean it was something he'd been looking forward to. After an awkward fifteen minutes, he changed into his new enforcer uniform. He stood before the bathroom sink mirror and took in his new appearance. The navy blue fabric was so much softer than his Old clothes, and it had no odor. It was likely made here by machines. And the enforcer hat was better than his Colorado Patrol hat. He liked the way he looked in uniform, even though the number nine on his cheek seemed to whisper the word *traitor* in the back of his mind.

He returned to the Registration Department on the second floor, as he'd been instructed. A man named Dallin sat behind a counter. To the left was an open space filled with desks. Dallin's black and yellow hair was amazing, and Omar imagined drawing him with insect wings.

"Have a seat, and I'll work up your ID," Dallin said.

Omar sat on one of the metal chairs. He could now see Dallin from the neck up only. "How do they decide what number we each get?"

"Our blood reveals to the Liberators which life we're in. A number one marks the first life. Nine marks the last. I'm a three, so I have six more lives before I reach *La Vie Dixième*. Most outsiders get low numbers. Your nine is shocking."

It was? "So I'm in my last life? What does *that* mean?"

"Just that you're nearly to the tenth life. So you should make this life count. Don't do anything foolish. Earn as much good fortune as you can. And, according to the Liberators, pairing up with anyone from your own life number angers Fortune — so stay away from other nines so you don't mess up your future lives."

Oh-kay. "So the tenth life is heaven?"

"Some call it that." Dallin slid a handheld computer, like the one Kruse used, on the counter and twirled it in a half circle. A picture of Shaylinn's fat face filled the glass. "I need you to verify any romantic relationships between these women and men, including yourself." Dallin swiped his finger across the glass a few times, and the pages turned. "Keep flipping through until you get to the end. Tap each face and type in the relationship."

Omar picked up the device, which had the word *Wyndo* etched across the top. His mother's face now stared at him from the glass, looking tired and sad but hard as always. She'd had to be hard to survive marriage to Justin of Elias. He wondered where she was now.

Tears stung Omar's eyes. "Why must I look at these pictures?"

"We need to know if there are any pairings."

"This is my mother." Omar set his finger on his mother's picture, and a list of letters appeared over his mother's face. He touched each letter until he wrote *mother*, then pressed the word "Done." The letters vanished, and the word *mother* was now visible under her picture. He took a deep breath and flipped to the next page, which held Naomi's image. "Naomi is Jordan's wife. They're expecting a child sometime this fall." He wrote Jordan's name below Naomi's picture. "What will you do with the women?"

"Most will serve a term in the harem and, should Fortune bless them, bear children for the Safe Lands. Then they'll task and play like the rest of us."

Omar thought of his fifteen minutes in the Donation Center and nearly choked. "They'll be bearing *my* children? All of the women?"

"Not necessarily. All men donate — it's Safe Lands law."

Omar paged back to where he'd left off, but his hand had started to shake. Clenching it into a fist, he reminded himself he had to complete this last thing, then he'd be free to find his new home and go with Skottie to the dance club. He forced himself to focus on the pictures on the screen. Nell was his cousin, as were Penelope and Lucy. Chipeta and Janie were his aunts. Mason was his brother. Jordan was Shanna's son, Jemma and Shaylinn's brother, Naomi's husband.

When Omar had completed marking the relationships, Dallin led him to stand by the wall and used the handheld computer to take his picture. "Now I just need your last name so I can finish your ID in the grid."

"I don't have a last name."

"Hold on." Dallin reached under the desk and pulled out a floppy book with thick white pages. "It really doesn't matter which name you choose. Take your time."

Omar leafed through the pages. They were organized by letter, but there were so many it was overwhelming. He flipped toward the end — startled by the number nine on the back on his hand — and stopped in the *S* section. His eyes fell on the perfect name. "Strong," he said.

"Omar Strong it is." Dallin tapped the name onto his glass screen.

Omar handed back the book. "Why do they mark the number in two places?"

"They put the number on your cheek so people can see it — your hair doesn't hide it. And they put the number on your hand in case you get too drunk to remember what's on your face." Dallin chuckled.

Omar laughed too, though he didn't understand why that was funny. "Alcohol was only used for sickness in our village." But he'd seen Levi drink when visiting Beshup in Jack's Peak.

"Yeah, well, you'll see plenty of it here. But I wouldn't drink too much if I were you."

"Why not?"

"Just trust me, okay? You take it easy out there. I'd hate to see a healthy kid like you be liberated before his time. Especially a nine."

Omar bristled. "I look like a child?"

Dallin pulled up Omar's picture on his computer screen. "You look fine. Women have a thing for the uniform and for skin like yours. Just don't question everything. It makes you sound like a shell."

"Right."

"Your identification is in your hand tag. Use it to open doors, to buy things, to power on appliances in your home, to start vehicles — pretty much anything. Task credits are posted to your account every Friday morning. Be smart with your credits. If you run out, you'll be hungry until credit day. Got it?"

"Yes." It seemed easy enough, anyway.

"Your apartment is in the Snowcrest Building across the street. Any questions?"

A million, but Omar said,"No."

"Welcome to the Safe Lands, Mr. Strong. Find pleasure in life."

It was dark when Omar left City Hall. He walked over to the Snowcrest, taking in the spectrum of electric colors everywhere, admiring how these people had embraced all life had to offer and challenged themselves to create new and exciting things. He shoved down the memory of his father, not wanting to think about what getting access to this fantastic world had cost.

Omar pushed past the glass doors of the apartment building and entered a chilly lobby.

A man in a red uniform approached. "Good afternoon, sir. Are you meeting someone?"

"No, I live here now."

The man held out a Wyndo displaying the image of a side fist print. "Identification, please."

Omar set his fist against the glass, and his picture appeared on the surface.

"Welcome to the Snowcrest, Mr. Strong. My name is Artie. You're in apartment number seven hundred sixteen. It'll be to your left when you exit the elevator. The even-numbered apartments have a spectacular view."

"I was told you could contact a friend for me," Omar said. "Can I give you his number?"

"Of course, sir."

Omar recited Skottie's number, and the doorman typed it into his Wyndo. "One moment, sir."

Footsteps clicked over the tile, accompanied by feminine murmurs and giggles.

"Good afternoon, Ms. Combs," the doorman said.

"Hay-o, Artie," a woman answered. "The girls are with me." Her low and raspy voice turned Omar's head.

Three curvaceous women approached the elevator, carrying with them a cloud of spicy scents. Omar suddenly realized he could breathe! No sniffles. And as far as first smells went, this one was amazing.

Omar had never seen anything like these women. All three wore short black skirts and spiky-heeled shoes, displaying nearly all of their legs. Their shirts were tight and strappy too. No woman in Glenrock or Jack's Peak ever bared so much skin.

The women stopped an arm's length from where he stood. The

nearest woman was a few inches shorter than him and bore the number seven on her cheek. Her hair was blood red, streaked with fluffy black feathers, and hung down in wide curls past her shoulders. Tiny SimArt flowers ran up the backs of her legs.

The other two women were blonde — both numbered five — one with shoulder-length hair that had been slicked back like she'd just taken a bath, the other a mess of tiny braids under a floppy black hat.

The redhead wore a purple top that was so tight her skin bulged out of the top. As if sensing that he was looking at her, the woman raised one eyebrow and fixed her eyes on Omar. How he wished for paint that deep sapphire color. The closest thing he'd ever made was from blackberries, and it was far too purple.

"Sir?"

Omar turned back to the doorman, who was holding out his Wyndo. Skottie's face was moving on the glass as if he were trapped inside.

"Hey, shell!" Skottie said through the screen. "Listen, we're going to come get you in an hour or so, okay? Your doorman says you're in the Snowcrest. What's your apartment number?"

"Seven sixteen."

"Got it. See you later, peer." The screen went blank.

"Thank you," Omar said to Artie.

"You're very welcome, sir."

Omar stepped toward the elevators and the beautiful women. The elevator button was already lit up. All three women held several bags in each hand.

"Would you like help carrying those?" Omar asked the redhead, proud that he'd managed to speak at all to such a beauty.

Her dark, painted lips curved into a smile, and she glanced at her friends, who giggled again.

The elevator doors slid open with a low buzz.

"You going our way?" the redhead asked Omar. She stepped into the elevator, her friends right behind her.

Omar followed, mesmerized by their flowery scent, their movement, their legs. He reached for the button for the seventh floor at the same time as the redhead. Their fingers touched, hers icy and small and tipped with violet-painted fingernails. Omar jerked back his hand.

The redhead pressed seven with her thumb and studied Omar, her dark eyelashes long and thick, enhanced somehow like the rest of her body, which looked like a canvas to be painted. "Visiting someone?" she asked.

Her attention so flustered Omar that he had to force himself to answer. "I live here."

"Since when?"

"Since today."

"Promotion?" She tilted her head closer and parted her lips in a way that made Omar's heart quicken.

"Yes."

"What's your rank?"

"Captain."

The woman's finger slowly traced the seam on the front of his jacket. "Really. What area?"

"Uh …" He rubbed the scar on his nose. It had been going so well. A longer conversation than he'd had with a female in a long time. The elevator stopped on the seventh floor. Omar followed the women into a wide hallway and glanced at the nearest door: 705.

"You go ahead and keep your secrets, trigger," the redhead said, walking to the right.

"We should invite him over!" the blonde with the braids whispered. "He's a cutie."

"Tonight's girl's night, Venita," the redhead said.

"So? Girl's night is more fun with a guy, especially one with such great skin."

"He's barely out of boarding school," the second blonde said. "And it's got to be Roller Paint."

"That's *not* Roller Paint." Venita turned to Omar. "How old are you, cutie?"

"Eighteen," Omar lied, puffing out his chest and trying to look like it was a fact.

The second blonde giggled. "Sure you are, baby doll."

"No guys tonight," the redhead said. "We're watching *C Factor*."

"We can zip *C Factor* for later." Venita turned back to Omar, her braids and hat swaying with her movement. "What's your apartment number, sweetie?"

"Um, seven sixteen," he said.

"We'll come visit later, seven sixteen. Once I talk Bel into it." Venita winked.

Not knowing what to say, Omar followed the numbers to the left. He stopped at door 716 and looked back. The redhead, Bel, and her blonde friends entered a room on the opposite end of the hall. The door thumped shut behind them.

Omar couldn't believe those women were infected with anything. Their skin had been flawless. No sign of the flakiness or veins. Would they really visit?

He pressed his fist to the pad on the door. It took him a few tries to get the angle right, but he eventually got inside. He spent the next five minutes trying to figure out which panel turned on the lights.

Once he could see, he discovered that his new home was as rich as the task director's office, but the brown and cream palette was more relaxing. There was a sitting area with a sofa and two chairs, a sheet of glass on the wall with the word *Wyndo* etched into the center top, a little kitchen, a table, a bathroom, and a bedroom with a huge bed, a dresser, and a GlassTop desk.

He inspected everything, wondering if the girls would knock on his door soon. However, once he discovered the SimPad that turned on the Wyndo, which turned out to be a TV, he became captivated by the color and movement. He could touch the glass to change what was playing—and they weren't movies of Old, either. Each program displayed the title along the top of the screen.

One show depicted two men trying to kill each other on a stage surrounded by cheering onlookers. On a cooking show, a woman taught Omar how to cook his own strawberry savarin, whatever that was. What Omar assumed was meant to be a beauty program showed fat people — bigger than Mary, Shay, and Megan combined — and how one woman wanted to go back in time and relive her third life to earn better fortune. On *C Factor*, a man with earrings was having relations with a woman. On TV! There had been a scene like that in the Old movie *Titanic*, but they hadn't shown it. A channel that seemed to be devoted to displaying things he could buy was selling something called a Personal Vaporizer that could be used to make candy, alcohol, medications, and stimulants — whatever those were — turn into a breathable form.

Omar found all he needed to learn in order to fit in as a Safe Lands National. Two hours passed before Artie the doorman's voice came through a panel near the door announcing that someone named Dane Skott had arrived.

Omar walked out of the Snowcrest's lobby and found Skottie waving from a sleek little red car that had bigger wheels in front than in back, so that the body of the car tilted backward. One of the back doors slid over the top of the vehicle to open, only these didn't look like mesh.

"Get in," Skottie said.

Omar barely fit in the backseat. A tall guy turned to face Omar from the passenger's seat, his head nearly brushing the roof. He had a thick neck and buck teeth.

"I'm Charlz," the guy said. "Skottie says you want more SimTags?"

Did he? Omar smiled. "Yeah, I think I would."

"Then let's do it!" Skottie steered the car out of the parking lot so fast, the momentum threw Omar across the seat.

The heaviness of the day drifted from Omar's mind. Everything was going to work out. Tonight, he could have fun and make friends. He leaned between the seats, trying to think of something flattering to say. "Thanks for taking me out. You seem to know everything about this place."

Charlz looked over his shoulder. "Skottie is decked. He knows everything and everyone. He says you're going to be tasking with the enforcers. I task there too."

"That's great," Omar said. *Great?* Why not *decked*? He needed to learn the language so he didn't sound like a shell. Dallin had told him not to ask stupid questions, but he felt like he needed to keep up the conversation. "Do you have extra SimTags too?" Omar asked Charlz.

"Just a SimTalk. I got the others taken out. They aggravated my skin."

"Charlz is a little sensitive about his skin," Skottie said.

"It's already flaking more than most. I don't need a rash too."

"What time you coming in to the enforcer's office tomorrow?" Skottie asked Omar.

"They told me to arrive at ten," Omar said.

"Come in early, and I'll show you something decked."

"One of Skottie's femmes works in surveillance," Charlz said.

"And here we are." Skottie slowed the car and parked along the side of the street. "Surface is the best SimArt shop around."

Omar found the door panel and pressed his fist against it, feeling less shell-like as he did so. Smells from the street gusted into the car: popcorn and something meaty. He climbed out onto a bright street. People were everywhere, moving along the sidewalk like two herds pushing in opposite directions. The lights from the storefronts on both sides of the street lit the pavement with vivid reds and blues. It seemed like videos were playing on every glass surface, advertising whatever might be for sale inside.

Omar inched his way across the crowded sidewalk, feeling stupid for finding this so difficult. But he managed to arrive at the doorway in one piece.

Skottie smirked at him. "Let's tag you up!"

Inside, Surface was dark and loud. The place smelled of strong incense, and Omar breathed in deeply. Glowing Wyndo screens covered every inch of the walls, flashing pictures of the types of SimArt a person could choose from: sleeve, fluorescent, cosmetic. Omar trailed after Skottie and Charlz, staring at the designs on the walls.

"We need to get this one into a chair," Skottie yelled.

Omar turned his focus to Skottie, who was talking to a shapely woman so pierced and marked up that Omar couldn't guess how she'd originally looked.

The woman dragged Omar to a reclining chair covered in black leather and pushed him into it. "How many you want and where?"

Omar glanced at Skottie.

Skottie waved his hand. "Go on, peer, tell Suli what you want."

Omar swallowed and panned the Wyndo screens. What did he want? Everything looked mad good.

"It's not that big of deal," Suli said. "You don't like 'em? You can turn 'em off or come let me take 'em out."

Right. This wasn't like the tattoos of Old. These weren't permanent. "I want a sleeve."

"Right or left?"

"Right." He caught sight of one of the screens, which showed a hawk on a man's back with the wings trailing down both arms. He pointed. "I want that!"

Suli smirked. "Let's start with a sleeve. You like it, you come get more. If I give you that many tags in one sitting, you're gonna be real sorry when you try and sleep tonight."

"Okay," Omar said, feeling stupid for being so eager.

Together with Skottie and Charlz, Omar chose the perfect SimArt for his first sleeve. He landed on a black web that wound its way up his arm and reminded him of an Old comic book hero.

"Lose your jacket and shirt," Suli told him.

Omar did, wishing he were as muscular as the pictures of the men on the screens. Compared to them, Omar looked like a half-starved child.

Suli twisted Omar's chair and pulled up a flap on the right side. She set a thick roll of plastic on the flap and unrolled it. "Stretch out your arm."

Omar set his arm on the plastic, and Suli covered it with the material, then grabbed the sheet and walked away.

Skottie and Charlz stood on Omar's left.

"She's getting a simulation of your arm so she knows where to put the tags," Skottie said.

"I love watching the gun," Charlz said. "Wish I could buy my own."

Suli returned with a thin plastic sleeve that she pulled over Omar's arm. It had circles and dots all over it.

"How many is he getting?" Skottie asked.

"Twenty-eight," Suli said.

Skottie threw back his head. "Aw, you long-armed ape. You beat me!"

Omar smiled, as if his having a longer arm that Skottie somehow made him worthy of friendship. He'd take every advantage he could get.

"Here we go," Suli said.

Omar looked back to his arm. Suli held a gun like the one the medic had used. She set it over one of the dots and fired. It made a soft clicking noise and stung. Only twenty-seven more.

Once they were all in, Suli programmed the tags and the design flicked on. Omar paid by touching his fist to a computer screen.

When they were done at Surface, Skottie drove them to a place called Main Event. It was dark inside, except for the pinwheels of orange and yellow light that spun on the ceiling. Omar's eyes slowly adjusted to the dim atmosphere. The room was filled with a maze of low counters and crowded with men.

"Is this a bar?" Omar asked, recalling the term from Old movies.

"That, and more," Skottie said.

Main Event turned out to be a bar where voluptuous waitresses walked on the counters to serve the drinks, and every time one of them was given extra credits, they all did a dance.

Omar liked watching them dance.

Omar had never drunk alcohol before, and he likely drank too much. The night passed in a blur. The last thing he remembered was Skottie escorting him to his apartment.

CHAPTER 12

Levi woke with his face in the dirt, sure he'd heard a noise. He was lying on the mound that was his father's grave. The realization brought back the heavy sorrow that sleep had numbed.

"Levi!" Someone grabbed his arm.

Levi pulled Sam's empty pistol from his waistband and rolled over, aiming the gun at ... "Beshup?"

"I thought you were dead, my friend." Beshup was a tall man of twenty-six with white-blond hair, which he'd grown long and wore in two braids, in accordance with the Native American traditions passed down by the founders of his village.

Levi let his head fall back to the dirt. "It seems like I'm the only one who's not." He always knew he'd be an elder someday. And here he was. But elder of what? Nothing was left.

"What time is it?" he asked Beshup.

Beshup looked up into the sky. "The sun is nearing the west, but there are several hours before it will get dark."

Levi pushed to his feet and walked away from the graveyard, toward the square. Seeing the stack of bodies again made him stumble.

So many dead. He turned to Beshup. "What can I do with the bodies? There are too many to bury."

"According to my elders, the coyote said that when men died, their friends should burn their bodies."

"It's too dry," Levi said. "I'd be setting fire to the whole valley."

Beshup pointed to the square. "The stage can serve as a pyre."

Levi set his hands on his hips and studied the stage. It *was* in a clearing with no overhanging branches.

"It's too soon, though," Beshup said. "We should wait so your people can pay their respects."

"I'm all that's left, Beshup!"

Beshup gestured to the bodies. "This is not all of Glenrock."

"I think they took the women and children into the compound. But I need to deal with the bodies before I go after them, or the wolves will get them."

Beshup stared at Levi, as if considering Levi's dilemma. "I will help you. Then come home with me to Jack's Peak and speak with Chief Kimama."

Levi nodded. Maybe Chief Kimama would offer to help rescue Glenrock's people. This could just as easily have happened there, after all.

Levi followed Beshup's every instruction. They covered the stage in two more layers of wooden planks, alternating their direction. Then stacked firewood. Beshup insisted it be four feet high, so Levi used his ATV and cart to gather firewood from every home until a massive pile covered the stage. They tried to keep the pyre as even as possible so the fire wouldn't burn lopsided.

As they worked, Levi distracted himself with a mental checklist. After this, he'd go with Beshup to Jack's Peak to ask Chief Kimama for help. Then he'd come back to gather supplies and check the cache to see if any ammo was left.

They poured ethanol over the wood. Levi worried he should save some, since he didn't know how to make more without Uncle Colton's or Penelope's help.

Then they were ready to move the bodies.

It was tricky getting all the bodies on the pyre. Twice, a chunk of firewood shifted under Levi's feet and fell off the side of the stage. Once all the bodies were on the pyre, Levi brought a couple of bedsheets from his house. He and Beshup draped them over the top.

When Beshup sat on one of the benches in the square, Levi asked, "That's it, then?"

"You must say farewell."

Levi took a deep breath and looked up to the sky, thinking back to the funerals Papa Eli had given. He spoke loudly, for all heaven and nature to hear. " 'Let not your hearts be troubled ... In my Father's house are many rooms.' He has prepared a place for you and now taken you there to be with him. 'O death, where is your victory? O death, where is your sting?' "

Levi's voice softened, emotion taking hold. "Take my people, Lord, into your heavenly home." Then he sang a verse from an old hymn.

So on I go not knowing, I would not if I might;
I'd rather walk in the dark with God than go alone in the light;
I'd rather walk in faith with Him than go alone by sight.

Levi and Beshup struck several matches and lit the pyre around its perimeter. It took a little while to get started, then the fire rose hot and fast, crackling, engulfing the stage in orange, yellow, and pink flames. Black smoke twisted into the sky like a tornado. The air became so hot that Beshup and Levi moved to the tree line, occasionally racing forward to douse a smoldering spark that leapt away from the pyre.

Even standing upwind, the village reeked of a sweet yet putrid smell, almost like tanned leather. Levi tried to ignore it, but the smell antagonized his stomach. These were his friends and family.

The entire pyre burned in less than an hour, but they waited longer for the coals to die down. Then Levi unhitched his cart from the back of his ATV, he and Beshup climbed on, and Levi pulled away, leaving the remains smoldering.

It was usually a two-and-a-half hour drive up to Jack's Peak, but without the cart — and in spite of all the potholes filled with rainwater — the ATV made it in two.

Jack's Peak sat on the edge of Mill Creek, which enabled them to get clean water before the Safe Lands collected it into their dam and compound. For some reason, Safe Lands enforcers had not attacked here … yet.

Levi rolled to a stop near the village fire pit, and a crowd of children and young men clustered around his rig. The people of Jack's Peak wore leather, fur, or cattail clothing, mixing in nothing Old. Some tattooed their bodies with clay, charcoal, and plant juices.

"Beshup!" Beshup's wife, Tsana, threaded her way through the sea of onlookers. "What news of Glenrock? Our elders were worried when they saw the smoke."

Beshup and Levi got off the ATV, and Levi glanced over Beshup's shoulder to the valley below. "Glenrock is destroyed, our elders are dead, and our young men, women, and children are taken. I need to speak with your chief."

The group gasped and stepped back.

"Come on," Beshup said.

Beshup led Levi around a dozen cabins and teepees. Chief Kimama allowed her people to build cabins, but many lived in teepees made of animal skins and bark.

"*Behne*, Levi!" A young woman with dark skin and hair waved from outside a teepee they passed. She stood over a washtub scrubbing a small red-headed child, and wore a leather dress with fringe and turquoise beads that clicked against the tub as she moved.

The sight of her stiffened Levi's posture, and he looked away. Kosowe. The woman they'd tried to match with Omar. Images from two years ago flashed in his memory. Finding the alcohol. Hiding it in his cart to bring to Beshup. Father making him take Omar along. The dancing. Sneaking away. The burn of the alcohol. Kissing Kosowe. Omar finding them.

Omar … His little brother was somehow mixed up in this attack by the Safe Lands. If Levi had been a better example, if he would have destroyed the alcohol when he'd found it, then he wouldn't have messed up so badly that night, and maybe Omar wouldn't have either. A village elder couldn't afford to make such mistakes. He had to be an example for his people. He'd blown it that night. He could never let that happen again.

Chief Kimama lived in the biggest teepee Levi had ever seen. He'd been inside it only once, when he was a boy and had come to visit with Papa Eli.

"Wait here," Beshup said. "I'm sure she'll see you, but ..." Beshup slipped into the teepee. A moment later he held open the door flap. "Go on in."

Levi ducked inside. The sun shone through the animal skins, creating a golden glow on the walls. Two rectangular mats woven in fat red and tan stripes covered a ground of wood chips. Between the mats, a circle of stones held the smoldering embers of a fire. The smoke trailed out a flap in the apex of the roof.

Chief Kimama sat crosslegged on a mattress behind the fire pit. Levi knew that Kimama was a bit younger than Papa Eli, but she looked the opposite. Thick wrinkles creased her tanned skin from the corners of her wide nose to the sides of her mouth. Her hair was white, parted down the middle, and twisted into two long braids that hung to her waist. Her posture was so hunched she reminded Levi of a hen nestled down to rest.

"Levi of Elias," she said in a hoarse voice. "I smell death on the air. The shadow of the owl has been circling the valley for days. Has it fallen on Glenrock?"

Her voice chilled him, but he kept his posture straight and his voice strong. "Yes, ma'am. Safe Lands enforcers killed our men and took the women, young men, and children captive."

"How many were killed?"

"Eighteen, ma'am."

"And Elder Elias?"

"Dead, ma'am."

She worked her mouth as if she were chewing something. "You're certain he's gone?"

The image of Papa Eli closing his eyes flashed through Levi's mind. "I buried him myself."

Her eyes narrowed. "Your father was Justin?"

"That's right."

She rocked back and straightened her posture, revealing that she did in fact have a neck. "Then you are no direct relation to me."

"No, ma'am." Maybe he should sit or kneel. What if standing was disrespectful in Jack's Peak?

"You are welcome to join us, Levi of Elias. Several females in Jack's Peak are old enough to marry. I grant you leave to choose a wife from my tribe and build a life here."

Great, now he had to tell the woman no. He searched for the perfect words. "You're very generous, Chief Kimama, but I'm not looking for a wife or a place to live."

She grunted and settled back into her hen-like position. "What is it you seek from Jack's Peak, then, Levi of Elias?"

"Your help, ma'am. I intend to free my people and bring them back to Glenrock."

Chief Kimama laughed, changing the shape of her face so drastically that Levi took a step back. She had no teeth at all, and when she laughed, her mouth curved like a U. Her laugh wheezed to a close, and she focused her dark eyes back on him. "No one who enters the Safe Lands comes out."

"All the same, ma'am, would you consider taking the matter to your tribal council?"

Again she straightened, her eyes stormy and dark. "I would not. What you ask is impossible, as are your intentions."

Levi set his jaw. Nothing would keep him from trying to free his people — from freeing Jemma. But it would be easier if he had help. "But your village sits upriver from the Safe Lands. If we built our own dam, cut off their water supply — "

"I have no quarrel with the Safe Lands. Cutting off their water would be an act of war."

Levi stepped forward. "Destroying my village was an act of war."

"To Glenrock, yes." She slouched again. "But not to Jack's Peak."

Levi squeezed his hands into fists. "Ma'am, please. Have mercy. The women and children. With his last breath, Elder Eli bade me get them back. I believe my brothers and mother were taken. And my fiancée."

She chewed her gums. "You are betrothed?"

"Yes, ma'am. To Jemma of Zachary."

Her eyes flew wide open. "Now that one is my blood. Did you know that?"

"Yes, ma'am. Jemma's grandmother was your daughter."

"That's right. Did you know that my dear Haiwee was named after my little sister, who perished in the Great Pandemic?"

"I did not."

She grunted, as if considering this new development. "This changes nothing. You've buried and burned your dead, and the shadow of the owl still circles. More will die, and soon."

Levi wouldn't give a bullet for her superstitions. "Likely the owl is circling those Safe Lands officials who'll die when I rescue my people."

Her lips curled and she chuckled. "You speak like a warrior, Levi of Elias. Are you one?"

"I'm whatever God asks of me."

She hummed long and soft. "I cannot involve my tribe in this mischief. We are few as it is."

What else could he say to convince her? "But Jemma is your blood, ma'am. And whatever the Safe Lands enforcers want with Glenrock, in time they'll come looking for it in Jack's Peak."

She shifted, ruffling her feathers again. "You cannot know that."

"Neither can you. Even if you refuse to help me, you should make use of my warning. Prepare against a raid such as the one that destroyed Glenrock."

"You are quite brazen for the last of your tribe, Levi of Elias, giving me advice." She pursed her lips, and her gaze traveled up and down his body. Then she spoke quickly. "But I will allow such words. You may stay here for as long as you need."

Levi did all he could to keep his expression solemn. "Thank you, ma'am. I meant no offense."

She rumbled one last time. "You may leave now."

Gladly. Levi strode out of the teepee, right past Beshup, and headed for his ATV.

His friend's footsteps plodded after him. "What happened? What did she say?"

"She said I can stay, but she won't help me get my people back."

Beshup grabbed Levi's arm. "Slow down, my friend. Come and eat dinner. No sense wasting what little food you have."

Levi stopped. He might not eat again for a while. "Very well."

"Good. Come with me."

Beshup lived in a three-room cabin on the edge of the village pit. They sat at a plank table in front of a cold hearth. His wife, Tsana, served bowls of fish stew and flatbread. Before Levi could finish his food, someone knocked on the door.

Tsana let in Kosowe, who approached the table, holding a wad of plain linen. She bowed to Beshup.

"*Behne*, Kosowe," Beshup said, gesturing to Levi. "You know Levi of Elias."

Kosowe bowed to Levi and said softly, "*Behne*, Levi."

He kept his eyes on his bowl of soup. "*Behne*."

She thrust her ball of fabric into Levi's lap and bowed her head. "For you."

Levi put down his spoon and unwrapped the bundle. A warm round of white bread. He nodded to her. "*Aishen*. But I'm not trading today."

"No trade," she said, glancing to the floor then back to his eyes. "Gift." She smiled and backed away from the table until she reached the door, then spun around and left, her bare feet padding over the dirt. Tsana followed her out the door and, just before closing it behind her, shot her husband the wide-eyed look of a hint.

Levi looked from the door to Beshup to the bread. "Want some bread? Smells good."

Beshup chuckled and set down his spoon. "Want a wife? I think Tsana is plotting."

Levi winced and set the bread on the table. "Our fathers tried to marry Kosowe to Omar a few weeks ago, did you know that? Omar was there that night she and I ... had our encounter."

"Kosowe will marry no one but you," Beshup said. "Her father keeps trying to make a match for her. It is not my fault that your brothers are the only other single men around. And you are fortunate I never told my father what I saw."

"Because you would be in as much trouble as me for drinking." Levi shook his head. "I don't need a wife. I have a wife ... Well, almost." And he wouldn't if Jemma ever found out about Kosowe. He pushed his bowl away. What was he doing here, wasting time? "You helped me with the pyre and fed me. Thank you. Now, I need to get inside the Safe Lands."

Beshup grimaced as if the very idea gave him indigestion. "You're greatly respected here. A successful scavenger. A wise trader. Stay with us." He gestured at the bread Kosowe had brought. "You may like what we have to offer."

"Beshup — "

Beshup held up his hand. "At least stay for the night."

"I can't." Levi pushed his chair back and stood, leaving the round of bread on the table, lest he encourage Kosowe further. "I'm going to marry Jemma, Beshup. I'll get her back." He went outside into the early evening.

Beshup walked with Levi to his ATV. "You aren't serious about going inside the Safe Lands, are you? There's no way out."

"If I can get in, I can get out."

"I've never heard of anyone who came out. Something inside those walls changes people. And even if you did, you'd probably bring the plague with you."

"There's a first time for everything, Beshup. I'm the patriarch of Glenrock at nineteen. It's my responsibility. I can't leave them in there. I won't. And I'm more than happy to die trying."

Beshup slapped him on the back. "May the wolf go with you, my friend."

Levi left Jack's Peak no closer to freeing his people. The trip had only served to increase the guilt of his mistake with Kosowe. He steered the ATV down the steep mountain trail and tried to come up with a plan.

He'd call Judson in Clean Creek, the only other village in the area. It was his last option. Papa Eli had said the rest of the world had perished in the Great Pandemic and that the water from Mount Crested Butte was the only safe drinking water on the planet. Levi's dad had doubted that claim, which was why he liked traveling to abandoned cities, hoping to find people or safe water sources. Not to mention, aircraft flew out from the Safe Lands every week, always headed north. They had to be going somewhere that had people and, presumably, good water. But Father's last trip had uncovered neither.

Levi arrived home and called Judson on his dad's two-way radio. When Judson heard what had happened, he offered Levi a place to stay but refused to help beyond that. Too much risk for his own people, just as Chief Kimama had said.

Levi was on his own. And it was getting dark.

He went to the two aspen trees with trunks that twisted together at the base and located the strip of braided twine in the grass underneath them. He yanked a sod-covered lid loose, pulled it aside, and jumped down into the village's emergency cache.

Cool air enclosed him. He located the flashlight on the far end of the top shelf. The beam was nearly dead, so he took the time to wind up the battery. Once the light was bright enough, he shone it around the cache, which was a four-by-twelve-foot rectangular pit. Shelves lined both sides. Guns and ammo were stored on the left; shoes, dried food, and medicine were stocked on the right. Tubs of clothing sat on the floor under the right-hand shelves.

Levi sat on the five-gallon bucket of jewels they'd scavenged from Denver City and dug through the clothing until he found some fresh packs of undershirts. He ripped open the package and traded a fresh one for his filthy red T-shirt then stuffed another clean one into his pack. He grabbed a bulletproof vest that Papa Eli had scavenged years before, and he changed into green camouflage pants and a long-sleeved matching shirt. The camo clothing smelled aged and would likely tear, but that didn't matter as long as it helped him stay invisible.

He placed the leather jacket Jemma had made him inside one of the tubs, snapped on the lid, then took stock of the ammunition. There was plenty for his rifle and the pistol. He strapped on a shoulder holster and put Elder Harvey's pistol into it — he hoped carrying the firearm would give him the fortitude he would need. He tossed two packages of bullets for his rifle up onto the grass and all the ammo he could find for the pistol.

Strips of beef jerky and some dried apples went into a cloth bag. He also gathered two more crank flashlights, a solar powered lantern, three wind-up two-way radios and two solar-powered ones, and a handful of jewels from the bucket in case he needed to buy something or bribe someone. He made sure to put his and Jemma's wedding rings on a chain around his neck, determined to place Jemma's on her finger at the first opportunity. Everything else he stuffed into a backpack and carried toward his family home.

It was dark now. Crickets sang, oblivious to the carnage that had taken place in the village of Glenrock. Levi wanted to go now, but he was exhausted. He needed a few hours sleep.

Then there was only one way he could think of to get inside the Safe Lands undetected: the sewers and storm drains.

CHAPTER 13

The enforcer closed in, charging through the village square. The sting of a bullet entered Shaylinn's back, and she fell. Still, the enforcer came. With every ounce of strength she crawled across the dirt ... until someone helped her up, lifted her into his arms. Omar.

But there was blood on his hands. Her blood. As he leaned down to kiss her, he said, "I told them to come. And I told them to shoot you first, ugly crybaby."

Shaylinn's eyes shot open. The clock glowed 3:34 a.m. on the mirror above her dresser. Her heart sprinted in her chest, and her stomach ached with the horror of such words. It was just a dream. It had been years since Omar had said anything so cruel.

It was too early to get up, but when she tried to go back to sleep, she couldn't. She crept into Jemma's room across the hall and climbed into her sister's bed. Jemma didn't budge. The girl could have slept through the enforcers' raid on Glenrock.

The thought pulled Shaylinn's mind back to the raid and then to her nightmare. She studied Jemma's room, which was identical to hers, but navy blue instead of cobalt. Omar had taught Shaylinn about the color cobalt one day while she watched him paint. She'd decided then it was one of the most beautiful colors in the entire world.

In an attempt to distract herself, she imagined better times in Glenrock: weaving wildflower wreaths with her sister, playing tag with her cousins, dancing and singing after a ceremony in the Meeting Hall.

When Jemma's mirror clock read 5:48, Shaylinn went back to her room to shower. Hot water shot out from three sides. If her stomach hadn't started pinging with hunger, she might have stayed in there all morning. As it was, when she came out the mirror clock read 6:35.

There were no clothes in Shaylinn's dresser drawers, so she put on her deerskin dress and went out to the living room. Kendall was already up, watching the wall of glass, which appeared to be a TV, her face aglow with the light of the screen.

"Good morning, Shaylinn," Kendall said. "Sona brought a tray. There's enough for everyone." She motioned to the table.

The tray held a platter of eggs and bacon, a bowl of berries and some sort of melon, and a platter of pancakes. Shaylinn put a little of each onto a plate then sat beside Kendall. "Are you watching a movie?" she asked, nibbling a piece of bacon that was very salty.

"No. *Finley and Flynn*. I don't know why I watch. All they do is gossip."

On the TV, a man and a woman were sitting on a purple sofa. The woman was wearing a skin-tight yellow dress with a wide black belt. The man matched her with his yellow jacket over a black shirt and a black-and-yellow-striped tie. Both had black hair and pale white skin.

"Why do so many people wear yellow and black?" Shaylinn asked.

"Because of Finley and Flynn," Kendall said. "They set the trends, and people mimic them."

Shaylinn looked at Kendall, who was wearing a blue shirt and black pants. "But not you?"

"I don't care what Finley and Flynn wear. I've got bigger things to worry about."

"Being a mom?"

"I wish. It's the Safe Lands, remember? As my medic made clear yesterday, I don't get to keep him. He'll be sent away right after I give birth."

So sad. "It's a boy?"

Kendall nodded. "I'm naming him Elyot. That, at least, I get to do."

"Are you scared?"

"Sometimes." Kendall set her hand on her belly. "It's not painful or anything. I mean, I felt nauseous at first. But now mostly I just feel big."

"I feel big every day," Shaylinn said. "If I really did get pregnant, I'd be humungous."

Once everyone had gotten up and eaten, Kendall led them downstairs to the main sitting room. Jennifer, Aunt Mary, Eliza, and Chipeta were there, along with Matron, who was wearing an emerald green pantsuit with orange and yellow platform shoes. Shaylinn wanted to try on a pair and see what it felt like to walk in them.

"Why aren't you wearing black and yellow, Matron?" Shaylinn asked.

Surprisingly, the woman didn't seem offended. "Don't get me wrong," Matron said, "Luella Flynn is as precious as can be. But I mimic no one."

Matron gave Shaylinn a small piece of glass called a Wyndo that she'd apparently given to everyone yesterday before Shaylinn had arrived. Kendall said Wyndos worked like Old phones, but could also be used to change hair, skin, or nail color or designs; monitor health; record conversations for playback; or identify any national's face. Wyndos also had a SimPal, in which you could choose from over a hundred different people or animals to use as a personal assistant or simulated friend, who would speak to you through the glass.

Matron led the Glenrock women and girls to the Registration Department, where they each took a test to determine which jobs they would do after leaving the harem. Shaylinn's results listed all sewing-related tasks. Figured. In Glenrock, women mostly did the mending and cooking and cared for their families.

Shaylinn also learned from the man in Registration that the SimTag in her hand could be used to purchase things, and that she received one thousand credits a week for serving in the harem. The news left her feeling both curious and unsettled.

On the way back to their rooms, Matron showed them the wonders of the Highland Harem. They took the elevator to the top floor to see a view of the city, toured a spa, visited an indoor swimming pool, tried ice cream — which Shaylinn found delicious — and looked at a movie theater, a game room, and a room filled with exercise machines.

"The Safe Lands is all about pleasure and comfort," Matron said. "And no place in the entire land offers more enjoyment and relaxation than the harem. So, sleep in and indulge in the comforts. Or if the idle life is not your fancy, you can begin task training. The choice is yours."

Wyndo screens hung everywhere. Big ones mounted in corners, little ones in elevators and hallways. Sometimes they were divided into four different images. Shaylinn also saw dozens of little yellow cameras throughout the building, which Kendall said were run by the enforcers for surveillance.

Back in the dormitory, the huge picture windows that had once looked out on the grassy lawn were displaying the image of the the Safe Lands logo, a gold bell within a circle on a black background. "How did the windows become a movie screen?" Shaylinn asked.

"Most of the windows in the Safe Lands use Wyndo technology," Kendall said. "If you ever want to know for sure, touch your fist to any glass surface and you'll find out."

Matron asked them to sit on the chairs and sofas that had been arranged to face the windows — Wyndos. So strange. Shaylinn sat between Kendall and Jemma.

A curvy woman in a pale yellow sleeveless blouse and flowing black pants stood in front of the windows. Her skin had a brownish orange tint and didn't look papery or veiny at all. Images of flowers and vines looked to have been drawn down the ridges of her arms.

Shaylinn leaned close to Kendall. "Why does the plague affect some more than others?"

"It's not that at all," Kendall said. "People like Tyra are just better than others at hiding it."

"Tyra Grant tasks as a beauty care specialist." Matron pointed to the tanned woman, then tottered over to a table and chair near the stairs and sat. "If anyone can work a miracle, she can."

Tyra eyed the girls and beamed, her teeth whiter than the carpet. She was holding a small Wyndo like Shaylinn's in one hand. "My job is to help you become beautiful, okay? So we're going to talk makeovers, then we'll go shopping."

"We get new clothes?" Mia asked.

"Yes, and don't use your own credits. Clothing is on the harem."

Shaylinn wanted to smile. Finally, something different than animal skins or faded dresses. But she reminded herself that they were prisoners. She wasn't supposed to enjoy it here.

"Now, I'm noticing a few things straight away," Tyra said. "Damaged hair ... oily complexions ... None of you shave or wax your legs?"

"Like candle wax?" Mia asked.

"Why would we?" Jemma asked.

Tyra wrinkled her nose. "Because hairy legs are ugly. And shaving your underarms decreases body odor."

Shaylinn twisted to smell her armpit. Smelled fine to her.

"Our goal today is to get you femmes beautified so you can meet the task director general on the Safe Lands ColorCast and attend the entertainment orientation," Tyra said.

"I don't want to meet the task director general," Naomi said. "He ruined our lives."

"This is mandatory," Tyra said, "so you may as well make the best of it."

"Fine," Naomi said. "When I meet him, I'll demand he take me to see Jordan."

"Where are the men being kept?" Shaylinn asked, wondering where Omar might be.

"*Please*, ladies," Tyra said. "The task director general is a wise man who deserves our respect. It's a privilege to meet him."

Naomi flubbed her lips. "None of you deserve my respect. You're clearly all insane."

"Let's get back on track, all right? Wyndo: slides." With Tyra's words the picture on the windows changed from the Safe Lands logo to a picture of three women captured mid-walk, laughing, dressed in clothing that hugged their curves and bared their arms and legs. They wore high-heeled shoes and clutched each other's arms as if they might fall over at any moment.

"Beauty," Tyra said. "It's every woman's birthright, if not duty. It makes us happy, desirable. But one mustn't judge beauty, for what's beautiful to me may not be to you."

Naomi coughed. "Hairy legs." Shaylinn snickered.

Tyra pursed her lips. "Wyndo: next." The screen flashed to a woman in a flowing red dress. "Wyndo: next." Three women wearing yellow and black. "Wyndo: next." A close-up of a woman's red lips exhaling black vapor. "Wyndo: next." An overweight woman dressed in a tight yellow dress that looked more like another layer of skin than clothing.

This time Mia giggled.

"Don't judge." Tyra scowled Mia's way. "Melana Georjan is the star of *Big is Beautiful.*" Tyra pointed to Mia. "You. Come stand beside me."

"What did I do?" Mia asked as she approached Tyra.

"You volunteered to be our first project, okay?" Tyra said. "One of the best things about living in the Safe Lands is the availability of glamour. The freedom to be beautiful."

Shaylinn scooted to the edge of her seat.

"We *are* beautiful," Jemma said, tossing her hair over her shoulder.

"But you do nothing to display it." Tyra's gaze roamed over Mia's body. Shaylinn had always envied Mia's looks, but Mia looked plain next to Tyra. Tyra was so sleek and vibrant in her black pants, while Mia looked faded in Old jeans and purple knit top. "Mia, you have so much potential beauty just waiting to be enhanced. You're tall and have a great figure. Your skin is relatively clear, your coloring is nice. You don't even need Roller Paint. You simply need some glossy clothes and to lighten that drab hair, maybe give it some curl. Perhaps some blue contact lenses or ... lavender?" She tapped on her handheld Wyndo. "What do you think, Matron?"

Matron exhaled a plume of green vapor. "She could use a posture class as well. She slouches."

Mia's eyebrows sank low, and her eyes flashed. "I'm the prettiest girl in Glenrock. Why don't you pick on someone who needs help? Like Shay."

The impact of Mia's words made Shay jump.

"*Mia!*" Jennifer said.

Jemma took hold of Shaylinn's hand. Shaylinn looked down at her lap, noticing how tight her big legs made her dress, and how chubby her fingers were compared to Jemma's.

"*Sor-ry,*" Mia said.

"You'll *all* take a turn," Tyra said, "then we'll go to the salon and get started. Shaylinn, why don't you come up next?"

Shaylinn shook her head. "I don't want to." She wanted help — to be beautiful. But she didn't think she could take the humiliation.

"I'll go next," Jemma said, standing up.

"No, I want Shaylinn," Tyra said. "I want to use Mia's comment to make the point that everyone has something beautiful about themselves."

"May as well get it over with, honey," Kendall said, giving Shaylinn a side hug.

Jemma sat down, and Shaylinn made her way forward. She was taller than Tyra by a full head. She was sure her girth and frizzy hair made Tyra look like a stick drawing.

"Let's see now." Tyra tapped her finger to her lips and examined Shaylinn. "You have a lovely complexion and lots of long, curly hair. And your features are nicely balanced. Threading that lip and those eyebrows will make a big difference right away." She made a quick note on her Wyndo. "Are you pleased with your weight? If so, you could work to gain more and audition for *Big is Beautiful*."

"I don't want to be on the TV," Shaylinn said. "And I hate being fat."

"Shay!" Jemma said. "You're *not* fat."

"I'll put you down for a cosmetic consultation, then." Tyra fiddled with her Wyndo. "And you might consider breast implants. I honestly don't know how you turned out so curvy with no breasts!"

"She's only fourteen," Jemma said.

"Right. Tall for fourteen. Wait to get implants until your body is done growing." She fingered Shaylinn's hair. "Your hair is quite damaged. Do you brush it?"

Shaylinn shrugged. "Sometimes."

"You should *never* brush curls like yours. Or, if you hate the curl, you can have it straightened. Truthfully, with your round face, the volume of your hair isn't helping."

Tears welled up in Shaylinn's eyes, and she hung her head. These were all things she knew to be true. Ugly, ugly, ugly, just like Omar had said when they were little.

"Your skin is beautiful. But most of you girls could use an acne program." Tyra lifted Shaylinn's hand to look closer. "Is that dirt under your fingernails?"

"It's probably leather. I was working a hide when the enforcers came."

"A hide? But you've showered sincc, haven't you?"

"Yes, ma — " Shaylinn stopped herself before saying ma'am. "I like the showers here."

Tyra sighed and tapped on her Wyndo. "Manicures and pedicures for all." She then launched into a long discussion of the best types of clothing to wear depending on each girl's body type, using Shaylinn's shape to call out ways to slenderize a waist or create correct proportions. Each term Tyra used was like a key to unlocking a strange yet hypnotic new language.

When Tyra finally let Shaylinn sit down, Jemma moved beside her and whispered, "I think you're perfect already."

Shaylinn blushed and leaned against Jemma's side. Maybe, just maybe, if she let Tyra make her beautiful, Omar would ask to paint her.

The public humiliation continued. Naomi disputed each criticism Tyra dished out, but Shaylinn felt like Tyra made many good points. Shaylinn would love to know how to make her eyebrows look sculpted, and while the idea of different-colored eyes and breast implants scared her, she couldn't help wonder how a cosmetic consultation could help her be thinner.

They spent the rest of the morning in the spa, where they all received new hairstyles, waxings, manicures, and pedicures. Kendall talked Shaylinn into getting bright red paint on her fingernails and toenails. Shaylinn thought it looked ridiculous, but Kendall said it was *glossy*.

Shaylinn loved her hair now. The stylist left it long enough that a few tendrils still reached her waist, but it no longer frizzed; instead, it curled in wide ringlets. It was so pretty.

Tyra's assistants wheeled carts of clothing into the spa, and the girls tried different outfits. Some of the clothing was so ugly that the girls refused to try it, no matter how much Tyra begged. Shaylinn didn't care. She had a great time trying it all. The most ridiculous was a fiery pink dress covered in matching feathers that made her look like a fluffy bird. She strutted out of the dressing room and chirped until she had everyone laughing.

"Fortune, have mercy!" Tyra ran across the room. "Absolutely not! Take if off! I told you simple and streamlined for your body, Shaylinn."

"I was just playing." Shaylinn went back into the fitting room and made a nasty face at herself in the mirror, mocking Tyra.

Someone tossed a blue and white gown over the door. "Try this one, Shay," Jemma said.

Shaylinn lifted it down to take a look. The fabric was a beautiful floral print of navy, cobalt, periwinkle, and white. The dress had a V-neck — maybe too deep — an empire inset waistband, and a full pleated skirt that stopped just above her knees.

Shaylinn sighed at its beauty, knowing that something like this would never fit. She put it on anyway. She stepped out of the fitting room, smiling so wide that she covered her mouth with her hand.

"Oh, Shay! I love it!" Jemma said.

"Me too, honey," Naomi said. "You look mad gorgeous!"

"It's not my favorite on you," Tyra said. "I'd rather see you in black, even a pale yellow."

"I mimic no one," Shaylinn said, quoting Matron, "and I love this dress."

"But your skin is dark enough that pale yellow would be glossy with your dark hair."

"I'm not changing." Shaylinn ran her hands over the skirt, admiring the soft fabric and the piping that edged the inset waist. It made her feel like one of Jemma's fairy tale princesses.

Shaylinn got to keep the dress. Jemma chose a lacy red dress with a black belt. Mia was wearing a slinky, floor-length black dress with bright yellow squiggly lines. Kendall picked a brown and orange floral chiffon dress. And Tyra talked Naomi into a royal blue satin dress.

Once everyone had shoes and jewelry to match, Tyra took the girls to a theater on the opposite end of the harem building. Shaylinn stumbled along in a pair of high-heeled white sandals. They'd seemed comfortable at first, but were soon pinching her toes and were becoming hard to walk in.

"Sit somewhere in the middle ten seats of the first three rows," Tyra said. "We want the camera to make the theater look full, and we've only got about thirty people here tonight."

A handful of people were already sitting in the front of the theater, including the older women from Glenrock — Jennifer, Chipeta, Aunt Mary, and Eliza. Mia hugged her mother. Naomi and Jemma ran to talk to the ladies. Shaylinn chose to stay beside Kendall in the middle of the third row. Seeing Mia and her mother together made Shaylinn miss her own mother, and Penelope and Nell too. Why weren't they here?

A bald man stood in the center of the stage, fussing over a microphone. He wore black gloves and had a funny black tattoo that covered half his head. "Testing, one, two, three, four ..."

Shaylinn glanced over her shoulder. In back of the room, in a small black booth, two men were working, one standing behind a camera as big as he was. Both men wore headsets.

"Those gloves he wears make me think of the evil Count Rugen, the six-fingered man from *The Princess Bride*," Jemma said, sitting down on Shaylinn's left. Jemma was always referring to that film. She lowered her voice to a whisper and seemed to say to herself, "Maybe it's a sign Levi will come for me like Westley did for Buttercup."

"Ladies," Tyra said. "In a moment Luella Flynn is going to film an intro. It's thrilling, I know. So I need you all to be quiet while we're taping, but applaud when you'd like, okay?"

Shaylinn wondered how many of the girls would clap. Mia seemed to be enamored with everything around them, but Naomi and a few of the other Glenrock women were sitting with crossed arms, staring at the stage. Shaylinn decided she would clap only if someone made her.

Tyra greeted a familiar-looking woman who stood on the far right of the stage. The woman was wearing a blood-red sweater and a tight, black, knee-length skirt. Her brown hair was twisted into a mound on the top of her head and studded with what appeared to be diamond flowers. She held a microphone with the letters *SLC* displayed on a square box under the foam head.

"That's Luella Flynn from the Finley and Flynn show," Kendall whispered. "I guess we're done with yellow and black. Just wait—everyone will be wearing those diamond flowers. And black and red. Jemma, you match her!"

Jemma groaned. "Now I'll look like I mimicked her."

Shaylinn thought back to the TV show she'd seen that morning. "But Luella had black hair."

Kendall smirked. "She changes her hair a lot. The brown is new. And so is the length. Probably a wig."

"Thirty seconds!" the cameraman yelled.

The women stopped whispering. Shaylinn continued to look back and forth between the stage and the men in the back, trying to understand what they were doing. Tyra ran onstage to retrieve one of Luella's diamond flowers off the floor.

"Ten seconds!"

"I keep losing those little beasties," Luella said, pushing at one of the flowers in her hair.

"In five, four, three, two …"

"Thanks, Finley," Luella said, her smile radiant. "Precious viewers, I'm live at the Champion Theater in the Highland Harem, juiced to meet the new conscripts. But first, the task director general is going to present a short greeting to the new nationals."

Luella went silent for a moment. "I haven't seen our newest queen. Yet. Rumor is she's *seven months pregnant*, which puts her delivery just two months behind Kendall Collin's. Now, I'm as stimmed as the rest of the Safe Lands about the prospect of two infant nationals, so I promise to get to the bottom of this to-*day* so we can see this miracle woman for ourselves."

The cameraman held up his hand. "We're clear."

Luella slouched and dropped the microphone to her side. "Just a little break for some product expos," she told the audience. "Did I lose any more clips?"

"No, you're fine," Tyra said from the side of the stage.

"Is the new pregnant girl out there?" Luella squinted into the audience.

"Right here!" Mia waved and pointed to Naomi.

"Thanks a lot, Mia," Naomi mumbled.

"Ug! I can't see you, femmy! The lights are too bright." Luella crouched and squinted at the audience.

"They aren't going to make me go up there, are they?" Naomi asked.

"Of course," Kendall said, "though they'll make me go up first."

"Why?" Shaylinn asked.

"Because I'm their spokesmodel. They want people to want to be like us."

"Pregnant?" Naomi said.

"Exactly."

"That's *so* weird," Shaylinn said. She hoped they escaped before that Ciddah woman summoned her, but after she got the magical cosmetic consultation.

"No, that's psychotic," Naomi said. "These people are nuts."

"Back in thirty!" the cameraman yelled.

"Kendall!" Tyra tottered up the aisle on her heels, waving. "I need you."

"Here we go." Kendall eased out of her chair and inched down the row, using the seat backs as a crutch. Tyra urged Kendall to hurry, but the girl had only one speed. Slow.

"In ten!"

Shaylinn watched Tyra help Kendall up the short flight of steps to the stage. A woman swooped in, fluffed Kendall's hair, and applied something to her face.

The cameraman spoke from the back of the room. "And five, four, three, two ..."

On stage, Luella lifted the microphone in front of her chin. "I give you the task director general of the Safe Lands, Lawten Renzor."

Scattered applause broke out from the small crowd. Shaylinn wasn't about to clap for the leader of her captors. The man walked to the center of the stage. He was wearing a black suit with a black shirt and tie underneath. He didn't look very special.

"Greetings, conscripts. As Task Director General of the Safe Lands, I oversee all facets of our beloved city. As you now know, female nationals are summoned to serve a term in the Highland Harem every two years. Since you're new to our city, we've asked you to serve immediately. This provides you with a safe place to learn our ways and a chance at a successful surrogacy."

"Before we all catch the plague and die," Naomi whispered to Jemma.

Shaylinn frowned. It was a morbid thought that seemed quite true.

"I'm sure you've discovered that the harem is a wonderful place to live," the task director said. "Matron Dlorah informed me you've been through orientation, task testing, and have been ranked for surrogacy. Congratulations on making it this far."

Jemma folded her arms. "Why's he trying to turn being kidnapped into some kind of competition? It's not like we chose to be here."

"He's just hoping we're as dumb as the people who live here," Naomi said.

But Shaylinn didn't think that Tyra or Kendall were dumb. Tyra was blunt, but she knew her job and did it well. And Kendall was so nice.

"As you all know, Kendall Collin is our beloved queen," the task director said. "You've likely seen her gorgeous face smiling at you from DigiBoards and Wyndos all over our city. My receptionist even has Kendall's picture as the background on her GlassTop."

This got a chuckle from the people in the front row.

"Let's give a warm welcome to Luella Flynn and Kendall Collin," the task director said.

Shaylinn looked back to the side of the stage. Arm in arm, Luella and Kendall walked toward the task director. He stepped back from the microphone and applauded. The Safe Lands nationals seated with the harem stood, cheering. One whistled. Another yelled Kendall's name. Shaylinn wondered if she should stand. Mia had, but Jemma and Naomi were still sitting.

She stayed in her seat as Kendall and Luella reached center stage.

The task director hugged Kendall and kissed her cheeks. "How are you, Ms. Collin?"

Kendall peered at the audience and said in a thin voice, "I'm doing good."

"You're looking good!" Luella said into her microphone, and nationals in the audience cheered.

"Naomi!" a voice whispered. Tyra stood at the end of the row, waving.

"I'm not going up there!" Naomi said.

"Ignore her, then," Jemma said.

But Tyra slipped down the aisle. "Naomi, I need you."

"I don't really care what you need."

Something hard flashed in Tyra's eyes. "I don't like to do this, Ms. Jordan, but I'm told your lifer is being held in the Rehabilitation Center. Your cooperation will assure his good treatment."

Jordan in prison? Heat flashed through Shaylinn's chest. She hoped her brother would try to control his temper. It felt like a futile hope.

Naomi's lips parted; her jaw twitched. "Did you just threaten me?"

Tyra swallowed and looked at the stage. "I'm afraid so."

Naomi shook her head and stood, pushing past Tyra and knocking the tiny woman down into a seat. Jemma followed Naomi all the way to the side stage. Shaylinn didn't want to be left alone, so she got up and followed. A lady with a brush approached Naomi.

"Don't touch me," Naomi said, and the woman skulked away.

Everything looked different from this position. Bright spotlights from the back of the room blinded Shaylinn, making the audience a white blur. She could see the stage perfectly, however, especially where the task director, Luella, and Kendall stood talking.

"Safe Landers," the task director said, "this baby is coming and soon! He's yours, and he's mine. Thank you, Kendall Collin, for your service to our great city."

Again the crowd applauded. Kendall walked off the stage, deflating a bit once she reached Shaylinn. "I *hate* being on the ColorCast," she said. "Especially with that man."

Luella spoke into her microphone. "Just yesterday, eight new women joined our nation. Like Kendall, they were once outsiders. And among them was their own queen."

Naomi crossed her arms on top of her belly. "I'm *not* going out there!"

"A queen as lovely as our Kendall," Luella said, though Shaylinn swore she'd heard the woman admit to never having seen Naomi. "A queen that brought with her the promise of a future. People of the Safe Lands, I give you Naomi Jordan, who's carrying a precious baby boy!"

"Go!" Tyra pushed Naomi onto the stage.

"Boy?" Naomi staggered the first few steps after Tyra's shove, then slowed to a standstill. Shaylinn understood why Tyra had insisted Naomi wear this fitted blue gown over the flowy one Naomi had preferred. They were putting her pregnancy on display for all to see.

"Come now, Ms. Jordan. Don't be shy." The task director held out his arms as if Naomi was his long-lost daughter.

The pale shock on Naomi's face hardened. She straightened, tossed her head back, and marched to the center of the stage. "It's *Mrs.* Jordan," she said.

The task director embraced her and kissed both her cheeks, though Naomi may as well have been a tree.

"Oh, you darling creature!" Luella said, taking Naomi's hands and holding them out to the side. She let go of one and twirled Naomi under her arm. "Finley, isn't she stunning?"

The audience applauded. Finley's reply, wherever he was, wasn't heard in the theater.

"What a joy," the task director said to the audience, "to introduce Naomi Jordan, our new Safe Lands queen."

"I'm not your silly queen," Naomi said. "What have you done with my husband?"

Immediately, majestic music rose, drowning out Naomi's unamplified voice. The task director turned to the left side of the stage. Shaylinn followed his gaze and saw two men walk out from the curtains, shirtless! One carried a fat red pillow that held a crown and a long ribbon. The other carried a bouquet of flowers.

The men stopped beside the task director, who picked up the crown with both hands and settled it onto Naomi's head. Then he put the ribbon over her head, which turned out to be a sash that fell across her body. It bore the words *Safe Lands Queen* in gold glitter. He took the flowers from the second man and handed them to Naomi.

"Surrogacy," the task director said. "Giving life. This is true beauty. This is true patriotism. This is the highest glory to be had in our nation. Naomi Jordan, you are highly favored. We thank you for your service. You're a Safe Lands hero. May Fortune bless you."

"Finally," Kendall said to Shaylinn. "Maybe now they'll start leaving me alone."

CHAPTER 14

That evening Shaylinn and the other harem girls attended the entertainment orientation, which was held in several ballrooms on the second floor of the Highland Harem. There was a room for dancing, a room for singing, a room for playing musical instruments, and a room for learning how to act. Tyra informed them that they must try everything once as part of their task training.

Kendall had been given the night off, due to what Tyra had called "the upcoming momentous occasion of giving birth," so Shaylinn stayed close to Jemma and Naomi. They decided to get the acting out of the way, then do the dancing, and end with instruments and singing, which they thought would be more relaxing. Mia tagged along too.

The acting room seemed twenty degrees hotter than the rest of the building because of all the bright lamps pointing at each of the stations. There were four stages set up in this room: a kitchen, a dance club, a living room, and a restaurant. Each had a row of seats for spectators.

"It's like a life-sized dollhouse!" Mia said.

Naomi pointed out a small table of food and filled a plate with stuffed chicken rolls. Once they all had something to munch on, the group sat by the living room station and watched Eliza, Jennifer, and Chipeta read a scene about three friends in the Safe Lands Boarding School. Shaylinn found the process of filmmaking fascinating, and asked one of the men running the station about camera crews, lighting, scripts, and how they put it all together.

"There you are!" Tyra said from behind Jemma. "I've been looking for you."

Naomi growled low, like a dog whose territory had been invaded.

Jemma flashed Tyra a hopeful smile. "You're going to let me take Naomi back to the dormitory because a pregnant woman needs her rest?"

"No," Tyra said, "but I'll make you a deal. The director wants to film some of the harem girls reading a scene for a thriller movie. He thinks it'll make great outtakes for today's 'behind the scenes with the new nationals' bit Luella's going to run on her show."

"They're filming this day?" Shaylinn looked around. She didn't want to be on TV.

"Of course!" Tyra said. "They film everything for the ColorCast."

"Good." Naomi shoved three chicken rolls into her mouth. "Whurs duh camma?"

Shaylinn cackled at how silly Naomi looked. The perfect woman for her brother.

"Be serious," Tyra said. "If you do this, and do it well, you can go back to the room."

"Done," Naomi said, gulping down her mouthful. "Where's my script?"

"Excellent!" Tyra handed them each a sheet of white paper. "I want Jemma and Naomi to read Mielle's parts and Mia and Shaylinn to read the kidnapper. Then if you want, you can switch. It's being filmed on the kitchen set. Byran Kester is the director. He's waiting for you."

"I want to switch," Mia said. "I'd rather play the victim over the kidnapper."

Shaylinn rolled her eyes and settled back to read it over.

29 INT. APARTMENT–KITCHEN–DAY

A FRIGHTENED MIELLE IS TIED TO A CHAIR. BEHIND HER, ON THE WALLS, ARE POSTERS DEPICTING REBEL PROPAGANDA.

MIELLE STRUGGLES WITH THE ROPES THAT BIND HER HANDS.

KIDNAPPER 1 APPROACHES MIELLE. HE IS HOLDING A KNIFE. ON HIS RIGHT, KIDNAPPER 2 IS SETTING UP A CAMERA ON A TRIPOD. KIDNAPPER 3 SITS ON A CHAIR BEHIND THEM BOTH, INHALING FROM A BLACK VAPORIZER AND BREATHING OUT BLACK SMOKE.

KIDNAPPER 1

We're going to record a little footage to send to your Valentine in the Highlands so he knows you're alive. That way he'll be more willing when we–

MIELLE

I'm not doing anything you say!

KIDNAPPER 1

Don't you think your lover has a right to know where you are?

MIELLE

Kale and I do what we want. We're not lifers.

KIDNAPPER 1

That's not what I heard. I heard you've scheduled your liberation for the same day. And you haven't been to your apartment in six months.

MIELLE

You've been following me?

KIDNAPPER 1

(to Kidnapper 3)

I think she's catching on.

(to Mielle)

Now, unless you want a knife shoved between Kale's ribs, you're going to help us out, you get me?

CUT TO:

30 INT. APARTMENT–KITCHEN–LATER

MIELLE SITS ON HER CHAIR FACING KIDNAPPER 2 AND HIS CAMERA. KIDNAPPER 2 LEANS IN TO RECORD.

31 CLOSEUP–MIELLE

MIELLE

(tearfully)

Hay-o, Kale. I'm sorry I got myself into this. I shouldn't have believed Tarme's lies about the Liberation Department. You were right about him. About everything. I miss you. The food is good, though.

(laughs)

Please do what they say. I'm afraid of what will happen if you don't. I love you.

Shaylinn looked at Jemma. "That's a scary story, isn't it?"

"Very. Let's just do it so we can go, huh?" Jemma said.

They walked over to the kitchen set and found Byran. He was a small man, dark-haired, with a thin face covered in scruff. He wore a black shirt with all of the buttons undone so that his bright yellow tank top showed. A thick gold chain hung round his neck.

"I've got the script on the prompters," Byran said, "so you can just read it. We're still trying to get a feeling for which lines are the best for this scene. Think you can act this out?"

"It's not much of a stretch," Jemma said. "We are kidnapped people, after all."

Byran's laugh sounded forced. "Let's take you first, lovely. That's a pretty dress."

"Right on top of the trends," Naomi said.

"Let's have you sit on the stool, femme," Byran said. "We're going to come in close on your face, but try not to fidget, because we want you as still as possible. Willa's going to put a little makeup on you, pale that tanned face a bit, give you some fake tears."

"Let's see, you other two ..." He looked to Shaylinn and Mia. "I'm just going to let you read how you want to. Try to sound mean."

Once Willa had finished applying makeup to Jemma's face, Byran said, "Both cameras are already rolling, so we can edit later."

"He's recording now?" Shaylinn asked, suddenly feeling awkward.

"Yep," Byran said. "I'm going to ask you all some questions to loosen you up a bit, help you get comfortable. Tell me, Jemma, how old are you?"

"Seventeen."

"And do you have a partner?" He looked at the script. "A uh ... *boy* friend?"

"Yes."

"Of course you do, lovely little flame like yourself. And what's your trigger's name?"

"Um ... Levi."

"Feeling a bit more comfortable?"

Jemma tittered and rocked in her seat. "No."

"How about you ... Shaylinn, is it?"

Had Shaylinn made a mistake? "You didn't ask me anything!"

Naomi snickered, and then Jemma laughed for real.

"No worries. Jemma, go ahead and read the lines off the prompter screen," Byran said, "Shaylinn, you read the kidnapper, but stand back by this microphone, out of the way. We're just filming Mielle now."

Shaylinn was relieved to stand out of the way. She and Jemma spoke their lines. Shaylinn didn't like the kidnapper's part. His words embarrassed her.

When they finished, Byran said, "Okay, that's *reading* the lines. This time, I want you to act them out. I want to hear your fear. I want to see real tears in your eyes. But I want a real fake laugh, okay? Make it sound like you're trying to make light of this horror you're living through. Make your lover believe it. Make Kale scared for you. Pretend it's your Levi, if it helps."

And so they read the lines again. Shaylinn tried hard to pretend she was an evil man, but it made her stomach tighten. She just wanted it to be over.

"Great!" Byran smiled at Jemma. "That was great, really great. Can you repeat that last line for me? But this time say, 'You were right about him. About everything. You were right.'"

Jemma repeated the line the way he asked.

"You're a natural, Jemma. Naomi, you're up. Shaylinn, let Mia stand where you are to read the kidnapper."

When they finished with Byran and the acting station, Naomi insisted they leave. Once they were out in the cooler hallway, Naomi said, "Can we go back to the room now?"

"Tyra said we could," Jemma said.

"But we haven't done the singing room yet," Mia said, "or the instrument one. I know neither of you are very good at either of those things, but I happen to have some talent."

"Who cares?" Naomi said. "We're prisoners in this place."

"So we shouldn't have any fun?" Mia asked.

"My father was killed, Mia," Naomi said. "Our mothers are missing. The children are probably terrified. You should treat this like a vacation."

"Are you trying to make me feel guilty because my mom is here and yours isn't? Fine! Go back to the room and cry. I'm going to have some fun." Mia stomped away, her tiny steps reminding Shaylinn of the way Matron Dlorah walked.

"I want to stay," Shaylinn said. "I mean, you're right, we are prisoners. But all I can do in my bedroom is feel bad about what happened. Here at least I can forget it for a few more hours."

Jemma hugged Shaylinn. "Okay, Shay. You stay with Mia. And keep her out of trouble."

"I heard that!" Mia yelled.

Shaylinn and Mia went to the dancing room next. It had six stations, three on each side of the room. Instrumental music was playing at the station to the right of the entrance where a ballerina danced, seeming to float across the floor on her toes, sweeping her arms from side to side. A small crowd had formed in front of the station, and the girls stopped to watch. When the song ended, the crowds applauded and the ballerina curtsied.

"Anyone interested in learning the steps of ballet?" the ballerina asked.

Mia raised her hand, naturally, and the next thing Shaylinn knew, she and Mia were learning "ballet positions."

After the ballet station, they visited a station for a dance that required them to move very quickly to thumping music, one where they made noise using their feet, and one for what they called club dancing, which forced them to do some things the elders in Glenrock might have frowned on. Mia seemed to pick them all up quickly, but Shaylinn's feet seemed too big and slow to do any of it right. Until they got to the one called ballroom dancing.

The flashing screen on the wall said their instructor, Maroz Zerrik, was a famous dancer. He had short blond hair, perfect posture, and broad shoulders. Every time he looked at Shaylinn, her cheeks tingled. He explained the waltz, the tango, the foxtrot, the jitterbug, performing each with a woman named Nelessa Kade, who looked almost naked in a light brown sequined dress.

"Now," Maroz said, "I will waltz with each of you."

Mia squealed and rushed up to Maroz as if he'd called her name. "Me first!"

Maroz chuckled. "As you wish, pearl."

Mia gasped at Shaylinn. "Did you hear that? He said 'As you wish.' I'll have to tell Jemma. Maybe I've found my own Westley."

By the look on Nelessa Kade's face, Shaylinn doubted that very much. As Maroz waltzed with Mia, however, she looked just as good at it as Nelessa. The longer their dance lasted, the more Shaylinn worried about her coming turn.

When Maroz's gaze fell on Shaylinn and he held out his hand, she nearly melted. Mia had to push Shaylinn onto the station floor. The man's touch made her stomach flutter. She couldn't remember if she was moving her feet or if Maroz had lifted her up for the entire dance, but somehow she glided along with him, both mortified and enthralled.

When the dance ended, Maroz looked at her with a wide smile. "With more practice, you could become quite good at this. You just have to — " But Shaylinn never learned what she would need to do, as Mia dragged Shaylinn to the singing room, which had one stage and a long line of people who wanted to sing. Shaylinn had no desire to sing in front of people, so she sat and waited for Mia, who, when her turn came, crooned on the center stage.

Neither of them had much success in the musical instruments room, but making funny sounds out of a trumpet made Shaylinn laugh.

"I have my cosmetic consultation tomorrow morning," Mia said. "What time is yours?"

"Nine thirty."

"Mine's at nine. You want to come earlier with me? I'll wait for yours to be over."

"Okay." It would be nice to have someone there to talk to, and she was enjoying spending time with tonight's kinder Mia. "I think I want to do it."

Mia laughed. "Do you even know what 'it' is?"

Shaylinn smiled. "Making me thin, I think. Why are you going? You're beautiful."

"I know, but there's so much I'd like to improve, and if these people are willing to do it, I'm not going to fight it."

Shaylinn understood. Everything about this place seemed wonderful. The food, the buildings, the beds, the showers, the clothes ... Granted, she was afraid of being pregnant and of catching the thin plague. But she was beginning to wonder if Papa Eli had been a bit mistaken about what happened inside these walls. She could get used to living here.

CHAPTER 15

The Safe Lands Rehabilitation Center, also called the RC, was located just north of City Hall. Omar arrived twenty minutes early for his meeting with General Otley, anxious to see what Skottie had wanted to show him. He checked in with the enforcer at the entrance, then waited in the lobby for Skottie. Pictures of people hung along the wall. Brass nameplates had been mounted under each, displaying the person's name and task.

Daniel Miller: TRST founder
Born 1983 — Final Liberation 2033

Taylor James: Founder of the enforcers
Born 1995 — Final Liberation 2045

Poet Levon: Theater entertainer
Born 2016 — Liberated to Seven 2066

Joie Champion: Communications anchor
Born 2021 — Liberated to Three 2071

Bristol Cruz: Engineering
Born 2032 — Liberated to Five 2072

Liberated. So strange. And too bad for Bristol Cruz. Skottie had said they'd changed the liberation date to forty back in seventy-two. Bad timing to lose ten years of your life, even if you were supposedly born into the next one.

When Skottie showed up, they took the elevator to the sixth floor. "You're going to love this," Skottie said. "One of my femmes tasks in Surveillance as a gatekeeper over the RC."

"What's a gatekeeper?"

"She's in charge of the locks. Nothing opens unless she says so. Now that, my peer, is a position of power."

The doors opened to the clamor of voices. Surveillance consisted of rows of narrow hallways lined with massive Wyndo monitors, three screens down and a dozen across, each screen divided into nine or twelve images. People wearing headsets sat on rolling chairs facing the screens, one person to every six screens.

Skottie led him to the far left of the room where there were several little offices behind glass walls. He walked straight ahead to the office in the left corner and tapped on the glass.

A curvy woman looked up from an L-shaped desk. She had lots of curly black hair that poofed out around her face. She grinned at Skottie and waved him in. Skottie opened the door and entered. Omar followed.

"Hey, Camella, how you doing?"

"Just working, trigger. Kind of quiet this morning. Who's your friend?"

"This is Omar. He's new to our world."

"New?" Camella's eyes shifted up and down Omar's body. "You look good, Omar. Where you from, baby face?"

Omar's chest filled with heat at her scrutiny. "Glenrock."

She laughed. "Yeah, I don't know where that is."

"Cammy, show Omar what you do," Skottie said.

Camella rolled her eyes. "Come on back, then."

Skottie grabbed Omar by the sleeve and dragged him around behind Camella's desk. She had three screens. One huge one hung on the wall on the long side of desk. It had nine images up at once, but they were changing every few seconds. The other two screens were side by side, built into the GlassTop desk. One showed a close-up of a door, and the other showed a screen that said *SimTag Authorization System* and had a keyboard beneath it.

"What happens is, I get a tap when one of the enforcers needs a door opened. Then I pull up the location on my GlassTop. The enforcer has to verify who he is, and I check each name in the Authorization System. Once I've cleared them all, I code in the entry, and the door will open. Then I log it in."

"No one can open a prison door without you?" Omar asked. "Not even Otley?"

She chuckled. "Much to Otley's chagrin, no. Even he needs — " Camella touched her ear and turned away. "Please verify identification."

"Who's she talking to? I don't hear anything."

"SimTalk. You should get one. They shoot it in your ear just like a SimTag, then you can talk without your Wyndo." Skottie waved Omar over to the office door. "Hey," he whispered. "Wait outside for me, will you? I want to talk to Cammy alone for a minute."

"Yeah, sure." Omar slipped out of the office and turned around. He didn't want Skottie to think he was eavesdropping, so he strolled down one row of monitors, then another, looking at images of pedestrians, streets, offices, medical facilities, holding rooms, and stores.

This must be where enforcers monitored the feeds from all those yellow cameras.

A man tapped Omar's arm. "Sir? Harem women in the hallway." He glanced up from his screen long enough to realize Omar wasn't the "sir" he'd been looking for. "Sorry." He called out to an enforcer at the end of the hallway, "Sir, the harem women?"

Omar leaned in to study the image of a group of women walking down a wide hallway. He recognized Naomi, Jemma, Mia, and … was that Shay? His heart thudded inside his chest. It was his first look at anyone from home. And they looked good, dressed in Safe Lands clothes. Omar felt a little lighter — clearly they were much happier here than Glenrock. His bringing them here had made it possible.

"There should be four heading back to the dormitory from the spa," a nasal voice said. "Tyra Grant and Kendall Collin should be with them. Can I help you?" the enforcer asked Omar.

"I'm just looking," Omar said.

"On whose authority?"

"Uh ... I'm meeting with General Otley in a few minutes."

"Then you should wait in the reception area on the first floor, Mr. Strong."

A rush of heat seized Omar. Was he in trouble? How'd this man know his name? "I'm sorry." He hurried to the elevator. Forget waiting for Skottie. He glanced back at the enforcer, wincing when he saw him talking to himself. Hopefully not speaking to Otley with one of those SimTalk implants.

Omar went straight to the first floor reception area, announced himself to the woman behind the desk, and sat down.

By the time the woman called him, he'd waited forty minutes.

Otley's office was plain and a tenth of the size of the task director general's. Bright lights glared down on a cracked GlassTop desk, three mismatched metal file cabinets, a set of black chairs on Omar's side of the desk, and Otley himself, sitting behind his desk with his beefy arms folded across his massive chest.

Omar would sketch Otley as a giant boar ramming its tusks into the side of a house. The children would like that. But the children were in the academy now.

Otley grunted. "Sit, little rat."

Omar sank onto the black metal chair and studied the tusk in Otley's nose.

"Don't like traitors," Otley growled, "so I don't like you. Don't want you in my department. Don't want you owning a rank. But I have little choice, so here's what's going to happen: Report to training every day from eight in the morning 'til five at night. Take an hour off for lunch. Training is closed Friday, Saturday, and Sunday, so stay home those days. Don't want to see you. My people don't want to see you. Snoop around again, and you're cleaning streets. Get me?"

That enforcer in surveillance *had* tapped Otley. "Yes, sir."

"Good. Get out."

Omar stumbled over the legs of his chair but managed to make it out of Otley's office alive. He went straight to the elevators and up to the second floor.

Training turned out to be school, which had started three weeks ago. There were twenty guys in the classroom, all sitting at GlassTop desks. Omar saw Skottie and Charlz in the back.

Enforcer Stiller, a thick man with a flat nose and squinty eyes, was Omar's instructor. He asked the class to read up on tactics, then sat with Omar at the back of the room.

"So you got your captain's stripes without taking one minute of classes," Stiller said. "I bet you're proud of that, aren't you?"

Omar shrugged one shoulder and fought a smile.

"Yeah, that's what I thought. TeleFlash, shell. None of us are impressed that Renzor pulled rank to get you a promotion, got it? So watch your back, *Captain*. The guys like to hammer cheats. And I won't stop a good hammering every now and then, if you get me."

Omar wanted to run, but he sat very still and forced himself to maintain eye contact.

"First, shell, get some muscle on those arms. I'm going to teach you pretty much everything you need to know for your head, but I can't make you strong and neither can your last name. Most of these guys have been training for years. So run to the gym. Move in, if you have to. You're going to hurt for a while, but stick with it. How old are you?"

Omar looked around and lowered his voice. "Sixteen."

"Walls. You should be at the boarding school, kid. All right, sit in back with Charlz. He's too thick to know you're a shell. You make friends with him, you might survive training." He nodded to where Charlz was sitting in the back row. Skottie was sitting just in front of Charlz, reading from a Wyndo. "The manual is on the GlassTop."

"Yes, sir." Omar sat at a GlassTop desk in the back row beside Charlz.

Skottie turned and whispered, "What happened to you upstairs?"

"An enforcer kicked me out and tapped Otley."

"My fault there," Skottie said. "Shouldn't have abandoned you."

"*Mr. Skott*," Stiller said.

Skottie turned back to his Wyndo.

Omar tapped on the surface of his desk, opening little folders until he located the manual. He perused the table of contents. There were sections on arrest and booking procedures, investigation techniques, radio communications, report writing, weapons care and safety, marksmanship, stress management, community relations, hate crimes, missing persons, patrol procedures, building searches, vehicle stops, use of deadly force, and shooting policy.

Overwhelmed, Omar closed his eyes. Levi used to leave him in charge of the lookout in Glenrock, which had always felt like a child's assignment. When Renzor had promised to make Omar an officer in the enforcers, Omar had imagined that someone would give him a gun and put him in charge of some men. His naiveté stung, as did the realization that he was again the youngest, that Otley hated him, and that some of his new classmates might resent him.

He wished he were standing in the lookout back home and that none of this had happened.

He shook the thoughts away. *This* was home now. And he had to prove to everyone that this place was better. Because if it wasn't ... If he'd done all this for nothing...

Later, while Omar, Skottie, and Charlz were eating lunch in the cafeteria, Charlz started in on a whole apple pie, the flaky crust the same color as his skin.

"They got the best desserts in this caf." He pushed his tray toward Omar. "Try it."

The mere idea that a flake from Charlz's skin had fallen onto that pie made Omar queasy. "Thanks, I'm full."

Skottie inhaled a long breath on his vaporizer, then tipped his head back and blew a plume of black vapor above his head, leaving behind a spicy smell. "Tonight, we take you out. *We* show *you* the Safe Lands DarkScene."

Charlz howled like some kid pretending to be a wolf. "Ginger Oak, please, Skottie, please?"

Skottie nodded in slow motion, his frizzy brown curls swaying over his eyes. "Oh, yes. Ginger Oak for the outsider. Pre*cise*. It'll be a night to remember. I still can't believe you've never paired up. That's prude."

Omar's cheeks burned. He wished he'd never told them.

"We should pair him up with Diamoniqua," Charlz said. "Think she'll do it?"

"For enough credits, she'll do anything!"

The guys roared at their private joke, Charlz laughing so hard his neck turned pink.

Omar wasn't certain he could be one of the guys — especially without violating the rules the task director had set him to. But he was certainly going to try.

After classes, Skottie drove Omar to a store where he purchased his own Wyndo transmitter. He paid extra for the program that would allow him to design his own SimArt and couldn't wait to learn to use it. Then they went to Surface, and Omar got a SimTalk installed in his right ear.

After that, Skottie dropped Omar off at the Task of Art store because he had planned to meet Camella for dinner. "I'll pick you up around nine for Ginger Oak, okay?"

"Yeah, thanks," Omar said.

Omar entered the store. Charcoal, pencil shavings, and the chemical smell of oil paints made him happy. He was more intoxicated by the sight of art supplies than he'd been from the drinks he'd had at Main Event last night.

He grabbed pads of paper, several canvasses, two sets of oil paints, paintbrushes, some turpentine, an easel, a palette knife, some charcoal pencils, a package of pastels, a pack of colored pencils, and some art markers. He stopped himself from taking one of everything in the store — unlike in his raids of the abandoned stores around Glenrock, these items would remain just as numerous and varied the next time he came.

When the clerk saw all that Omar intended to purchase, he asked, "You sure you can afford all this?"

Was it a lot? Omar wished he'd paid more attention when Dallin had explained costs. "I think so."

"Most enforcers only make four hundred credits a week."

"Oh. Well, I've been saving up," Omar said.

The clerk raised one brow and added up Omar's purchases. "Okay, that comes to 1,349.29 credits."

All this stuff was worth three weeks' credits? He pressed his fist against the pad and waited. He had millions of credits. Didn't he? Maybe the task director had taken them back or hadn't given them out yet.

The clerk suddenly gave him a wide smile. "Thank you, Mr. Strong. Let me put all this in some bags for you."

Since Omar didn't really know where he was, he wasn't sure how to get home. He walked for several blocks, carrying his art bags, then, after seeing several people wave down a taxi, he tried it. The taxi cost him only twelve credits.

He carried his bags up to his Snowcrest apartment and set up his easel. He wanted to play with his new Wyndo, make a SimArt owl, or tap someone to try his new SimTalk implant, but he wanted to paint more. He hadn't drawn or painted in days. Omar stood at his easel and used a piece of charcoal to sketch his neighbor Bel, from memory, from the waist up onto one of his new canvases. Once he was happy with the outline, he squeezed red, brown, orange, and white onto his pallete and started to paint her hair. He instantly noticed how soft the paint was, how smoothly it moved over the canvas. The colors came out exactly how they looked on the tubes, not like Old paints that were dull and thick and goopy or his homemade paints that were so thin.

When Artie tapped to tell Omar that Skottie was waiting downstairs, Omar almost didn't want to leave.

Almost.

CHAPTER 16

Levi parked his rig in a grove of aspen, swung his rifle over his arm, and crept to the edge of the trees. A rocky expanse with tufts of wild grass separated his location from the northern edge of the Safe Lands. The outer wall stood three stories high and was wide enough to support a two-way road on top. Beyond that wall was the canal, then the inner wall. A Jeep was driving south along the outer wall at the moment, and Levi waited for it to pass out of sight. He'd be exposed as he approached the storm drain, but he couldn't risk waiting until nightfall to get inside. Who knew what had happened to Jemma and the others already.

Once the trill of the Jeep's motor had faded, Levi scrambled down the hill, keeping to the tall grass. He still wore the camouflage clothing he'd put on last night but had added the bulletproof vest, his backpack, a pair of gloves, and brown rubber chest waders he'd scavenged from a house in Denver City. They'd keep him dry from what he was about to wade through.

The sun was high in the sky; no sign of rain. That, and his own adrenaline, had him in a full sweat. He'd never been inside the Safe Lands, no matter how many times he and Jordan had dared one another. Elder Eli had instilled a fear of this place that Levi knew not to toy with.

Blackberry bushes scratched at his boots as he started up the hill to the wall. Overflow fed out of the bottom of the concrete wall in four large drains, evenly spaced around the bell-like perimeter. Each was a half circle, about six feet wide and four feet tall, covered with grates of crisscrossed iron. There was no way to swim through such small openings and no way to cut the iron that wouldn't call attention to his presence. The grates had hinges on one side, padlocks on the other. The hinges were Levi's way in. He repeatedly struck them with a hammer, checking his surroundings after every five blows to make sure no one was approaching. After about an hour his strikes began to crush the concrete around the bolts into powder.

From there it wasn't long before the bolts were loose enough for Levi to pull them out with his hammer, like nails. He pulled back the grate until he was able to slip past. His boots slushed in the water, and he tried not to think about what he was wading through.

Chest waders and gloves had been wonderful inventions of Old.

But it didn't smell like waste water. It even looked clean. With great care, Levi pulled the grate back into place and edged through the flow, careful to make as little noise as possible. The tunnel that passed under the outer wall looked to be about fifteen feet long, though he couldn't see where it let out from his position. All he could see was the inner concrete wall.

When he reached the opening, the sun warmed his face again. He stood in ankle-deep water in the mouth of the tunnel that branched off the main canal: a concrete gutter that cut a four-story gash around the Safe Lands compound, a manmade path for the river that was open to the sky. Levi's storm drain had let him in at water level, leaving three stories of walls towering overhead. Why were the walls so deep? The water would never reach such a depth. He supposed the real reason was to keep people from getting out, which made him very aware of how exposed he was to anyone who might be patrolling the wall above.

The water didn't look deep or fast, but he supposed the dam held back much of the flow. Still, he turned and slowly lowered himself off the storm drain's ledge feet first, and was thankful to feel the bottom quickly. When he stood on the bottom of the canal, the water reached his waist. The surface was mucky under his boots. He swung his arms, slogging upriver, toward the city for what felt like miles upon miles. It was hard to tell from his position, but he knew from looking through his rifle scope up on the mountain that the Safe Lands had three areas separated by huge walls and gates. He should be in the middle area now, and guessed that Jemma and the others would be in the upper city, the farthest away from escape.

He stayed close to the outer wall, hoping such a position would make him invisible to patrols above. Every few yards, pipes opened into the canal from the inside wall, discharging trickles of brown waste water into the river. Most were about a foot in diameter, but there were a few bigger ones: some two feet in diameter, some about four. Levi hoped to find a six-footer, like the one he and his father had explored in Denver City. Large drains tended to lead right under city streets.

Levi reached a dividing wall that separated the middle area of the Safe Lands from the upper portion and was stopped by another large grate—hinged on one side, padlocked on the other, just like the first one. Slowly and with as little noise as possible, he worked the bolts over with his hammer until he was able to pass through and continue up river.

On the other side of the dividing wall the canal inclined some, climbing the foothills of the mountain. The water flowed faster here, washing trash and leaves past his ankles. In the distance, the canal turned slightly, obscuring itself as it curved around. Sounds from inside the city drifted to his ears: engines, music, laughter.

For some reason the laughter stopped him. He leaned against the outer wall and closed his eyes, only to envision images of a destroyed Glenrock. His father's face. Papa Eli dying. Emotion threatened to take over his body; his knees trembled. He sucked in a deep breath. He could mourn later.

He hiked up the curving incline, the sound of falling water music to his ears, but when the six-foot drainpipe came into view, it had no more discharge than a tiny creek. What, then, was that watery roar?

Levi passed by the drain, seeking the source of the noise. Another hundred yards around the curve of the canal and he caught sight of the dam, built into the wall at the crest of the bell. Water shot out from one of three spillways and into the canal. A cement ladder ran through the water and up the right side of the dam. Above, a bridge connected the dam to a roadway. A generator rattled somewhere close by, perhaps the very one that got its power from this contraption.

"Hey!" A man in a gray jumpsuit looked down from the wall, standing above the dam. "You can't be in there, shell!"

Levi turned and ran. He made it three steps before he slipped and fell onto his side, sliding down the canal faster than he wanted to go. He turned his head away from the water and tried to stop himself. Something sharp snagged his hand through his glove, and he cradled his palm against his chest. He managed to slow himself to a stop before reaching the six-foot pipe. He pushed himself up, his legs shaky. A blaring siren brought his attention to a flash of sunlight gleaming off the windshield of a Jeep cruising along the top of the outer wall, approaching from the west.

With a deep breath, Levi inched toward the six-foot pipe on the inner wall. About three yards before he reached the opening, bullets plopped into the water around him like stones skipping on the surface of a lake. His careful steps became lunges. Bullets cracked against the inside wall, shattering tiny dents into the concrete. Panicked, Levi dove into the pipe, twisting so that he landed on his side, lifting his head as he skidded through the water. The gunfire ceased.

He scrambled up, dripping, and started down the tunnel, slipping twice. His movement upset a swallow, which fluttered toward him. He crouched to let it pass.

The water was only inches deep, spanning a couple of feet in the bottom of the pipe. The only light in the tunnel was the sunlight at the entrance, now twenty yards behind. He swung off his pack and fumbled for his solar lantern, only to discover the bulb had broken in his fall. Stifling a groan, he dug for a crank flashlight. The beam lit little of his surroundings, but the light was better than nothing. Squaring his shoulders, Levi headed deeper into the tunnel.

The storm drain was concrete on the bottom half and rusted corrugated steel pipe on the top. He slipped again, catching himself just before he took another bath.

Maybe the chest waders weren't as ingenious as he'd first thought.

He decided to avoid the water by walking on the dry sides of the pipe, which offered better footholds but burned his leg muscles. He moved carefully, shining his flashlight at the water. Now that he wasn't kicking it up, he could see it was cloudy brown with bits of trash and the occasional beetle. Stripes of rust on the pipe's sides marked past higher waterlines. Good thing he wasn't trying this after a heavy rainstorm.

After a while, he came to a square opening where three new pipes shot off in different directions. All were smaller than the one he stood in — two four-foot pipes and one two-footer. Thick chains draped across the openings of the larger pipes, and sheets of spider's webs filled the corners of the room and covered half the opening of the middle pipe. Graffiti above the smaller hole said "Black Army will prevail" over a drawing of bird's wings.

Levi chose the pipe on the far left, hoping to head toward the upper part of the city. He had to crouch to navigate this smaller drain and kept his feet on either side of the water and his left hand on the wall to steady himself. This pipe was solid concrete, smooth but spotted with algae and the occasional graffiti. Every so often, he passed a rib where two concrete pipes butted together and thin, brown water dripped down.

He came to an indentation shooting off to the right, and he stopped to explore. A square chute ran straight up and looked to be two stories high. Rusty iron rungs jutted out from the wall, providing footholds. Levi tucked his flashlight into his mouth and started to climb. A third of the way up, a shell of rust crumbled off the rung, revealing a thin spindle of metal underneath that snapped under Levi's weight, causing him to drop to the previous foothold. He held tightly with his left hand and, once his heartbeat returned to normal, reached for the rung above the broken one. He tugged it first, and it snapped. Frustrated, he climbed back down.

The beam of his flashlight flickered over the walls. The tunnel curved, and he worried he'd come out back in the middle section of the Safe Lands with no way of getting through the second inner wall. An occasional foot-wide pipe dumped into the larger one, sending a stream of water down the chute. More pipes split off from the main one, but Levi stayed on the straight course. No sense in getting any more lost.

The next ladder he came to ran up the wall to a manhole. Light pulsed through a cluster of tiny openings in the lid, and thuds of tires and music echoed down the chute. Flashlight back in his mouth, Levi climbed slowly, checking each rung before putting his weight on it. When he came to the top, the rhythmic *thump-thump*, *thump-thump* of tires lowered his spirits. He'd be a fool to exit in front of the vehicles that were looking to capture him or might simply run him over.

He climbed down and continued up the tunnel. Some of the connecting ribs rained steady streams of water over his head, cooling his sweaty body. The tunnel forked into two. Levi kept to the left, inching down a steep grade. The water rose quickly, and he noticed several cockroaches on the walls, moving in the opposite direction.

"If it's bad enough for roaches ..." he said, marveling at the sound of his voice in the dark place. He turned back and took the right fork. This tunnel was cleaner and smooth. He passed some graffiti that said, "Lonn for Task Director General." The smell of fried food wafted down, and his stomach growled. He wondered how long he'd been in the drains and if he should stop and eat some beef jerky. Just ahead, red and blue electric light danced at the bottom of the tunnel. Another ladder up?

A shadow suddenly flashed long in the distance across the tunnel walls. A light shining behind him. He ducked down, then ran for the indentation in the concrete where the colored light originated. Hidden in the nook, he peeked back down the tunnel. Two powerful lights shone his way, ten times brighter than his crank flashlight. A voice drifted down the tunnel. He couldn't understand what was said, but it didn't sound urgent. Perhaps they hadn't seen him.

Levi started up the rungs, testing each quickly, and climbed to the top. Above, a rectangular grille blocked his exit. The sky was dark already. Levi could see the tops of lit-up buildings but little else. He didn't hear any vehicles, so he put one hand flat against the grille and pushed. Unexpected dirt and rust sprinkled into his eyes. He ducked and blinked, trying to clear his vision. Far below, the tunnel glowed bright and footsteps splashed. The men were almost beneath him.

Keeping his head down, he pushed again, pressing his shoulders and head against the iron. It shifted. Dirt and rust tickled his neck and slid down the back of his shirt. He pushed harder and groaned under the strain. The iron popped free, upsetting a glass bottle that rolled on the ground above, clanking over what sounded like asphalt — maybe a road? He could barely slide the grille aside. It scraped over the ground.

"He's there!"

Light blinded him from below. He scrambled out of the hole and crawled onto asphalt. He lay between two buildings in a narrow ditch filled with bottles, broken glass, smashed paper cups, some kind of plastic, and crusts of half-eaten food. Music pulsed nearby, thumbing in time with Levi's heartbeat. He pushed to his feet, covered in rust and dirt, which had practically turned to mud due to how wet and sweaty he was.

"See that? I must be vaping high, 'cause a man just climbed out of the trash."

"You ain't vaping, peer. I see him too."

Two grubby men were sitting on the curb across the street from the ditch, smoking.

"You the trash man, shell?" one asked, then said to his companion, "Them cleaning men get to go more places than enforcers!"

Levi stood on the corner of an alley and a narrow road that divided a wall of buildings from a grassy expanse, searching for somewhere to hide. He inched into the road, looked both ways, then sprinted around the two men and into the grassy area.

"There he goes!" a man called from the hole Levi had just exited.

Levi dodged around bushes and couples sitting on blankets on the grass. His feet were wet inside his boots, slipping on the rubber and making each step uncertain. A concrete wall loomed ahead, somewhat camouflaged in a thick array of trees and bushes. He turned sharp, to run alongside the perimeter, but lost his balance and fell, sliding into some bushes near the wall. He lay still and peeked back, hoping they'd lost sight of him.

No such luck. Five Safe Lands enforcers approached, each with a gun aimed his way. Think! He wouldn't be a help to Jemma if he was dead. He crawled deep into the cover of the bushes, slipped his rifle over his head, then shrugged off his backpack.

"Come on out of there, shell! Nice and easy. We'll get you cleaned up."

"His SimTag isn't registering on my reader," another voice said.

"Mine either," said the first. "He must be a ghost." Then louder, "Pull your stunners!"

"Nothing to see here," a third voice said. "Go on back to your pleasure."

Levi hid the rifle and backpack under a large, thick bush. He pushed onto his hands and knees and crawled along the wall.

"He's moving!"

"Then stun him, fool."

Something scuttled over the back of his chest waders. He lay still, listening to the crackling sound. When the sound stopped, the enforcers moved in. Levi drew the pistol from the holster on his chest, flipped off the safety, and fired the gun.

They enforcers dove for cover, so Levi popped to his feet and carefully trained the pistol on the men. In turn they aimed their weapons his way.

"We don't want to hurt you, sir."

Levi wasn't certain they could. Their strange guns had had no effect on him, and if some shot actual bullets, he was wearing the bulletproof vest. He was safe ... unless they shot for his head.

"Let me go on my way then," Levi said. "I don't want to hurt anyone either."

"Can't do that. Least not 'til we log this disturbance. And it's illegal to to go without a SimTag. Now put that gun down, and we'll go talk this over at the RC."

Levi's gaze fell on a streetlamp behind the enforcers, and after a moment of consideration he aimed and shot. The lamp went out with a pop, and Levi sprinted between two of the enforcers, heading for the streets, hoping he could get lost in another drain or pile of trash.

"Aim for his shoulders!"

Another crackle lit the air. His body stiffened, and he fell. He hit the grass hard on his face and chest, sliding a few feet. His muscles cramped tighter and tighter until he thought he might explode. Then the crackling stopped. He grunted and tried to move. Someone knelt on his back, pulled his wrists behind him. His limbs were still tingling. He felt lightheaded.

" ... violation of Safe Lands laws," a man's voice said from above. "You'll appear before the Safe Lands Guild to plead your case. Anything you say or do can and will be held against you at trial. Do you understand?"

Levi grunted, unable to form actual words.

The enforcers put him in the back of a van with the quietest, smoothest engine he'd ever heard. They transported him to what they called the "RC," a three-story brick building with a sign over the entrance that read *Safe Lands Rehabilitation Center.*

The enforcers took Levi into an elevator then to a white room that was barely larger in size. It was empty but for a small table with two chairs in the center of the room. Some folded, light blue fabric sat on the table.

"Change into the jumpsuit," one of the enforcers said before shutting the door.

"Why don't you make me?"

No one answered. Levi sat at the table and shuddered under a constant stream of cool air pouring through a vent above the table. He climbed onto the table, careful not to let his rubber boots slip on the shiny surface. He found no way to shut the vent. He pulled off his gloves and tried to pry the vent free, but only succeeded in ripping his thumbnail.

He gave the vent one last bang with his fist and fell back into the chair, shivering, sucking on his throbbing thumb. He noticed the gash on the top of his hand from when he'd fallen in the canal. If Mason where there, he'd probably claim it was infected.

His hands were trembling, a sign that he was breaking down. He squeezed his fists. He was in their world now. At their mercy. The realization sent him into a rage. He stood, knocking back his chair, grabbed the edge of the table and pushed it over, screaming as he did. He ran to the door and pounded and yelled for them to open it.

He sank to his knees and set his forehead against the door. He'd failed his people. His first day as elder, and he'd already failed. What could he do?

No compromise, Papa Eli had said. Levi would not do what they asked. He would not put on their clothes or obey their commands. He would not compromise.

But then the gas came.

The next thing he knew, Levi was waking up on a stiff mattress.

He sat up, queasy, and looked around. A small yellow camera peered down on him from above. When he stood, he realized he was wearing a light blue jumpsuit and a pair of sissy black slipper shoes. As far as he could tell, he was in a jail cell. Rows of cells ran along two walls and on both sides of him, separated by a narrow aisle.

The cut on his left hand was bandaged, but his other hand itched, as did his cheek. He caught sight of a faint white glow of *9X* on the back of his hand. "No!" They had *no right* to mark his body like he belonged to them.

He tugged at his hair and screamed until he lost his breath. Unable to stay still any longer, he ran to the bars of his cell. "Hey!" He gave the bars a good shake. "Hey! You people have no right to keep me here! Let me out!"

"You won't get out of here that way, shell," a man said from the cell diagonal from Levi's. He had a wide forehead; a short, graying beard; and shoulder-length wavy dark hair that hung in his face. "Name's Lonn. What's yours?"

Levi slowed his breathing slightly. "Levi."

"That X on your face new, Levi?" Lonn asked.

Levi touched his cheek again, nodded. "If it matches the one on my hand, it's as new as the number. What's it mean?"

The man's eyebrows rose. "Outsider, huh? Well, the X is a strike. It means you've been a bad boy. Three strikes are all you get in the Safe Lands before they put you away for good."

Lonn had three Xs on his cheek. Anyone with three strikes was all right by Levi. "So you're going away for good then?"

"Soon, yeah. But hopefully not without giving them one last expression of my distaste."

"So ... I only have one X. Does that mean they'll let me out?"

Lonn swept the hair out of his eyes. "Maybe. Depends if you give them what they want."

Then he'd likely be in the cell forever. "They killed my people."

"That doesn't surprise me."

"Hey there, raven," a woman on Levi's left said, her voice a husky rumble. She was standing against the bars that separated the side of his cell from hers; she was bone thin and was wearing a pale-blue jumper three sizes too big, which she'd unbuttoned to reveal impossible cleavage for someone so malnourished. Her face might have been pretty once, but her cheeks were gaunt and gouges circled her eyes.

Levi turned back to Lonn. "How often do the enforcers come down — "

"Don't look away, Valentine," the woman said. "Come on over here and let me trigger your stims."

Levi yelled as loudly as he could, "Anyone from Glenrock here?"

"Me!" a small voice cried from the cell on the other side of the crazy woman. Levi stepped closer and peered through his neighbor's cell. A dark-haired girl in a pale-blue jumpsuit. It couldn't be. "Penelope?"

"Levi? Oh, Levi! What are you doing here? You were supposed to free us!" his cousin said.

Her words made him feel like he swallowed his heart. "I will, Pen, don't worry. Give me some time to figure this place out, will you? Is, uh, Jemma — ?"

"She's okay, I think. She was with us in the transport. Your mom too. But Omar did this, Levi. Omar is a traitor."

A chill flashed over Levi, Omar's lies fresh in his mind. "You sure?"

"The enforcers gave him a gold envelope. Auntie Tamera said it was for a job."

No, no, no! Levi ran his hands through his tangled hair. Omar responsible for the death of their father? Of little Sophie? Sure, his brother had lied, but . . . "Anyone else from Glenrock in the jail, Pen?"

"Jordan. But he's unconscious. They put him down toward the front cells."

Yes! Hope surged in Levi's chest, and he craned in hopes he'd see his friend.

The gaunt woman stepped in front of Levi, blocking his view of Penelope. She reached past the bars and grabbed the sleeve of his jumpsuit. "Come on, Valentine. Let's you and me share a little love, huh?"

Levi stepped back, pulling his arm out of her grip. "I'm trying to talk to someone here."

"Natachah just wants a kiss," Lonn said. "And she won't shut up 'til you give in."

"I let her kiss my hand," Penelope said, her tone somewhat ashamed.

The people here were worse than Papa Eli had said. "Well, I guess I'll have to raise my voice, then," Levi yelled into the woman's face, "because I'm not touching you!"

Natachah screamed, threw herself on the floor, and began to shake as if having a seizure. She must have been faking it, but it sure looked real. Levi backed away from the bars and sat on his bed. Two guards ran down the corridor to the woman's cell.

"Give us a break, Natachah, will you?" one of them said as he opened the door. "You'll never get out of here if you keep this up."

The second guard secured Natachah's hands behind her back while the first held a white tube to her lips. Natachah pursed her lips around it and sucked in the longest breath Levi had ever seen. When the enforcer removed the tube, Natachah exhaled a plume of white smoke, blowing it out in a long stream, her face frozen like a skeleton's.

"Sleep it off, Natachah, huh?" the guard said, grabbing her by the arms.

The guards helped Natachah onto her bed, removed the handcuffs, and left her cell.

"You just think about giving her a little peck when she wakes up," one guard said to Levi. "Or she'll just start in with you again and none of you will get any sleep."

The guards left the cell and walked back the way they'd come.

Levi jumped up. "Hey!" he yelled after them. "I have some questions!"

The guards ignored him.

"Levi!" Penelope still stood at the bars on the side of her cell.

Levi knelt at the bars that divided his cell from Natachah's. "Why you in here, Pen?" he asked, noticing they'd put the same number—9X—on Penelope's cheek.

"I got in trouble in science class. We went outside to collect leaves from one of the grassy areas, and while I was looking for a pretty one a boy asked to kiss me, since I was new. I told him no thank you, and he called me a proo dish."

Levi frowned and double-checked the word. "Do you mean prudish?"

"A prude dish," Lonn said. "That's an attractive person who won't play love games."

Levi didn't want to know what kind of love games were played in a school for thirteen-year-olds. It had better not be more than kissing in trees. "What happened, Pen?"

"He wouldn't leave me alone. And he tried to kiss me anyway. So I kicked him where you taught me and tied him to a tree with his belt."

"Ha!" Levi slapped his thigh and grinned. "That's my girl!"

"The teacher saw, though. Said I was unloving and sent me to the assistant educator, who lectured me on hateful behavior, added an X to my number, and put me in here for the day."

If Levi ever saw that kid or the educator ... "That's you and me, Pen. I guess 9X is the number to be, huh?"

"But, Levi, I don't want to go back to the school. I want to go home."

"Me too. And we will soon. Tell me about this boarding school."

"It's for all kids under fourteen. We have to live there. They said we can't see our moms again. Nell is in my dormitory. I hope she's okay without me. The boys were teasing her too, and I don't think she'll fight them off."

"Tell me everything that happened yesterday, Pen. In the village."

So Penelope did, starting with the attack on Glenrock: gathering in the meeting hall, the gunfire, the enforcers getting the women's names, Omar arriving with Jemma. "The enforcer gave Omar a gold envelope. Then they took us to this city and marked us with numbers. Levi, they took my mom somewhere — they have all our mothers. One of the men told me I won't see Mom until I'm fourteen or pregnant."

The word *pregnant* pulled Levi away from dwelling on his idiot brother. "*Excuse me*? Explain what you mean by *pregnant*."

"Exactly what I said, Levi. I'm not dumb. They took the older girls and moms to something they called the Highland Harem, to take turns having babies. Nell said she was going to volunteer to get pregnant so she could see her mom again sooner."

"No, Pen. No, no, no. You tell Nell to be smart. I'm going to get us out of here, okay? Don't let these people get to you. You fought today, Pen, and that was great. I'm proud of you. That was Papa Eli's blood in your veins. You keep on fighting, okay? But be careful too."

"But I'm scared."

Penelope's words — *take turns having babies* — caused his stomach to lurch. "I know, Pen. I'm scared too."

"Dog-faced, manure-eating cockroach!"

Levi perked up at the familiar sound of Jordan's insults. He ran to the bars that separated his cell from Natachah's. Thankfully, the woman had been let out yesterday, the same day they'd released Penelope. He peered out and watched as enforcers dragged a somewhat limp Jordan through the door of a cell about six away from Levi's. The enforcers heaved his friend onto the bed and left.

When their footsteps faded, Levi called out. "Jordan!"

Jordan groaned and lifted his head off the mattress. "Levi?"

"Are you okay? What happened to you?"

Jordan blinked twice, squinted at Levi, and screamed "No!" so loudly that Levi crouched and covered his ears.

"What's the matter with you?" Levi asked. "You want them to come back and sting you again? Shut up!"

"*You're* supposed to rescue us, you droppings of a donkey... How'd you end up here?"

"They caught me sneaking into the city through the storm drains."

Jordan cursed another long, drawn-out, completely illogical phrase.

When he stopped, Levi asked, "What about you? What happened?"

Jordan pushed himself up so he was sitting with his legs dangling off the side of the bed. He rubbed his hands over his face. "They want me to join their people, so I tried to kick some enforcer's face in. But those electric guns! Hog's teeth, those things mess me over. By the way, they've got Mason up there somewhere. He decided to play along to see what he could learn."

"Why didn't *you*?"

"Are you mad? I'm not letting those maggots push me around.

They already put their mark on me." He looked at the back of his right hand. "What does 4X mean?"

"Don't know about the number, but X means you're trouble," Levi said.

"Good. They'll cover me in Xs for what I'm going to do when I get my hands on that hairy, spike-nosed, vole-loving — "

"There's no way out of here," Levi said.

"Can we dig a hole like that Shawshank guy?"

"It's all cement."

"The drains then. Rip out that sink and follow the pipes."

"They're too small, Jordan."

"But we could get to the dirt that way and dig a hole."

"The cameras, Jordan. They're watching us."

"Shame what they do these days," Lonn said from his cell across the way. "They bring outsiders in here, make all kinds of promises, but most people end up dead before the Guild even gets what they want."

"What do they want out of us?" Levi asked.

"Babies. Uninfected ones if they can get 'em."

Levi stared at the older man, bewildered. Why did the Safe Landers want their children? And if that was their goal, why were they keeping everyone separated? But before Levi could ask, Jordan jumped off his bed and walked to the bars of his cell. "The enforcer said the same. That our women would bear children for this place. Why?"

"Because our people can't," Lonn said.

"I don't give a pile of rotten robin's eggs about what your people can and can't do," Jordan said. "They took my wife. They will *not* keep her. Or my son."

"I like your fire, boy, but you've gotta be careful. Their so-called liberation ain't gonna get you what you want."

"So what will?" Levi asked. "They have my fiancée too."

"Patience and wit." Lonn grabbed a scrap of paper and scribbled something on it, then casually tossed the now-crumpled wad toward Levi. Being just as discreet, Levi leaned down and grabbed the missive, quickly reading the words:

If you boys get out of here, go to the Midlands and ask for Bender. When you see Bender, tell him I said, "Rose."

Levi looked at Lonn and nodded, then turned to Jordan and said in a low voice, "Looks like we have an ally."

"That's right," Lonn said.

"Why should we listen to you?" Jordan asked.

Lonn swept his hair over his head. "Trust me?"

Jordan laughed harshly. "I ain't trusting none of you maggots."

"The problem is, we won't get out of the city unless we find a way out of this cell," Levi said.

"Getting out might not be as hard as you think. They'll do something to convince you to comply and play nice," Lonn said. "It's how they operate."

Levi couldn't imagine anything convincing him to comply with these maniacs, unless it involved Jemma. He might be able to play the game for a little while, to keep Jemma safe. But if they hurt her in any way, they'd forever regret it.

CHAPTER 17

The redheaded guard, Ewan, escorted Shaylinn and Mia to their cosmetic consultations in a blue luxury car. The Plaza Medical Center was a huge white building several blocks away from the harem. It was six levels high — bigger than the entire village of Glenrock.

Tyra Grant's office was on the third floor in the Beauty Care Department. As they entered the waiting room, Shaylinn couldn't stop staring at the silver walls that were covered with pictures of beautiful women. Did they plan to make her look like them?

While Mia went in for her appointment, Shaylinn settled onto a cushy black sofa and tried to settle her nerves by playing with a GlassTop table that recommended a variety of hairstyles and clothing choices "that will make the new you sparkle even more." She was just starting to relax when she heard Tyra's voice.

"I really think you'll do great, Mia," Tyra said.

"I can't wait to get everything done," Mia said.

"Come on in, Shaylinn," Tyra said, waving Shaylinn to follow.

Tyra's office took a moment to get used to, due to the light pink walls and Kelly green shelves and accents. Even the glass desk Tyra now sat behind was incredibly shiny and bright. The chair Tyra motioned her to sit in was the most interesting of all: pink and green polka-dots covered every inch.

"Adorable chair, right?" Tyra said. "Shaylinn, you're going to love living here. The Safe Lands has everything a girl could ever want."

Shaylinn wanted to believe her, but things were moving so quickly. "I'm not sure I want to have a surgery." She'd been caught up in the makeovers yesterday, but actually changing what she looked like...

"Oh, Shaylinn! You're not here to talk about a surgery. Fortune, no!" Tyra chuckled and reached across her desk for a roll of white plastic. "These are just some simple InstaWraps. You seem to have a slow metabolism, and these will burn away the extra fat, tone your muscles, and remove toxins so your body will be healthier too. I'm also going to get you on a special diet so we can keep the weight off. I think you'll be very pleased with the results."

Shaylinn didn't like the sound of the word *burn*. "Will it hurt?"

"Not at all," Tyra said. "Stand up."

Shaylinn slowly pushed back the polka-dotted chair and stood. Tyra grabbed the hem of Shaylinn's shirt and rolled it up, baring her belly.

Shaylinn gasped. "What are you doing?"

"Showing you how to apply the wrap. Now, these are very advanced and quite expensive, but while you're in the harem, they're free." Tyra pulled off the top layer from the roll of plastic, which left her holding a rectangular sheet about the size of a pillowcase. "This is what you'll be using. Once you get the backing off, all you have to do is press the moist side against your skin." Tyra peeled off a plastic layer. "Ready? It's going to be a little cold."

Shaylinn nodded and lifted her arms. As the wrap was pressed to her belly, she tensed against the coldness, but it was uncomfortable for only a moment.

Tyra began to smooth it over Shaylinn's skin. "You can do more than one at a time if you have help. The wraps need to stay smooth against your skin. No wrinkles or bubbles, okay?"

"What do they do?" Shaylinn asked.

"The formula on the wrap absorbs into your skin and speeds up the cells in your body—the fat cells shrink down like you've been exercising for a month. Now, I want you to do some other things for me daily. A half hour in the sauna to keep your metabolism going—but if you become pregnant, the saunas will have to stop." Tyra reached onto her desk and grabbed a few thin cylinders. "These are SkinnySticks—you can use them as little touch-ups on places where you need a little more toning, or, Fortune forbid, in places where there was a bubble in the wrap and the fat didn't burn completely. Also, drink lots and lots of water. Follow the diet I'm going to give you, and eat smaller meals, and more frequently."

Tyra quickly wrapped Shaylinn's arms then fetched what she called a compression jacket. "This will hold the wraps in place while you wear them. They only require twenty minutes, but you can wear them longer. Some women sleep in leg or neck wraps because it's more comfortable. I'm also going to give you a face mask so you can wrap your chin and neck."

Shaylinn had to remove her shirt to put on the compression jacket so that the jacket would fit tightly. But she was able to put her shirt on over it—which was a small relief.

"You'll likely see a major difference in just a few days," Tyra said. "Especially if you start exercising and eating well."

Tyra sent Shaylinn home with enough wraps for the next two weeks.

She showed them to Mia on the car ride back to the harem, whispering so Ewan couldn't hear.

But Mia leaned toward Ewan and practically screamed, "Did you hear that? Shay is finally going to be skinny." She turned back to Shaylinn. "Just think—if we'd never come here, you would have stayed chubby and plain forever. Now you're going to look so amazing! I wish they could do implants and acne treatments as quickly as body wraps. I'm so jealous. We have to go out tonight and celebrate. Rand said he'd take me and my friends out anytime. What do you say?"

"Who's Rand?" Shaylinn asked.

"A piano player I met at the entertainment orientation. He promised to introduce me to some professional dancers. Do you remember that man who waltzed with us? Maroz Zerrik?"

"How could I forget?" Shaylinn had relived that dance over and over.

"Well, Rand plays for Maroz's show." Mia grabbed Ewan's arm. "Ewan, didn't you say you would take me to meet Rand?"

Ewan looked at Shaylinn and fluffed his cloud of hair. "I said I *could*."

Mia squealed. "I'm going to tap Rand right now." She removed her Wyndo from her jacket pocket. "I keep forgetting that I can talk to anyone with this. Isn't it amazing?"

"I forgot mine at the harem," Shaylinn said, running her hands over her belly. Was she getting thinner right now? She couldn't tell.

"Someone there?" A man's picture was moving on Mia's Wyndo screen.

Mia lifted the Wyndo. "Rand! It's Mia from the harem."

"Hay-o, pearly girl. What you doing right now?"

The leer in Rand's voice made Shaylinn shiver. She listened as Mia made plans to go out to a cab-array, whatever that meant. Shaylinn wasn't sure how she felt about this Rand guy; but the look on Mia's face made her wonder if she was worrying over nothing.

By the time Ewan escorted Shaylinn and Mia back to the harem, Jemma, Naomi, and Kendall were eating lunch at the kitchen table in the Blue Diamond Suite.

"Just in time for food!" Naomi said.

Jemma pulled out the chair on her left. "Come sit down, Shay. How was your morning?"

"It was good," Shaylinn said, thinking she should go remove the wraps to see if she was thinner. "Tyra gave me InstaWraps to help me lose weight."

"You're not fat, Shay," Jemma said. "You're perfect."

Sisters were supposed to say things like that. No *man* had ever told Shaylinn she was pretty, much less thin. In fact, several had told her the opposite, including her own father.

Shaylinn unfolded the approved food list Tyra had given her and scanned it. Fruit was the only match she could find on the table. With a deep breath, she took a wedge of melon and nibbled on it.

"My consultation was more than good," Mia said. "It was ah-mazing. They're going to get rid of my acne, and perform a breast enhancement."

Shaylinn's eyes bulged. Mia had mentioned implants but not the location.

"What on earth do you need implants for, Mia?" Naomi said. "You're bigger than me, and I'm pregnant!"

Mia simply rolled her eyes. "Look around you. If you want to get noticed, you need more than nice eyes and a decent figure." She ate a grape. "And I intend to get noticed. I even have a date for tonight."

"Like in the Old movies where a boy comes by and gives you flowers?" Naomi asked.

"Sort of. But since boys can't come to the harem, I'm going out."

"With who?" Kendall asked.

"His name is Rand, and he plays piano for Maroz Zerrik."

"Maroz has a bad reputation, but so does everyone here," Kendall said.

"I don't like you spending time with a Safe Lander," Jemma said. "How well do you know this piano player?"

"That's what dates are for, Jemma." Mia nudged Shaylinn and whispered, "And your sister's the one who watches all those movies." She looked back to the group. "He's taking me to a musical show — I forgot the name — and he said I'd love it."

"What about Mason?" Jemma asked.

Mia ate another grape. "I could care less about Mason."

Jemma gasped, but Mia just rolled her eyes.

"How can you go anywhere?" Naomi said. "We're only allowed to leave the harem for doctor appointments. And then only with Ewan or some other enforcer glued to our sides."

"Ewan and Rand are friends," Mia said. "Ewan's going to take me to meet him."

"Then we all should leave!" Jemma said, suddenly excited. "If Ewan isn't guarding the door, we could get Kendall past the wall and into the outer lands before she goes into labor and — "

"Like that would even work, Jemma," Mia said. "All this is going to be is a date — Rand and *my* date. If you went, you'd get Ewan in trouble, and then Rand would be mad at me."

"Mad at *you*?" Jemma said. "They're going to take Kendall's baby, Mia. We've got to help her."

"*I* don't have to do anything." Mia stood up, grabbed her plate, and walked to her bedroom.

Silence descended over the table.

Jemma jumped up from the table and ran from the suite, headed toward Mia's mom's room.

Shaylinn watched the front door swing closed, torn. Jemma was right. They should do all they could to escape. But Shaylinn wanted to give her InstaWraps and SkinnySticks time to work, and she was really looking forward to the cab-array.

Mia's mom forbade Mia to go out with Rand, so Mia dragged Shaylinn into her room where on Mia's insistence they tried on their new clothes, parading one outfit after another out into the living room for Jemma, Naomi, and Kendall to see. Shaylinn kept the InstaWraps on and was able to hide them under every outfit. Mia did Shaylinn's makeup and curled Shaylinn's hair into bobbing ringlets. When Shay looked in the mirror, she felt . . . attractive.

She desperately missed Penelope and Nell and hoped they were doing okay in the boarding school. But Shaylinn was actually having fun — with Mia. Maybe they'd become friends.

"That's the one," Mia said when Shaylinn had put on a short black strapless dress that flipped out in a full skirt. "Put this over your arm." She hung a thick purse across Shaylinn's body, then Mia made her put on a thick, floor-length bathrobe over the dress. "Say nothing."

Mia likewise put a bathrobe over her hot pink halter dress. She pulled Shaylinn into the living room. "We're going to get a snack from the kitchen. Anyone want anything?"

"We have snacks in our kitchen," Naomi said.

"I don't want those. Since my date was ruined" — she glared hard at Jemma — "I want something special."

"I was just looking out for you, Mia," Jemma said. "You seem to forget we're prisoners here. I don't want you to get hurt."

Mia set her hand on her hip. "Do you want something or not? It's a simple question."

"No, thank you," Naomi said.

"Fine." Mia pulled Shaylinn toward the door. "We'll be back."

They walked down the stairs in their bare feet, crossed the harem sitting room, and entered the dark kitchen. One light above the stove and a green emergency exit sign barely lit the room. The chef was gone for the night.

Mia threw off her bathrobe and straightened her skirt. "Give me the purse," she said.

Shaylinn took off her robe and handed the bag to Mia, who dumped the contents. Two pair of shoes clattered onto the floor.

Mia stepped into the gold heels. "Put on the black ones, and hurry!"

"We're still going?" Shaylinn asked.

"What do you think? Come on."

Mia dragged Shaylinn through the emergency exit and into a cold stairwell. A man stood in the darkness, and Shaylinn screamed.

Mia clapped her hand over Shaylinn's mouth. "It's just Ewan. Walls, girl!"

When had Mia started saying walls?

"There are no cameras this way," Ewan said.

He led them down the stairs. Shaylinn couldn't move very fast in the high heels and trotted after Mia and Ewan, down, down, down.

"Come on!" Mia whispered.

"I'm trying!"

The stairs let out into a large warehouse. Ewan led them through it and out a door where a car was waiting. Mia climbed into the back, Shaylinn got in beside her and sat in the middle, then Ewan jumped in and slammed the door shut.

"The Venetian Room," Ewan told the driver, then leaned back and put his arm over the back of the seat, behind Shaylinn's head. He leaned close to Shaylinn, and his hair tickled her face. "Hey, shimmer. You look pretty," he whispered.

Her eyes flew wide. "I do?"

He let his arm fall around Shaylinn and pulled her against his side. She stiffened and shot Mia a worried glance.

Mia raised her eyebrows as if to say, "Go along with it."

Shaylinn didn't really want to go along with it, though. She didn't know Ewan enough to be so close, and she didn't like the way his poufy red hair kept itching the side of her face.

"Expect greatness tonight, femmes," Ewan said. "This show does something for the soul."

Well, that sounded nice, at least.

It didn't take long to reach the Venetian Room. Outside, the building was nothing more than a narrow white storefront with a flashing marquee, but once inside, the place looked like an Old concrete warehouse. It was dark, and red and blue lights rotated in bands across the walls and the high ceiling. The music was loud and thrummed through Shaylinn's body straight to her heart. The floor was filled with little round tables, and they all looked full.

Shaylinn followed Ewan and Mia to a table in the very front, where a handsome young man with slick yellow hair was waiting. He kissed

Mia on both cheeks and they spoke, and though the music was too loud for Shaylinn to hear what they said, Mia giggled and touched the man's arm, then pointed at Shaylinn. The man smiled and, before Shaylinn knew what was happening, he was kissing both her cheeks as well. He smelled good, and she enjoyed the way the scent lingered even after he moved away.

He and Mia sat beside each other at the front of the table. Shaylinn sat in back beside Ewan. He scooted his chair close as if he might put his arm around her again. She leaned on the table in the opposite direction so he couldn't reach her.

A waitress came and took drink orders. Shaylinn didn't know what to order, so she shook her head. Then the show began.

The music seemed to wash over her, the notes alternatively fading and coming in strong as the band played. The lights danced and swayed and changed colors, all perfectly timed with the music. Then suddenly, everyone was looking up.

A man hung from the ceiling, wearing only black underwear. And a woman! She wore a white bra and flimsy white skirt. The man swung from a metal bar by the backs of his knees, then the tops of his feet, his arms and legs bulging with muscles. The woman tangled herself in yards of shiny red fabric, twisting and splitting and dropping right over the tables but never falling.

The music changed, and dancers ran out onto the stage, wild and stomping. Women wore black bras and fishnet stockings. Some had mustaches and some had clown noses. Men tumbled across the stage in their underwear, twisting their bodies and rolling together as if they were one person. More performers danced from ropes and strips of fabric, metal rings and squares, sometimes in pairs. Lightning flashed and flashed, white and red. The music thumped.

Shaylinn couldn't blink.

It seemed to go on forever, yet when it ended, Shaylinn felt like it had barely begun. It had been mesmerizing ... and it made her feel wild and giddy inside.

The silence brought by the end of the show was somewhat odd.

Shaylinn focused on those around her and was shocked to see Mia and Rand kissing more than each other's cheeks. Their faces seemed glued together. Shaylinn stared until she realized she was staring, then she looked away only to find Ewan watching her with a hungry look in his eyes. She jumped and pulled her curls towards the front of her face so he couldn't see her.

She was suddenly cold and wanted to go back. She leaned across the table and poked her friend. "Mia," she said. "Mia!"

Mia and Rand's lips broke apart, and they both turned to look at Shaylinn.

"I'm ready to go," she said.

Mia scowled. "I'm not."

Shaylinn stood. "Well, I am, Mia. Let's go. Now!" Shaylinn couldn't explain the confusion she felt. She only knew she needed to leave. And she wasn't going to let Mia bully her into staying.

Mia's eyes sprang wide, and with that Shaylinn felt strong. "I'm sorry," Mia told Rand. "My friend isn't feeling well."

"Tap me when you get home?" he asked.

"Of course."

Shaylinn suffered through one more Mia and Rand face-sucking episode before she managed to drag Mia away. Ewan followed her like Mason's dog sometimes had, and Shaylinn kept Mia between them as a buffer, even once they entered the car. She didn't like the look in his eyes.

They drove back in silence.

Ewan escorted them into the harem building through the regular entrance. They passed through the revolving door, walked across the orange and blue lobby, went up the elevator to five, and walked down the red and black carpet to the golden door engraved with the creepy cat-bird-woman. There they stopped. Shaylinn pressed her fist against the door. Nothing happened.

"Why didn't it open?" she asked Ewan.

"It only opens for staff," he said. "But touching it rings the bell, so someone will come."

"Well, thank you for bringing us back," Shaylinn said.

"You promised me a kiss," Ewan said to Mia.

Eww. Shaylinn looked from Mia to Ewan and back to Mia.

Mia clicked her tongue and prodded Shaylinn's arm. "Go on, Shaylinn."

"Me?" Shaylinn backed against the door. "I didn't promise to kiss anyone."

Mia sighed. "The only reason Ewan agreed to take us out tonight was because you'd give him a good-night kiss. Do it so we can go inside."

Shaylinn glared at Mia. "You had no right to promise that!"

Mia grabbed Shaylinn's arm and squeezed. "You already ruined my night," she said through gritted teeth. "Stop embarrassing me."

Shaylinn pulled away. "You're embarrassing yourself, Mia. Letting that Rand man kiss you in public like that. You don't know hardly anything about him."

Mia rolled her eyes. "That's why I'm getting to know him."

"The music was too loud for talking, so I doubt you learned anything except how well he kisses. You're going to get hurt. My mama says a girl should protect her heart."

"Like you with Omar?"

Shaylinn's chest smoldered. "You don't know anything about me."

Mia smirked. "I know you're always staring at Omar."

"I am not!"

"Shut up," Ewan yelled.

Shaylinn jumped and turned to face him.

"I'll take my payment now." He grabbed Shaylinn's arms, pushed her against the wall, and forced his mouth onto hers.

He smelled stale and bitter at the same time, and he pressed so hard that Shaylinn's own teeth cut into her lip. She turned her head to the side and screamed as loud and long as she could.

Ewan let go and glared at her. "What's the matter with you?"

Shaylinn pulled off one of her shoes and threw it at Ewan's head. "You're a terrible — "

"Ow!" Ewan cowered under his arms.

"—rude, horrible, disgusting—!" She yanked off the other shoe and hit him with it.

"Stop it, you crazy femme!" He tried and failed to dodge her blows.

"Shaylinn, stop." Mia grabbed Shaylinn's arm and pulled her back. "Matron's here."

Sure enough, Matron stood in the doorway, looking at Shaylinn like she was a disobedient child.

CHAPTER 18

The clink of iron woke Levi. Before he could gather his wits, his hands were bound behind him and he was dragged to his feet. From down the hall, he could hear rustling and a few grunts.

"Get off me, you dung-wielding rot face!"

Apparently Jordan was being moved as well.

The enforcers took them to a cell on the third floor, which had a huge TV screen on the wall opposite the entrance. A steel bench in the middle of the room faced the screen. They sat Levi and Jordan on the bench, side by side, and attached their restraints to metal loops on the back. A quick yank of the chain confirmed the bench was bolted to the floor.

A third enforcer ducked through the doorway. He had dark, frizzy hair, parted down the middle, which tangled with his bushy mustache and beard. His eyes were a freakish yellow. Even weirder, two coils of gold metal pointed out from each nostril like feelers on an insect. Medals and bars and fancy patches — including one that said *Otley* — covered his uniform. The number eight glowed on his cheek.

"Still like to get your cooperation voluntarily," Otley said to Jordan.

"You're not getting anything from us, you grizzly pukepile of a man." Jordan turned to Levi. "He's the maggot who killed your father, Levi. I saw him do it."

Levi turned his head slowly until he met Otley's gaze. He attempted to stand, but his restraints were so short that his body jerked back to his seat. He set his jaw, fighting to hold back his anger, then closed his eyes and tried to breathe calmly like Jemma had taught him. Recite his verse: *Refrain from anger, and turn from wrath.* His breaths came short and hard, but with them some clarity surfaced. He was the village elder. He had to help his people.

"Something you want to say to me, rat?" Otley asked.

Levi opened his eyes. Took a deep breath. *Refrain from anger, and turn from wrath.* "Not … yet."

Otley walked to the back of the room. "Wyndo: power. Play, pause." The TV powered on, black at first, but slowly colored to reveal Jemma from the shoulders up, wearing a red dress and sitting in a kitchen, frozen and slightly fuzzy. On pause.

"Jemma," Levi whispered.

"What are you doing with my sister?" Jordan yelled.

Otley's cheeks balled up in a smirk. "Wyndo: play."

Levi's chest heaved, his anger growing again, but the screen moved, and Jemma spoke.

"I'm sorry I got myself into this. You were right. Levi. About everything. I miss you. The food is good, though." She chuckled as if making a lame joke. "Please do what they say. I'm afraid of what will happen if you don't. I love you."

"Wyndo: pause," Otley said.

The screen stopped on Jemma's face, misty eyes wide, lips frowning slightly.

Levi could hardly breathe. "You threatened her?"

"Someone else would like a word. Wyndo: play."

The screen went black a moment before showing Naomi in the same kitchen. The angle of the recording, her tight blue dress, or the way she held her hands over her huge belly made her look like she might explode.

"No!" Jordan stood, arching his body backward and pulling at his bonds. His face reddened, veins popped out on his neck.

"Jordan? Baby? I'm so sorry this has happened."

Jordan wilted at Naomi's voice and fell back to his seat. "No, baby, no."

"They're treating me well. But I don't want to be here anymore. Some of them scare me. I'm scared for our baby." Naomi started crying.

Jordan moaned, and it slowly morphed into another scream of rage.

"Wyndo: stop," Otley said. The TV went black.

"Put her back!" Jordan yelled. "Please!"

"Naomi is correct," Otley said. "We're currently treating them all very well. But that ends if you continue to cause problems. You both must become Safe Lands nationals, obey our laws, or your women will be killed." Otley looked to Jordan. "We'll wait until your baby is born before killing her, of course. This is nonnegotiable. You have a few minutes to decide."

With that, Otley and the enforcers left the room.

"We have to do what they say." Jordan's voice was small.

Levi felt like his brain was going to explode. *Refrain from anger. Refrain from anger.*

"Levi! Say something," Jordan said.

"I'm thinking!" What Jemma had said didn't make sense. "What was I right about? And why would she apologize? This wasn't her fault."

"You think they faked those movies?"

"I don't know. But being stuck in this prison isn't getting us anywhere." Levi leaned close to Jordan. "So let's play along, like Mason. And we make a plan to get out of this place. Good?"

Jordan sniffled. "Mad good."

Levi and Jordan were taken for a medical examination, after which enforcers escorted them to the Donation Center. Which, from Levi's perspective, was wishful thinking on Otley's end. Jordan lost control again, broke a door, and ended up restrained, but for some reason the enforcers released him when they reached the Registration Department. They had their pictures taken, chose last names — Levi Justin and Jordan Harvey, after their fathers — and were instructed to sit at glass desks and task test.

"What's a task test for?" Levi asked Dallin, who worked in Registration.

"And why's your hair look like a bumblebee's butt?" Jordan asked.

"Task testing determines what task you will perform in the Safe Lands," Dallin said. "And I'm updating my hairstyle tomorrow — the yellow and black is so yesterday. I should really get HairTags."

Tapping one letter at a time, Levi entered his name into the glass computer. Dallin walked back to his desk.

"Hey," Levi whispered, "just don't forget how much we both like to clean things."

Jordan looked his way, eyebrows raised. "Clean fish?"

"Clean up messes. I saw a guy in the park. Said that cleaning people get to go more places than enforcers."

"I got you," Jordan said. "Cleaning is my favorite."

"No talking!" Dallin said, then muttered something about crazy outsiders.

Levi answered the questions carefully, trying to guess which selections might result in a cleaning placement. He wondered how Jordan was faring. His friend wasn't very methodical.

Nearly an hour had passed when Jordan pushed back from his desk. "Ha! Beat you!"

Levi leaned over and read the words off Jordan's desk: *Task test complete. Please report to your test director.*

"All done?" Dallin asked.

"Yeah." Jordan swaggered to Dallin's desk.

Levi continued to answer questions, watching Jordan and Dallin between each answer, wanting to be done too. Thankfully, it wasn't long before his test ended.

Levi walked over to Dallin's desk and found the man talking to himself. "Yes, sir ... I haven't run the other one yet ... I understand. Thank you, sir." He turned to face Jordan. "Okay, Mr. Harvey. You'll serve your first six months in maintenance for the Grand Lodge. The task director general says this will allow you to visit your lifer, uh, I mean, your ... wife."

Jordan gripped the end of the counter. "Can I see her now?"

"After you're fully processed, we'll set up an appointment."

"An appointment to see my own wife?" Jordan yelled.

Levi elbowed him. "That's good, Jordan. You'll get to see Naomi."

Jordan frowned, but reined in his temper and released the counter.

"You'll be housed in the Grand Lodge," Dallin said. "Your room number is 345. First thing tomorrow, report to the maintenance room in the Grand Lodge to meet your task director."

"What about me?" Levi asked.

"If you'll be patient ..." Dallin fiddled with his glass computer screen in what seemed like slow motion. "Mr. Justin, your first run is street cleaning in the Highlands. Your task director is Dayle Mardon at Highlands Public Tasks. Go see him today, and he'll get you a schedule. You'll reside in the Larkspur Building in the Midlands. Has a great fight club called the Hunter. I spent a lot of time there as a graduate. They put little arrows in all their drinks."

"When can I see Jemma and my mother?"

"Surrogates are not permitted visitors."

"What? How come Jordan gets to see Naomi?"

"Mr. Harvey's lifer is already pregnant, so she cannot complete surrogacy duty."

"What does that matter? I want to see Jemma and my mother."

Jordan elbowed him. "Naomi can tell me how they're doing."

Levi bit his tongue so hard he tasted blood. "Fine. But why does Jordan get to live in the Grand Lodge, and I have to live in the ... whatever you called it?"

"The Larkspur." Dallin shrugged. "I'm not a programmer, Mr. Justin. I just do as the computer says."

"Of course you do," Levi said.

Dallin handed Levi a sheet of paper with his task test results. "Use the SimTag in your hand to open doors and to make purchases, including meals."

Levi held up his fist. "How many things can I buy with this?"

"You're given four hundred credits to start. Nationals are paid every Friday. You won't get more until credit day, so be smart about what you purchase."

Levi and Jordan left City Hall and stood on the sidewalk in front of the building.

In the light of day, people filled the sidewalks, the majority wearing red or black and sucking on metal cigarettes. The streets were clean — no sign of trash here. And the cars...

"What kind of rides are those?" Jordan asked.

Levi watched the vehicles. Strange and sleek, shaped like bullets, the roofs and doors tinted glass, the carriages shiny. Taillights and headlights were rimmed in glowing tubes of red, blue, or green light, and fat tires spun like pinwheels. "They don't make any sound."

"Let's get one and drive it," Jordan said.

"Focus, Jordan. See that place?" Levi nodded toward the grassy expanse adjacent to the City Hall building. "Let's meet there tomorrow, just after dark. I'm going to see if I can find my pack. I had some two-way radios in there. Wouldn't mind scavenging up some of those electric guns either."

A yellow car that had *Safe Lands Taxi* written on the door stopped at the curb in front of them. A video of a half-naked woman dancing over the words *Ginger Oak Gentleman's Club* showed on the car's windows, turning the side of the vehicle into a TV screen. A man got out of the taxi and yelled at Levi over the front hood of his car, "Hey, you need a ride, or what?"

"Suppose I do." Levi slapped Jordan's shoulder. "Say hi to Naomi for me. And don't get into any fights." Levi walked to the passenger's door of the taxi. No door handle.

"The back, shell!" the driver yelled. "Get in the back!"

The back door had slid up onto the room, so Levi obeyed, though he felt ridiculous sitting in the back seat when the front was empty. Once the door shut, Levi marveled that he could see through the windows — no dancing woman on this side of the glass. The car was so silent that the fuzzy static of a radio caught his attention. He looked between the front seats at the dashboard, which appeared to be a giant computer.

"ID?" The driver tapped a black square on the console between the two front seats.

Levi stared at it a moment, then set the side of his hand on the pad. Something beeped, and Levi's picture appeared in a little square on the windshield.

"Where to, Mr. Justin?" the driver asked.

"Uh ..." Levi fumbled for his task test results and read from the sheet of paper. "I need to go see Dayle Mardon at the Department of Public Tasks."

"You got it."

Looking over his shoulder and out the back window, Levi watched Jordan and City Hall shrink away. He was glad Jordan would get to see Naomi, but the idea of his not seeing Jemma was unacceptable. And he certainly couldn't allow her to become a baby machine.

"Dispatch to all cars. I've got a man at the Whetstone looking for a ride to the Midlands."

"Taxi 248, I can get him."

"Thanks, 248."

"Is that a two-way radio?" Levi asked the driver.

"It's the cab company's private frequency," the taxi driver said.

"You can talk to other drivers?"

"Yeah, but it's not a Wyndo, shell. Dispatch can hear everything we say."

Of course it wasn't a window, but before Levi could clarify, the taxi stopped in front of a gray building. Inside, Levi found Dayle Mardon in a huge garage filled with a half dozen bullet trucks that read *Department of Public Tasks* on the doors. Dayle was a short man with cropped black hair and muscular arms that were painted in black, red, and blue tattoos.

Dale gave a gruff speech about basic cleaning protocol and took Levi before a wall map of the Safe Lands. "I'm gonna assign you Mornin' Glory Way, Sunflower Drive, and Buttercup Lane." He pointed at a section of streets. "You got four days to clean it each week. Three days off, then back on for four and so on."

"I clean streets?"

"Sure, shell. You get down on your hands and knees and scrub 'em real nice like."

"With what?"

"Fortune, save me. Look kid, I was jokin', right? You sweep leaves off the streets, pick up trash, mop up spills, paint over graffiti, blow leaves off the sidewalks in the fall, shovel snow off the sidewalks in the winter, knock icicles off street signs, stuff like that. Stay out of the buildings. I don't care if some dandy pearl asks you to carry in her shoppin' bags. You on duty, you stay out of the buildings. Got it?"

"Can I clean the streets by the Grand Lodge?"

"Rewl cleans them streets already. I need you on Mornin' Glory, Sunflower, and Buttercup." He walked to a metal cabinet filled with gray jumpsuits and work boots. "When you work, wear your uniform and boots. Check out two in your size and take the extra home, got it?"

More flimsy Safe Lands clothes. The boots were nice though. "Yeah, Mr. Task Director, I got it."

"Don't call me Mr., and don't call me Task Director. It's Dayle."

"Got it, Dayle."

"You can drive, right?"

"Sure." Though Levi had only driven an actual car a couple times. He mostly drove his ATV.

"I'll assign you a truck. Use it as your private vehicle if you want. Just call in when you arrive and when you're ready to go home for the day. If I find out you aren't fulfilling your task, I report you. And you don't want to be reported. It's a trust thing. Can I trust you?"

"Yeah ..." Until he couldn't anymore, of course.

"They always be sending me Xs. What you get yours for, kid?"

Levi stared at Dayle. The guy was crotchety, but there was something real in his eyes. "They've got my girl over in the harem."

"What's your problem, then? She's having the time of her life up in that party house. Don't you worry 'bout her. And don't you go snooping around the harem, neither. They don't like uninvited guests."

Great. Levi checked out two uniforms — gray jumpsuits with the letters *DPT* embroidered on the front pocket — and put one on. He loved the feel of a pair of sturdy boots on his feet and tossed the sissy slipper shoes.

Dayle took him to the parking lot and assigned him a shiny white bullet truck, then quickly showed him how to start it with the SimTag in his hand and how to tap an address into the dashboard computer and get directions to wherever he needed to go.

Levi left his clothes and second uniform on the passenger's seat while Dayle showed him the supplies in the back of the truck — trash bags, cleaning sprays, brooms, a leaf blower. Then he showed him the dumpsters in the parking lot where Levi would dump his trash bags, and the supply closets in the garage where he'd get new supplies when he ran out.

The truck had a radio that allowed Levi to talk to what Dayle referred to as the dispatcher for the Highlands Public Tasks system, or talk to other Highlands DPT taskers. "You can tap channel two and talk to Midlands Public Tasks, though you got no business doing that unless I tell you to. Dispatch will let you know if there's a problem in your area."

"What kind of a problem?"

"I don't know. Accidents, fire, flood, some rebel with a gun. It's rare, but stuff happens."

Once Levi found his pack, he'd have to be careful to find an unused channel.

He entered his assigned street names into the GPS and started the truck. It felt big and smooth beneath him. He steered it out the driveway, waited for a break in the line of moving vehicles, then pressed the gas — make that electric — pedal. The truck shot out into the lane and over the yellow stripes in the center, headed straight for another vehicle. Levi wrenched the wheel to get back into his lane, narrowly missing the other car, which honked its horn.

His arms shook, and he gripped the steering wheel with both hands. He recalled his father explaining the freeways in Denver City and how there had been rules to driving in the Old Days. Levi should've listened better. Road rules made sense with so many cars around.

The words *Highland Harem* captured his attention. A beige building with a brown roof peeked up over a wall of thick bushes. Levi could barely see curls of barbed wire poking between the thick green foliage. A car horn jerked his attention back to the road. How'd he get in the other lane again? He steered back to the right. The harem was behind him now. He saw City Hall ahead on his right, then the Grand Lodge, and just past it, the Rehabilitation Center.

Well, this was all good to know. Jemma and the others weren't far. He just needed to locate the boarding school Penelope had told him about. And find a way to keep in steady connection with Jordan. He suspected Otley had intentionally separated the two of them so they couldn't plan an escape. As strange as Otley looked, the man clearly wasn't a fool. Levi supposed he'd better do his job if he wanted to stay out of the RC long enough to make a plan.

The GPS told him to take Marcellina Road west. He obeyed and quickly located his route. It was a residential neighborhood, but instead of little homes like the Old ones near Mt. Crested Butte, these looked like metal shoeboxes standing on their ends. Some lawns were green and colorful like the field of wildflowers outside Glenrock. And some were . . . odd. One had pink grass and black flowers. Another was a checkerboard of grass and dirt.

He started on the east side of Morning Glory Way and drove his way down one side of the road until he reached a dead end, then circled around the other side until he came to Sunflower Drive. He picked up litter and swept leaves off storm drains, tempted to climb down one and escape. It wouldn't do him any good to be free without the others, though.

He came across some graffiti on the sidewalk that looked like *FFF*. He found a can of gray paint in his truck and sprayed himself in the chest while trying to figure out how to open the thing.

People were everywhere, walking, driving, riding bicycles, but Levi could rarely guess where they were going by how they were dressed or what they carried with them. Weird that people dressed so similarly. Mostly red and black. Were they uniforms of some kind? He didn't see any other DPT uniforms.

Sunflower Drive took him to Buttercup, which made him think of Jemma. Buttercup brought him back to Sunflower, which turned out to be a long road. He worked his way along one side, around the dead end, and all the way back until he arrived back on the opposite side of Morning Glory Way.

The sun was now low in the sky, and he figured that meant he was done for the day. Plus, he was aching for food. He picked up his "wet paint" sign and drove out onto Marcellina Lane. A few blocks down he pulled into a parking lot, drawn by the words *Marcellina Steakhouse*.

The one-level log structure with a red slate roof was dwarfed by all the tall buildings around it. Inside, the aroma weakened his knees. Most of the red-clothed tables were occupied, and Levi stood feeling helpless until a woman, whose nametag said Londie, greeted Levi and sat him at a table by a window. Londie looked normal compared to most of the women he'd seen today, except that she had orange eyes. Levi tried not to stare, but he couldn't help it.

"How do you make your eyes look like that?" he asked her.

"They're contact lenses, dim."

That didn't bring Levi any closer to understanding.

"Did you order in advance?" Londie asked.

"How would I do that?"

"On your Wyndo." Londie pulled a leather book out of her apron pocket and handed it to him. Inside it was a glass screen with pictures of different food options. "Our special today is a bacon-wrapped sirloin for ten credits."

She'd won him at bacon. "Can I have that, please?"

"Sure thing. You want salad with that?"

"Okay."

"What kind of dressing?"

"What's good?"

"I like the ranch."

"Uh ... that sounds fine." He closed the leather book and handed it back to her.

She reached out for it but hesitated. "And what can I get you to drink?"

"Water?"

She took the leather book and slid it into her pocket. "Sure thing. Be right back with your water."

Levi examined those around him. Red or black clothes dominated the wardrobes here as well, and many had tattoos and odd-colored eyes, skin, or hair. Perhaps it was the culture here to paint yourself in as many ways as possible. Levi certainly felt plain with gray overalls, brown hair, and skin-colored skin.

Londie returned with a glass of water. She also set down a plate of lettuce, tomatoes, carrot shavings, and purple cabbage drenched in white sauce. "There you go. Your steak will be out in a few minutes."

"Thank you." Levi picked up the fork off the red cloth napkin and ate a bite of the salad. It was almost icy on his teeth. The milky sauce was cold too — and delicious. Salt and pepper and herbs flavored it, greatly improving the taste of lettuce. By the time Londie returned with his steak, Levi was wiping the extra sauce off his plate with his finger.

"Careful," Londie said as she set a platter in front of him. "The plate is hot."

One look at the steak and the word *beautiful* came to mind. Dark grill lines had been seared across the meat, and three strips of crisp bacon had been cooked around it.

"Would you like a side of ranch for your steak?" Londie asked him.

"Yes," he said, elated to have the chance at more of the sauce.

"I'll get that for you. Anything else?"

Levi shook his head, waiting for her to leave. When she did, he picked up his knife and cut a bite off one end of the steak. He put it into his mouth. Never before had meat melted in his mouth like butter.

Londie brought him a tiny dish of the sauce. "You need anything else?"

"This is delicious," Levi said. "What does it take to cook steak like this? Refrigeration?"

Londie laughed in a short, high trill. "I'm glad you like it. But if I told you the secret, we wouldn't have a very successful restaurant, now, would we?"

Levi scarfed down his steak then used his spoon to finish eating the bowl of ranch dressing. A woman at the table next to his stared. He wondered what he was doing to earn such a look from a woman with six gold rings pierced around her bottom lip.

"I need to get some real clothes. I can't keep wearing this uniform everywhere," a young man's voice said from behind him.

Something about the voice was familiar. Levi looked to the entrance. There, standing just inside the doorway with two men, was Omar. All three were dressed in enforcer uniforms.

Levi's mouth went dry. He stood and strode to the entrance. "Omar."

When Omar's eyes met Levi's, his neck flushed pink. "Brother! I was hoping you'd decide to come inside the walls." His eyes shifted to the floor, and he rubbed the scar between his eyes, revealing a black tattoo that crisscrossed from his wrist around his arm until it disappeared into the sleeve of his uniform. He had the number nine on his cheek. No Xs. Not surprising; Omar had always been a follower. The name on his uniform said *Strong.* Levi couldn't suppress a smirk.

Omar's enforcer friends studied him, their eyes questioning.

"It's okay," Omar said. "Why don't you get us a table?"

The enforcers glared at Levi and walked to Londie's counter.

"So, I guess you know that Beshup never showed at the cabin," Levi said.

Omar rubbed his scar and stepped toward the enforcers. "I don't have a really long lunch break, Levi, so I should get going."

"You're an enforcer, huh? What's 'strong' mean?"

"My last name."

"*Omar Strong*? So it's a play on words, huh? An oxymoron?"

Omar scowled. "You're the moron."

The enforcers came back to stand beside Omar.

"Marcellina's a little out of a cleaner's credit range, isn't it?" the enforcer with the sissy mustache and the name *Skott* on his uniform asked. "How much they give you to start?"

"Four hundred credits," Levi said.

Skott laughed. "Better stop eating at steakhouses, shell."

"He just means that those credits have to last you until you get paid again," Omar said.

"What about you?" Levi asked. "You're eating here."

The other enforcer snorted. His name badge read *Charlz*. "Enforcer *captains* make a great deal more credits than street cleaners."

"Hey, Skottie." Londie walked toward an empty booth. "Got your table ready."

"Okay, thanks," Skott said, trailing after Londie. "You free tonight, femme?"

Omar waited until the enforcers were across the room. "Look, Levi. It's not a good idea for us to spend time together. People will think we're up to something. I'll see you later." Omar started to follow his friends.

But Levi grabbed Omar's collar and pulled him close. Despite the intimidating uniform, Omar was still scrawny. "Why'd you do it?" Levi whispered.

Omar tried to pull away. "Get your hands off me, Levi. You can't touch an enforcer and get away with it. It's my job to maintain order."

Levi held tightly. As much as he wanted to beat his brother into mud, Omar was right. Levi would likely end up back in the prison with a second X on his face. "Our elders are dead because of you. Our father's dead because of— "

"It wasn't supposed to happen that way!" Omar blinked back tears.

Refrain from anger, and turn from wrath. Levi pushed Omar back and released him. Omar stumbled against a table where a man and woman were eating, knocking over a pitcher of water. "I didn't mean for things to happen the way they did, brother," Omar said. "I'm sorry. Truly I am. But … life is so much better here. You'll see."

"You're a fool, Omar. A pathetic, sissy— "

"Don't call me that!" Omar drew a gun from his belt and pointed it at Levi. "I'm sorry so many died, but I fit in here. And we all know that was never going to happen in Glenrock."

Destroying an entire village to fit in? "Just make sure that the thing you're living for is worth dying for, Omar. Enough people have lost their lives for you to *fit in*. But everything has a cost, and you had better be ready to pay up."

"You know what I'm ready for, 'brother'?" Omar said with a new edge to his voice. "I'm ready to hammer you for the first time in my life." He waved his arm at his lapdogs. "Take him out back."

As the enforcers hauled Levi from the steakhouse, Skott told Londie, "Hold our table, femme. We'll only be a minute."

CHAPTER 19

"We need to up the dosage on her fertility stims," Ciddah said. "Change it to 150 milligrams."

Mason made a note on the CompuChart. "But isn't that a lot of hormones? Won't that affect her body in other ways?"

"I'm the senior medic here, Mason. Let me worry about that."

"But — "

Rimola leaned around the doorframe. "Enforcers just dropped off a patient in exam two." She'd been Roller Painting her skin dark pink ever since Luella Flynn started wearing red and black. Her spiky black hair hadn't changed. "He's been arrested for assaulting an officer."

Ciddah looked away from the CompuChart. Mason watched her profile as a strand of her wispy blonde hair fell from her hair clip. "What'd they do to him?" Ciddah asked.

"Don't know," Rimola said. "His face is pretty bloody. They said to keep it quiet."

"Wonderful." Ciddah patted Mason's back, her hand lingering there longer than necessary. "Why don't you assist me, Mason?"

"Sure." Mason followed her out of the office. So far, he'd done little but enter data into CompuCharts, weigh patients, and take blood pressure measurements, all of which constituted a multi-stepped process Ciddah called *taking the vitals*. Ciddah allowed him to do some *saliva tests*, but no *blood draws* until she had time to teach him. All of it was fascinating.

But Mason never met a more bewildering woman. Or more beautiful. Her wisdom and care with patients impressed him greatly. Yet with him, her words were all business, her eyes communicated a longing to be elsewhere, yet her hands touched him more than was necessary. So many contradictions.

None of it mattered, of course. Mason needed to focus on his goal of getting his people back to Glenrock, not how long Ciddah's eyelashes were, how tightly she wore her scrubs, or how her hair swayed against her waist as she moved down the hallway.

Having seen her medical history, Mason knew she was Levi's age and that she'd had four miscarriages. *Four.* After having learned about embryonic transfer from Ciddah on his first day, he knew that four miscarriages didn't necessarily mean she'd been intimate with a man yet, but Mason wondered. He also wondered about the psychological impact of such losses.

He followed Ciddah inside exam room two. A man in a gray uniform had been secured to an exam table. His face was purpled and bloody, the bridge of his nose cut open.

Levi.

"Looks like the enforcers paid him back double," Ciddah said. "Dumb shell. Why don't you get him cleaned up, then I'll check him over?" Ciddah left Mason alone to deal with the patient.

Mason looked his brother over, wondering what had happened. He must have snuck into the city compound, trying to free them, and, like Jordan, discovered that fists wouldn't work against these people. They were too strong to defeat that way. And the numbers on his face and hand already had two Xs behind them. From what he'd learned through seeing reports on the ColorCast about some guy named Lonn, that wasn't good.

Mason put on a pair of rubber gloves and located the bottle of sterile water. He poured the water over Levi's face and wiped it with fresh gauze. Levi jerked his head to the side, which startled Mason. He'd thought his brother was unconscious.

"My name is Mason Elias," Mason said in a voice louder than necessary.

Levi's eyes, somewhat hidden behind his swollen face, shifted until they met his brother's. "Mason." His voice croaked, and he panted in a few short breaths before speaking again. "It was Omar. He did this."

"Omar? He beat you up?"

"No. Well, yes. But … it's his fault we're here. All of us."

"What?" How could any of this be Omar's fault?

"The little maggot sold out our village …" Deep breath. "For a job with the enforcers. To *fit in here*, he told me."

Mason groaned, remembering Levi and Jemma's engagement party, when Father had mocked Omar. "I knew he was unhappy. But … you're sure?"

Levi coughed and worked to clear his throat. "He all but confessed … wearing his enforcer … uniform … with his enforcer buddies … smiling before he stomped on … my face."

Mason squeezed the bottle in his hand, and sterile water overflowed, slapping onto the floor. *Keep it together.* "Hold still. I've got to clean you up before the medic comes back." Mason grabbed some fresh gauze and some paper towels, tossed the paper towels onto the floor and stepped on them, then mopped up his mess on the exam table.

Levi's eyes found Mason's again. "Aren't you the medic?"

"Uh, no. Just a lowly assistant." Mason wiped under Levi's nose.

"Was I really that bad to him?" Levi paused to gasp in a breath. "Mother and Jemma both said I needed to be nicer, but they're girls, and I figured … what do they know about men, you know? About brothers." Another large breath. "Did he ever say anything to you?"

"He said he wanted to be included. With you and Father. He wanted to go along."

"Even if he hated us … Even if that hatred was justified … why betray the entire village?" A tear ran down the side of Levi's face, pooling in his ear. "I found eighteen dead, Mase ... Papa Eli died in front of me. I buried him myself."

Mason inhaled slowly, fighting back his emotions. He'd failed to save Papa Eli.

Stop. He needed to stay focused. This wasn't his fault.

Levi seemed to be pleading with Mason through his eyes. "If I would've been nicer ... Do you think Omar would've ... ? Is it my fault that ... ?"

Mason wanted to smile. Stage two of the grieving process: they were both blaming themselves. "This is not our fault, Levi. The Safe Lands is the enemy. Not Omar. He's just their pawn. General Otley killed Father and Papa Eli, and Lawten Renzor sent Otley and the enforcers. And they'll likely kill us if we aren't more careful."

"Mase, I can't breathe too good."

Mason stopped swabbing and gave Levi a chance to breathe. "Your nose might be broken."

Levi's shoulders shook. Tears pooled in the hollow between his eyes and the ridge of his nose, mixing with the blood.

"Try to stay calm." Mason tossed the bloody gauze then started on the other side of Levi's nose.

"Have you seen Mother?" Levi asked.

"I haven't seen anyone but you since they took Jordan away."

"They brought him down to the RC." Levi paused to gasp in a breath of air. "That's where I was ... They showed us movies of Jemma and Naomi ... We had no choice but to — "

"How's it coming?" Ciddah asked, appearing at Mason's elbow.

Mason jumped, wondering how much she'd overheard. "Almost done."

"It's fine." She stepped in front of him so that her body brushed against his, filling his senses with the smell of vanilla and cinnamon. "I can work with that."

Mason stepped out of her way and set the bottle of sterile water on the counter.

"Here." She handed him the CompuChart. "See if you can fill in more of that."

Mason looked over the chart. Levi had chosen the last name Justin. Not surprising — Levi and their father had been close.

"My name is Ciddah." She smiled down on Levi, gloved hands held out to the side, no unnecessary touching. "I'm going to take a look at your nose, okay?"

"I can't breathe through my nose," Levi said.

"That could be due to swelling, or maybe it's broken." Ciddah slid one of her gloved hands behind Levi's neck and tilted his head back to examine him. Mason watched, intrigued by everything Ciddah did, especially her gentleness with patients. As much as Mason didn't want to be in the Safe Lands, he longed for Ciddah's medical knowledge. She was a level nine medic. And from what she'd told him, the highest medic ranking was a twenty.

Mason desperately wanted to rank a twenty.

"Looks like it's broken, Levi." Ciddah released her hold on his neck. "Come back in a few days if you'd like to have your nose reset. I don't like to set the cartilage until the swelling has gone down. Later on, if your nose looks crooked and you're interested in reconstruction, we can set up an appointment with the Cosmetic Center."

"I don't care," Levi rasped.

"Maybe later, then. Mason, finish cleaning him up." She left the room, blonde hair swaying. All business again.

Mason pushed away his confusion with Ciddah, got some fresh gauze, and resumed cleaning the blood from Levi's cheeks and neck. Levi needed a shave. "They have stores here. G.I.N., which Ciddah says stands for Get It Now. Anyway, you can use your ID to buy razors and soap. They have special cream to shave with too. Keeps away the rash."

"Penelope said the women are in a place called the Highland Harem." Levi fixed his bloodshot eyes on Mason. "Jordan says they're going to make them have babies. Explain *that*, Dr. Mason."

Mason grunted, still somewhat confused at the process. "They call it surrogacy. With the thin plague, most Safe Lands nationals are sterile, so they reproduce by using a medical procedure, selecting those who are still healthy enough. Ciddah explained it to me. They harvest seed from the males — "

"The Donation Center?"

Mason shuddered. "Yes. Did you?"

Levi choked on a breath. "No!" Another cough. "Did *you*?"

"Not *yet*." Mason thought of those all-knowing eyes on the top floor of City Hall. "I had to get clever. But the task director general is watching me. It's important to the survival of their people that they get us to comply. They need uninfected nationals to repopulate their city with uninfected people. Without us, they'll die."

Levi groaned and shifted his head on the exam table. "Wish they'd die quicker."

Ciddah came to mind then. Mason didn't want someone so smart and beautiful to meet that fate. "Well, despite the reason they're doing it, the whole process is pretty amazing." He wiped away a bit of crusty blood on Levi's cheek.

"Amazing?" Levi's eyes flashed. He grunted, pulling against the restraints until his face and neck were flushed purple. "They're going to make Jemma pregnant, and you're amazed?"

Mason hated this side of Levi, the part that reacted in anger like their father. He stepped back and tossed the bloodied gauze toward a trash can. "I'm just saying the technology is amazing. I don't want anything to happen to Jemma or anyone else."

Levi closed his eyes, breathed in and out, silent for several calming breaths — a trick Jemma had taught him to calm down. Mason sent a silent thank you for her wisdom. Levi opened his eyes and said, "So if *you* visit the Donation Center, Jemma could carry *your* child?"

"I ..." The question knotted Mason's thoughts. "I don't know. I suppose it's possible."

Levi lifted his head off the exam table as if trying to sit up, but the restraints caught him again and his head slapped back against the table. "You'd like that, wouldn't you?"

"Of course not!" Mason glanced over his shoulder, saw the empty doorway, then whispered to Levi, "I'm trying to learn so I can help the women. I have a … plan … to deal with the donation issue, should it arise again. You and I need a way to communicate. And you've got to be careful. You've got two Xs already."

Levi choked out a cough. "Two? I only had one this morning. How'd they change it?"

"It's a computer chip. They just change it. Three Xs and you'll be liberated."

"What does that mean?"

"I don't know. But liberated people go away and don't come back."

Levi panted in a breath. "I've got some radios in my backpack. I've just got to find it."

"What building did they put you in?"

"Larkspur. It's in the Midlands, I guess. Haven't gone there yet though …"

Leave it to his brother to get in a fight before even spending one night inside the compound. "I'm in the Highlands, at the Westwall. I'll send you a message. I'm pretty sure all messages are read, so I won't say much. But send one back, okay? Don't write anything you don't want the enforcers to see. If we can message each other, we can communicate. Maybe we can use a code or something."

"And I can tell you if I get the two-way radios — "

"Mason?" Rimola knocked on the doorframe. "Ciddah needs you in exam four."

"I'll be right there." He turned back to Levi. "Keep in touch."

Mason found Ciddah in the exam room standing over a girl who was crying.

"What took you so long?" she asked.

"Sorry." Mason stopped on the other side of the exam table and glanced at Ciddah, whose wide blue eyes were focused on the patient.

"This is my third miscarriage." The girl couldn't have been more than eighteen.

"Your best bet is to keep trying," Ciddah said. "And next time you conceive, come to the harem right away. I can't promise we could have done anything to save the baby, but we do have methods to assist with delicate pregnancies."

The girl's words came out in a mournful sob. "I promise."

Ciddah swept a strand of hair from the girl's face. "I'm going to give you a med that will help your body recover, and might even help prepare you to carry a child again." She motioned Mason to follow her to the counter against the wall.

In a very soft whisper, she said, "Mason, what I'm about to give her is going to hurt her — a lot. I'm going to need you to grab her and keep her as still as you can once she inhales." Ciddah then reached into a drawer and removed a small disposable vaporizer.

They returned to the patient's bedside, and Ciddah administered the drug. As Mason held the girl's arms, he looked up to see tears welling in Ciddah's eyes.

As soon as the girl was still and breathing steadier, Ciddah left the exam room. Mason jogged after her.

"You interested in Rimola?" Ciddah asked without turning around. "I hear she's gratifiable."

Mason stopped in the hallway. "What? No. I barely know her."

Ciddah glanced over her shoulder, eyebrows raised. "What's *that* matter? She's attractive, you're attractive ..." She continued down the hallway.

I'm attractive? Mason started after her again, killing this bizarre line of questioning with one of his own. "Do you know why that girl miscarried?"

"They all miscarry these days," Ciddah said as she turned into her office. Mason stopped in the doorway. Ciddah settled behind her desk and tossed her hair over her shoulder. "The plague weakens the body so much that women can't carry a pregnancy to term. I've been asked to explain this to you. I think now is a good time. Have a seat."

Mason moved a stack of papers off one of the chairs in front of Ciddah's desk and sat down. Ciddah didn't speak, simply stared at him, and a Bible verse came to mind: "Who is this that appears like the dawn, fair as the moon, bright as the sun, majestic as the stars in procession?"

The thought embarrassed him. Why suddenly wax poetic over a woman he'd just met? A confusing woman. He stared at his hands, unable to look at her again until she finally spoke.

"The thin plague ravages the immune system," Ciddah said, "which in turn affects the reproductive systems in both men and women. What you told your outsider *friend* about Safe Landers being sterile is not completely true."

A rush of heat seized Mason. "You heard that?"

"Some nationals are sterile. Some are not, but their donations are too weak to survive fertilization, which amounts to the same thing. And some women just don't have the strength to carry a child to term, even with the help of fertility stims. You were also mistaken about pregnancy. Many women become pregnant in the Safe Lands, but they always miscarry. There hasn't been a child born to a Safe Lands national in over three years."

"But Kendall Collin — " Mason said.

"Kendall is an outsider. Like your women, she came to the harem uninfected. But the male donor was infected, so her child will be too." Ciddah's eyes were suddenly hard and angry. "I'm not a member of the Safe Lands Guild, but I do know that outsiders are brought here to save our people. We're dying. And if you and your outsider friends refuse donation, we have no chance of survival."

Mason sat up tall in his chair. "Your government holds our people against our wills. We don't owe you anything. And we've survived, uninfected, all these years by having a wiser way of life."

Ciddah huffed and shook her head. "So *you* say. But you can't imagine what it's like for a woman to lose a child."

Mason *could* imagine, actually, more than most men. But he didn't see her point. "What does that have to do with us? *You* can't imagine what it's like to have your freedom taken away."

"There's freedom in the Safe Lands," Ciddah said simply. "If you comply."

Mason scooted to the edge of his chair. "Forced compliance is the opposite of freedom."

She raised her eyebrows and looked down her nose. "Not if you choose it."

"Choosing compliance over death is not freedom," Mason said, grabbing the edge of her desk and leaning up against the smooth glass. "It's blackmail."

Her tone became heated. "You're a healthy male. It's your duty to donate!"

Mason didn't know what to say. Clearly Ciddah was upset. He realized he'd practically climbed onto the end of her desk, so he sank back in his chair, wanting to understand. "You resent me because I won't donate?"

"Because you're selfish and narrow-minded." The words felt like a slap, and Mason didn't know why. "Thousands of women desperately want to bear a child, yet since it's not your *belief* to donate, you refuse. And you leave hundreds brokenhearted."

Mason took a few short breaths. "I'm sorry women have to experience that kind of pain. But it's not my wish to mate with hundreds of women."

Ciddah growled. "You don't have to! Don't you get it? The Surrogacy Center does it for you."

Couldn't she see how awkward *that* statement was? "Yes, but it's still my child. My children."

"No, it's not," Ciddah said, softening her voice. "Children belong to the nation, are raised in the nursery and boarding schools until they're fourteen."

Wait, this was what Kendall Collin had been talking about. She'd said that she wanted to hold her child, and Ciddah had said that the child belonged to all of them, but Mason hadn't understood fully until now. "What of their mothers?"

"Surrogates are given six weeks of rest, then they return to their lives."

Questions tumbled in Mason's mind. "What about bonding? What about breastfeeding?"

Ciddah wrinkled her nose. "Bonding is a myth. And breastfeeding isn't sanitary. Plus, the plague passes through a surrogate's milk. All infants are given formula. There's no reason for the mother to stay with the child. The true reward of giving birth is knowing you helped your community survive."

"The mothers never see their babies again?"

"Surrogates can apply for a revealing. And when a child comes of age, if the child also applies for a revealing, they can meet. Male donors may also apply for a revealing. But both surrogate and child, or donor and child, must apply before a revealing is granted."

To never know family? To have no parents or siblings? How horrible. The Safe Lands had many good things — excellent medical care, the technology to do things Mason had never imagined — but they were misguided about so many more important things.

Mason looked directly into Ciddah's eyes. "So you've grown up all alone? Never saw your parents together?"

"Like I said, no one does. It's not how things are supposed to work."

"In my village," Mason said, "a man and woman grow fond of one another, spend time with one another, and if they decide they'd make a good match, they appeal to the elders for marriage. If the elders grant their request, a three-month waiting period begins. Then the man, if he hasn't already, must choose a trade and build a home. And the woman, if she hasn't already, learns a trade as well. Both are mentored by an elder as to how to be a good husband or wife. At the end of the three months, the man stands before the entire village and announces his intention to marry." Unless, of course, no one wanted him, and his parents arrange the marriage.

Mason went on. "If no one objects, the wedding is scheduled. Then the mentoring elder joins the couple in marriage and they are declared man and wife. Should they have children, those children live with them in their home until they're old enough to choose a spouse of their own. That's the way of my people."

Ciddah's cheeks pinked, and she folded her arms. "Some of that sounds comforting, but isn't it a lot of work to have to have two tasks? Raising a child *and* working a trade?"

"My mother never complained. And she was a doctor *and* taught school."

Ciddah shook out her hair, something Mason now realized she did when nervous. "You're of age. Did you appeal to your elders to marry?"

Mason didn't want to mention Mia to Ciddah. It hadn't been his idea, anyway. "No."

Again she tossed her hair, this time with a flutter of eyelashes. "Why not?"

Now that Mason *could* answer. "I didn't feel ... I hadn't found the right woman yet."

Ciddah transformed before him then. Gone was her honest anger and vulnerability and personal questions. Her eyes became distant again, her posture stiff. "You must think my people cold and lazy to only work one task."

"Some of them, yes. But not all of them. Not you."

She came back to him then, instantly softening at his compliment. "Have you witnessed a birth? A natural birth?"

"Hundreds — of animals." He chuckled. "But only one human birth."

This time Ciddah leaned over her desk. "Tell me about it. Please?"

Was she serious? She'd never seen one? Heat crept up the back of Mason's neck. "It's ... difficult to describe."

She slapped her palm on the top of her desk. "Mason Elias, you exasperate me with your modesty. Just tell me what you saw!"

Now she was mad again. Ciddah's moods were like the weather: sunny days, wind, thunderstorms, lightning, and if he waited long enough, the sun would come out again. "Okay," he said. "But I hope it'll help you understand why I'm here in the SC."

CHAPTER 20

When Mason came to work Monday afternoon, Ciddah sent him up to the task director general's office. "Lawten wants to see you," she said.

Lawten? As Mason rode the elevator to the eighth floor, he pondered the reasons Ciddah might be on a first name basis with the task director general. Nothing he came up with pleased him.

Kruse led him inside the office. "It's the intellectual one, Mr. Renzor."

See? Even Kruse called the man *Mr. Renzor.* Without waiting to be asked, Mason sat in the red leather chair in front of the task director's desk. The man looked … weathered. Mason didn't really know what made men handsome to women. Muscles seemed to matter. And that sort of rugged, courageous hunter thing Levi and Jordan had going on. Lawten Renzor had neither. Surely Ciddah wasn't romantically involved with this man.

"We've taken the time to show you why donation is important to our survival," the task director said. "Now, will you comply?"

Not going to happen, *Lawten.* "I understand why you ask me to donate. But not why I should help. You killed my father, all the elders of my village. You claim to value life, yet you willingly destroyed it. And to clean up the mess you've made of your city, you ask me to reproduce with my friends and family. It's completely unacceptable."

The task director looked at Mason, his eyes dark, unnerving. "What *will* make it acceptable?"

"Nothing. Let my people go back to our village to rebuild our lives as best we can."

"We can't do that, Mr. Elias. If we let you go free, we die."

"And you have yet to show me why that's my problem."

Those eyes stripped Mason, making him feel exposed. "If you refuse, we'll be forced to use infected donations on your women. Then their children will be born infected and the process will likely infect the surrogate as well."

Anger shot through Mason, but it was short-lived. The man was bluffing. "Then you gain nothing. You need uninfected donors if you're to survive."

"Yes ... You know, we are receiving regular donations from Omar Strong."

Omar! That foolish, careless ... "Sounds like you got what you want, then."

"I cannot excuse you from donating simply because you have a brother," the task director said. "There are no such relationships in the Safe Lands. You must do as every other national does."

Mason clenched his teeth. This man was cruel. Insane. Depraved. "Your actions ... Your procedures ... You don't need donations — you need to find a cure."

"You're our cure, trigger," Kruse said, flashing a glowing smile.

Mason stood up and leaned on the task director's desk. "If *I* find a cure, will you release me and my people?"

The task director laughed. "What makes you think you can find a cure?"

Mason had no idea how to cure anything, but he said, "What makes you think I can't?" *God, I hope you plan to help me with this one.*

"Uh, let's see now, shellie ..." Kruse said. "Our scientists have been looking for a cure since the end of the Great Pandemic and keep failing. Yeah ... that's pretty much it."

"We do healing differently where I come from," Mason said, as if his head were filled with secret knowledge. "At least let me try."

The task director leaned back in his chair and folded his arms. "Very well, Mr. Elias. I'll allow you to see our history and research. But unless you offer something constructive in one month's time, this experiment will end and Kruse will take you to the Donation Center himself."

"I don't understand," Ciddah said when Mason returned to the Surrogacy Center and found her sitting at her desk in her office. "Contributing to the population is our responsibility as citizens of the Safe Lands. Every male national *must* donate. Every female *must* be a surrogate. Why would Lawten excuse you?"

Lawten again. "Because I'm going to find a cure, somehow," Mason said as he sat in the chair in front of her desk.

Her eyes flew wide, baring every bit of the whites. "For the thin plague?"

When Mason nodded, Ciddah burst into deep laughter, a sound that should've annoyed him since she was mocking his plan, but somehow endeared her to him instead.

She stopped laughing. "There *is* no cure, Mason. Everyone knows that. Most people don't even want one."

Not want a cure? So people really were insane here. "Ciddah, if I find a cure, the task director promised to free me and my people."

Ciddah frowned, her eyes growing distant. "Why do you want to leave so badly? How can you stand living in the dirt?"

Man, she got mean when she was angry. "How can you stand living in a gilded cage?"

Her eyelashes fluttered. "A *what* cage?"

"Gilded. It means covered in gold."

She shook her head, tossing her hair over one shoulder.

"It's a metaphor, Ciddah. I'm saying the Safe Lands is a beautiful cage, but it is a cage nonetheless."

Her brow scrunched up, wrinkling her forehead as she tried to think of a retort. Mason liked arguing with her just to see her facial expressions.

She finally said, "We stay inside the bell to be safe from the dangers outside."

"What dangers? Do I look dangerous?" Mason clapped his hand against his chest. "I'm not even infected! The plague only exists inside your walls. The only serious dangers outside these walls are your enforcers murdering or abducting innocent people and bringing them here. You can't even leave. It's a cage."

She lifted her chin. "Some have left, but they always come back and say it's dangerous."

"Probably because they don't know how to survive without all the gilding. The way everything is handed to you here ... Who does your hunting? Butchering? Who plants your food? Who makes your clothing? Even I could kill an animal if I had to, though I'd probably live off tubers and vegetation instead."

Again with the forehead wrinkle. "Must every word from your lips be a riddle?"

Mason grinned. As fun as it was to debate with her, he had work to do. "No more than the words from yours. If you don't need me for anything else today, I'd like to leave. *Lawten* said I could work on a cure, but only on my free time." He stood up and walked toward the door.

"Wait. You're not going to the HC, are you?"

"If the HC is the History Center, then yes. *Lawten* gave me permission to read the information on the computers there. Don't worry. They'll be monitoring me. I can't ruin anything."

She crossed the room and stopped inches from him, bathing him in the smell of vanilla and cinnamon, but she looked down, not to the floor but sort of into nothing, mumbling to herself. "*So* unfair! Months away from HC access. Stupid Lawten." She looked up at Mason, forehead crinkled. "You've been here two weeks!"

He couldn't help but smile. "I'll tell you what I learn, if it means that much to you."

"How will you even know what you're looking for?"

Mason shrugged. It was a good point. "I don't know. But I have to try."

She grabbed his arm in both hands and tugged. "Take me with you."

He wanted to. "I don't have permission to take anyone along. I don't want to abuse *Lawten's* trust."

Ciddah released his arm. "Why are you calling him that?"

"You do." Mason waited to see her reaction.

She just stared. Her left eye twitched. "Fine." Ciddah shoved past Mason and strode down the hall toward the front desk. "I'll work harder," she said without looking back. "I'll reach level ten by the end of the year. Then I'll have access to the computers too, but *I'll* be able to work there during the day. And *I'll* have an HC task director to mentor me." She glanced back, her hair a golden cape swirling with her movement. "You won't."

He chased after her. "Ciddah, I don't want to compete with you."

She waved her hand over her head. "I know. You're just trying to rescue your people from us *caged* barbarians." She turned around and started to walk away. "Well, I'm sorry that you hate us so much. That you hate me so much!"

Mason felt completely lost by her reaction. Had he insulted her somehow? Insulted her people? Taken the Lawten comment too far? She was clearly jealous that he could visit the History Center. But calling her jealous wouldn't temper the situation. He could think of nothing to say that would help, so he simply remained silent and followed her to Rimola's desk.

When he reached her side, she folded her arms and scowled. "You have nothing to say?"

"I don't hate you."

Ciddah slouched, then switched her weight to her other foot, her expression softening again.

How long did he have to stand here? "Um … Do I have your permission to leave?"

"Sure, Mason. Have a fun time." She flashed an ugly smile and patted his arm.

"O … kay. Thanks." He headed for the elevators.

Behind him Ciddah growled, walked back down the hall, and slammed her office door.

Mason glanced at Rimola, who seemed to be fighting a smile. Embarrassed for reasons he couldn't define, he pushed the button to call the elevator.

Women made no sense whatsoever.

CHAPTER 21

The fight with Omar had earned Levi a broken nose, a second X, three nights in a solitary jail cell, and now a meeting with the man who'd killed his father. Levi sat shackled to a chair in a holding cell across a metal table from General Otley.

"Behavior like yours is only permitted in fight clubs, little rat."

Levi imagined breaking free from his restraints and strangling Otley. But he couldn't do that even if he had the strength. He was village elder, and so far, he'd done a pathetic job of upholding that rank. His business with General Otley would have to wait until his people were back in Glenrock. For now, it was time to buck up and do what he had to do to get back on the streets.

"Got two Xs already," Otley said. "One last chance to get it right. Got more rage to let out, join a fight club. But no attacking enforcers, whether they deserve it or not."

Levi stared at a dent in the shiny tabletop, wondering if a captive with a temper like Jordan's had put it there. "I won't hit Omar again." There was no point. The kid was drunk on his own ignorance.

"Want to go back and task?"

"More than anything."

"Sarcasm does not assure me of your compliance."

"I guess you'll just have to be surprised, then."

"Let him go," Otley told the enforcers. "Return to your tasks and play, rat. I see you again in this room, you'll be liberated."

"I look forward to it."

The enforcers led Levi downstairs and uncuffed him in the lobby. "Good fortune, shell," one of them said.

Outside, it was pouring rain. It was Monday. Levi had missed his meeting with Jordan in the park. Now what? He wanted to go look for his pack, but with two Xs, it would be better to wait for dark.

He took a taxi to the steakhouse, but his truck was gone, so he took another taxi to the Highlands Public Tasks building and went inside. Maybe Dayle would tell him to leave and he'd be free to find his backpack and look for Jordan.

But when he found Dayle in his office, the man winced and set his hands on his hips. "Two Xs, huh. What'd you do?"

"Got in a fight with an enforcer."

"Yeah, that'll do it. Look, kid, I don't want to make trouble for you, but I need people to show up to task, otherwise I look bad. And I don't want no Xs on me."

"Yeah, I'm sorry. It won't happen again."

"That's good to hear. Now, I got a flood down at the end of Morning Glory Way. Need you to go check it out."

"What am I supposed to do about a flood?"

"Check the manhole. Sounds like the one in the cul-de-sac isn't letting water into the storm drain. Could be plugged up with leaves or trash. I'll get you a hook. Come on."

Dayle got Levi a manhole hook and showed him the pressure washer feature on his truck. "You only need to use the pressure washer if you can't get it open with the hook."

Once Levi had restocked his truck, he set out. His route was cleaner than it had been last Thursday, though he did find three little diamond flower-shaped hair clips Jemma would like. Who would throw something like that away?

He discovered that the flood at the end of Morning Glory Way had been caused by a plastic sack covering the drain slots on the manhole's cover. Levi removed it within seconds, and the water started to trickle through. At that rate, the flood would take all day to drain. He tried to remove the cover with the manhole hook but couldn't get it to budge, so he drove his truck next to the manhole and tried the pressure washer. The lid came free, and the water poured through.

When he finished his route, it was just after four. He was hungry but figured it was about time he saw his new home. He needed a base of operations. He typed his apartment address into the GPS and drove where it told him to. He found himself nearing the wall that separated the Highlands from the Midlands. Another wall between him and Jemma.

The road widened before the wall to the Midlands, splitting into four lanes with a tiny booth and gate at each. Levi took the lane on the far left, still a little shaky steering around so many moving vehicles. He stopped before the gate and fisted three squares on the dash before he found the one that rolled down his window. The man in the booth stared. Levi stared back.

"ID?" the man said, pointing to a black pad sticking out from his booth. "You're not vaping and driving, are you?"

"No." Levi reached out the window and fisted the pad. "I don't even own a vaper."

The man chuckled as the gate started to rise. "Find pleasure in life, shell."

"Yeah, you too." Levi steered through the gate. A black car honked as it raced by on his left, nearly crashing into him. Levi took a deep breath, looked over his shoulder for other vehicles, waited for two more to go by, then steered back into the single lane that tunneled through the wall to the Midlands.

Going from the Highlands into the Midlands, Levi left behind the wonder and color of the magical city and returned to stark black-and-white reality. The buildings were clean, but shorter and shabby: rows of houses, shops, and apartment buildings. And where the buildings in the Highlands were crammed together, there was more land out here.

More open space. There also seemed to be more billboards. Levi tried to read one of the signs but ended up swerving out of his lane.

He passed a graffiti-covered wall. He managed to make out the words, *Virus*, *FFF*, and what looked like *Black Arm*, though some street cleaners were painting over it.

The GPS led him nearly to the next wall. To the Lowlands, perhaps? Or outside? Before he came to the gate, the GPS told him to turn right, which sent him parallel along the wall.

The Larkspur was a log building, four stories high. He found a slot to park in and got out of the truck. There was a spinning door in the front, but Levi found a regular one and went inside. The lobby looked like it came out of an Old Western movie: roughhewn furniture and wagon wheel chandeliers. The place smelled like woodchips.

A doorman met him inside and checked his ID on a handheld computer. "Welcome home, Mr. Justin. My name is Colter. If you need anything, please use the help on your Wyndo."

Whatever that meant. "How do I find my room?"

"You're in room 206. You can take the elevator or stairs to the second floor. Your apartment will be to your right. If you'd like something simple, the Hunter serves a great hamburger. There are also two restaurants down the block: Wingers and Café Eat, if you don't mind InstaFood."

"What's InstaFood?"

"It's frozen. Already been cooked, then they heat it up. No waiting."

Bizarre. Levi took the stairs to the second floor. His new home was a hotel room of Old: narrow and clean. It had a bed, one of those glass-wall TVs, a separate indoor bathroom, a sink, and a small refrigerator.

Seeing no reason to hang around, he decided to find food. He took the stairs back to the lobby, and as he descended, his gaze caught sight of the words *Black Army* that someone had written in dark ink on the back of the steps above his head. He'd eat, and afterwards he'd see if he could find out what some of this graffiti stood for. And maybe he could find Bender, like Lonn from the RC had suggested. He had to be careful, though. He couldn't afford another X.

“Is everything okay, Mr. Justin?” Colter asked when he entered the lobby.

“Just looking to get some food,” Levi said. “How do I get to that instant café?”

“Café Eat is to the left. It’s on the corner before the next light.”

Levi started for the door. “Hey, how do I send a letter to a friend in the Highlands?”

“I can call a messenger for you, sir. They do charge a fee.”

“Will they read it?”

“Certainly not, sir.”

“Where can I get some writing materials?”

“There’s a G.I.N. store just before Café Eat.”

“Thanks. Hey, one more question. How can I look someone up, to see where they live?”

“You could use your Wyndo to access to the grid, or you could leave the individual’s name with me and I’d be happy to try and locate them.”

“Yeah, okay, well, his name is Bender. I don’t know if that’s his first or last name.”

Colter’s eyes widened. “For the record, Mr. Justin, residents of the Larkspur are law-abiding nationals. I hope you aren’t involved with the Black Army.”

“Bender is connected to the Black Army?”

“Oh, yes. He’s one of their leaders. But I must warn you ...” He glanced at Levi’s cheek where the two Xs were bared for all to see. “Spending your time with people who associate with the Black Army will only get you liberated before your time.”

Levi definitely needed to find this Bender fellow. “Look, I’m an outsider who just moved here. Some guy told me to see if I could find Bender. I didn’t know he was trouble, and I certainly don’t need any more. Sorry if I upset you. And thanks for setting me straight.”

“Not at all, Mr. Justin. Enjoy your lunch. And find pleasure in life.”

“Yeah, I’ll do that.” Levi walked to the truck but could see the Café Eat sign from where he stood, so he decided to walk. A wall of cement lined the sidewalk. Thick gray paint had recently covered large sections of the wall. He strained to make out the covered-up words but couldn't tell what had been written underneath. Street cleaners in the Midlands did good work.

He waited at the intersection for the light to change. The G.I.N. store sat kitty-corner from where he stood. He'd stop in there on his way back to his apartment.

Café Eat had a very different atmosphere from the Marcellina Steakhouse. No fancy tablecloths. Everything was red and white plastic. The patrons were loud, laughing and yelling across the room at people on the other side.

Levi waited inside the door, but when no waitress showed up, he wandered to one of two vacant seats at a counter where he could see the cooks cooking and a waitress on the other side. She set a plate of food in front of a man, then stopped in front of Levi.

She was wearing a short red dress with a white apron. "Know what you'll have?"

"Beef with ranch sauce?"

"How about a bacon ranch burger?"

"Sure."

"You'll have it in three, or it's free." The waitress walked away.

Three what? Minutes? Could that really be safe? Levi inspected the man sitting at his left. He was tall and bony, and his arms were covered in tattoos. He had two Xs on his cheek.

"How'd you get *your* Xs?" Levi asked.

The man glanced Levi's way and grunted.

The waitress stopped by Levi again. "What can I get you?" She wasn't looking at Levi, though.

A kid had claimed the stool on Levi's right. He looked about Omar's age, and was wearing black gloves, had brown hair like a trimmed porcupine, three tiny gold hoops on one side of his nostrils, and was missing his left ear. Bummer. A five was inked onto his face. The only thing he seemed to lack was an X.

"Chicken sandwich with honey mustard and some onion rings," the kid said.

"Back in three, or it's free," the waitress said.

Levi tried not to look at the kid's ear when he asked, "Know where I might find Bender?"

The kid started to laugh. "Seriously? Look, peer, you're going to have that third X by the end of the day if you go around saying that name."

"Bender?"

"No, bacon ranch burger," the kid said, still chuckling.

"Well, how am I supposed to find the guy?"

"Don't know why you'd want to, you dim shell, but unless you want to end up in this month's liberation ceremony, you'd better think of a plan B."

"Live here all your life?" Levi asked.

"Yep."

"How did you manage to lose an ear and not get at least one X?"

The kid's jaw twitched. "You really have to burn someone to get one X, let alone three."

"Yeah, but I'd guess you'd really have to burn someone to lose an ear too."

Levi's burger came then, as did the kid's chicken sandwich and onion rings. Levi figured he'd done enough damage with his mouth and stuffed his face.

The food satisfied but didn't compare to the steak from Marcillina's. The man on Levi's left finished long before he did and left without saying a word. Levi was only half done eating when the earless porcupine got up to leave. He'd eaten barely half his food.

"Another time, shell," the kid said. "If you last that long."

Levi finished eating and headed for the G.I.N store. The place resembled Old stores he'd scavenged over the years, but this one was bright, clean, cobweb free, and filled with fresh products. Levi found a rack of greeting cards and grabbed a few different ones, including one for Jemma with kissing birds that looked like hearts. He wondered if a messenger would deliver it to her.

By the time he left G.I.N., it was dark. From the sidewalk, he could see the tops of some Highlands buildings over the wall. He hated that

Jemma was so close but he couldn't get to her. He prayed she was safe, that all the Glenrock people were. He needed to learn how things were done here. He needed a friend who could explain. The earless porcupine had been nice enough but obviously didn't want to associate with Xed people.

Levi went back to his apartment, where he wrote cards to Jordan, Mason, and Jemma, and took them down to Colter for delivery.

Patience and wit was what Lonn had told him he needed. Perhaps he'd go out and watch for graffiti artists, follow them to see if they led him to Bender. If he didn't see anyone, he'd take his truck back to the Highlands and look for his backpack.

It felt mad good to have a plan.

He forced himself out into the night. He walked the opposite direction from Café Eat, came to an alley, and decided to explore it, but without streetlamps it was too dark to see anything. As he started back for the main road, bright headlights startled him. He moved to the right. The vehicle passed by, and he saw that it was a taxi. Just as he continued on, tires skidded over gravel behind him. Car doors creaked open.

Two masked men ran toward him. He sprinted for the main road. No way was he going back to the RC. Another vehicle turned down the alley, lights blinding him. Levi paused only for a moment, trying to decide what to do, but it was all his pursuers needed. Stun wires bit into his back, and he hit the ground.

The masked men taped his hands and ankles and put a fabric sack over his head, and he felt his body lift off the ground and plunk on a somewhat soft surface. A door slammed. Apparently he was inside the car, which quickly sped away. Levi lay across the seat on his stomach trembling and trying to think of how he'd get free before they inked his third X.

The car turned once and stopped. The sound of car doors opening, then someone climbed on Levi's back and several sets of hands grabbed him, pushed him down against the seat. Someone cut the tape on his hands and squeezed his right wrist.

“Get off me you filthy, depraved maggots!” Levi tried to wiggle free, but he may as well have been buried alive.

“Don’t move, and this won’t hurt as bad,” a man said.

A scratch tickled Levi’s hand, then throbbed like a bee sting.

“What are you doing?” Levi yelled. “Get off me!”

The same man said to someone else, “Here, go have a drink at the Hunter. And don’t lose that.”

“You got it,” a younger voice said.

“One drink, Rewl,” the man said.

“Yeah, yeah.”

The man on top of Levi pressed something over the sting on his hand, then wound tape around Levi’s wrists again. The weight left his back. Both car doors slammed. The car lurched forward. Several minutes passed this time. Levi tried to calm down. To think. Enforcers wouldn’t do whatever this was. He just needed to stay calm and be smart.

The car turned at least five times before stopping again. Levi allowed himself to be pulled out and dragged between two people, his boots scraping over a smooth surface until one of his abductors said, “Sit.” A different man’s voice. Older.

Levi squatted carefully until he felt the edge of a chair press against the backs of his legs. He lowered himself onto the chair. “Bender?” It had to be.

A man chuckled. “What makes you ask?”

Levi’s breath made the fabric stick to his face. He blew it away and said, “I’ve been a guest in the RC twice now. This isn’t how they do things.”

“Right you are, boy. Sorry we had to cut you, but they track SimTags these days. Take off the bag, Zane.”

The sack came off Levi’s head. He sat on a metal folding chair in front of a desk in a dark office that had Old wood paneling. The place looked as old and forgotten as the man sitting behind the desk — older than was allowed in the Safe Lands. The man’s face was wrinkled and shaded with a few days’ growth of a gray beard. A burn scar pinched his left eyebrow down over his eye so he looked as if he were winking. Levi glanced over his shoulder and saw a kid standing in the corner, arms crossed.

Turned out Zane was the earless porcupine.

"Chicken sandwich," Levi said.

Zane nodded once at Levi. "How's it going, bacon ranch burger?"

"You following me?" Levi asked.

Zane grinned. "How'd you guess?"

"I hear you're looking for me," Bender said, pulling Levi's attention back.

"Lonn told me to. I met him in the RC."

Bender took a deep breath. "I don't suppose he sent a message?"

A message? Who was Lonn anyway? "He said you'd help me if I told you 'Rose.' I thought it was a code or something."

"That's it?"

"Yeah."

Bender sighed and rubbed his eye. "We can do that for Lonn, but since he's not here to tell us why, we're going to ask a favor. See, we've been watching you. Got our own surveillance tapped into the grid. Saw you came in carrying a rifle. Lost you in the park, but we know the rifle didn't come out. You didn't have it, the enforcers didn't have it, so where is it?"

"I hid it."

"That's what we figured. But even with my excellent trackers, we haven't found it."

"That's what this is all about? You want my rifle?"

"Not exactly," Bender said. "Very few enforcers are trained as snipers in the Safe Lands. And with Lonn in the RC, I don't have a sniper. So I want to know if you can shoot."

Levi huffed a laugh. "Can I shoot my own rifle? Yeah."

"How do I know you're not lying?" Bender asked.

"Why would I?"

Bender stared at Levi for a moment, then opened a desk drawer and pulled out a pistol with a silencer attached. "Cut the tape, Zane."

Zane pulled a knife and cut through the tape on Levi's wrists and ankles.

Bender handed Levi the gun. "Why don't you tell me if this is loaded?"

Levi gripped the gun in his right hand, which triggered the laser sights on the wood-paneled wall. He popped out the clip, saw that it was empty, shoved it back in, pulled back the action, pretending to chamber a round. "It's empty." He flipped the safety on and off, aimed it at the wall to check the sights. "Can I have this?"

Bender looked at Levi, impressed. "No, you can't have it. But you can help us."

Levi handed the gun back to Bender. "I'm not killing anyone."

Bender put the gun back in the drawer. "Not even Otley? We heard he killed your caretaker. People tend to have strong attachments for their caretakers."

"I miss my caretaker every day," Zane said.

A chance to take out Otley? "I'll think about it," Levi said.

Bender sat back down. "Think fast. We've only got a few days to make our move."

"But you're going to help me, right?" Levi asked.

"This about a femme?"

Femme meant girl, didn't it? "What makes you think that?" Levi asked.

Bender grinned, flashing a few rotten teeth. "Lonn is a, uh ... What's the Old word for softies, Zane?"

"Romantic." Zane fluttered his eyelashes and laughed.

"Right. Lonn had a lifer named Martana Kirst. But he called her Rose."

Thank you, Lonn. Maybe these were the friends Levi needed. "Enforcers attacked my village and brought us here. Our women are in the harem. I need to get them out."

"I could maybe get one or two out," Bender said. "How many are up there?"

"I'm not sure. Ten, maybe? Twelve? And our village's children are somewhere too, but I don't know where. There's about a dozen kids."

Levi really needed to make a list. If he did manage to pull off a rescue, he didn't want to leave anyone behind.

"Hold the flavor. I don't do kids," Bender said. "They got high security up in that school — spies too. Listen, this is going to take time."

Levi wanted to scream. "I don't know how much time I have."

"I get that. I'll be thinking how I can help you out. And you let me know what you decide about being our sniper." Bender leaned back in his chair and knocked on the wall.

A woman walked in. She had short, spiky red hair that curved around her face instead of sticking up like Zane's. She was holding a pair of black gloves.

"This one goes by Red." Bender gestured to the woman. "Come here, femme."

The woman bounced up to the desk and handed the gloves to Bender. She was pretty, though her skin was ashen, and her body was all sharp angles where it should be soft.

"The right-hand glove has a pocket for your SimTag," Bender said. "The one we cut out of your hand."

Levi looked at his hand. A sticky bandage clung to the side. "And the one in my face?"

Bender shook his head. "You can get a hundred SimTags in your body. They all answer to the one in your hand. And once they're more than twenty feet apart from the host tag, they lose their connection. You see any numbers on my face?"

"No."

"But when you saw Zane in the café, you saw his numbers, right? He was wearing his gloves. Be smart about this. Going out in public? You wear your gloves, even to eat. Don't want enforcers knowing where you are? Leave the gloves someplace you spend a lot of time. Where the gloves are is where the enforcers think you are. Right now your SimTag is having a drink in the Hunter." He tossed the gloves to Levi. "So when you get back and my guy gives you your tag, put the tag in the pocket. Get me?"

"Yeah. Can you do that for a couple of my people?"

"If I can get to them, I can do that for all your people. Zane, get him a Wyndo."

"You didn't say he was such a raven, Zane," Red said, staring at Levi like he was steak.

"You didn't ask." Zane walked to a shelf across the room.

Red touched Levi's cheek with her index finger. "How can he be so soft?"

"'Cause he's not infected," Bender said. "And don't you be changing that."

A slow smile spread across Red's face as she studied Levi. "I've never seen eyelashes like those on a guy. Most *femmes* can't even pull off eyelashes like that without three coats of mascara. That your real hair too?" She combed her hand through his hair.

"Stop touching me." He didn't want any woman touching him but Jemma — especially not someone with a plague.

"Walls, you're so blessed," she said. "Mine's half plugs."

Levi watched Zane digging for something on a shelf across the room. "I don't know what that means."

Red twirled her finger around a lock of Levi's hair. "It means half my hair fell out, and I got it replaced with fake hair."

Levi grabbed her wrist and pulled her hand away from his hair. "I have a fiancée."

She laughed. "Now *I* don't know what you mean. What's a fiancée?"

"A lifer," Bender said.

"Lifer?" Red pouted. "Walls, raven! She must be some lover."

"Her name's Jemma." Levi tugged the cord with their rings out of his shirt and held it out so they could see. "I scavenged these rings from Denver City. We were supposed to get married last Friday."

"That's sugar sweet." Zane handed Levi what looked like an Old cell phone. The letters *CB* were engraved at the top and designed in a way that created two people's profiles, talking.

Levi touched the screen, and it lit up. "So it's a phone?"

"Phones are ancient," Zane said. "A Wyndo is way better than a phone. Play with it tonight, and learn how to use it. It's already got Red's and my numbers in it. You can use it to talk to us, but if you use it to talk to others, be careful. Don't tap in your SimTag. The Guild monitors all transmitters, and since ours are off the grid, putting your SimTag in or talking to someone whose transmitter is on grid will only call attention to your big bad illegalness."

"I got it. What if I need to talk to Bender?"

Bender glanced up. Levi had forgotten his scar and thought he was winking. "You tap Zane or Red, and I'll tap you. That's all the time I've got for you tonight, shell."

Zane held up the fabric sack. "Sorry. Gotta put this on again."

Zane left Levi's arms and legs free for the drive to the Larkspur but made him lie in the backseat to avoid being seen.

"Be careful with Red," Zane said.

Levi lay on his back this time, with his knees up. "Careful how?"

"She wants you."

"Wants me to what? Wait ... aren't you and she ... together?"

Zane snorted a laugh. "No way. I mean, we traded paint a few times when I first started working for Bender, but ... she's a lot to maintain."

Sometimes Levi could barely understand what these people said. "What's that mean?"

"She gets gummy, you know? Wants you to be with her all the time. It's weird."

"Well, I'll be careful." The last thing Levi needed was more guilt.

"Good plan. And don't drink anything she gives you. She stimmed me a few times to get what she wanted. She's one crazy flame."

It was almost ten at night by the time Levi got back to his apartment. He got in his truck and drove toward the Highlands, hoping his backpack and rifle were still in the park. But when he got to the gate, they wouldn't let him through.

"Sorry, Mr. Justin. You have a work ID only. Unless you enter the Highlands with a Highland resident, you're only permitted to enter between seven a.m. and five p.m."

Oh, come on! This place had more rules that the book of Leviticus. "Fine."

Levi turned around and drove back to the Larkspur. He'd just have to look for his backpack tomorrow after his shift. Once he got the two-way radios, he'd figure out a way for Mason and Jordan to meet Bender and lose their SimTags. Then he could rescue Jemma.

CHAPTER 22

Shaylinn was sitting with Jemma, Kendall, Naomi, and Mia in the Blue Diamond living room, watching the Safe Lands ColorCast program *C Factor*. Jemma had barely spoken to her since the night she and Mia had snuck out. Shaylinn kept looking for an opportunity to talk about it, but her sister was always with Naomi, as usual.

Shaylinn was torn. She liked looking pretty. She liked the clothes. But she hadn't liked Ewan's behavior at all. Her first kiss. Stolen by a bully.

"Why's Page kissing Bolton?" Jemma asked. "Doesn't she love the earring man?"

"That's Fivel," Kendall said. "She only paired up with Fivel to make Bolton jealous. But Bolton is using her to get horn implants."

"What are horn implants?" Shaylinn asked.

"They're silicone horns that you can get implanted under your skin. They're scary."

Shaylinn wrinkled her nose. If the Lord had wanted her to have horns, she'd have been born with them. She frowned. Wasn't the same true of her body? If the Lord had wanted her to be thin, he'd have made her thin.

On the screen, Bolton pulled Page's shirt over her head, leaving her in just her bra.

Jemma shrieked and covered her eyes. "Don't want to see!"

Shaylinn leaned closer to the screen, staring at two lines of gold rings on Page's back. "What are those things on her back?"

"That's a surface corset," Kendall said. "You should've seen her in the gown she wore two weeks ago. It was backless, and her corset looked so glossy with satin laces."

"She laced up the rings in her back?" Shaylinn asked. "Doesn't that hurt?"

"Naw. They put a silicone layer under the skin and permanently numb the pierced areas. I saw an edudrama about it called *Cosmetic Confessions*."

"Someone should make an edudrama about the Safe Lands called *Psychotic Confessions*," Naomi said.

There was a knock at the door. Jemma jumped up. "I'll get it."

She opened the door to a young man dressed in green shorts and a white T-shirt with the letters *SLMS* on the upper right. "Messenger service," he said.

Kendall shrieked and reached toward him. "Hay-o, Chord!"

Chord jogged around the sofa and leaned down to give Kendall a hug and kiss both cheeks. "How are you, femme? Walls, you're famous now. Your face is everywhere."

Kendall groaned and patted her belly. "I know. Almost done, though."

"You're huge!" He laughed.

"Thanks," Kendall said. "Chord, this is Jemma and Naomi and Shaylinn and Mia. Girls, this is Chord. We were messengers together in the Midlands before I came here."

"Nice to meet you." He stared at Naomi, his gaze shifting from her face to her belly. "You're famous too."

Naomi pursed her lips and looked back to the ColorCast.

"Can't stay," Chord said. "Lots of messages to deliver. Oh my fortune! You guys are watching *C Factor*. I can't stand that show, Hey, which one of you is Shaylinn Zachary or Jemma Harvey?"

Jemma gasped.

"I'm Shaylinn."

Chord handed Shaylinn a gold envelope, then held out a black touchpad that was attached to his belt. "ID?"

Shaylinn pressed her fist against the pad.

"Got it." Chord tapped on his Wyndo, then looked up. "And Jemma?"

"Right here!" Jemma stood, waving both hands. "It's from Levi. I know it is!"

"How?" Naomi asked.

"Because here my last name here is Levi. But Levi wouldn't know that. He might assume I chose my father's name instead."

"So might your mother," Naomi said.

Jemma's grin faltered. "True. A letter from my mother would be good too."

While Jemma gave Chord her ID, Shaylinn opened the gold envelope.

Jemma squealed and grinned and cried all at the same time, waving around a colorful card. Chord and Kendall were talking, but Shaylinn wasn't listening. Her heart fluttered like a flag in the wind.

The Safe Lands Guild Surrogacy Center
OFFICIAL SUMMONS
To: Shaylinn Zachary
It is your responsibility to be in the Surrogacy Center on Wednesday, June 23, 2088 at 11:00 a.m. Failure to appear will result in the issuance of a warrant for your arrest.

Being ranked first in line, she'd known it was coming; but she'd shoved aside the reality and indulged in all the fun things this place had to offer. And now, here was the price. They were really going to make her pregnant.

Chord hugged Kendall again and left. Shaylinn tucked her summons between her knees and tried to pay attention to the others.

Naomi slid to the edge of the couch. "Stop screeching, and tell me who it's from."

"Levi sent me a card!" Jemma hopped up and down and giggled, but it morphed into a confused cry. "That means he's okay. Right?"

"I'd say so." Naomi patted the couch beside her. "Come, sit. I want to hug you, but I'm not getting up."

"'I wish I had no heart, it aches so …'" Jemma sat beside Naomi, who gave her a side hug. "I'm going to write him back." She read the card again.

"Can I see it?" Shaylinn asked.

"Sure." Jemma thrust the card to Shaylinn.

The front said *Love* and had two red birds flying toward each other. Inside, the birds were kissing and their touching bodies formed the shape of a heart. The pre-printed words said, "I'm glad we're in this together," but underneath, in black pen, "I miss you, Buttercup. Write me back. Your Westley. Larkspur, Room 206, Midlands."

A tear ran down Shaylinn's cheek. She gasped and quickly wiped it away. She never cried. *How annoying!*

"Shay, what's the matter?" Jemma asked.

Shaylinn returned the card. "I always wanted to be a mother. Someday though, you know? Not now. I know none of the boys like me. But I don't want to have a baby like this!" Her bottom lip trembled in a terrible frown, and she turned her head in case her eyes betrayed her and spilled more tears.

Jemma got up and knelt on the floor at Shaylinn's feet, put her hands on Shaylinn's knees. "Shay, what's wrong?"

"Was it your letter?" Kendall asked. "Was it the summons?"

Shaylinn pulled out the envelope, now slightly crumpled, and handed it to her sister.

Jemma read it. Her expression hardened. "No! Honey, this is *not* okay. We have to do something." She passed the paper to Naomi.

"Oh, Shaylinn," Naomi said. "I'm *so* sorry. We'll think of something."

"We can try and sneak out!" Jemma said. "Make that Ewan guy help. He owes Shay."

"Sometimes the procedure doesn't work," Kendall said.

"Yes!" Jemma said. "Way to think positive. The procedure might not work."

Shaylinn looked to Kendall. "It worked on you."

"Yeah, but you never know," Jemma said.

"Easy for you to say, Jemma. Everyone has always loved you. Levi, Mason, Omar — they all would have chosen you. I don't have anyone. And now I'll have a baby, and it will be worse. No boy will like a girl with a baby."

Jemma started to cry. "I'm sorry, honey. I don't know what to do or say to make this better."

"You guys are looking at this all wrong," Mia said. "It's not a big deal, Shaylinn. You're forgetting that it's the Safe Lands' baby, not yours. You won't be a single mother. Once you have it and they take it, you'll be free and have a lot more credits and fame."

"I don't want fame or credits. I want what Jemma has."

"You like Levi?" Jemma asked, her voice a high squeak.

"No. I just want someone to love me. To think I'm beautiful." Even though he'd turned in the entire village, her heart still wanted Omar, but she'd likely never see him again.

"Ewan thought you were beautiful," Mia said. "And you were. You *are*. I don't know why you don't think so. I'm kind of tired of hearing about it, frankly."

"Shaylinn, you have all of us. We're all getting out of this place long before you'd deliver this baby." Jemma glared at Mia. "That's a long time from now, and, Kendall's right. You're not pregnant yet. Let's pray about this, okay?"

"But what about Kendall's baby?"

"My baby will go to the nursery, and I'll go back to the Midlands Messaging Office." Kendall smiled and blinked so rapidly that Shaylinn knew she was trying to be strong. "I've gained a ton of weight. Trust me. I need the exercise."

"Kendall, you said you were a messenger before coming here," Jemma said. "Don't you have to change jobs every six months?"

"You can apply for an extension if you like your task, and I did. When I first got here, I tasked as a runner for City Hall. I think they like to keep new outsiders close at first."

"Then why did the task director make Levi live in the Midlands?" Jemma asked.

"He probably got a strike," Kendall said. "And maybe to separate him from his friend and from you. The enforcers have enough trouble with the rebel groups."

"There's a rebellion in the Safe Lands?" Shaylinn asked.

"Think Levi has already found them?" Jemma asked Naomi.

"Knowing him, I wouldn't doubt it," Naomi said.

"Tell us about them," Jemma said to Kendall.

"There are some groups that protest the government. They're pretty violent. I found out about them when I worked for City Hall, and once I moved to the Midlands, I saw their graffiti everywhere. They set bombs and kidnap people. Sometimes they kill. They want to change things. I guess they figure if they can kill off the Safe Lands Guild, maybe they can take over."

"We should start our own rebellion," Jemma said. "A more peaceful one. Plot a way to get out of here before Shaylinn's appointment and Kendall has her baby."

"Careful, Jem," Naomi said. "You're starting to sound like me."

"Jemma, it's too dangerous," Kendall said.

"No it's not. They need us. We're too valuable to kill. And what's the worst that can happen? Kendall still loses her baby? Shay and the rest of us get pregnant? We've got to try."

"What do you have in mind?" Naomi asked.

"We start by sending Levi a message," Jemma said. "I need some paper and a pen."

Shaylinn tuned out. Jemma's letter to Levi wouldn't reach him before her appointment in the morning. She read her summons again and closed her eyes. *God? Is this what you want for me? Why?*

Someone sat beside her on the couch. Shaylinn opened her eyes. Mia.

"I think you're so lucky," Mia said.

Shaylinn scowled. "You're such a liar."

"You're going to be famous. Everyone is going to worship you. And I'm not lying."

"Then trade places with me."

"I already asked. They said our numbers are based on our biology or something like that. Nothing can be done. But they said we'll all be pregnant within the next six weeks, so it won't be long."

Shaylinn stared at the summons again. Tomorrow. No, it wouldn't be long at all.

Shaylinn sat on her front porch, knitting a hat for her baby. Her belly was huge, the perfect table for her project. It wouldn't be long now, and they would be a family of four.

The children ran past the porch, giggling, holding fistfuls of dandelion clocks, loose seeds drifting behind them.

She watched them run, her heart light and free and very full. They ran straight to their father, jumping up and down at his feet and begging him to blow, blow.

He did, and the seeds danced in the air to the laughter of the children, bringing a wide smile to Shaylinn's lips.

She woke as if someone had gently nudged her shoulder. It had been only a faceless dream, yet she felt calm and peaceful. *Is everything going to be okay, God? Could it be true?*

CHAPTER 23

Omar pressed the down arrow and stepped back from the elevator to wait, staring at his scabbed knuckles as he pulled his hand away. It had felt good to hurt Levi — to dominate him for the first time ever. But it hadn't taken long for the thrill to turn to guilt. Skottie and Charlz had taken Levi to the medical center and told Omar that Levi had gotten a second X for assaulting an enforcer.

They were trying to comfort him. But Omar knew that Levi's anger was justified. He scratched at the smallest scab on his middle knuckle. If only no one had died. If only the enforcers had come to Glenrock peacefully when Omar had told them to.

No matter how Omar tried to shift blame, it always came back. *He* was responsible for many deaths. His father and uncle ... nine men total, two women, a child, and possibly more.

"What are you doing?" a velvety voice asked.

Omar whirled around and saw Bel, his red-headed neighbor, standing behind him. She was wearing a short gold dress that draped off the edges of her shoulders and clung to her body like it was trying not to slide off. Square nets of gold and black metal dangled from her ears.

And she wore black boots that came up to her knees. There were no feathers in her hair today; she'd straightened it into a silky red curtain.

He liked that Bel never seemed to mimic everyone else's styles. Skottie had talked Omar into buying a lot of black clothes because he could mix them with the color trends and still fit in. Today, he was wearing shiny black pants and a stiff red shirt that buttoned only halfway up.

"Could I paint you?" Omar asked, bolder after several nights out with Skottie and Charlz. "Your portrait, I mean."

She blinked her thick, dark lashes. "Walls! You move kind of fast, don't you?"

"I'm an artist," Omar said. "And you're beautiful. It would be wrong not to paint you."

The elevator dinged. Omar jumped. Bel laughed, her shoulders trembling with the movement. Omar wasn't sure if she was laughing because he'd asked to paint her or because the elevator had startled him. He stepped toward the open doors, but Bel caught his hand and pulled him back. The elevator closed.

Her lips curved in a slow smile. Still holding his hand, she lifted it toward her face and examined his knuckles. "You got into a fight." She kissed each scrape, then released his hand. "I hope she was worth it."

Omar couldn't breathe. His hand seemed to tingle, which *had* to be his imagination.

"You meeting a femme tonight?" She withdrew a purple metal vaporizer from her purse, put the end to her lips, and breathed in.

"No."

"You're an outsider, aren't you?" she asked, her voice hoarse as she held in her breath.

"I'm a Safe Lands national."

She turned her head, blew out a stream of bright green vapor, and fixed her gaze back to Omar. "But you *were* an outsider, right?"

"I'm that obvious?"

She laughed again. "Yes."

"What am I doing wrong?"

"I wouldn't say *wrong*. You just look so healthy. And lost and lonely and … intense. I'm Belbeline, or Bel, by the way. But I guess you heard my friends call me that already. What's your name?"

"Omar Strong." He pressed the down button again.

"Where you headed right now, Omar Strong?"

"To a club."

"I'm going to need a little more than that. Which club?"

He was meeting Skottie and Charlz at Ginger Oak again, but a girl might not like that. He shrugged. "First one I come to."

She clicked her tongue. "Oh, that'll never do. Come with me tonight, trigger. I'll be your guide. What's your stim?"

Omar glanced at the purple vaporizer delicately balanced between her long, pale fingers. "I like beer."

She rolled her eyes. "Do you have a vaporizer?"

"No." Skottie kept telling Omar he should get one, but he wasn't sure he was ready for whatever they held.

"You'll need a good one." Belbeline squeezed his arm. "Are you *really* of age?"

No. But Omar said, "Yeah."

"You look so young, you blessed thing."

"You look young too."

"Flattery will get you … exactly what you want, I imagine," she said, giggling.

He grinned, not knowing if he was supposed to reply.

"For a guy who asked to paint me, you're still a bit of a neo."

He stiffened, not understanding her criticism.

"But *my*, you have a quick temper. Don't be so serious. I'm teasing you. Stick with me, and I'll take good care of you tonight, Valentine."

The elevator arrived then. In the lobby, Belbeline called a taxi, which carried them to a dance club called Blue Heaven. Omar tapped Skottie and told them not to wait for him.

As the taxi slowed to a stop outside the club's entrance, Omar could hear the thump of bass inside the car. "It must be really loud inside," he said, watching the way the blue lights pulsed in the night sky.

"It is." Belbeline slid across the seat and opened the door. She said something to him with a wink, but Omar couldn't make out the words.

He followed her into the dark interior, where the sound intensified until the beat was like a physical force, almost pushing him back to the entrance. At first he couldn't see, but his eyes slowly adjusted.

Shards of colored light slashed from the ceiling across the dance floor. Squares of light dotted the dance floor, and those dancing on them seemed on fire, while the rest of the crowd appeared as fragmented limbs and faces, their bodies lost in the darkness until the colored light cut across them.

Belbeline took his hand and pulled him through the bouncing mob, past bare skin, long legs, black leather, red dresses, a cloud of perfume, and couples whose bodies were tangled together. Some girl's hair slapped his face. A guy brushed up against his side. It wasn't possible for Omar to not touch someone. Skottie and Charlz had never taken him anywhere so ... fast.

Belbeline released his hand and spun around. Blue light slashed across her face, highlighting her features. She smiled slowly, swayed, moved her feet, grabbed the sides of her skirt and swished it around. Omar's stomach seemed to slide down one leg of his pants and onto the floor as she lifted her arms over her head, shaking out her curtain of hair. This was *not* how people danced in Glenrock.

She moved closer and put her hands on Omar's waist. He hugged her close, liking how she felt in his arms. They danced through several songs, moving in time with the mob. Omar felt connected, included. This was all he'd really wanted: a beautiful woman to choose him.

She leaned close and yelled in his ear, "I know something that will really make your night wild." She tugged him by the hand through the crowd.

Omar would have followed her anywhere.

They left the dance floor and walked down a narrow corridor, up a flight of stairs, and down a wider hallway. The walls were painted black, lit by twinkling lights that zigzagged along the ceiling.

"Where are we going?" he called.

"Somewhere more quiet," she said.

Halfway down the hall, Bel stopped at a door, knocked twice, paused, then knocked five more times. The door swung in, revealing an imposing man in jeans, a black jacket, and dark sunglasses. He stood beside a black podium that held a SimTag pad.

Belbeline set the side of her hand against it, her other hand still clasping Omar's. "How are you tonight, Dag?"

"Decent." The man looked at Omar, then down at the pad, then up again, and Omar swiped his fist as well. The man gave him a nod. "Enjoy."

"We will."

Belbeline led Omar into a dark room clouded with vapors that smelled sweet and minty, and of something else that tickled his nose. The room was filled with small tables and chairs, couches, oversized pillows, and recliners in black and silver that were arranged on either side of a low, two-sided glass bar that stretched down the center of the room and glowed brightly with blue light — the only light in the room. The barkeep stood on a floor that was lower than the one Omar was walking on. Dozens of people sat vaping, talking, kissing.

Belbeline walked to the bar and set her vaporizer on the counter. The purple metal tube rolled a little over the glass. She spoke to the barkeep. "Give me my usual, and vape me with a five. Pink, strawberry, grass. And my man here, I'm going to buy him a PV. You have a silver bullet?"

"Yeah."

"Okay, fill it with grass ... a two. Black. No flavor. And get him a — " She looked at Omar. "A black velvet to start."

"You got it." The barkeep held out a pad, and Bel pressed her hand against it.

"We'll be in the corner." Belbeline took Omar's arm and led him to the far side of the room, where they claimed a black leather sofa and a tiny square table. "Girls where you live probably don't dress like us or dance like us, huh?"

"Uh, no." He laughed, trying to picture Shay in Bel's dress.

"You and I, Omar ... We're going to have so much fun together."

Omar ran his fingers over the scabs on his knuckles, wondering what kind of fun Belbeline had in mind. It didn't seem fair that so many were dead because of him, yet here he was with this beautiful, friendly woman. He'd expected God to punish him for what he'd done, but his life here only seemed like a reward.

That bothered him more than he cared to admit.

The barkeep arrived with a tray. He set two glasses on the square table before them. One was a goblet-like glass filled with clear liquid; several olives rested inside. The other glass was tall and thick, filled with two stripes of dark liquid and froth on top. He also set a silver plate between the glasses. The vaporizers sat propped on little indentations in the plate, Belbeline's purple vaporizer and a thick silver one. "You guys behave, now."

"Oh, we will." Belbeline reached for the glass with the clear liquid. She took a sip, then set the glass back on the tray. She pushed the other glass toward him. "Find pleasure in life."

Omar picked up the glass, which was cold in his hand, and took a sip. His top lip sank into the froth, and the liquid below was cold, fizzy, and had a bitter, creamy taste. It also tasted smoky, a bit like unsweetened chocolate, but it seemed like some sort of beer. He started to put down the glass, but Belbeline set her hand on his arm.

"Don't give up. Give yourself a chance to get used to the taste."

He took another sip, liking the way the drink seemed alive and whispering.

Belbeline picked up her vaporizer and took a long breath. "Since you're so sweet, I bought you one," she said on an exhale, her words hoarser than normal as a pink cloud of vapor seeped from her lips. "It's a personal vaporizer. Most people call them PVs."

"Thanks." Omar wasn't certain he wanted one, but it did seem as though he was the only national without one, and the guys had wanted him to try it. He wasn't sure what was holding him back. "But what are they for?" Omar had watched an entire show about it and still didn't know.

“Whatever you need, or want,” Bel said. “You can vape anything. People take their meds this way. Some also like to vape stimulants.” One side of her mouth quirked up. “There are all kinds of juices from plain flavors, which is like candy, to harder stuff. You order a hit level, which is how powerful the vape will be. And if you want, you can also ask for color, which will color your fog.”

“Fog?”

“Your breath when you blow out.”

Omar stared at the silver tube. “So what’s in mine?”

“I got you grass, only a hit level two. You ever tried marijuana?”

“No.” Some people in Jack’s Peak smoked marijuana. And Omar had heard stories of Jordan’s grandpa smoking it. “It wasn’t allowed in our village.”

“Well, *everything* is allowed here. And grass will help you relax, so we can go downstairs and really dance.”

Omar swallowed, embarrassed by his hesitation. He’d much rather go back to the dance floor now. “Don’t you smoke marijuana, though? I guess I don’t understand how a vaporizer is different.”

“Smoking is against Safe Lands law. It’s unhealthy, and it gives you bad breath. Plus it can start fires. Vaporizers don’t even have a smell, unless you get flavor.”

Was that why marijuana was bad? Papa Eli had never said why. Perhaps the Safe Lands had found a way to eliminate all the dangers. Doubts nagged him, but would it hurt to try it once?

Omar picked up the silver tube, wanting to please Bel. “How do you do it?”

Belbeline snatched the vaporizer from his fingers. “I’ll get it started for you. New PVs don’t work quite right at first.” She put her lips around the end and took a few quick breaths. The tip lit up bright blue with each draw. With almost no emotion on her face, she blew out a quick puff of black vapor, sucked longer, then blew out a long stream of vapor that felt cool as it hit Omar’s face. “That’s better.” She handed it to him, a ring of red lipstick around the end of the silver tube. “Now you try.”

He put the end into his mouth and sucked. Nothing happened.

"Push the button," Belbeline said.

He tried again, this time pushing the small circle on one side. Hot air filled his mouth and burned the back of his throat. He opened his mouth and croaked, "It's hot."

"Take shorter breaths until you're used to it. They have cold PVs too, you know. They're kind of fun if you want chilled vape."

Omar took a short breath, and the hot moisture filled his mouth like breathing in steam from the sauna. He held it there, not sure what to do. He swallowed and choked.

"Don't swallow it, dim. Breathe it all the way into your lungs."

Omar tried again. The hot air passed into his mouth, down his throat, and filled his chest with a slight burning.

"Now blow it out," Bel said, her sapphire eyes more like black diamonds in the low light.

The stream of vapor came out in a black plume, like a curl of smoke from a dirty chimney. He smiled and tried it again.

Belbeline inhaled on her own vaporizer, and exhaled a bright pink stream into Omar's black one. He laughed, and for a while they simply sat and blew vapor at each other.

The nerves in Omar's body began to tingle, even behind his eyes. He could feel his heart thudding in his chest, faster, it seemed, as if he'd been running. "Did they turn up the music?" he asked Belbeline, who was fishing an olive out of her drink.

"That girl is waving at you." Belbeline put the olive in her mouth and tucked it into her check. She nodded over Omar's shoulder. "Do you know her?"

Omar squinted across the dark room. Mia sat at a little round table with two men and a woman. Mia smiled, spoke to one of the men, then stood and walked toward him.

Lights seemed to flash as Mia came over. Omar squinted against the brightness and leaned against the sofa, feeling like he could melt into it. His arms prickled like static was in the air.

Mia stopped before their couch, her posture straight as a lamppost. "I just wanted to say that even though the way you did this was wrong — that people shouldn't have had to die — I do agree with you. Life here is better than it was in Glenrock." She glanced at Belbeline. "Who's your friend?"

Omar turned to look at Belbeline and remembered that she'd wanted to dance.

"I'm Belbeline Combs."

"Are you a dancer?" Mia asked.

The sound of Belbeline's laugh warbled in pitch from high to low and back to high. Omar winced and shook his head to get rid of the sound.

"Right now I task as a masseuse at the Highland Grove Spa. I've also tasked as a barista. I love to dance, but just for fun."

The olives in Belbeline's glass reminded Omar of tiny frogs sticking out their tongues. He snorted, trying not to laugh.

"Well, you're pretty enough to be a stage dancer," Mia said.

"Thank you . . . ?"

"Mia. I'm from Omar's village. I'm here with Rand MacCormon. He's a piano player for Maroz Zerrik and Nelessa Kade."

"I've seen their show. They're amazing. And Rand is quite the Valentine." Belbeline ate another olive. "He and I go way back."

"Oh." Mia's smile faltered. "He took me to a steakhouse. The food was so good!"

Omar fought back another desire to laugh but failed, chuckling deeply.

Mia turned her gaze to where Omar sat, which made him laugh harder for some reason. "What's the matter with him?"

"First time trying a vaporizer."

"Oh."

Was that it? The vaporizer was the reason he felt silly?

"Well . . . enjoy your night," Mia said. "Bye, Omar."

Omar watched her go, giggling at how she wobbled on a pair of very high-heeled shoes.

"I think you've had enough." Belbeline snatched the vaporizer from Omar's fingers.

"Hey!"

"I'm just glad I only got you a two." She tucked his vaporizer into her purse and took a long drink from her frog-filled glass. "Let's go dance." She bounced up and pulled Omar by his hand.

He stumbled after her, out of the dark room and down the stairs.

"These stairs are steep. I wonder if people ever fall down them." He concentrated on the last two, feeling proud to have made it. "How do you walk in those shoes?"

"Carefully. But it's worth it — I feel gorgeous in high heels."

"You're mad gorgeous."

Belbeline giggled. The thumping music grew louder as they neared the dance floor. Then, as if missing a few minutes of his life, Omar and Belbeline were back in the mass of writhing bodies.

The night went by in erratic time. Some moments lingered in Omar's mind: dancing with Belbeline and eating something called an orange. Others were a rush of images: meeting up with Belbeline's friends, swimming in an indoor pool with his clothes on, kissing someone — not Belbeline — more dancing, drinking, and vaping. Like a child, Omar felt like he could do whatever he wanted forever and ever and ever.

Omar awoke on the floor of a strange apartment, clutching his vaporizer to his chest and shivering violently. His sleeves were rolled up to his elbows, his clothing was damp, and his socks and shoes were gone. He pushed up to his feet and almost puked. Breathing through his nose to keep the nausea at bay, he brought the vaporizer to his mouth, then thought better of it, worried it might make him feel worse.

Where was he? Soft music played nearby. Across the room, a man danced alone in front of a mirror. A soft snore lowered Omar's gaze to where a couple lay in each other's arms, sleeping on the length of the sofa. The rest of the apartment looked empty.

Through an opening in a wall of fluttering curtains, a swimming pool glowed, the lights beneath its surface making it look bright and electric. Omar walked outside, but the slightest movement made his head throb. A cool breeze gripped him, his moist clothing making the chill worse than it likely was. The pool was on the roof of the building. How did they keep it from accidentally flooding the rooms below?

The stars were dim overhead, muted by the city lights. Only two rooftops away, a vehicle passed through the sky. A second, more careful look proved that it was actually driving along the top of the wall that divided the Highlands from the Midlands. On the Midlands side, an image of two dancers hung on the side of a building, their sweaty bodies knotted together, caught in an intimate moment that looked vaguely familiar.

Why would people allow themselves to be photographed while they were doing that? They'd probably had too many stimulants and couldn't remember what they'd done. The thought sent a shock of panic through Omar. Had he done anything like that last night? He recalled the task director's warning. Surely he'd remember being held that way. And he hadn't vaped anything really strong, right?

He spotted one of his shoes on the edge of the pool and picked it up. It was full of water, which he dumped out onto the deck. It took him much longer to locate his other shoe, eventually locating it on a chair with his balled-up socks. He tucked his socks into the dry shoe and looked for Bel. He couldn't find her and figured it was time he left the apartment.

It was even colder in the hallway and elevator. The air-conditioning, he supposed, ran constantly. Omar shuddered, goose bumps appearing on his forearms. He tried to use his vaporizer, but it merely tasted like ashes. The cylinder was warm, though, and he pressed it against his cheek.

The elevator stopped in the lobby. He walked toward the exit, and a doorman opened the door for him. "Good evening, sir."

"Can you call me a taxi?" Omar asked, trembling.

"Of course, sir."

"Thanks." Omar started toward a bench, then turned back and

asked the doorman, "Is there somewhere to get this checked?" He held up his vaporizer.

"The bar is through that doorway, sir."

Omar wove his way into the bar and collapsed onto one of the stools.

A somewhat kind-looking man walked over and leaned his elbows on the counter. "How can I help you?"

"I, uh, was wondering if my vaporizer is broken. Nothing's coming out."

"Your first time, eh? It's just empty. You want me to fill it?"

The marijuana had been fun at first, but Omar didn't like not remembering where he'd been or what he'd been doing. Maybe he could vape something else. "Yeah."

"What's your juice?"

Juice? Was that the same as stim? "Can I have beer?"

The barkeep sighed. "I can get you a beer to drink or alcohol to vape."

"Oh. I want to vape it."

"Alcohol then. What level?"

"How many are there?"

The barkeep laughed. "Ten, shell."

"Let's go with a five, then," Omar said, feeling mature.

"Any flavor? Color?"

"Sapphire. No flavor."

"I got blue." The barkeep slid a SimTag pad toward Omar.

Omar tapped his fist against it, and a few minutes later was sitting on a bench outside what turned out to be the Django Building, waiting for his cab, eager to see if his vaporizer could help him get a little warmer on the inside.

The first puff burned the back of his throat and made him cough. His second breath was more careful. The stream of hot vapor hit his tongue, and he held it in his mouth a moment before breathing it into his lungs. At least it didn't burn the back of his throat this time, and it definitely warmed his insides.

The taxi arrived and carried him to the Snowcrest Building. Not too long after, he entered his apartment. The carpet was inviting under his bare feet. He'd barely closed the door when his doorbell rang. He opened the door, and Belbeline walked inside.

"Magnificent Fortune!" She grabbed him in a hug. "You're freezing! What happened to you?"

He took a quick puff and blew a cloud of blue vapor into her face, then chuckled at her surprised expression.

She snatched the PV from his hand. "You refilled this. When?"

"It was empty. Give it back." He pried it out of her fingers.

"You have to be careful, Omar. You can make yourself sick vaping too much grass. Too much anything. No more tonight, okay? I don't want you getting liberated before your time."

"I'll be careful." He felt clever to have filled his PV with alcohol. "How'd you know I was back?"

"I asked Artie to tap me when you came in. I thought you left me!" She slapped his arm.

"I woke up in some strange apartment, on the floor behind the couch."

Belbeline started to laugh, but it trailed off as her eyes went wide, looking past his arm. "Is that me?" She pointed to where his easel was set up in the kitchen.

Omar's cheeks burned. "Uh ... yeah. I couldn't stop thinking about your hair."

She walked into the kitchen and stared at the canvas. "You really *are* an artist."

Omar joined her. "It's not done." He suddenly felt heavy and exposed and wanted to cover the canvas. "I'm sorry. I should have asked first. Are you mad?"

She turned those gorgeous eyes back to him. "I'm not mad. I want you to paint me again."

The heaviness fell away. "Really?"

She ran into his living room and crawled onto his couch. She twisted and turned and settled onto her side, shaking back her hair and making his breath catch. "How's this?"

A thrill bounced through him. She wanted him to paint her now? "Okay." He lifted his painting of Bel's face off the easel and leaned it against the wall, then put up a fresh canvas.

CHAPTER 24

Mason woke up at five thirty and showered. He didn't have to go to the SC until ten thirty, which gave him several hours of free time. Perhaps this morning would be a good time to explore a little. Take another look at the harem before Levi made contact and wanted to plan a rescue.

He again read the card Levi had sent him. Despite the silly message, which featured a cartoon of a pile of body parts — "I'm falling apart without you" — Levi had written only, "Write me back. L," and his address in the Midlands. Mason would have to pick up some cards at the G.I.N. after his shift. Not much was open at this hour.

He took a taxi to the Snowcrest and walked across the street. The harem took up several blocks in the center of the Highlands and was surrounded by a fence topped with coils of barbed wire. Were the fences meant to keep people out, or the women in? Mason walked the perimeter, taking note of the entrances and the locations of each yellow camera.

The drop-off zone in front was in public view, but the loading docks in back might be a possibility. They all let out onto Snowmass Road, but an alley that cut between the Axtel and the Whetstone buildings connected the harem's loading docks to Emmons Road. If the women were somehow able to get to the loading dock, they could easily be picked up. Still, a bright yellow camera looked down on the loading dock.

The cameras were a problem.

Mason walked toward City Hall, just people-watching at this point. The skin colors and piercings, the bizarre hairstyles, the clothing, the extremely well-endowed women … So much rested on personal appearance here. He passed a group of women who were sitting on a bench and blowing different color vapors into the air and giggling.

He stopped and turned back. "Excuse me," he said. "I'm conducting a little experiment. I wondered if you ladies would mind telling me what substance each of you are vaping."

"Grass," they said together.

"Thank you." Mason continued along his path to City Hall, asking the same question of anyone using a vaporizer. The majority answered that they were vaping a combination of caffeine and alcohol or grass, which Mason figured out was marijuana. After being in Jack's Peak, he'd recognize that smell anywhere. Mason thought several were vaping candy, until he asked some follow-up questions. It turned out that in most cases, *candy* just meant *flavor.* The other fluffy-sounding answers were much more daring substances: brown sugar was heroin, golden ice was methamphetamine, and white cocoa was cocaine.

Mason knew a bit about narcotics from the book *Addiction Medicine* his mother had on her shelf in the sick house. It had intrigued him because of the thick layer of dust covering it. He'd asked his mother why she kept an obsolete book that she never read. "Knowledge is never obsolete," she had answered.

So Mason understood the damage that the habitual use of stimulants could impose upon many organs in the body that were already burdened by the thin plague. Surely, Ciddah would know that such substances were harmful to pregnancy.

But what if she didn't?

Perhaps he could use this observation to his advantage. He had visited the History Center once and been unable to find much medical knowledge at all. Perhaps a medic with a higher rank would be permitted to see more. He would simply have to take Ciddah with him.

He sighed. Time to see *Lawten* again.

"I have some theories I want to talk to you about. I think it might prevent miscarriages."

Ciddah looked up from the CompuChart on her desk. "Don't you knock anymore?"

Her angry tone deflated Mason's confidence. "When I knock, you don't let me in."

She swept three little black plastic rectangles into her top drawer and slammed it shut. "Fine." She shook out her hair, fluttered her eyelashes, and — finally — made eye contact. "What are your theories, O brilliant outsider man?"

Mason flushed at her insult but stuck to his plan. He needed her help. "Only if you come to the History Center and read the files with me. The task director said you could join me."

Ciddah swelled with a deep breath, smiling wider than Mason had seen yet. "When did you ask him?"

"I just came from his office. I had to wait an hour to get in to see him."

Ciddah snorted, and it turned into a silent laugh. "An hour is *amazing*. Some people wait months to see Lawten. Some never get in."

"Oh. Well, he didn't mind about you coming with me to the HC. Said it was fine. See?" He handed her the letter the task director's receptionist had given him.

The paper trembled in Ciddah's hand. "Why would he agree to this?"

"Because I can be very convincing." Mason bared his cheesiest smile. "He really thinks I might be able to help. And I have a theory I wanted to — "

"Well, I don't." She crumpled the paper and threw it toward the trash. It bounced off the rim and onto the floor. "How could you possibly know more than Safe Lands medics? You were raised in the woods by rabbits or something." She twisted a strand of her hair. "There's no way ..."

There she went, being cruel again. Something had upset her, but what? "That's pretty narrow-minded for someone who calls *me* narrow-minded."

She softened a little. "Fine. I can do it on Friday, but then you have to give me your theory. And it had better be amazing, Mason. Because if it's not ... I won't waste more time explaining things to you."

He grinned, electrified by the idea of seeing her outside the SC. "Thank you, Ciddah."

"You can leave my office now," she said without casting even a glance his way.

Not wanting to push his luck, Mason stepped out into the hallway and shut the door. He didn't understand Ciddah's rolling hills of emotions — he was just glad she'd agreed to come along. With her help, he should be able to find the medical data in the History Center.

"Here's the information for the one in the waiting room," Rimola said, jerking Mason out of his thoughts. She handed him a CompuChart and walked back out to her desk.

Mason read the patient's name. "Shaylinn Zachary?"

"Mason?" Shaylinn's voice came from the waiting room.

Mason walked out past Rimola's desk and saw Shaylinn sitting in the waiting room. She looked different, older. They'd done something to her hair. Or maybe it was the clothes.

"Mason!" Shaylinn squealed and jumped up waving both hands.

"Does she know why she's here?" Mason asked Rimola.

"Said she was here because of her summons."

Mason's stomach twisted into a knot. "Why was she summoned?" He found the answer on the chart the moment Rimola answered, "ETP."

Embryo Transfer Procedure. "No!" The task director general had promised.

"Something wrong?" Rimola asked.

"Everything." Mason strode to the elevator and hit the button.

"Mason?" Shaylinn asked. "Are you okay?"

He squeezed his hands into fists and hit them against the sides of his legs. Where was the elevator? "I'll be right back." He opened the door to the stairwell and ran all the way to the tenth floor.

The task director general's receptionist was talking to someone on her GlassTop. Mason walked right past her.

"Excuse me!" she yelled, then said to her GlassTop, "Can you hold, please?"

Mason pushed open the door to the task director's office and went inside.

"Sir!" The receptionist chased him inside. "You can't come in here without an appointment."

"Clearly that is a false statement."

The task director sat at his desk across from a man in an enforcer's uniform.

"We had a deal," Mason said, ignoring the enforcer and hoping he didn't have any weapons nearby. "You said the Glenrock women wouldn't be made into surrogates until I had a chance to look for a cure. You said a month."

The task director's flaking face became animated, fixing into a smile that revealed a row of shiny, small teeth further dwarfed by his massive nose. He looked at the enforcer. "My apologies for the interruption, Colonel Stimel."

"Would you like me to remove him?" the colonel asked.

"This will only take a moment. Then, depending upon his reaction, perhaps I will require your assistance." The task director fixed his eyes on Mason. "Mr. Elias, I allowed you to postpone *your* donations for a month while you searched for a cure. But I don't need your donation to start procedures on the women. As we discussed, I have an uninfected donor in Omar Strong."

Once again, Omar had sabotaged things. But was this arrangement really what they'd agreed on? Mason tried to recall the exact wording of their conversation, certain he'd bought everyone some time. "You intend to make all the women carry Omar's children?" Not that he could even call Shaylinn a woman. The girl was only fourteen.

"Omar's donations will provide us with as many children as I deem prudent. But if you are concerned about the similar DNA, never fear. I've recently located another uninfected male donor."

"From where?" Mason asked.

"Wyoming, where Kendall Collin came from. He has been tested and has already made donations. Now all the females from Glenrock can be scheduled for surrogacy without delay, and you are free to conduct your research. And you are also free to leave my office."

Mason suddenly felt unable to move.

"Mr. Elias, that wasn't a suggestion."

CHAPTER 25

Shaylinn sat on the exam table, wearing another thin white gown and swinging her legs. This room looked just like the first one she had awakened in. The door, the cupboard, the strange screen were all in the same place. Behind the exam table was a counter and sink with a mirror above it.

Shaylinn slid off the table and stood before the mirror. She studied the mirror clock, leaning close to see how it worked. No use. It was simply magical, like all glass in this place.

She drew her hair in front of her shoulders and twisted the curls together to form a fat ringlet on each side. She ran her hands over her waist, admiring how thin it seemed after so many InstaWraps and tiny meals. With so many major changes, why didn't she feel pretty? She could tell she was pretty. Prettier anyway. Not like Jemma or Mia, of course. But she wasn't ugly.

Then why did she still feel ugly?

Maybe because she was going to get pregnant? But that didn't make sense. Both Kendall and Naomi were beautiful even with their bulging bellies.

Shaylinn sat back on the exam table. Eighteen minutes passed by on the mirror clock before someone knocked twice and cracked open the door.

"You ready, Shaylinn?" Mason's voice.

She smiled, eager to see someone else from their village. "Yes, come in."

Mason pushed in the door and closed it before meeting Shaylinn's gaze. His eyes were fierce and moist and had circles under them.

"What's wrong?" she asked.

He scratched the back of his neck and looked just about every place in the exam room he could but at her.

"Mason, look at me."

So he did, drumming his fists against the sides of his legs. "I can't stop it, Shaylinn. I tried. I mean ..." He stepped up to the exam table and lowered his voice. "We could run. But they can track our SimTags, so they'd catch us and just do the procedure anyway."

"It's okay, Mason." Shaylinn lifted her chin. "I'm ready."

"What?" His eyebrows sank low. "How can you be so calm?"

Shaylinn shrugged. "You're going to laugh."

"No, I won't."

"I ... I had a dream. A beautiful dream. And ... I think God is going to do something big. This place needs hope. I mean, there's so much wonder in this city, and it looks good at first, but it's empty. I can't explain it very well, I guess. But I just wonder, what's the point of looking beautiful on the outside if you're dead on the inside?"

Mason's posture wilted. "Shaylinn, do you feel dead inside?"

Did she? "Sometimes. There are things that poison me, I think. Words I tell myself. But I was thinking, if I didn't know that God loved me the way I am, if I didn't believe he made me who I am for a reason, I'd feel dead all the time. Every little thing would poison me, and I'd do everything I could to try and make it better."

"Shaylinn, you can't fix yourself. You're not broken."

"I know. I do. It's hard to remember sometimes. But I think God is going to turn death into new life. It's what he does, right?"

Mason's face softened. "I didn't expect you to behave so calmly, Shaylinn. Your maturity is quite impressive."

For some reason the word *maturity* embarrassed Shaylinn, and she looked at the floor.

"Okay," Mason said, "let's get you weighed." He helped her lay back then extended the table to its full length. "Put your feet up, please."

Shaylinn swung her legs up onto the table. "Mason?"

"Hmm?" His gaze shifted between the scale's readout on the edge of the bed and his CompuChart.

"Do you think I'm pretty?"

He looked at her and swallowed.

She pursed her lips. "Don't worry. I'm not in love with you."

He fought a smile. "Thank you?"

"I ask because it's one of my poisons — thinking I'm hideous and fat," Shaylinn said. "And I thought if a man told me how pretty I was, everything would be okay. But the other night a man did say I was pretty, but it didn't change anything. Maybe because I didn't want *that* man to say it. What's wrong with me?"

"There's nothing wrong with you, Shaylinn. You're human." He tapped on his CompuChart and helped her sit up. "We all believe lies about ourselves. Something likely happened to make you believe you were hideous and fat — which I don't think you are, by the way." He paused. "I hope my father's words didn't make you think you were ugly. You never were."

She remembered when Elder Justin had called her fat. But there had been many such things before then. And none had ever bothered her as much as when Omar had called her an ugly crybaby. "Do *you* believe a lie, Mason?"

Mason moaned out a laugh. "Shaylinn ... I do, but you can't tell anyone."

She shook her head. "I won't tell a soul."

"Okay." Mason took a deep breath. "I believe that I'm ... backward somehow. Girls don't like the smart boy. They like muscles and who can kill the biggest bear, so … when we were in Glenrock I used to always think, who would ever love me? No one."

Shaylinn's eyes glossed with tears. Again, she was about to cry. "That's not true, Mason."

He grinned and lowered his gaze. "Yes, I know. And your lie isn't true either. Shaylinn, you're a beautiful young woman. Believe anything else, and you're believing a lie."

"Thank you, Mason."

"Glad to help."

The door opened, and Ciddah entered. "Are we ready to proceed?"

"Uh … no," Mason said, his cheeks flushing. "I'm not quite finished."

Ciddah folded her arms. "What's taking you so long to get her vitals?"

"We were — "

"Mason was counseling me on a personal matter," Shaylinn said. "He's very wise. And handsome. And loveable."

Mason glared at Shaylinn.

Ciddah raised her eyebrows. "Yes, well. We all love Mason." She glanced at him and flipped out her hair. "Please come get me when you're ready."

"I will," Mason said.

Ciddah left and closed the door behind her.

"You like her!" Shaylinn said.

Mason edged away and tapped on his CompuChart. "Another lie you believe, I think."

"*No* … I saw the look on your face when she walked in. You blushed."

Mason set down his CompuChart and picked up the blood pressure cuff. He took Shaylinn's hand and slid the cuff up her arm. "I *don't* blush."

She laughed and kicked her feet. "Oh, sure. No boy blushes more than you, Mason of Elias. So? What are you going to do? Are you going to kiss that pretty doctor?"

Mason squeezed the bulb again and again, and the cuff got tighter and tighter. "If you don't stop, I'm going to sphygmomanometer you to death."

"What?"

"Sphygmomanometer." He tapped the blood pressure cuff. "It's what this is called."

"That's a crazy long name. Say it again."

A smile grew on Mason's face. "Sphygmomanometer."

Shaylinn giggled. Mason took off the cuff and turned to set it against his CompuChart.

"Will I get the thin plague like Kendall?" Shaylinn asked.

"That's doubtful," he answered, his back still facing her.

"Why?"

"The thin plague is passed through blood. Or bodily fluids," Mason explained. "And supposedly the donor ..." He paled, and his eyes lost focus.

Shaylinn thought of Mia and Rand sucking each other's faces. "You mean kissing?" She gasped. "Is *that* why you won't kiss the doctor?"

Mason snapped out of his daze and rubbed his temple. "No, Shaylinn, I don't mean kissing. Mostly, uh ... relations. As long as you aren't intimate with an infected person, you can't contract the thin plague."

Shaylinn pondered that. "Strange that I can have a baby but never have ..."

"Yes," Mason said, nodding at the floor. "It is strange." He picked up his CompuChart and faced her. "Um ... I'm finished, Shaylinn. So I'm going to leave now. Ciddah will be in momentarily, I'm sure. I'll be praying for you. I'm glad God gave you peace about this, but, well, I'm still nervous for you."

"Thank you, Mason. When will I know if it worked or not?"

"Ciddah says you're to come back on Monday to find out."

"Monday," Shaylinn said.

"That's right."

Shaylinn swung her legs from side to side. "Until Monday, then."

Shaylinn didn't feel all that different after the procedure. It had been awkward and cold, but it hadn't hurt. And now she was tucked into bed, being spoiled by Jemma, Naomi, and Kendall. She even ate a bowl of ice cream Jemma had brought her, despite it not being on Tyra's list of approved foods.

Mason had said that the thought *Shaylinn is hideous and fat* was a lie. And Shaylinn refused to believe any more of those. Something big was going to happen soon, and Shaylinn was holding on to that dream of a calm and peaceful future.

CHAPTER 26

Dayle called Levi on his truck radio while he was working his route. "Rewl needs some help with a big graffiti job over in front of City Hall. They want it covered fast. Go help."

"Yes, sir." Levi drove over to City Hall and parked along the street. The graffiti was hard to miss. The words *Free Lonn* had been painted across the second-floor windows.

A Highlands Public Tasks truck had been parked up on the sidewalk right in front of the doors. A man wearing a gray jumpsuit was shooting water at the graffiti with a hose that was attached to the truck. He had wide-set brown eyes, big lips, and very little brown hair.

Levi walked over to Rewl. "Dayle said you need some help."

The man lowered the hose and stopped the water flow. "Nah, I got this, shell." He spoke like he was pinching his nose. "I just painted it a few hours ago, so it's coming down nice and easy."

Levi looked around them, but there was no one. "You did that? How'd you get up there?"

"That's my secret." Rewl grinned, baring teeth that were etched with black stripes. "Listen, I'm the guy who held your SimTag last night." Rewl lifted his fist. He was wearing gloves too. It had been so dark in the Hunter last night, Levi hadn't gotten a good look at the guy. "Bender says to tell you, 'Where's your transmitter, shell?' Says he can't help you if he can't reach you."

Levi had left the piece of glass at the Larkspur. "Sorry. I mean, tell him I said sorry."

"Tell him yourself, shell." Rewl raised the hose and turned it back on. Water shot out at the graffiti and sprinkled on Levi's head.

A distant chorus of voices captured Levi's attention. He strained to make out the faint sound, but the water from Rewl's hose was too loud.

"Do you hear singing?" Levi asked.

Rewl shut off the hose again and tilted his head. "It's coming from the Harem Gardens."

Levi blinked at Rewl and sprinted toward the harem.

"Hey, shell, where you going?"

Levi darted down the sidewalk and over a grassy lawn that led up to a wall of bushy green trees. When he got closer, he found that the spaces between the foliage were filled with chain link fence. Through the links Levi could see nothing but a wall of trees on the other side. The coil of barbed wire on top of the fence ended the brief thought that he might climb over.

He could hear the singing more clearly now.

Let not your heart be troubled,
His tender words I hear;
And resting on His goodness,
I lose my doubt and fear.
Tho' by the path He leadeth,
But one step I may see,
His eye is on the sparrow,
And I know He watches me.

"Jemma!" Levi slipped between two bushes and edged along the fence looking for a break in the wall of green, any place that would allow him to see inside.

Someone grabbed his arm from behind. "Hey, *softie*," Rewl said.

"It's illegal to talk to the harem girls. You're going to earn that third X in a hurry."

Levi's heart was beating so fast his hands were trembling. "I can hear my fiancée!"

Rewl's gaze flickered between the fence and the street. "I'll keep watch, but if I see anyone coming, you've got to run, hear me?"

Levi pressed deeper into the tangle of trees. The singing had stopped, but the bubbling sound of women's voices reminded him of passing the meeting hall on a tanning day: a lot of talking and giggling, and little he could pick out of the conversations. A gap in two trees revealed the women sitting in a circle on the grass. There was Jennifer! And Chipeta and Mia and ... Jemma sat between Mia and Naomi. She was wearing a light blue dress.

"Jemma!"

Her head twitched, turned to the back fence.

"On the other side of the fence!" Levi yelled. "In the trees!"

The other women's heads turned; the entire circle focused on the back fence. Jemma stood and helped Naomi stand. Levi couldn't help staring at Naomi's belly. She looked like she'd swallowed a small boulder.

The women began to sing again, all but Jemma and Naomi, who slowly made their way toward the fence, stopping to pick a flower here and there. Their pace was maddening.

Finally, they were close enough that he heard Jemma ask, "Who's there?"

"It's Levi, Jem."

"Oh!" She ran into the trees then leaving Naomi behind. He lost sight of her a few yards to his left. "Where are you?" Her voice sounded panicked.

He scraped through the tangle of branches, trying to reach her more quickly. "Here."

She stepped into view between two bushy trees. Her beauty stole his breath, and he threaded his fingers through the chain links and squeezed, wanting to rip away the metal barrier.

She slid her fingers over his and pressed her face against the fence. He kissed what he could of her lips and face, tasting the bitter metal between them.

She finally pulled back and her brown eyes flit over his face. "Oh, Levi! Your nose! What happened?"

Levi scowled and rested his forehead against the chain link. "Omar."

"Oh, love. Thank you for the card." She reached her finger through the bars and rubbed his prickly cheek. "Two Xs? You look … scary."

Not exactly the words he was hoping to hear. "Yes, I'm a regular Dread Pirate Roberts."

She jerked on the fence and pursed her lips. "I meant scary because you only have one more chance."

"Don't give up on me, Jem. I'm going to get you out of here.

Her chin quivered. "I'm afraid for you. I'm afraid you'll do something foolish."

"I've been good, Jem. I've been doing your breathing trick to keep my temper in check. I need you to trust me. Remember when we were out looking for berries and we saw that black bear?"

"He wanted to eat us."

"He wanted the berries, Jem, and you didn't believe me, but you trusted me. And you were so brave. Now I need you to keep being brave, okay? Here." Levi reached into the neckline of his shirt and pulled the chain over his head. "You take these. Keep them safe. As soon as I get you out of there, we'll get married, okay?"

She pulled the chain through the fence and started to cry.

"No, no. I didn't give them to you to make you sad."

"They're just so beautiful, Levi." She fingered the diamond on the woman's ring. "It's cut like a teardrop."

"You hold all my tears."

"I won't let them fall." She gripped his fingers. "I want you to hold me."

"Soon, Buttercup. Listen, if I hide some two-way radios in these trees, can you get them?"

"I think so. Which ones?"

"I'll mark the spot somehow. With a ribbon or something colorful."

"Won't that draw attention?"

"How about I stash them in the branches of the tree to the right of the one I mark?"

Jemma nodded. "When?"

"I don't know. I'll try to come back tonight or tomorrow. Don't talk until I test it. Can you get one to Mason?"

"I think so. Shaylinn said he's working in the doctor's office."

"He is. Tell him the same. And keep them on channel four."

"Okay." She sniffled. "They did something to Shaylinn today." Several tears fell down Jemma's cheek. "They're trying to make her pregnant. I'm so scared for her."

Not Shaylinn. Levi fought back his rage with a growl. "What about you?"

She shook her head. "I don't have to go in for another two weeks."

"I'll get you out before then." He kissed her again. What else did he have to say? "Oh, I met some people."

"The rebels?" She smiled — so beautiful. "When Naomi and I heard about them, we knew you'd find them."

"Well, they want me to kill Otley."

"What!" Her eyes flew wide. "Levi, you can't kill anyone. You mustn't!"

He wasn't sure he had a choice. "It might be the only way to get the rebels to help."

"No." Jemma shook her head.

"Otley is the one who killed my dad and Papa Eli."

"Oh …" She sniffed back tears. "Still, Levi, that doesn't make it right. Revenge? That's not what Papa Eli would have wanted. You can find another way. I believe in — "

"Time to go!" Rewl said.

He kissed her again. "Be careful, Jemma. Remember, I'll always come for you."

She grinned past her tears and played along. "But how can you be sure?"

“Because this is true love. You think this happens every day?” Levi kissed her fingertips, her lips, then forced himself to turn, to claw his way out of the trees. He saw Rewl running down the street with an enforcer on his heels. Levi turned and sprinted toward his truck.

Levi lingered in the Highlands until after dark. He parked his truck by a dumpster at the edge of Champion Park and walked inside, carrying a trash bag and a can of spray paint in case anyone spotted him. His biggest concern was hiding his rifle as he walked back to his truck, assuming the rifle was still there.

Please let it be there!

The park was about a half a mile wide and consisted of a forested area, a lake, and paved walking trails. One side of the park ran alongside the Highlands-Midlands wall. Levi realized he had originally come up through the grille at the northeastern corner of the park, only a block from Marcellina Steakhouse.

He kept to the shadow of the wall and quickly found the area where they’d caught him. Crickets were singing. He could hear the distant murmur of voices but saw no people. He kicked every bush he came to, peeked underneath trees, and had almost given up when he tripped over the barrel of his rifle.

He shoved the pack and rifle in the trash bag and carried it to his truck. Then he drove to the Snowcrest and parked in the lot that faced the harem. The garden fence was well lit. He considered using his rifle to shoot out some streetlamps but couldn’t risk anyone coming to investigate the noise while he was hiding the two-way radios. Better to just come at the gardens from the other side.

The darkest location seemed to be on the far end where the fence met the back of a building called the Whetstone. Levi drove to the Whetstone lot and looked in his pack. He’d give the windups to Jemma and Mason; Jordan could have a solar one. He shoved two windups and a pair of wire cutters into a trash bag and darted along the back of the building.

When he reached the fence, he was on the far right of where he'd talked to Jemma. It would be easy to hide the radios in the bushes here, but he couldn't risk her missing them. So he threaded his way through the trees that hid the fence, slowly making his way to the other side.

When he reached the general location of where he'd spoken to Jemma, he cut through enough links in the chain fence so he could push the radios through and tuck them into the lower branches of a bush on the other side. Then he cut some wires by the next bush over and tied the length of trash bags to a branch. The black plastic draped all the way to the grass, then blew in the gentle breeze. Not exactly colorful, but less obvious was better.

By the time he'd mended the fence and drove back to the Midlands, it was almost ten o'clock. Apparently Midlanders could leave the Highlands at any house, just not enter. He parked his truck and started across the parking lot toward the front doors of the Larkspur, carrying his trash bag-covered rifle and backpack.

A car pulled in front of him. The window slid down and Red said, "Get in."

Levi desperately wanted to take his stuff into his apartment, but he couldn't afford to ignore Bender. He got in the passenger's side, holding the trash bag with his backpack and rifle on his lap. Red pulled out onto the street.

"Where are we going?" he asked.

"Nowhere." Red turned left out of the lot. "Heard you saw your lifer today."

"Yeah." Levi smiled at his fresh memory of Jemma.

"Still floating for her, then?"

Levi didn't know what "floating" meant but wasn't about to let Red know that. "I've known Jemma all my life. She and I, we . . . I don't really know how to explain. It's like we're a match. We help each other be better people."

Red drove past the G.I.N. and turned left before Café Eat. "Better than who?"

"Better than how we are alone."

Red grunted. "Sounds boring. Like you let a computer match you up or something."

"There are no computers where we're from."

"Well, being with the same person forever doesn't sound fun to me."

Why was he talking about this with Red? Why was she so nosy? "Where I'm from, if a man marries a woman, he stays with her his entire life. No matter what. They're a team. And they never give up on each other. Even when it's hard."

"Sounds like unnecessary trouble." She drove into a left turn lane and stopped to wait for the light. "But it's your life, shell. I just think you'd be wise to shop around."

"That would only destroy what we have." The guilt from his night with Kosowe was heavy enough. He didn't need any more of that.

Red turned at the light and turned right again at the next one. She was circling back to the Larkspur. Good. "Listen, Bender says to tell you that hanging around the harem and talking to surrogates is against the law. He says you do that again, he isn't going to help you."

"It won't happen again because we're going to get her out."

Red rolled her eyes. "You're so strange. Bender also said to tell you that he's going to rescue your boys on Saturday — that medic and your angry friend. That's the earliest he could coordinate it with their task schedules."

"Saturday will be fine." Saturday was well before Jemma was scheduled for her procedure.

Red pulled the car into the Larkspur's parking lot. She powered off the vehicle and scooted to the middle of the seat, roughly pushing Levi's trash bag aside before placing her hand on his knee. The smell of her perfume pulled his gaze to her lips.

"What do you want to do now?" she asked.

Red's hand was sliding higher up his thigh. He looked down and seized her wrist. He wasn't going to make a mistake like this again.

He tapped his fist against the doorplate, and the door glided open. Seconds later he'd grabbed his stuff and slid out of the car.

"I'm going to go to bed. Alone."

CHAPTER 27

A knock woke Omar. His head throbbed between his ears, and he grabbed a pillow to muffle out the noise.

The knock sounded again, sharper. He should sit up. Go deal with whoever that was.

"Just a minute!" a woman's voice said. Belbeline.

He opened one eye. He was at Bel's apartment. In her bedroom. The realization of his weakness brought on a sudden panic, and he searched the ceiling for bright yellow cameras, wondering if the task director knew he was here. Again. Or that he'd failed. Again.

He didn't care. He was going to marry Belbeline anyway. And she couldn't possibly have the thin plague. She was too pretty. Too soft.

Muted voices carried from the far side of the apartment. He squinted at the bedside table. *Yes.* His vaporizer was there. He reached for it, but his arm didn't obey. It felt like it was encased in steel.

What time was it, anyway?

Must. Move. He propped himself up onto one elbow and peered at the open bedroom door. The voices became clearer.

"Left you five messages, Bel-bel, and — Who painted that?" A man's voice. Deep.

"You're not my task director, Ollie," Belbeline said. "I don't have to report to you."

"And those! Whose shoes are those?"

Belbeline clicked her tongue. "I don't know. People come over a lot. I can't keep track of who leaves their stuff here."

"You're not alone."

It's wasn't a question. It was a realization. And it didn't sound happy. Omar raised his eyebrows and looked around the dark room, wondering where he might hide.

Wait. Why should *he* hide? Belbeline was his girlfriend. And he was an enforcer. He should storm out there and confront this jerk who was hassling her. He threw off the covers, but the cold air clapped around him, and the throbbing in his head intensified. He grabbed his vaporizer and burrowed back under the covers. One deep breath later, his head cleared.

Until the lights flashed on. Omar shut his eyes and pulled the covers over his head.

"That who I think it is?" the man's voice said.

The blankets were pulled away, leaving Omar cold and half naked on the bed. He strained to see the large, hairy man who loomed above the bed.

General Otley! What?

Omar could only stare, his PV pinched between his thumb and two fingers. Soon the cylinder was at his mouth, and he took another long drag. The stims were helping him wake, but his brain felt foggy, loose. Or maybe his brain was fine, and this was more of a communication problem between his brain and limbs.

Otley grabbed Omar's ankle and pulled him off the end of the bed. Omar's back hit the floor first, then his head. Otley held his ankle in the air and shook it, glaring down. "Those are *my* pajamas, little rat."

Omar looked himself over. He was shirtless, wearing the black satin pajama pants Bel had given him. No wonder they were so big. He looked to Bel, and his voice came out raspy, the blood rushing to his head. "You said these were a present."

Otley threw Omar's leg down and kicked him, his heavy boot like a hammer to Omar's ribs. The blow flipped him onto his stomach. "This ends now, *rat*. Don't even look at Bel-bel again."

Omar crawled around the side of the bed, wanting only to get away from that boot.

"Don't be a prude, Ollie," Bel said. "I can see who I want."

"And I can task who I want."

"I'm *not* going back to that club."

"Keep away from the shell, and you won't have to." Otley strode out of the bedroom.

Bel followed. "You don't own me, Ollie. Why do you have to be such a fun-downer?"

"I'm the enforcer general. All part of my image. And I'm taking this painting."

The front door slammed, shaking the windows. Omar's stomach throbbed. He still clutched his PV in his fist, so he took another long drag and pulled the blanket over himself, curling into a ball on the floor. Some of the pain ebbed away, but the ache still held him in a fist. *This can't be real. It just can't.*

Bel's footsteps pounded into the bedroom. "He's *so* controlling. You'd think an enforcer would know all about a person's rights, but *no* ... Omar?"

"Here," Omar said from the floor.

Bel's steps pattered this time. She knelt at his side and pushed her hand back over his hair. "Oh, trigger, I'm sorry. Are you hurt?"

Just his pride. "These are really my task director's pajamas?"

Bel rolled her eyes. "What's it matter? They fit, don't they?"

"Not really." Omar took another drag, desperate to float again. "And are you and my boss ...? Did you ...? With him?"

Belbeline sat back on her heels. "Did I *what*? Spit it out, Omar."

He took a quick puff on his vaporizer for courage and sat up. "If I'd known you were involved with Otley — my *task director* — I never would've pursued you."

She raised her eyebrows and laughed. "*You* pursued *me*, did you?"

"Looking for a wife. I've got to be a better choice than Otley."

She cackled now, the expression of amusement on her face like a knife to Omar's bruised torso. "I see now why you never paired up in your outsider village."

"What does *that* mean?"

"You're delusional, Omar. *I* picked *you* up. *I* showed *you* how to have a good time. If it wasn't for me, you'd still be standing at the elevator staring at your knuckles."

That wasn't how it happened. "I had a good time before I met you."

"With who?"

"Charlz and Skottie. We went to the Paradise Saloon and the Ginger Oak Club."

Belbeline stood up and sat on the edge of her bed. "Those are tasked clubs, Omar. Those girls are credited to play with men."

Omar shook his head. "No, they're not."

"Look, Omar. It's been a party, okay? But we need to take a break."

Omar's head became light, but not in the way he'd hoped. "I thought you liked me."

"I do like you. But it's been two days, and you're already way too gummy."

He felt insignificant lying on the floor while she was on the bed. Though it hurt his head and the growing ache in his side, he forced himself to sit up, to stand. "You like Otley better?"

She pulled her curls back from her face and twisted them. "It's not like that. Ollie does me favors, I do him favors. People say he's going to be the next task director general, and I can't afford to cut that tie."

She wanted Otley for his position of power. Things here weren't that much different from Glenrock after all. "Then how could you have betrayed him?"

Bel stood up and paced to the door. "Omar, you're so caught up in the Old ways. Relationships aren't exclusive here. We have fun. We pair up. We see someone else we like the looks of, we play with them. Ollie gets that. He does the same. He'll get over his little jealous phase, and then maybe you and I can pair up again."

"You're really leaving me?" Omar hated the sound of his voice. The hint of a whine. He gritted his teeth. *Be strong*, he reminded himself. *You are Omar Strong now, not some sniffing little kid.*

Bel sighed. "Why are you making this into a big deal?"

"Because it *is* a big deal! I want to marry you." At her blank look, he said, "Be a lifer."

Her laughter came so fierce and fast that she snorted. She held her hand in front of her mouth until she stopped, and her hair untwisted and fell loose around her face again. "I'm not going to fight over this. If you can't accept it, fine. I won't tap you again."

How could she dismiss him so easily? "Just like that?"

"Just like that," she said, walking out the door. "Go home, but leave the pajamas."

After his shift, Omar went straight to the Regal Lounge, which was a theater club in the Highlands. A woman holding a tray of shots greeted him. He took two of the little glasses and made his way to a table in front. He shrugged out of his enforcer's jacket. Time to relax.

A man and woman were in the middle of the stage, singing about some kind of disagreement. The man had wanted the woman to dance exclusively for his cabaret, but the woman liked to work many clubs. Sounded familiar.

The song shifted into a big dance number, and a half-dozen dancers filed out onto the stage wearing skimpy, sequined outfits and doing high kicks. Omar swallowed his first shot and studied the women. One caught his eye.

Mia.

Elbows on the table, he held his face in his hands, watching her through his fingers. From the look on her face, she was enjoying herself. See? The people of Glenrock liked living here. But watching Mia made him feel ill. The way they had dressed her...

Relationships aren't exclusive here, Bel had said. Is that what Mia would discover? Would she fall for some entertainer, then be cast aside when he became interested in someone else? Is that what Omar was supposed to do? Look for someone else?

He didn't want anyone else. He wanted Belbeline.

The Regal Lounge had a hitroom, so Omar went upstairs and set his PV on the counter. The barkeep was speaking with a blonde woman at the far end of the bar. She had skin that glittered like gold.

"Brown sugar four, plain," the woman said.

The barkeep took her PV and paused in front of Omar. "Know what you want?"

"I'll have the same," Omar said, tossing his jacket on the stool on his left. "And a black velvet."

The barkeep set a SimTag pad on the counter, and Omar tapped his fist.

The woman got up and moved to the stool on Omar's right. "You a sweet tooth for brown sugar too, baby face?"

"Naw," Omar said, clueless as to what she was referring to. "But it turns out I need to try some new things."

The woman traced her sparkling gold finger up along the lines of his SimArt tattoo. "What kinds of things?"

He glanced at her and met a set of eyes that were golden brown. "All things."

Omar and the woman, whose name turned out to be Lexanna, relocated to a set of pillowy chairs, reclining on either side of a small table where the barkeep set their PVs.

When Lexanna leaned over and kissed him, he wanted to cry. He didn't know this woman, and he didn't want to know her. He pretended she was Bel for a few minutes, but that just made him feel pathetic. Plus, she was getting gold glitter all over his uniform. He broke away and inhaled a long drag on his PV. Nausea gripped him. He held his breath and let his head fall back on the chair. What in all the lands was brown sugar, anyway? And why would anyone want to feel sick like—

A sudden rush of velvety euphoria sent tingles swirling over Omar's body, a powerful, yet completely peaceful feeling. He was sitting on the top of a hill in a white haze. He could see the silhouettes of people around him, and while they were unrecognizable, he knew it was Levi, Belbeline, and his father. They swam through the haze on the top of that hill, trying to reach one another but not really caring if they ever did. In fact, nothing mattered at all now. This was a safe place. Like being inside one of his paintings.

Lexanna spoke, but Omar didn't comprehend her words. Or maybe he did but forgot what she'd said. All he wanted to do was be on that hill.

The feeling faded a bit, so Omar took another long breath through his vaporizer. His stomach clenched against the nausea, but this time he waited for it to pass, waiting for…

Euphoria drenched him again. He closed his eyes, doubting he could have kept them open even if he'd wanted to. He was standing on the roof of a building, the wind blowing hard against him. He leaned into it until he was parallel to the ground, the wind so strong it held him there.

Strong.

But he wasn't on a roof. He was in the hitroom of the Regal Lounge with Lexanna. His body felt hot, melting almost, from the inside out. He felt his head droop until his chin nearly touched his chest. He must look asleep. And maybe he was, nodding in and out of sleep. It was a nice feeling. No guilt. No loneliness.

Until Lexanna started talking again, pulling on his arms, slapping him. He kept his eyes closed, wishing she'd go away, wanting to tell her to leave him alone.

There was a man's voice and the sensation of standing. Someone shook his arms. Bright lights. Movement. More people he didn't recognize, looking at him, talking to him.

Mason?

Omar awoke in a white room under glaring lights. He was wearing a white dress. Something beeped. His arm itched. A small needle was taped just below the inside of his elbow. It had a hose attached to it that ran up to a bag of liquid hanging on a stand.

Was this the medical center?

His mouth was dry; his lips felt cracked; his body hurt all over, a dull, heavy ache in his nerves. He scanned the room for his vaporizer but didn't see it. A quick taste would ease his discomfort. Why had they taken it away? He needed it.

Someone passed down the hallway outside the open door to his room.

"Hey!" He reached out and noticed that his hands were coated in gold glitter.

A woman stepped through the doorway. An angel, white and glowing with sapphire eyes. Eyes like Belbeline's. "Good!" she said, leaning against the doorframe. "You're awake."

Not Belbeline. A blonde. A medic. "Why am I here?"

"You OD'd," the angel said. "And since you were in uniform, they brought you to me."

Omar frowned. "OD?"

"Overdose. Too much. Your body couldn't handle what you put in it."

Omar bristled at the insinuation he was weak. "Really? It felt good."

The medic gave him a one-sided grin. "It usually does the first time or two. If I were you, I'd quit while I was still alive. There are much safer poisons." She glanced out the door. "Someone wants to see you." She pushed off the doorway and left.

Let it be Belbeline, sick with worry and begging his forgiveness.

But seconds later, Mason appeared, looking clean in a turquoise medic outfit, hair neatly combed. "Hey, brother," Mason said. "Glad to see you up. You've been trying the vaporizers?"

Mason tasking as a medic — figured. "Yeah, I have." *And you can't control me, Mason, so don't try.*

Mason walked up to Omar's bedside and examined the bag of fluid. "Which stims? Do you even know?"

Mason's tone filled Omar with a rush of anger. "Do *you*? I'm not stupid, Mason."

Mason tipped back his head and smiled. "Right. I forgot how you planned all this and got half our village killed. Good one, Omar. Brilliant, really. My favorite part was when you almost killed yourself too."

"Are you just going to stand here and lecture me?"

"A little, yes. So you're trying the PVs and drinking. And what about women, Omar? Have you been intimate with women too?"

"Why's any of this your business?"

"You have the thin plague, Omar. You're infected."

Nausea rolled in Omar's stomach. He fought to keep his features even, calm. "So give me the cure."

Mason coughed out a half laugh. "You know very well there's no cure, brother. That's why we're all here. Thanks to you. But it's a slow death, if that makes you feel better."

"Why are you being so mean?"

Mason winced, as if thinking it through. "Papa Eli used to say, 'A person becomes wise by watching what happens to himself when he's a fool.' I love you Omar, and I can't let you do this to yourself. You've made some really bad choices. But now you have the chance to become very wise — if you learn from your experiences." He patted Omar's leg and left.

Omar lay back on the bed, exhausted, longing for the peace he'd felt last night in a breath of brown sugar. Especially now that he knew he'd contracted a death sentence. He cursed and wondered if the task director general knew his girl had the plague. Belbeline was so beautiful, and she used those body paints that made her skin smooth. But of course, she was infected. They all were. Their dying nation was the main reason they'd talked Omar into helping them. Well, as the task director had predicted, he wasn't very useful to the Safe Lands anymore, was he?

He never *had* been very useful.

Omar wanted his PV. Now. Would Mason return it when he left the medical center? If not, he'd just buy a new one. He was dying anyway. No reason to suffer more than necessary, right? In fact, the sooner he could numb himself, the better.

CHAPTER 28

Mason slipped the CompuChart into the slot beside the door of exam room two and peeked into Ciddah's office. "Exam two is ready."

"Thanks," she said.

Mason walked toward reception to see if Rimola had any new arrivals for him to check in. He stopped when he heard her talking with someone at the front desk.

"You're one of the new outsiders?" Rimola asked.

"Yes," a female voice said.

"Good. None of us know what to do with the male conscript they sent us, Mason Elias. He's so raven we can't breathe, and he won't flirt with anyone. It's *so* prude."

Mason slowed his steps. He was prudish?

"In fact," Rimola went on, "he's the prudest dish I've ever met. The things he says! It's like he's talking in another language."

"Yes," the mystery woman said. "I know exactly what you mean."

Mason recognized the voice. Jemma! Suddenly his feet couldn't move fast enough.

Jemma was standing on the other side of Rimola's desk. Her eyes flashed wide, and a smile stretched across her face. "Mason!" She ran around the desk and wrapped him in a hug.

He stiffened, not used to such physical affection. "How is Shaylinn?"

Jemma released him. "Better than I would be. She said you guys had a nice talk. Thank you for being so kind to her."

His cheeks flushed, and he looked at the floor. "I wish I could have done something to — "

"Is there somewhere private we can talk?" Jemma asked.

Mason glanced at the enforcer sitting in the waiting room. Why had Jemma come? She had no appointment. Rimola was tapping on her GlassTop, her eyebrows lifted as a sign of her intention to eavesdrop. Mason took Jemma's sleeve and pulled her down the hallway.

"Where are you going?" Rimola called after them.

"We'll be right back," Mason said.

He led Jemma to the end of the hall. When he was sure no one had seen them, he opened the supply closet door and flipped on the light. Jemma followed him inside and pushed the door shut behind her, bumping Mason so that he almost fell backward over the mop bucket. He grabbed the shelf to catch himself.

"Here." She pulled a wadded-up trash bag out of her purse and thrust it into his arms. "It's from Levi. A two-way radio. I have one too. He said you'll have to wait until he calls you."

Mason's heart leapt at the thought of speaking with Levi. He wrapped the excess bag around the radio until it was a small roll and tucked it under the supply shelf so that it was completely invisible. "No one should find it there. Where'd you put yours?"

"Under my mattress."

"Take care, Jemma. There are cameras everywhere."

"Not in my bedroom. But if Levi doesn't get us out soon, I'm going to have to plan an escape. Kendall and Naomi don't have much time."

"It's too dangerous," Mason said. "And what about the others? How will — "

The door flew open. Jemma screamed.

Ciddah stood in the doorway and stared at them. "What are you doing in here?"

Mason started talking without thinking. "Exam room two needs a fresh gown, but Jemma came and needed, uh ..." He lost his train of thought.

"Mason was just showing me where he works," Jemma said. "Then he was going to refill my prescription. I broke one of the vials."

"Mason doesn't fill prescriptions," Ciddah said. "I do."

"That's what I was telling her." Mason grabbed Jemma's sleeve and pulled her out the door, cursing his stupidity and hoping Ciddah didn't decide to search the supply closet.

Ciddah's footsteps clicked behind them, but Mason didn't dare look back. They made it halfway back to the reception desk when Ciddah spoke.

"I'd like to speak with you and your femme in my office, now, Mason."

He took a deep breath and led Jemma into Ciddah's office.

"Messy in here," Jemma whispered.

Ciddah brushed past them to stand behind her desk. Mason couldn't look at her, for fear of the expression clouding her face. Granted, it *had* looked bad.

"The Safe Lands Guild does not oppose pair-ups during breaks, but only when approved by the office task director. And I *never* approve of physical displays of affection in this office. People who come ... many have miscarried. They don't need to feel worse about their situations because of your carelessness."

"Doctor, Mason and I are not ... romantic," Jemma said as if the idea was ridiculous, which, he supposed, it was. "We grew up together. I'm engaged to marry Mason's brother Levi. I'm sorry we didn't ask permission before he gave me a tour."

"I see." Ciddah's posture relaxed. "Thank you for your honesty. It may interest you to know that the man called Levi was brought here a few days ago for a broken nose. He'll recover. But he was taken to the

RC for assaulting an enforcer, and he received a second X. Forgive me if my words are harsh, but if he were my lifer, I'd want to know."

If Jemma had seen Levi, she must have known all this. Still, tears pooled in her eyes and she said, "'I am not afraid of storms, for I am learning how to sail my ship.'"

"Yes, well, if you'll excuse me, I have a patient waiting." Ciddah walked around her desk and held open her office door. Mason and Jemma walked out, and Ciddah followed, closing the door behind them. "If you leave your information with the receptionist, I can have your new prescription delivered to the harem this afternoon."

"Thank you," Jemma said.

Ciddah glanced at Mason then stepped across the hall and entered exam room two.

"Wow." Jemma elbowed Mason. "She *really* likes you."

Jemma's statement set off fireworks in Mason's head.

"No access?" Ciddah tapped on the GlassTop, her fingernails clicking with each stroke. "I can't access the history files either. That's so strange. Why would they hide them from people anyway? Are you even listening?"

"Yes." She was annoyed now. Ever since Jemma had confirmed Ciddah's affection for Mason, he had been overanalyzing everything she said and did.

They were alone in the History Center, which took up the entire third floor of the Treasury Building. It reminded him of the libraries in Old movies the scavengers had found. There were rows of shelves filled with books, real books that were not allowed to leave the room. But he and Ciddah were sitting at one of a dozen GlassTop desks that were around the perimeter wall, and the glow from their screens was brighter than any bulb on the ceiling.

"I have questions of my own that I want answers to," Ciddah said.

"It's clear I can't trust Lawten. I can't trust anyone. I should never have agreed to any of this. I knew better!"

She was mumbling now, talking to herself. Mason watched her. The attraction he felt toward her was making him irrational. He'd never shared such stimulating conversations with anyone. But if she were to declare her affection, what would he do? She was a Safe Lander. There could be nothing romantic between them. He'd rather have her friendship than risk her avoiding him because he had to reject her.

He didn't think he could reject her.

His heart started up again. What would he do if she said something? How would he respond? There was far too much risk in all of this. Risk of rejection and loss. Risk of infection like Omar.

Ciddah looked at him. Their eyes met, and Mason felt awkward.

"Why are you staring at me?" she asked.

Why indeed? He looked away. *Completely irrational.*

"What's the matter with you?"

He was a logical prude, right? Well, he could provide her with a logical answer. "I'm sorry," he said. "I was thinking about the women. The task director found an uninfected donor from another location."

Ciddah laid her hand on his thigh. "I'm sorry this is so difficult."

Her touch and sympathetic words confused and thrilled him, and he fought to keep focus. "I wonder why he complied. Was he blackmailed in some way?"

"Maybe he hates his life in Wyoming. Maybe he's simply more open-minded about saving lives."

That statement was like cold water; they'd already had this discussion. It would be enjoyable to debate it again, yet here was the perfect opportunity to discourage her affection. Mason picked up the notebook he'd been compiling his theories in and stood.

Ciddah stood with him. "Where are you going?"

"Home." Mason started across the darkened room toward the elevator. As much as he loved being in her presence, it would be a relief to put distance between them tonight.

"Why are you being like this?" Ciddah asked.

He turned back and found her right behind him. "Like what?"

"You owe me your theories," she said. "It's not my fault I don't have access to the files. I kept my side of the bargain by coming tonight."

"A valid point."

She took his hand and tugged him back to his chair. "Why did you decide to study medicine?"

"I thought you wanted to hear my theories. Why are you changing the subject?"

Ciddah pushed out her bottom lip. "I want to understand you better. Please?"

Her expression made him chuckle. Why did she have to be so alluring? He sat back down. He should return to his apartment, turn on the radio, and listen for Levi, not linger here with Ciddah Rourke.

"I never liked killing, but I was born into the Elias tribe, and the Elias tribe are hunters. My friend Joel, he wanted to be a hunter more than anything and often tagged along on hunting trips. One day, the men set out to track a bear. Joel wanted to go. Wanted me to come too. I refused. But I loaned him my gun because it was a better weapon."

Mason's pulse was too high. Why was he telling her this in so much detail?

"Something happened?" Ciddah asked.

Indeed. "Yes. An accident. Joel's gun — my gun — backfired." Irrational. He was out of control around this girl. The logical thing to do would be to protect his own mental state and pride by fleeing.

"I'm so sorry." Ciddah squeezed his hand.

He made himself pull away. "People who lose a loved one, Ciddah … it's hard to get over. Feelings run deep. I don't want Shaylinn to have that pain." Which reminded him of his theories. Omar must be Shaylinn's donor. Unless it was the man from Wyoming. "Why do they take babies away from their mothers? Have they always done this?"

"As far as I know."

Perhaps this is why Ciddah was so moody and insecure. "One of the first textbooks I read was a child psychology book. Did you know that when a child is born, it needs to bond with its mother, and the sooner the better? Studies of Old showed that babies who bonded with their mothers were more secure in life and had better relationships with others as adults."

"Our children seem to get along together just fine."

More facts poured into his brain. "Infected women should avoid narcotics and alcohol. They burden an already weak immune system. Everyone I see seems to be vaping. They're only killing themselves faster."

Ciddah rubbed her eyes. "Thank you, O wizened one."

"Wait—you know this? Then why don't you do something about it?"

"It's not that easy, Mason," Ciddah said. "Our way of life . . . people like it."

"You could at least let the women know that drugs and alcohol are bad for them."

"I do. They know. And I've reminded many. Some women do avoid stimulants. But it's never made any difference. People are just trying to enjoy this life and get to the next one with as much good fortune as they can earn."

Fortune indeed. "'For it is by grace you have been saved, through faith.'"

Ciddah fought a smile. "That's, um, lovely. What's it mean?"

"That you can't earn your way to heaven—or Bliss. It's what I believe."

She leaned back in her chair and folded her arms. "Now wait a minute. You just said you became a doctor out of guilt for the death of your friend. It sounds like you're trying to earn fortune, just like the rest of us."

Her comment rocked Mason to his bones. *Was* he obsessed with works? He'd never meant to be. He thought of the lies Shaylinn believed. Was he punishing himself for Joel's death? Serving a life of penance? "Sometimes it's not easy to live out your faith."

"Then why bother?"

"Because I believe there's only one life before eternity. Not ten."

"Nine," Ciddah said. "The tenth life is eternity in Bliss."

Ah, the tenth life. "I'm sorry, but that begs the question, how do you explain transmigration along with your population decrease?"

"Excuse me?"

"When your people die and those souls are transferred to new bodies for new lives, wouldn't there be a shortage of bodies? Where do all the souls stay while they wait?"

"I don't . . ." Ciddah scowled at him. "Why are you always arguing with me?"

She was upset again. "*Argue* is the wrong word choice, Ciddah. There is no anger or frustration involved. I'm simply trying to help by pointing out where your logic is flawed."

"You're trying to help me by criticizing me?"

This was pointless. His goal in coming here tonight had been to get Ciddah's assistance in accessing the medical history of the Safe Lands. If she couldn't help him, Lawten had never intended to allow Mason to learn anything here. Though why the task director had made the offer at all, Mason still didn't understand. "I'll see you tomorrow."

"Wait. Do you want to share a taxi? I live in the Westwall too."

She did? And how did she know where he lived? He'd never said. "Not tonight, no."

But as Mason sat alone in the taxi, riding back to the Westwall — Ciddah's face and smell and touch heavy on his mind — all he could think of was *Come back, come back, so that I may gaze upon your beauty!*

She was the wrong woman for him in so many ways, but the words still rang in his head.

Come back.

Once Mason was home, he turned the two-way radio to channel four and set it on his kitchen counter. He watched TV for a bit and had nodded off when he heard Levi's voice.

"This is Jackrabbit with a call out to Eagle Eyes. Do you copy?"

Mason scrambled to get up from the couch and grabbed the two-way radio off the counter. "This is Eagle Eyes. I copy. Over."

"Eagle Eyes, you beautiful bird, you. Where you been?"

"Tasking mostly. The experience has been both fascinating and discouraging."

"I hear you, brother. This place is like that. Look, I want you to take a walk tomorrow morning at nine. There's a place where you and Jem and Mother would have spent a lot of time. A big place. Behind that place is a cactus. Wait for a ride out front."

"Can you confirm that, Jackrabbit? A cactus? Over."

"Affirmative. Don't worry, you won't get pricked. Well, yes, you will, actually."

A cactus? Levi's riddles were never that difficult to solve. Mason tapped his forehead. A place he and Jemma and their mother would have spent a lot of time? The hospital, of course. Ah yes. There was a restaurant behind the hospital called the Green Cactus Grill. "Understood, Jackrabbit," Mason said. "I'll visit the cactus at nine tomorrow morning."

"Mad good. Oh, and Eagle Eyes? Stay calm. It'll only hurt for a moment."

Hurt? Mason hoped he wasn't going to get stunned. "Copy that, Jackrabbit. Over and out."

CHAPTER 29

Levi parked his truck at the Department of Public Tasks and went into the garage to get more bags. He'd been looking over his shoulder since he left the Larkspur, anxious about seeing Jordan and Mason. When were Bender's people going to show?

Levi had talked to Jemma for hours on the two-way radio the past two nights. Being able to hear her voice on a regular basis made things seem almost normal. He opened the cupboard that held the trash bags and pulled one out.

"Hey, Levi!" Dayle called from his office. "Come on in here a minute, will you?"

Levi wrapped a half-dozen trash bags around his arm to keep them from slipping all over the place and walked into Dayle's office, which was a closet-like room at the end of the garage.

Dayle waved him around to his side of the desk. Once Levi was standing beside Dayle's chair, Dayle tapped his finger against his computer screen. It showed a picture of the empty garage. Dayle hit a key—on an antique keyboard Levi hadn't noticed before. The screen blinked but kept the same image ... until Levi saw himself leave Dayle's office and walk out the garage doors and into the light of day.

Whoa! "How'd you do that?"

"Bender thought it best if we do your meeting here. All my guys are out on jobs, so we've got at least two hours."

A chill ran up Levi's arms. "You work for Bender?"

"For Bender ... *with* Bender ... Bender tasks for me. There's really no boss now that Lonn is in the RC. We all just keep doing our part."

He looked Dayle over. Could this be a trap? "You're not wearing gloves."

"I still have my SimTag in place. Not all of us can live underground."

"How do I know you're telling me the truth? You could be an enforcer."

Dayle folded his arms behind his head and leaned back in his chair, displaying his brightly colored arm tattoos. "Why don't you go ask *him*?" He nodded at the open doorway.

Levi peeked out. A black car had pulled into the garage. Levi ran out of Dayle's office just as Bender climbed out of the driver's seat and smoothed out his jacket. He was dressed like some fancy businessman, but the scar over his eye made him look like an Old mobster. What did Levi know? Maybe Bender was a new kind of mobster.

"You got Jordan and Mason with you?" Levi asked, looking toward the car.

"They're coming in a different vehicle."

"So what's the plan?" Why had Bender come out of hiding for Levi's meeting?

"That's what I need to decide, outsider. And it all depends on you."

The sniper thing. "I can't kill anyone," Levi said. "At least not premeditated."

Bender sighed and leaned against the back of the car. "I'm sorry to hear that."

Levi didn't like the guy's tone. He also didn't trust Bender not to call off bringing Jordan and Mason to see him. "But I've been thinking," Levi said. "I can cut the power to the Highlands. Then you and your people can swoop in to rescue Lonn while the cameras are off."

Bender looked skeptical. "And how are you going to cut the power?"

"With my rifle. Shoot out the transformers."

"You can do that?"

"Yep. That's my diversion plan for when I get the Glenrock women out of the harem. But I'm not particular on when I do it, so long as it's soon. I could time it with Lonn's liberation ceremony."

Bender pushed off the back of the car and walked toward Levi. "Take Zane with you when you enact your plan, and you've got a deal."

"Fine by me."

Bender clapped his hands and laughed. "Lonn is coming home!"

Levi sat on the hood of a DPT truck, alone in the garage, and watched a black torpedo car pull inside. Dayle and Bender were in Dayle's office, talking business Levi hadn't been invited to hear. Fine with him. With Dayle's pre-recorded footage being fed into the system, the enforcer's surveillance cameras could see nothing of what was really transpiring at the Department of Public Tasks today.

Once the garage door had shut all the way, the driver got out. It was Rewl. He was wearing his Highlands Public Tasks jumpsuit. He smirked Levi's way and opened the back door.

" — sagging piece of cow liver!"

The sound of Jordan's voice made Levi chuckle. Zane got out of the passenger's seat, and together he and Rewl dragged Jordan out.

Rewl then helped Mason out of the car as well. The sight of Jordan and Mason with sacks over their heads amused Levi almost as much as the contrast in their behavior. Mason wore a bluish-green outfit that looked like Old pajamas, and stood like a statue just where Rewl had left him. Jordan wore a black and red uniform from the Grand Lodge. They'd taped his wrists together. He knocked his elbow into Rewl's gut and tried to pull away. Rewl pushed him, and Jordan stumbled to a stop in the middle of the garage.

"Pulling a knife on *me*? You maggot-kissing, beetle! Cutting *me*?"

"He's wrapped tighter than a cabaret corset," Rewl said. "I'm done." He walked into Dayle's office and, apparently, was allowed inside.

Zane came to stand beside the front of the truck. He handed Levi two sets of gloves: a black pair like Levi's and a brown pair. "Brown for the medic. But he's going to have to do something else when he tasks. Wrap his hand in a bandage or something. He can't wear these in the SC."

Levi set the gloves on the hood and jumped down. "Jordan!" He walked up to Jordan and patted his back. "I'm going to take this sack off."

"*Levi!* Argh!" Jordan kneed Levi's thigh and tried to head butt him.

Levi just laughed and backed out of the way. "I'll leave it on if you don't play nice."

Jordan fell onto his knees, his head sagging down to his chest. "Come on, Levi! Some guy put a bag on my head and cut up my hand. What would you do?"

"He cut out your SimTag so the enforcers can't know where you are. Sorry they didn't explain first." Levi took Mason's pillowcase off first. "How are you feeling, brother?"

"Fine." Mason narrowed his eyes. "But you look terrible. You never had anyone fix your nose?"

Levi shrugged and grinned. "Haven't had time."

"*Levi!*" Jordan's tone oozed with frustration.

"*All right.*" Levi darted behind Jordan, pulled off his pillowcase, and snapped it at Jordan's back.

Jordan twisted around still on his knees. "How come Mason isn't taped up?"

"Because Mason isn't an angry mule. Calm down. We don't have much time."

Jordan hopped to his feet, hands still taped behind his back. He sucked in a deep breath that made his shoulders look huge, then blew it out in a growl. "I'm calm."

"Zane, can you cut his bindings?" Levi asked.

"If you're sure. If he lashes out, it's on you." Zane pulled a knife from his pocket and walked slowly toward Jordan, creeping as if approaching a bear. "Easy now, shell boy, I'm not going to hurt you."

Jordan shot Zane a dirty look. "Shut up, maggot."

Zane straightened, then cut through the tape on Jordan's wrists.

Jordan jumped on Levi, tucked Levi's head under his arm and squeezed. Levi tried to pull back, but Jordan had him. Of all the immature ...

"You want to go back to rehab, brother? Lose your visits with Naomi? Time to be serious. Let go!"

Jordan obeyed, and his voice became mopey. "Those rat-eating maggots make me talk to her through a window. I can't even touch my own wife."

"At least you're both still living," Mason said. "And healthy."

Levi straightened his jumpsuit and brushed a hand through his hair. "We're going to get her out, Jordan. We're going to free the women on July first, during Lonn's liberation."

"Really?" Zane said. "How you going to do that?"

"I'm going to kill the power in the city. You're coming with me, Zane."

Zane grinned and the rings on his bottom lip spread apart. "Sounds like a stimming adventure."

"But what about Kendall?" Mason said. "She's scheduled to deliver on Monday."

This Kendall girl wasn't Levi's concern. "Nothing I can do about that. So here's how it's going to work: Zane and I will take the storm drains to shoot out the transformer. Mason, when the power goes out, I need you to get the women. Bender's people will get you a van or something. You'll drive them to the back of the Bradbury, which is between the Gamble House and that BabyKakes bakery. Take a walk over there to check it out so you know what you're doing. Get some cupcakes. They're good."

"What do I do?" Jordan asked.

"You're going to meet Mason and lead the women through the storm drains to some underground bunker that Bender's setting up. That way Mason can take back the van and keep his cover."

"If we're escaping, why do I need a cover?" Mason asked.

"We have no way to get the kids yet. So you need to stay where you are. Look like a proper Safe Lands national."

"If our women escape, they'll know I had something to do with it."

"They'll suspect you did — that's why you need an alibi. Think you can get one? Maybe the doctor? Jemma says she likes you."

"A girl likes Mason?" Jordan cackled.

Mason's face paled. He looked like he might puke. "I'll think of something."

"Good. Call me on the radio. They monitor the Wyndos," Levi said. "My only concern is that once the women are free, they might put the children in the RC."

"Not the RC, but they'll be guarding them for sure," Mason said. "Still, I don't see another option. We won't know the results of Shaylinn's procedure for a few more days, but we can't risk waiting for — "

"What procedure?" Jordan asked. "What happened to my sister?"

Mason shook his head. "If we don't do this now, it'll be too late for the other women."

"Too late is not an option," Levi said.

"I'm still not sure how we'll get out," Jemma said over the radio. "Even without the power, there will still be enforcers in the hallways."

"You have to think of a way," Levi told her. He was lying on his bed in the Larkspur, staring at the ceiling. It was late Saturday night. Levi had spent the early evening with Jordan, Zane, and Rewl, slogging through storm drains between the Highlands and the Midlands, so that Jordan could learn how to get the women to Bender's underground bunker.

"I'll try. You know, 'It's all very well to read about sorrows and imagine yourself living through them heroically, but it's not so nice when you really come to have them, is it?' "

"No, Jem, it's not."

Levi's Wyndo started to sing a techno beat. He sat up and grabbed it from his bedside table. Red's picture covered the screen. He tapped it. "Hello?"

"I'm out in front of the Larkspur," Red said, as if she was stuck inside the glass. "Bender needs you. Come on out."

Levi checked the time on his mirror clock — 1:34 a.m. "Now?"

"Yes, now. And wear something normal, shell." She disconnected.

Static fuzzed on the radio. "Levi? Are you there?"

He pressed the talk button. "Yeah, but I've got to go, Buttercup. Bender needs me."

"Be careful. 'All my heart is yours, it belongs to you.'"

He smiled. "I'll take good care of your heart. I promise."

Levi put on his Old jeans and one of the fresh white tank tops from his backpack. He doubted that was what Red had meant by normal, but it was normal for him. It was a little chilly when he got outside, and he wished he had his leather jacket.

He found Red sitting on the hood of a black car in the parking lot. She was wearing what looked like a black towel, lacy fingerless gloves that likely held her SimTag, and clunky shoes with heels as long as Levi's hand.

"Aren't you cold?" he asked.

"Aren't you?" She slid off the hood and opened the driver's door. "Get in."

Levi climbed into the passenger seat. "So where are we going?"

Red started the car and drove out of the lot. "A club called the Savoy. Our mission tonight is to be seen together. One of my contacts, Nash, who tasks on the ColorCast gets jealous. Bender needs a few more details about Lonn's liberation and thinks I can get them from Nash."

"I don't like it," Levi said. "What if the guy jumps me? I can't afford another X."

"Nash won't hit you. He'll just buy me a drink and ask me to ditch you."

"Then how do I get home?"

"Take a cab."

Great. "Why didn't Bender mention this earlier?"

"He won't always tell you everything, shell."

Levi wanted to tell Red to eat dirt and Bender to feed it to her. He didn't appreciate such beckon-and-call moments. And he didn't trust Red. But until his people were freed, what choice did he have?

Red drove them into the Highlands and parked the car. While they waited to get into the Savoy, Red fluffed her hair, took some kind of purple makeup crayon out of her cleavage, and drew the color on her lips. She handed it to Levi. "Hold this for me?"

"What's wrong with putting it back in your . . . ?" He motioned to her chest.

"It will fall out when we're dancing. You've got baggy pockets."

"Fine." Levi pocketed the crayon.

When they finally got inside, it was like some kind of torture chamber. Dark, hazy, with blinding bluish-white lights flickering from the ceiling. Bodies everywhere, packed in and wiggling like they all had to pee. Deafening noise with a steady thumping rhythm and a wailing voice that needed to be put out of its misery filled the space, all masquerading as music. Madness. *Give me a grassy clearing and the Glenrock women singing any day over this.*

Red took Levi's hand and dragged him through the wiggling bodies. She stopped in the center of the mob and slid her arms around his waist, tucking her hands into his back pockets. He grabbed her arms and pulled them out.

She yelled into his ear. "We have to look like we're together."

"We are together." He couldn't believe how he had to scream just to be heard.

"Like we're pairing up." She moved in close and ran her hands over his chest. "Like you want me."

With Red this close, Levi's view revealed way too much. "I'm not comfortable with — "

"There he is! Dance with me." She pressed against Levi, rocking her body against his.

Levi reached up and grabbed his hair, anything to keep his hands off this crazy woman. He squinted at the flickering faces around him, looking for a man who might be watching them.

"You have to *dance*, shell!" Red pulled Levi's arms down and around her waist.

Levi felt exposed and embarrassed standing in this crowd with a half-naked woman rubbing up on him like a bear scratching on a tree. She was both repulsive and alluring.

Too long, they danced. Too much, Red touched him. And when she pressed up onto her toes to try and kiss him, he turned and left the dance floor to get far away. He made it all the way outside before she caught up with him.

"What was that about?" she yelled.

"I'm done. I don't care about your mission. Call Zane to be your scratching post."

Red's eyes glinted, her face sallow under the lights of the Savoy sign. "I can't. Nash knows Zane."

"If Nash isn't jealous by now, he never will be."

She shot him a nasty glare. "What do you know?"

"I know I'm going to take my cab now."

"Bender will hear about this, shell."

Levi considered that. But Bender had understood about Jemma and had told Red to leave Levi alone. "I'll explain the situation to Bender." It was worth it to get away from the temptation Red's roaming hands had awakened in him. He took a cab back to his apartment in the Midlands, but it was hours before he managed to fall asleep.

CHAPTER 30

"Jemma?"

Shaylinn opened her eyes. She lay in her bed in the harem, and when she looked over to the clock it read 2:12 a.m.

"Jemma?" Kendall's voice called out in the hall. "I think the baby is coming."

Shaylinn sat up, slid off her bed, and searched her floor for something to wear.

"Did your water break?" Jemma asked.

"I don't think so. How will I know?"

"You'll know."

Shaylinn pulled on a pair of stretchy pants under her nightgown and ran across the hall to Jemma's room. Kendall was sitting on the edge of Jemma's bed, her face pinched, gripping her belly with both hands.

Jemma held the radio to her mouth. "Buttercup to Jackrabbit. Come in." She looked to Shaylinn. "Go fetch Naomi and Mia and tell them to come here."

"But what are we going to — ?"

"Shh. Go, quickly." Jemma tried the radio again. "Jackrabbit, are you there?"

Shaylinn slipped out the door and woke Naomi, but Mia's room was empty. That girl was likely out with Rand again. Shaylinn had no idea how Mia had managed to talk Ewan into helping her. She was just thankful not to be a part of it.

Naomi was already in Jemma's room when Shaylinn got back. "Mia isn't here."

Jemma closed her eyes and sighed. "Fine."

"Mason then?" Shaylinn said. Jemma nodded and spoke into the radio. "Buttercup to Eagle Eyes, come in." She clutched the radio to her chest. The four of them remained frozen: Jemma sitting up in bed, Shaylinn standing just inside the doorway, Kendall sitting on the foot of Jemma's bed, Naomi standing beside her, rubbing her shoulders.

Kendall suddenly moaned and rolled forward, clutching her belly. The sound scared Shaylinn, and she hugged her own stomach, wondering if life was growing inside her.

"What are we going to do?" Naomi whispered.

"I don't know," Jemma said. "Shay, go fetch Aunt Chipeta. She'll be able to help."

"Just tap them," Kendall said.

Shaylinn ran back to her room, happy to get away from Kendall's pain. She found her Wyndo on the floor beside her bed and brought up Jemma's aunt's picture. It rang and rang and rang before a sleepy Chipeta answered.

"Shaylinn? Is something wrong?"

"Kendall is in labor. Jemma wants you all to come to our suite."

"Oh, dear. We'll be right there."

Shaylinn sat for a moment to catch her breath. She set her hand against her abdomen; something told her there was life inside even though she didn't feel any different. The peace she'd had the day of the surgery fled, and fear gripped her like the bite of an electric gun. She didn't want to have a baby, and she didn't want any pain. But if she was going to have a baby, she really didn't want anyone to take her baby away.

Her Wyndo vibrated in her hand. She tapped Chipeta's image. "Hello?"

"Come let us in!" Chipeta said.

Shaylinn ran to the front door and opened it. The women filed inside and went to Jemma's bedroom. Aunt Mary gave Shaylinn a hug.

"No one is answering my calls!" Jemma said.

"Then we need to leave on our own," Chipeta said.

"Where's Mia?" Jennifer asked.

"She snuck out again," Shaylinn said.

"Please," Kendall said. "I don't want any of you to get into trouble. Let's call Ciddah."

"No." Jemma threw back her covers and got out of bed. "We'll just have to deal with this ourselves. There is no way I'm letting them take Kendall to the hospital, not when they'll take her child away." She squared her shoulders. "I know Levi had a plan, but I think we should try to leave the harem tonight. Even if it's only to hide somewhere until Kendall's baby is born."

"We'll get caught if we try to escape with her," Naomi said. "The cameras are everywhere."

"We could try and go out through the kitchen," Shaylinn said.

Jemma stepped into a pair of shoes. "What do you mean?"

"The night Mia and I snuck out, we went through the kitchen," Shaylinn said. "Stairs back there lead to a big garage in the back of the harem."

"Are there cameras?" Naomi asked.

"Ewan said there weren't."

"If you're determined to do this, we'll need to split up," Chipeta said. "You young girls will go Shaylinn's way. Us older women will go out the front, create a diversion just in case Ewan was wrong about the cameras."

Jennifer folded her arms. "I'm not leaving without Mia."

"We won't actually get away, Jennifer," Chipeta said. "They'll catch us."

"But what if they don't? What if we get away and Mia comes back and we've left her?" She shook her head. "I'm not leaving my daughter."

"I'll stay with Jennifer," Aunt Mary said.

"We should leave the radio with you, in case we do get away," Jemma said.

"No!" Aunt Mary said. "How will you reach Levi or Mason without it? Besides, it will be my turn to visit the Surrogacy Center soon enough. We can speak with Mason there."

Another painful moan from Kendall silenced any further discussion. Chipeta planned to give the girls a five-minute head start, in case there was an enforcer outside the harem's front door. Everyone exchanged hugs and kisses, then Shaylinn, Kendall, Jemma, and Naomi each filled a pillowcase with belongings and crept downstairs. Shaylinn had packed her favorite new dresses, though if she were pregnant, she doubted they would fit much longer.

Shaylinn led them across the main sitting room, hoping and praying this would work. When she reached the kitchen door, she pushed it open just a crack. It was dark inside. Jemma entered and held the door for Kendall and Naomi. The light above the stove and the green emergency exit sign gave them enough light to see. Shaylinn led them through the exit door and into the stairwell.

When the door closed behind them, their surroundings were pitch black. Shaylinn fumbled in her pillowcase until she located the Wyndo. She tapped the glass and it lit up, illuminating the stairwell with a dull gray glow.

Shaylinn took the stairs slowly, trying to be quiet, but the scuffing of their shoes over the concrete steps seemed terribly loud and convinced her that an enforcer would catch them any moment.

Kendall stopped and cried out, and the sound seemed twice as loud in the confined space.

Jemma ran to her side. "Another contraction?"

Kendall nodded. Several strands of her tangled brown hair were sticking to her flushed cheeks. "I don't like it."

Jemma sucked in a wincing breath. "Shaylinn, what time is it?"

Shaylinn glanced at the time on her Wyndo. "Two thirty-three."

"Be sure and tell me when the next one happens, Kendall," Jemma said.

"I'm sure you'll know." Kendall limped a few steps, stopped, and whimpered.

Jemma hooked Kendall's arm with hers. "We'll wait until you're ready."

Kendall's lips pressed into a thin line. "I'm ready."

They continued down the stairs very slowly. Shaylinn braced herself for another outburst from Kendall, but it didn't happen. They reached the bottom without meeting anyone. Maybe this would be simple. Maybe there was truly no one up at this hour. Maybe the enforcers had never thought of guarding this door or putting cameras in this place.

She peeked through the door at the bottom of the stairwell, saw no one, and led the girls into the warehouse, keeping close to the wall. Only a few lights were on, making the room appear to be lit by a full moon. The air smelled oddly of cardboard boxes. Shaylinn put the Wyndo into her pillowcase and moved along the edge of the wall while trying to keep in the shadows. The door was here somewhere.

She walked until they came to a corner, then followed the next wall. The bright glow of an exit sign quickened her breath. She could see it clearly at the end of the row. Though she wanted to run, she forced herself to move slowly.

The exit door let out into a narrow street between the harem and another building. It was dark to the left. To the right, Shaylinn could see the Harem Gardens, beyond them, a busy street and the huge Medical Center. Shaylinn walked to the left, hoping that staying in the shadows would be wisest.

They reached the end of the alley. An expanse came into view on their right. The Noble Gardens. City Hall stood beyond the gardens like a watchful eye. They needed some place quiet where Jemma could try to call Levi on the two-way radio again.

They walked along the sidewalk edging the gardens. Shaylinn's gaze fell onto a truck idling at the curb. The driver's door was open, and the seat was empty.

"The truck?" she whispered to Jemma. "I think I could drive it. It looks empty."

"The truck, go!" Jemma ushered Kendall and Naomi toward the vehicle, but a maintenance man stepped out from around the front of the truck, ducked in the driver's door, then moved back to the front hood, which Shaylinn now saw was opened. A tool box sat open on the driver's seat.

Jemma backed away from the vehicle, grabbing hold of Kendall and Naomi as she moved. "That's not going to work, Shay."

"Evening, femmys."

Shaylinn whirled around. An enforcer was making his way across the grass, coming at them from behind.

"Any fortune?" he asked the maintenance man.

"Not yet. It just won't hold a charge."

"Well, a tow is on its way." The enforcer stopped beside the truck and turned back to the girls. "You femmes lost?"

"No. Just taking a walk." Shaylinn turned her back to the enforcer and mouthed the word "Go" to Jemma, Naomi, and Kendall. They turned, and Jemma helped them hobble over the wet grass.

"Wait, are you femmes *pregnant*?"

The question sent fire through Shaylinn's veins. "I'll catch up with you." She turned back to the enforcer. He was walking toward her, his brows furrowed. She smiled and tried to sound calm and confident while holding her pillowcase behind her back. "I'm sure you've seen ColorCasts of Kendall Collin and Naomi Jordan, the two women about to deliver babies to the Safe Lands. They get stressed being caged in the harem all the time. It's bad for their pregnancies, so I bring them out for a walk each night when it's not so crowded and people won't mob them."

The enforcer's brow furrowed. "But that's not allowed."

"Not officially, no. But you know how the harem is. Anything for our queens. As long as we're back before sunrise, Matron looks the other way."

His face relaxed into a smile. "Oh, well ... I guess I will too, then."

Shaylinn offered her biggest smile, trying to bat her eyes the way Mia did. "I appreciate that."

"Sure thing. Hey, is Matron Dlorah your task director?"

"Yeah." She'd have to be if Shaylinn were out walking the surrogates.

"I've heard she's tough," the enforcer said.

"Oh, she's not so bad once you get to know her."

"What are your off days?"

"Um ... they're different every week. You know, surrogates and their medical appointments and such. This task doesn't really allow consistent free time."

The enforcer pushed up his sleeve, revealing a Wyndo watch. "Well, maybe next time you're free you could tap me? It seems every woman I've met this year is a two. But you're a four. Maybe we could pair up sometime."

Shaylinn's cheeks burned, but she forced a smile. "Oh, thanks." She touched the screen of his Wyndo watch and read his name. "Reglan Brown."

"That's me."

"Well, I should catch up to them. Don't want them getting lost."

"You didn't tap."

She swallowed. "Oh. Sorry." She set her fist against the screen of his watch. It clicked, and Shaylinn's picture filled the glass. All it said was her name, ID number, and Highland Harem. Maybe he wouldn't—

The radio clipped to Reglan's shoulder crackled and a female voice said, "Calling all units. We've got a 10–98 at the harem. Be advised, suspects are four women in their late teens, all dark-haired, two pregnant."

Shaylinn turned and ran.

"Hey!" Reglan called after her. "Stop!"

Shaylinn quickly caught up to Jemma, Kendall, and Naomi. "They're coming. We've got to hurry."

"I can't go faster," Kendall cried.

Jemma slowed some. They reached the other side of the Noble Gardens and jogged across the street. It was mostly deserted, though one car was forced to slow because of Jemma and Kendall in the road. The driver honked and yelled as he cruised past.

"Here!" Jemma handed Shaylinn the two-way radio. "Call Levi. See if he answers."

Shaylinn took the radio and started for the Snowcrest apartments, but an enforcer's car pulled into the parking lot. Shaylinn reversed their direction, but before they reached the next building, another enforcer's car pulled off the road right in front of them, emergency lights flashing. The officer climbed out and started toward them.

Shaylinn fumbled to press the button on the radio. "Levi? Are you there?" She turned back to the Snowcrest and yelped at the nearness of two enforcers coming their way. She tugged Jemma and Kendall off the sidewalk and through a circular flower bed. Before they reached the other side, one of the officers cut them off. The three officers were closing in. Shaylinn didn't know what to do.

"Levi," she said into the radio. "Levi, we need help."

"Get away from us, you creeps!" Naomi yelled.

"Don't be upset, girls," Kendall said. "I love that you tried to help."

Shaylinn shoved the radio into her pillowcase and hugged Kendall. "I'm so sorry we failed."

Jemma hugged Kendall next. "I love you, sweet girl. I'll be praying for you."

"I love you too, Jemmy," Kendall said.

An enforcer pointed his gun at Shaylinn. "Don't move! Put your hands behind your neck."

Shaylinn obeyed. And with that, the enforcers arrested them all.

CHAPTER 31

Kendall's in labor!" Ciddah's yell carried all the way to exam room three, where Mason was cleaning the Wyndo screen. It was very early in the morning, and the place was dead. "I'll contact Luella at her private number and let her know to meet me over there."

Mason ran to Rimola's desk in time to see Ciddah call the elevator. "Can I come?"

Ciddah turned and frowned. "I'm sorry, Mason. Outsiders are prohibited from the procedure."

"Why?"

The elevator dinged and slid open. Ciddah stepped inside and set her palm against the door. "Since an outsider tried to kidnap our babies tonight."

Outsider? Levi? Jemma? Mason ran around the desk. "Tell me what happened? Was anyone hurt?"

"Jemma, Naomi, Shaylinn, and Kendall tried to run," Ciddah said. "Don't worry. They're all fine. They took Kendall to the Medical Center and the others to the RC."

"Rehabilitation Center?" Mason stopped in front of the elevator.

Ciddah lowered her hand, and the door slid closed.

Mason mumbled to the closed elevator, "Kendall and Naomi's babies are *not* yours."

He ran to the stairwell and pulled open the door, completely abandoning the SC. He took the stairs down the five levels and hailed a taxi to his apartment in the Westwall. By the time he held the two-way radio, he had to catch his breath before he could speak.

"This is Eagle Eyes calling Jackrabbit, come in." There was no answer, so he repeated his call. He glanced at the clock. It was 5:49 a.m. Levi had to be home. "Jackrabbit, you copy?"

The radio crackled, and a weak voice spoke. "Jackrabbit here. What's your tidings?"

"Uh ..." Mason scrambled to come up with some kind of code. "Buttercup and her little sister and Stampede's other half and uh ... Buttercup's friend, uh, Springing Heifer. They made a run for it because Springing Heifer was about to ... uh ... spring. Now Buttercup is in the fishtrap. Over." Mason rubbed his eyes and hoped Levi could translate that ridiculous message.

"Did you say Buttercup is in the fishtrap? *My* Buttercup?"

"That's a 10–4, Jackrabbit. Buttercup, her little sister, and Stampede's other half are all *in* the fishtrap. Over."

A stretch of silence passed. Mason pictured Levi either destroying his apartment or sitting up in his bed with his forehead wrinkled as he tried to figure out what Mason was talking about in the middle of the night.

"That's a 10–4." Levi said finally. "We stick with the plan and hope they get out. Cut some Zs, Eagle Eyes. But let me know if you hear anything else. Copy?"

"Copy. Over and out."

Mason made his way back to the SC and finished his shift, then went home.

He slept until his doorbell buzzed at almost eleven thirty in the morning. Who would ever visit his place? Levi?

He rolled out of bed and opened the front door, eyes half closed.

Ciddah stood outside his doorway holding two bags. The smell of eggs mingled with Ciddah's everyday scent of vanilla and cinnamon knocked him back a step.

She took advantage of his surprise and swept past him into his kitchen. She looked tired, but he'd never seen her smiling so wide. He liked it.

"Good morning," she said as she reached into her bag. "I hope you're hungry."

He awoke quickly then. "I … well …" He surveyed his apartment. Not too bad, actually. The shirt he'd worn last night lay on the floor in the doorway to his bedroom. He swiped it up, then realized he was wearing only his scrubs bottoms. He clutched the dirty shirt over his bare chest. "Uh … be right back."

He darted into his bedroom, tossed the shirt into his laundry pile, and pulled a fresh one over his head. Green shirt, navy blue pants. It would have to do.

When he returned to the living room, Ciddah was setting out omelets and toast.

"You brought me breakfast," he said.

"You're welcome. I felt bad about the way I left you alone in the SC."

"How's Kendall?"

"Good. Very good. I'm sorry you weren't able to witness the birth. It was incredible. The surgeons said she was too far along to stop labor, so they let her deliver naturally. They were as nervous as I was. There hasn't been a natural birth in the Safe Lands in ten years."

"The baby's okay?"

She squealed and clapped her hands. "He's absolutely precious! He's in the nursery already getting comfortable."

Mason closed his eyes. He wanted to yell, but this wasn't Ciddah's fault. It was so much bigger. *How can I possibly do any good in this place?* Were his people and other outsiders like Kendall doomed to a life here, slowly killing themselves and being bred like cattle?

A sniffle caused him to open his eyes. Ciddah stood in his kitchen, one hand on the counter, the other covering her mouth. She was crying.

Without thinking, Mason was at her side. "Hey, what's wrong?"

"I lied." Ciddah sniffled. "It was awful." Another sniffle. "Kendall was completely out of control. The birth went fine, but not what happened afterward. Lawten had promised she could hold the child, but in light of her attempted escape, he said there was no way he could allow that to happen. But she was awake when the baby came and — " She broke into another long sob.

Mason stared at her face as it transformed before him. Her tears washed a stream of black from her eyes, down her cheeks. He handed her a wet cloth to clean her face, and the eye makeup smeared with cream-colored liquid, becoming gray goo. All this time, the smoothness of her skin had been painted on. In the clean streaks on her cheeks, Mason could see her real skin, cracked, transparent. He'd always known — in his head, at least — that she was infected, but her perfect appearance had made it seem possible that she really was just a healthy young woman.

To see hints of her true face ... he wanted to hold her. But he also wanted to push her out into the hall and shut the door. No, he wanted to wash away the paint and see what she really looked like.

He didn't know what he wanted.

Ciddah went on, oblivious to her exposure. "Kendall ... I've never seen anyone fight off sedation." She sniffled. "We had to give her three doses before she calmed down."

"It's a terrible crime," Mason said, thinking of the thin plague that made Ciddah hide behind so much paint, thinking of Kendall mourning the loss of her child.

"I know!" Ciddah choked in a few calming breaths. "Jemma and Shaylinn and Naomi. Their twisted priorities robbed Kendall of her chance to hold the child."

Mason set his jaw. "I wasn't talking about that, Ciddah." He walked into the living room to put some space between them. "A woman's child was taken. It's the worst crime I can imagine — the greatest evil."

Ciddah stomped toward him, her face a glistening mess. "Don't you *dare* call me evil, Mason Elias." She shoved his chest with both hands. "I did my job." She shoved him again. "I can't help that you don't understand."

When she came at him again, he caught her wrists and held them. "I understand. You're only doing what you've been taught is right. But, Ciddah." He pulled her hands against his chest. "What if you were taught wrong? Ignorance is no excuse for evil."

Her bottom lip trembled. "*Again* you call me evil."

"Not *you*, Ciddah."

She tried to pull away, but Mason held tightly.

"I thought you were starting to understand," she said. "I thought tasking in the SC was helping you see that our ways aren't *so* bad." But then she moaned, a soft sound like a distant wasp that slowly grew into jagged sobs. It reminded him of his aunt last spring, who'd wailed after her child came stillborn. He wrapped his arms around Ciddah and held her close, wondering what she was mourning the loss of.

CHAPTER 32

A messenger brought me this," Omar said, holding up a gold envelope so the task director general's receptionist could see it. "It said to come at nine this morning."

"Have a seat. I'll let him know you're here."

Omar sat and patted his chest pocket, comforted by the feel of his new vaporizer. He'd vaped in the elevator, but he was so nervous he wanted another puff. Why had he been summoned? He bet the woman doctor Mason tasked for had told Renzor that Omar had gotten infected. Some angel.

Twenty minutes passed before the receptionist sent him in. He knocked on the door out of respect. Or maybe it was guilt. Trying to suck up to the big task man.

"Enter." Kruse's voice.

Omar took a deep breath and entered the office, stopping before the task director's desk. Kruse stood in his usual place by the task director's side.

Omar sat, annoyed at how soft the chairs were, as if comforting his backside was going to make this any less painful. "You wanted to see me, sir?"

"Mr. Strong, General Otley is unhappy with your recent behavior, as am I."

Omar swallowed. "It was an accident, sir. I didn't know brown sugar could kill me."

"A captain should possess more common sense than to ingest high doses of stimulants, especially when in uniform and committed to weekly donations."

"I'm sorry. It won't happen again."

"It's too late for apologies, Mr. Strong. You disobeyed my orders and have contracted the plague. You're useless to us now. General Otley wants you out of the enforcers, and I have no reason to disagree."

Tears wouldn't help matters, so Omar clenched his teeth to fight them off. "You're demoting me?"

"Discharging, actually. Report to the Registration Department to turn in your enforcer badge and personal ID for reassignment."

"That's not fair!" Omar yelled, the pitch of his voice that of a swindled child. "Otley's just mad at me because of Belbeline."

"You failed us. That's all that matters."

"But you still have all the women in the harem. Because of me."

"You were compensated for those women. It is not my fault that you threw it all away. Good day, Omar Strong."

While sitting in the Registration Department, Omar looked over his task list:

Construction: Painter
Enhancement: SimArt designer
Entertainment: Makeup artist
Communication: Graphic illustrator
Entertainment: Set designer

The only task Omar knew was SimArt designer. "What's a makeup artist do?"

"Makeup for programs on the ColorCast," Dallin said from behind his desk. He'd changed his hair from the black and yellow stripes to dark red. "But you aren't there yet. Painting in construction is hard physical labor. You paint walls inside and out. If I were you, I'd do your six there, then try to get into enhancement. Or do six in entertainment and try to get an extension. I wish I could work in entertainment."

"Couldn't you just retest and cheat? Say you're interested in entertainment?"

"You have to be careful cheating. It can anger Fortune and the task directors. Some get away with it, but if you fail your task, you can get discharged. And if you get discharged three times, you get an X." Dallin looked Omar directly in the eye. "So I also suggest you don't pair up with any more of Otley's flames."

Omar was convinced his new task was the worst possible assignment one could draw. His task director, Radcliff, a short, wiry man with brown skin, put him on a paint crew. Omar had worked six hours straight, painting the walls of some apartment blue over green. Omar wanted to ask, *Why?* But he'd had his fill of disciplinary action. Besides, it was all he could do not to beat in the wall with his fist.

When he made himself stop thinking about Radcliff, Belbeline's face kept appearing before him. He'd painted her eyes on the wall then painted over them three times now. Why didn't she want him anymore? No women wanted him. What was wrong with him, anyway?

"Hey, Strong!" Radcliff yelled. "I think you got that spot, all right? Keep moving."

Omar kicked his paint tray down a few feet and started on the next section.

Belbeline.

When Omar got off for the day, he met Charlz and Skottie in the hitroom of a Highlands club called the Savoy. Once they settled in at a table on a balcony overlooking the dark dance floor below, he told the guys about the brown sugar, his discharge, and Belbeline.

"Forget that prude!" Skottie said as he stroked his mustache. "Why do you want to make a fashion of her? Get you some stims, and we'll find you a new flame."

"There's Yedra," Charlz said. "She's gratifiable. And Janique. One of my favorites who's always willing. Know what? Forget you. Janique's mine tonight." Charlz got up from the table and headed for the stairs.

Omar watched Charlz approach the tangle of swaying bodies that were mostly wearing red and black. Mimics. Belbeline wasn't a mimic.

"Janique *does* fill the need," Skottie said. "Wish I'd seen her first."

"You've paired up with her too?" Omar asked, a little surprised at that coincidence.

"We've all pretty much paired up at least once, except with our same numbers. There are a few femmes I haven't been with. Highbrows. Entertainers." He slapped the table, and the beer in Omar's glass swelled over the side of his glass. "I paired up with Luella Flynn back in boarding school. She won't even look at me today, the prude."

Omar pointed at a blonde woman with spiky hair. Venita, Belbeline's friend. "Her?"

"Venita, sure. She's deluxo. Great legs."

Omar pointed to another woman, short and round with curly black hair.

"That's Camella. You've met her. Tasked in massage? Now she tasks in surveillance? Covers the RC? I took you up where she works, remember? She's a favorite of mine."

"Belbeline tasks in massage," Omar said.

"Enough!" Skottie called the barkeep and handed him Omar's PV. "Fill it with brown sugar— "

"No!" Omar said. "I can't— "

"A *one*. Plain," Skottie said as he raised one eyebrow at Omar. "A one won't hurt nobody, and you need a hit of something."

Omar's heart felt heavy, like it held the weight of all his poor decisions. All of the dead in Glenrock, everything he'd done living here.

He *did* want that feeling again. That free, happy, light feeling that nothing mattered. He pressed his fist against the barkeep's SimPad and watched him walk away, knowing he was making a mistake yet not really caring.

His gaze flitted down to the dance floor where Charlz was dancing with Janique and Venita. Did pairing up with different women bring pleasure in life? Was Omar a prude for wanting only one? Would this heaviness in his heart double and triple and quadruple until he needed a hit of brown sugar at level ten to make it go away?

Skottie and Charlz lived that way, but they didn't look depressed. And Omar already had the thin plague, thanks to Belbeline. He may as well see if he could find this elusive pleasure everyone else seemed to already have. When the barkeep returned, Omar took a long drag from his PV and headed for the dance floor.

CHAPTER 33

An enforcer opened the door to Shaylinn's cell. "Let's go, femme."

Shaylinn stepped out into the narrow hallway that separated the two rows of jail cells from one another. Naomi already stood beside a second enforcer, the X after her number a sobering reminder that they were property of the Safe Lands. Shaylinn's X had been there when she'd awakened that morning.

"What about my sister?" Shaylinn asked.

The enforcer motioned for Shaylinn to walk toward the exit. "Just you two today."

Shaylinn turned and looked past the enforcer to Jemma's cell, which was at the very end of the row. "Jemma!"

"It's okay, Shay," Jemma said. "Go with them. Don't worry about me."

Shaylinn's heart swelled within her chest. "I don't want to leave you here."

"And I don't want to stun you, but I will if you don't move along," the enforcer said.

Shaylinn inched toward the exit. "I love you, Jemma!"

"I love you too, Shay!"

The enforcer pushed Shaylinn's shoulder, and she barely caught her balance. "Let's go, femme. Today!"

The enforcers took Shaylinn and Naomi to the lobby where Matron was waiting. Her black pantsuit with a bright green scarf almost made her look more severe than normal. "I'm very disappointed in you girls," she said.

"What about Jemma?" Shaylinn asked. "Why does she have to stay?"

"Jemma can sit there until summoned to the Surrogacy Center," Matron said. "You two are far too precious to breathe the same air as the vermin who inhabit the RC."

Shaylinn glanced at Naomi, who shrugged. *What makes me so special all of a sudden?*

The thought sent a chill over Shaylinn. "I'm pregnant, aren't I?"

Matron smiled. "Get your things from the enforcer, girls, and let's go. Luella Flynn is meeting us at the SC, and I don't want to keep her waiting."

For Shaylinn, the day passed by in a blur, starting with a trip to the SC for confirmation and prenatal prescriptions, three interviews with Luella Flynn, a shopping trip with Tyra, and ending with a coaching session on the proper foods to eat each day.

By the time Matron dismissed her, Shaylinn was exhausted. She entered the Blue Diamond Suite and found Mia watching TV in the living room. "Where's Naomi?"

"In her room," Mia said. "Congratulations, by the way."

The word made Shaylinn queasy. Nothing would be the same without Jemma and Kendall here. She realized this place had never been close to being a home; all the comforts had been a distraction. Shaylinn started down the hallway wanting nothing more than the peace of sleep.

"I saw Levi," Mia said.

Shaylinn turned back. "Where?"

"At a club Saturday night while you guys were sneaking out."

Shaylinn narrowed her eyes.

"He wasn't alone, either. He was dancing with someone. It was pretty wild."

"You just think you saw him." Night after night, she'd tolerated Mia's stories of the dancing and the fancy drinks she'd tried at the places Rand had taken her. She believed Mia's story of seeing Omar, though it had nearly broken her heart, but Mia had to be lying about Levi. "Levi would never go to such a place. He's not like that."

"*Such a place?* The Savoy is wonderful. Stop judging these people because they live differently than we used to. And I know what I saw. I saw Levi dancing *badly* with some gorgeous Safe Lands national."

"Mia, we're prisoners here. And there's nothing more dangerous than an enemy claiming to be your friend. These people mean to use us and throw us away!"

Mia tipped back her head and moaned. "*Shaylinn* ..."

"Ever since we got here, you've loved everything they've placed in front of you. But your turn is coming. And I know you think being pregnant will be amazing, and you might be stronger than me, but no one is strong enough to survive this place."

Mia looked back to the TV. "You try and help a person ..."

"My thoughts exactly," Shaylinn said as she went to her room.

Shaylinn cried, and it felt good. She lay in bed, burrowed under her covers. Forget stupid Omar calling her an ugly crybaby. Forget Mia and her obsession with Rand. Omar and Mia could just stay here forever with these horrible people.

"Jack ... it to ... uttercup, come in."

Levi? Shaylinn sat up and wiped her eyes. She looked around her room, and leapt out of bed once she spotted her pillowcase by the door. She dumped the pillowcase out. Her Wyndo snapped into three pieces, but the wind-up radio bounced over by the dresser.

She picked up the radio and pressed the talk button. "This is Shaylinn."

A bit of static, then, "You need … it."

She held the speaker to her lips. "What?"

"Wind, wind … ind!"

Oh, wind it. Shaylinn grabbed the handle and cranked it in circles until her arm was sore. Then she tried again. "Levi? Is that you?"

"Copy, yes. Hello, Shaylinn. Is Jemma there?"

"No. She's in the prison."

"I was afraid of that. How long you think they'll keep her there?"

"Matron said until her appointment."

Everything seemed terribly quiet while Shaylinn waited for Levi to reply. He was probably upset. Jemma's appointment was scheduled days after Levi's planned rescue.

He finally responded. "Ten-four, Shaylinn. I'm going to need someone to help get our people out of there. Can you help me?"

"Yes." Shaylinn would do anything to get away from this place.

"Good girl."

CHAPTER 34

Announcements for the Lonn Liberation were playing more frequently on the ColorCast. Mason spent almost every spare moment talking with Levi, Jordan, and Shaylinn on the radio, and soon a detailed plan was made, all the way down to a secret knock.

But Mason still had to work out some sort of alibi that would keep the enforcers from suspecting his involvement in the escape. Ciddah was his only hope. They hadn't spoken much since her visit to his apartment last Sunday morning. Perhaps she was embarrassed about having literally fallen apart in his presence, or perhaps he'd finally driven her too far away with his beliefs. He didn't know. But he waited all day for an opportunity to broach the subject.

It came that afternoon. He finished cleaning exam room four, and when he walked into the hallway, Ciddah was standing outside her office reading a CompuChart.

"You going to watch the liberation?" he asked.

She looked up from the CompuChart, met his gaze, and smiled. "Of course."

"I've never seen one," Mason said, hoping his voice sounded casual.

Her smile faded, and her eyes grew distant and cold. But she said, "Would you like to watch it at my apartment?"

There it was, the moment he'd been hoping for. Yet something felt wrong: the look in Ciddah's eyes. The coldness. Could she somehow know what he and Levi were planning? She'd invited him awfully fast. Mason pushed away his paranoia and tried to keep his smile small, not wanting to appear eager. "Sure. If you don't mind explaining every little thing to an outsider."

"I'd be honored." Her expression faltered, and for the briefest moment an authentic, shy smile appeared. But it vanished just as quickly. Perhaps he'd imagined it.

He wished he hadn't. He wished for a world without disease and prisoners and lies and theft. A world where he could spend each day trying to coax such a smile from this lovely girl. A world where she wasn't the enemy and he wasn't the captive.

On the day of the liberation, Mason arrived early to Ciddah's apartment. She answered the door in a short peach-colored dress that had one sleeve and a crooked hem. Mason had never seen her wear anything but scrubs. He couldn't stop staring.

Since they lived in the same building, their apartments were almost identical. Ciddah's walls were brown rather than blue, and she'd decorated with a food theme, specifically baked goods: cookie-shaped pillows on the sofa, framed pictures of cakes and pies, curtains over the windows with tiny cinnamon rolls on them, and decorative bowls filled with wax pastries.

The place even smelled like vanilla and cinnamon — of course — and of sautéed onions and something else sweet.

"Sit wherever you like," Ciddah said as she went back to the kitchen. She turned on the faucet and scrubbed a dish. "I was just cleaning up. I hope you're hungry, because I made us a feast."

He glanced at a steaming pan on the stovetop as he sat down on her sofa. "You did?"

"I did." She gave him a real smile then. It distracted him a moment before reality caused him to sink back against the cookie pillows. If Ciddah made dinner, he couldn't volunteer to fetch it from the Blue Bell Diner — which had been his plan to slip away just long enough to free the women. Dessert maybe? That cupcake place?

Ciddah banged around in the kitchen, opening and closing cupboards, checking whatever was cooking in the oven. "I hope you'll extend a little mercy my way, Mason. I'm not a bad cook, but I'd never tried to roast beets before. I think I should've peeled them after they were cooked." She held up her hands, the palms of which were stained dark pink.

So preoccupied with the crisis in his agenda, Mason's laugh came out forced. "Shanna was the dye expert in Glenrock. I think she had us all help her with red and purple at some point."

Ciddah crouched out of sight behind the island counter. "Did you all help each other with tasks?"

"Whenever someone needed help, they'd ask."

Ciddah carried two plates into the living room and set them on the table before the couch. There was a thick steak, a sautéed red and green vegetable dish that Mason guessed was part beets, and a thick slice of brown bread topped with a hunk of melting butter. She sank beside him on the sofa, so close their arms rubbed together.

How could he tell her that he didn't eat meat? "This ... looks amazing, Ciddah. Thank you. Did you bake the bread yourself?"

She touched her finger to the butter on her slice of bread and swirled the lump over the surface. "Baking is my favorite, especially anything that's kneaded. It's relaxing." She picked up her bread and bit into it.

Mason did the same. It was excellent. "Do people live in the lowlands, where the animals are?"

"I've never heard of anyone living there. I think it's just farmland."

"People must be tasked there, right?"

"Sure." She shrugged one shoulder. "But everyone I know is a medic."

"Except Lawten," Mason said.

She stiffened beside him. "He was a level twenty medic in the SC when I did my first internship. He got me into the program."

"Oh." Ciddah and Lawten had known each other for years then.

"It's starting! Wyndo: increase volume: twenty-three." The volume came on.

Mason hadn't known he could set voice commands for his Wyndo. He tried a bite of the roasted beet salad and found it quite good. "Mmm, this is—"

"Shh!"

On screen, Finley Gray and Luella Flynn were standing in the center of a packed auditorium, and were dressed to match, as always: Finley in a white suite with a silver vest and Luella in a silver gown that glistened like it was made of glitter. Tomorrow the Highlands would be coated in white and silver mimics.

"So many celebrity nationals have shown up for this historic event," Luella said. "I'm simply thrilled."

"I'm still in awe over Lawten Renzor's suit!" Finley whistled.

An image of Lawten in a satin blue-and-black-printed suit flashed on the screen.

"He looks amazing," Luella said. "He'll be inspiring his own mimics with that look."

"Walls! I hope so." Finley chuckled. "You know, I might even be one of them."

"Well, we're almost there, Safe Landers," Luella said, gazing into the camera so that it seemed like she was looking right at Mason. "Only five minutes until show time. Stay tuned."

The Colorcast went to a bit about silver glitter Roller Paint. Apparently the trends weren't so random after all.

"You're not eating your steak," Ciddah said.

Mason glanced at her and winced. "I'm a vegetarian."

Her eyes widened. "Oh."

They stared at each other a moment, then Mason said, "The beets and bread are really good."

Ciddah's cheeks turned pink. "Well, there's more, so have as much as you want."

The program started again. The screen displayed pictures of the dozen or so Safe Lands nationals who Finley claimed were going to be liberated today.

"Wait," Mason said, "I thought this was just for Lonn. Who are these other — " His words fell away as he recognized some of the portraits. Five were older women from Glenrock, including his own mother, Tamera.

Mason stood up so fast he knocked his plate to the floor. He stepped forward. Stopped. Walked to the door. Turned back.

Ciddah set her plate on the sofa and stood. "Mason, what's wrong?"

What could he do? He'd left the radio in the van. Even if he ran down there, Levi probably had no way of contacting Bender at the moment.

"Mason?"

Could he just sit here and watch them kill his mother? Maybe Bender would free everyone who was being liberated tonight. But what if he didn't? "Liberation is death?"

"I don't know; I think so."

"Ciddah, please! Tell me what exactly is going to happen to these people. It's important."

She wrung her hands. "Liberation is a mystery. That's part of its splendor. We don't know what happens, only that it's wonderful."

"Basing your death on hearsay is illogical. Who says it's wonderful? Has someone been liberated and returned to tell the tale?"

"No, but — "

"Then how do any of you know it's wonderful?"

"Mason, please sit down. You're frightening me."

He glanced back to the screen. His mother's picture was displayed alone. She'd been a number nine at thirty-nine years old, so Luella led a chanting prayer to Fortune to have mercy on her as she entered the tenth life.

"That's so sad," Ciddah said. "Entering Bliss before age forty. Did you know her?"

"Yeah." Mason prayed he could expose liberation for whatever it truly was, that his mother was still alive, and that he could hold himself together in front of Ciddah. The other women were counting on him. He knelt and started to pick up his food that now covered the floor. His hands were shaking.

"Let me help you." Ciddah ran into the kitchen and returned with some napkins. When the mess was cleaned up, Mason sat back down on the couch.

The last national highlighted was Richark Lonn. Majestic music played as pictures of Lonn flashed and text listed facts about his life. Born in 2037, he excelled in mathematics and science. After graduation, he'd entered medic training, was the fastest national to reach a level twenty at age twenty-three. He'd maintained a steady relationship with Martana Kirst that had started in boarding school. She and Lonn had gifted the Safe Lands with eight children. Most of the pictures had both she and Lonn in them.

Luella Flynn's voice spoke over the montage of images. "Martana was liberated suddenly in 2068 in a complication with her tenth pregnancy."

"That's not exactly true," Ciddah said.

"How do you know?" Mason asked.

"It's kind of an urban legend amongst medics. They say that Martana did miscarry the tenth child, but she didn't die from it. She killed herself afterward."

"That's terrible!"

"She and Lonn made seven babies together in a span of twelve years. She wanted to be done, but the Guild said no. She was still strong, and they wanted to keep her as part of the harem. She completed one surrogacy term — baby number eight — then had a ninth child by Lonn. At that point, she was on meds for depression. When she didn't conceive again on her own, she was conscripted for surrogacy, but when she lost that tenth baby, it was too much. She took her own life. And that's why Lonn started the Black Army — so they say."

"Because really, the Safe Lands killed her," Mason said.

Ciddah leaned back against the couch. "That's a strange way to put it."

"If I were the man who loved her, I'd see it that way. She wanted the pain to stop, and the Safe Lands refused. What you saw Kendall go through, Martana suffered that nine times. I told you, Ciddah, a mother and her child have a bond. To be kept apart from your child nine times ... I can't imagine how she must have suffered. Lonn too."

"You think a donor suffers as well?"

"Lonn was more than a donor in a closet in City Hall. He loved Martana. And he knew those babies were his. Of course he suffered."

Applause brought Mason's attention back to the ColorCast. The history montage had ended. Lonn stepped out onto the stage to a thunderous reception, but Lonn was not smiling. He walked to the center of the stage, where Luella Flynn sat on a sofa, and sat down beside her.

"You have a special message you want to share tonight, don't you, Richark?"

"I do." He looked into the camera. "A revealing is a wonderful experience. If you've ever wondered who your donors were, fill out a revealing waiver today. And if you learn that I'm your donor, I love you very much."

"Love is so special, Lonn," Luella said. "Isn't liberation a wonderful time to communicate peacefully with all the Safe Lands?"

Lonn chuckled. But they cut away without letting his reply be heard.

Mason glanced at Ciddah. Tears streaked down her cheeks from eyes so suddenly bloodshot they looked more red than white. "You think Lonn and Martana are your parents?" Mason asked.

She laughed. "No!" She tried to laugh again, but it came out more like a gasp. "You're so dim."

"How can you be so sure? The ages fit."

"Because my donors live in the Midlands. In the Prospector."

Mason swallowed; she'd never mentioned anything so personal before. "How long have you known?"

"I applied for a revealing on my fourteenth birthday. Found out who my donors were that same day. Met them the day after that."

"They had both filled out waivers?"

"The day I was born."

"And they were together? Lifers?"

She nodded and smiled. "They're a lot like Lonn and Martana were. According to my donors, I have three siblings out there. But none of them have come looking."

"That's exciting, isn't it? Knowing your parents. Knowing you have family."

"Some days. Some days it's only depressing." She used her fork to move her beets around her plate, then jumped up suddenly and walked to her Wyndo screen. She picked up a small black object from the top of the screen then put it back. Her shoulders rose and fell in a deep breath, and she returned to the couch, eyes glossy with tears.

Mason wanted to ask what that was all about, but the look on her face made him wait.

"I have to admit," Ciddah finally said, "when I found out my donors knew each other, that I was a product of love, not donations and schedules, I was so overcome with joy. Does that sound stupid?"

"Not at all. It's natural to love one person, to create life together, to help it mature to the point when it's ready to love and produce its own life. Family is a good thing." Most of the time.

"I believe you."

Knowing how difficult it must have been for Ciddah to admit that, Mason's heart cracked. He could feel her nesting inside. He refocused his gaze so he could see their reflection in the Wyndo screen, sitting side by side on the sofa.

He pictured himself standing at a crossroad. One way, the road ran smooth and straight. Mason discovered the cure for the thin plague, cured the entire Safe Lands population, and changed the confining laws of this place. He married Ciddah, started a family, and they grew old together.

The other road was rocky with steep twists and turns. Mason

found no cure and was forced to make donations. He filled out revealing waivers each time in hopes of meeting any children who might result. The Safe Lands remained a controlling place, stealing women for surrogacy from all corners of the world and wresting babies from their mothers' arms. Mason continued to work as a medic and after ten years reached level twenty. He pledged his life to Ciddah, and he contracted the thin plague. She continued to miscarry, and that hardship haunted their relationship until they were liberated together when Ciddah turned forty.

"My father knew Lonn," Ciddah said, jerking Mason from his daydream. "The first time my mother was conscripted for surrogacy, my father got involved with the Black Army. It was pretty new back then, so no one really thought of it as a rebellion against the Safe Lands."

"Your father's a rebel, and he told you?"

"He's not a rebel anymore. He was warning me that fighting back isn't worth it. That the Safe Lands will always win."

Lawten clearly was good at controlling the people through fear—he could even weaken a father's resolve. "That's a pretty negative outlook."

"Not when you've seen what he has. My father was there when Arris died."

Mason looked at Ciddah, unable to remember that name. "Who?"

"I forget sometimes you are so new and haven't heard all our history. Arris and Lonn started the Black Army together. Arris had a memoriam liberation because he was killed. They all were—around twenty of them. My father was the only one left alive. The enforcers told him to make sure the rebels knew what happened to traitors, and if any of them told a word of the deaths, they'd all die with bad fortune."

"But I don't understand. I've never seen any reports of death on Finley and Flynn's show. In fact, I've never seen any reports of crime."

"People do die here. And there are bar fights, overdoses, heart attacks, and murder. And when death happens, there's a memoriam liberation. But only the positive parts of life are shown on the ColorCast. You won't hear any mention of Lonn's three Xs or the Black Army in this liberation ceremony, unless Lonn says something. But violators never do. It's strange. I wonder what stops them."

Lonn's voice came loud and clear through the Wyndo screen. He stood at a podium before a huge crowd and spoke into a mounted microphone. "I lived my life the best I could. I learned, I loved, I played, but I also questioned. If we accept everything in life without question, we forfeit the chance to reach our potential. The Safe Lands can be a better place if you insist on it."

The camera focused on Luella Flynn. "Some ways you can make a difference, Safe Landers? Retest in tasking to see if you're serving in the right area. Adopt a pet from Pet Squad. Or join Safe Watch, an organization committed to keeping our city safe."

It seemed to Mason that Luella had turned what Lonn had said into something else. "Sounds like Lonn still thinks people should fight back."

Ciddah grunted a response, staring at the screen, her arms folded.

"You still think I should make a donation?" Mason asked.

She didn't move. "Yes."

"Why?"

"Because the Safe Lands could only be benefitted by having more nationals like you."

He felt himself blush. "Well, uh, thank you, Ciddah. But I'm going to keep on questioning, like Lonn said. Find a cure instead. Won't that be better for every— "

A shrill siren rang out. Mason clapped his hands over his ears. What was that?

"Oh no!" Ciddah ran to the kitchen and opened the oven. Smoke billowed up to the ceiling. She screeched and jumped back.

Mason grabbed a potholder, pulled the pan from the oven, and dumped it into the sink. Ciddah flipped on the faucet, then turned back to the oven and switched it off. She stared at him with wide eyes as she used a towel to fan the air until the noise stopped.

"Oh!" Ciddah frowned, looking into the sink.

"What was it?" Mason asked.

"A cake."

He chuckled. "I think it's done."

She swung at his chest, but he caught her fist in his hand. She tried to pull free, but he held tight. Something about her smile and the way her eyes sparkled made him glance at her lips. He could kiss her. See what it was like. Or he could be smart.

He released her hand and glanced at the clock. It was ten minutes before he needed to leave. *Close enough.* "How about I run and get some cupcakes from BabyKakes?"

"You'll miss the rest of the speech!"

"I'm kind of missing it already."

"I'm sorry."

"Don't apologize. I'll be quick, okay?" He glanced in the sink. "You like chocolate?"

She swatted him again. "It was a spice cake."

He raised his eyebrows at the black lump. "If you say so. Be right back." He darted out the door before she could say another word.

Mason had parked the minibus in the Westwall's uncovered lot. He started it and shakily steered onto Gothic Road. It had been years since he'd driven a vehicle, and he'd certainly never handled something this large. A horn honked, and a car sped around him. He pressed the accelerator harder to try to keep up with the rest of traffic. To make matters worse, the roads were wet from the rain.

He eventually parked in the alley between the Highland Harem and the Noble Gardens. Once the power went out, he'd circle around to the alley that led to the loading dock where the women were supposed to meet him — if Shaylinn managed to get them out. He should've driven slower. Hopefully, no one would ask why he'd parked here. Everyone was likely watching Lonn's liberation anyway.

He reached back to the first passenger's seat, grabbed his two-way radio, and pressed the talk button. "Eagle Eyes to Jackrabbit, you got your ears on?"

The answer came instantly. "This is Jackrabbit, go ahead."

"The ark is in position," Mason said.

"Glad to hear it, Eagle Eyes."

"Saw Mother and four other Glenrock women on the liberation program. Think we can get them out too?" *Please say yes. Please.*

"I'll look into it right now. Jackrabbit over and out."

Mason dropped the radio on his lap and leaned back against the seat, hoping it wasn't too late for Levi to help their mother. He had never been so thankful for a burned cake. Not only had it given him the opportunity to fulfill his part in the escape and possibly help Mother, but it also had gotten him out of Ciddah's apartment before he'd done something he would've regretted. His feelings for Ciddah were only getting stronger, but she had the thin plague. To love her would mean his own death. He could just hear his father mocking such a choice.

His father wasn't here anymore, but Mason was leaving the Safe Lands soon and had a list of logical reasons against pursuing her, so despite his overactive imagination about the future, there really wasn't anything to decide.

CHAPTER 35

"I don't like it," Zane said.

"It's not your problem," Levi said as he carried the manhole hook toward the hole.

"There's no exit." Zane gestured down the dark alley to the drive that circled the Mountaineer. Grass and a fence of trees met them on one side, the building on the other. "We come back up out of here and someone sees us — enforcers see us — we're dead."

Levi leaned on the manhole hook like it was a cane. "Dead? Not liberated?"

"Hey, not everyone goes in for that tenth life juice. I'm a rebel, aren't I?"

"Yeah, yeah." Between Jemma being in the RC and his mother and the other women in the liberation ceremony, Levi found it almost impossible to stay focused on Zane's words.

"Look, I picked this alley because no one will see us," Levi said. "And it's closest to the dam. Stop criticizing and help me open this."

Levi inserted the hook into one of the slots in the manhole cover and lifted the edge. He'd made a point to clean it yesterday, so it came up easily. He pulled it toward him while Zane squatted on the other side and pushed, and together they slid the cover across the pavement and onto the grass. Levi traded the manhole hook for a road construction sign he'd nabbed from the Highlands Public Tasks. He set it up beside the manhole, and once they had both climbed through the opening, Levi pulled the sign over the hole.

The stagnant odor of algae and mud brought him back to the day he'd come into the compound. It hadn't been that long ago. As his feet lowered into the water, icy liquid sucked through his pants legs and onto his skin. He slowed until his foot felt the ground, then he let go of the rungs.

The water at the bottom of the storm drain reached his knees. Almost twice as much water as there had been on the day he'd tested the route. He readjusted his rifle that he'd slung over his back, then dug his flashlight and Red's makeup crayon out of his pants pocket and darkened the X on the tunnel wall before the exit chute split. He'd marked the exits on his test run but figured they could stand to be more visible.

"What are you doing?" Zane's face, barely illuminated by Levi's flashlight, appeared to Levi's right. Dressed in a gray maintenance uniform, Zane's head looked like it was floating in the darkness.

"Marking the way." Levi waded past Zane. The water was too high to walk on the sides of the pipe and avoid getting wet. Yesterday, it had taken him twenty-two minutes from the road to the canal. They were already moving slower. At least it had stopped raining.

Their footsteps sloshed through water as Levi led the way down the storm drain. He stopped to darken his hash marks at each exit shaft but tried to move as quickly as possible.

"I'd like to have a look at that gun later," Zane said. "It looks like you made it out of wood."

"I didn't make it — it was my great grandfather's. But parts of it are wood. It came from a place called Arizona, which is pretty far south of here."

Thinking of Papa Eli reminded him of home, which made him think of Jemma. Shaylinn had told him how they'd tried to reach him on the radio the night Kendall went into labor. If it hadn't been for Red's dance mission, Levi would have heard their distress calls.

"Do you know if Red managed to get the information she needed from Nash?" Levi asked. "She said it was important to Bender for tonight."

"Nash!" Zane started to laugh. "Oh, you're so dim. What'd she talk you into?"

Levi turned and pointed his flashlight at Zane. "She took me to some dance place and said we had to make Nash jealous so he'd pick her up. That was the night Jemma got arrested."

Zane's laugh dwindled. "Walls, I'm sorry. I *told* you to be careful."

Heat burned into Levi's cheeks and chest. "She made it up?"

"That flame is tricksy," Zane said.

Of all the insane ... Levi spun around and splashed through the water. He breathed hard and fast and could almost taste rusty dirt on the air. *Refrain from anger, and turn from wrath. Refrain from anger...*

They passed some graffiti that said *Arris & Lonn: For all lives.* The closer they got to the exit, the shallower the water became. By the time the tunnel's opening appeared in the distance — a circle of night that swallowed his flashlight's beam — the water was only a foot deep, gushing toward the main canal.

Levi looked back at Zane. "How much time do we have?"

Zane pulled out his Wyndo and glanced at the screen. "About twelve minutes 'til Bender makes his move."

"Then we'd better make ours." Levi waded the rest of the way out of the storm drain and up the canal. The moon was fuller than he'd have liked. Thankfully, numerous clouds in the sky dampened its glow. They reached the dam and the fish ladder that ran up the powerhouse wall. Levi stepped carefully in the sides of each pool, hoping his footing stayed sure.

At the DPT office, Levi had discovered that unlike in Old cities, the Safe Lands electrical substations weren't located in the center of town. Aesthetics mattered more than convenience to Safe Landers, so the substations were on the top of the wall, on appendages that shot off the roadway like Old scenic lookouts. There were eight substations for the Safe Lands: two for the Highlands, two for the Midlands, and four for the Lowlands. Levi had guessed that the eastern one fed power to the ColorCast studio, since it was closer, but he didn't know for certain. He prayed his guess was truly an educated one.

Halfway up the fishtrap, they climbed over the railing to a concrete ledge that separated the fish ladder and powerhouse from the roadway. The trill of the generators buzzed through the powerhouse walls, vibrating the ledge under Levi's boots. They jogged along the ledge until it met the wall that surrounded the roadway and stopped to look out.

Streetlamps lit the roadway, spaced about one hundred feet apart and alternating on each side of the road. Inside the walls, the city glittered. Outside, the land was pitch black, disrupted momentarily by a set of taillights that receded far out near the western wall. Levi could see no other vehicles.

The distant substation was a tangle of gray metal on a field of black maybe three hundred yards out. The four gleaming spotlights that towered over the station didn't cast their glow far.

"Nowhere to hide," Zane said.

"We won't be here long enough to need to hide." Levi jumped down onto the roadway and crossed to the inner wall. It came up to his waist. He lifted the strap of his rifle over his head, set the rifle on the wall, and crouched to look through the scope, turning the zoom until the substation glowed in the lens. After locating the row of transformers, he tried to figure out which way they ran. If he could hit the first transformer in the series, everything else would go out.

Levi pulled back the bolt and loaded a round into the chamber. "Keep an eye on the studio's location, and let me know if it goes dark." He flipped off the safety and took aim at the transformer on the far left. One deep breath, and he pulled the trigger.

The shot cracked around them, echoing off the concrete walls of the dam. Through the scope, Levi saw no sparks or evidence that he'd hit anything. He glanced up at Zane.

"Prospector apartments went dark," Zane said. "All the way to ... Wow, that's weird. The power went out in the Highlands all along the edge of the Highland–Midland wall."

"It's an arch." The first one must be the other end then. Levi chambered another round and aimed for the transformer on the right end. Just as he pulled the trigger, Zane spoke.

"Someone's coming."

The shot rang out, but Levi knew he'd missed. He cocked the gun and straightened, looking where Zane was pointing. Two sets of headlights were heading their way from the other side of the inner wall. They'd just passed the other Highland substation.

Levi crouched and aimed for the transformer again. "Don't talk." He took in a deep breath and held it, then fired. He straightened to glance toward the city below.

Zane yelled, "You got it!"

Levi tucked the rifle strap over his head. "All I needed to hear. Let's go."

As they sprinted across the road, the headlights from the approaching enforcer vehicle lit their way. Levi boosted Zane up onto the roadway wall, then Zane pulled up Levi.

"Stop!" an enforcer yelled.

Levi followed Zane along the wall to the ledge that separated the powerhouse, over the railing, and into the fish ladder. Zane flipped on a flashlight, and they splashed down through the fish ladder as carefully as they could. A door on the powerhouse above opened, but Levi didn't look back.

"They went downriver!" a man yelled.

Zane tripped on the last step of the fish ladder and fell into the canal. Levi jumped over the last two steps and pulled Zane to his feet. They splashed downstream, staying against the inner wall. Above, enforcers' flashlights roamed the water.

Gunfire pelted water around them, urging them to move faster. Zane stopped in front of the storm drain and shone the light into the tunnel, waving at Levi to hurry.

"Don't wait for me!" Levi yelled.

Zane hoisted himself into the tunnel and soon cried out and dropped his flashlight, which slid out of the pipe and plopped into the canal, dimly illuminating the brown water from below.

Levi lunged up into the tunnel, took hold of Zane's waist, and pulled him into the drain.

Zane's voice was a whisper. "I think I cut my leg."

"Hold on." Levi helped Zane sit, then skidded back out the drain. He squatted down for the glowing beam of the submerged flashlight, grabbed it, and crawled back into the pipe. Zane was slumped along the curve of the tunnel, his waist submerged in the flow of water, his legs elevated on the other side. Levi shone the light on Zane's face, turned the beam to his legs, and then to the water, which ran red from Zane's legs and past Levi's boots.

Levi looked up to Zane's welling eyes. "It's no cut. They shot you."

CHAPTER 36

Only lights I see are headlights." Charlz's voice came from the darkness across the room, his form a black shadow before the pale outline of the window. "Power's out everywhere."

Omar shifted on Charlz's couch. Before the power had gone out, they'd been watching Lonn's liberation and listening to Charlz's enforcer scanner.

The scanner crackled and a male voice said, "B46, 11 – 99. Highland Substation Beta, 11 – 99. Shots fired."

"Rebels, I bet," Skottie said from Omar's right. "They're all worked up about this Lonn thing."

"That makes sense," Omar said. "Think they're trying to free him from liberation?"

"Nah, the guy's old," Skottie said. "It's the way of things."

Mad lot of sense that made. "Lonn's a rebel. What if he doesn't agree with liberation?"

"Why would anyone disagree?" Skottie asked. "Liberation is the highest honor."

The radio buzzed again, and this time a woman spoke. "B46,

11 – 99. Highland Substation Beta, 11 – 99. Shots fired. All wall units respond. Code 3."

"Too bad I'm not out there," Charlz said. "I'd pop those prudes with my stunner and watch them twitch." Charlz drew an imaginary gun and pretended to shoot it.

"You'd miss," Skottie said. "And Otley would use you for the next target practice."

"Shut it," Charlz said, shooting Skottie with his nonexistent stunner.

A fizzle of static. The female voice again. "Units responding to wall, suspects are two white males, wearing gray Department of Public Tasks uniforms, last seen near the powerhouse."

Omar slid to the edge of the couch.

"It *would* be the cleaners," Charlz said. "Hey, Omar, maybe it's your outsider brother. He's mad 'cause you broke his nose, and he wants payback."

"Why wouldn't he come shoot up Omar's apartment, then?" Skottie asked.

The radio crackled, and Omar yelled, "Quiet!"

The female voice. "Units responding to wall, suspects entered a storm drain, pursue with caution."

Omar's thoughts tumbled together, recalling Levi's two Xs, his promise to free their people, and how he'd entered the Safe Lands through the storm drains. He stood up. "We need to find a DPT radio. Now."

"Why?" Charlz asked.

"Because I'd bet you my PV that my brother is using them to make trouble. And I think I know how to locate him."

It took longer than Omar had liked to find a maintenance worker. None seemed to be working at this hour. Thankfully Skottie remembered that his friend Nash tasked for the DPT, so they went to Nash's

Mountaineer apartment and borrowed his radio. Not that they moved much faster once they got to Nash; Charlz kept complaining they were missing the rest of the liberation.

"It's not on anyway. The power is still out," Omar said.

"Still, we could be doing something better than chasing after your hunch. You're not even in enforcement anymore, remember?"

"At least I'm doing something."

When they were back inside the car, Skottie asked, "Where to?"

"Just wait a minute." In the back seat, Omar flipped through the channels on the radio, listening. One: nothing. Two: some guy at a malfunctioning fire hydrant. Three: nothing. Then he hit station four.

"—to stop the blood flow. Then get moving. Over."

"10–4, Eagle Eyes," Levi said. "Meet in the dead-end alley behind the Mountaineer."

"Negative," the other voice said. "I've got to fill the ark and deliver the cargo. You're on your own, Jackrabbit, so hurry. Over and out."

"Copy, Eagle Eyes," Levi said. "Over and out."

Channel four went dead. *Sweet mercy.* "They're coming here," Omar said.

"Who's coming here?" Charlz asked from the passenger's seat. "And what's a Jackrabbit?"

"A code name for my brother. We've got to stop them." This was it: Omar's chance to get back in with the task director general and Otley.

"What's that mean, *cargo*?" Charlz asked.

"It means they're stealing something," Omar said. "You guys got your weapons? They took mine."

"I've got stunners at home," Charlz said. "Been collecting them a while."

"Not enough time for a trip to your place," Omar said.

Skottie reached across the car and opened the glove compartment. "We've got one," he said, removing a stunner.

"One will have to do," Omar said. "Now let's find that alley."

CHAPTER 37

Shaylinn kept everyone in the downstairs sitting room watching Lonn's liberation, so that when the power went out, they'd be close to the kitchen and the stairs to the garage. Seeing her mother's face on the screen with the other women of Glenrock almost made Shaylinn too frightened to lead the escape. But by the time the lights blacked out, her fear had turned to anger.

They were getting out of here tonight. No more of this friendly imprisonment.

They reached the garage without incident. Shaylinn saw a transport parked in the alley where Mason was supposed to be. She just needed to make sure. She lifted the two-way radio to her mouth. "Eagle Eyes, give me your signal. Over."

The lights on the transport flashed on and off.

Shaylinn waved Naomi forward. "Go, go!"

The transport had steps. Mason came down to help Naomi up the first one.

Naomi hugged him. "Thank you, Mason."

Eliza hugged Mason as well. Aunt Mary pinched his cheeks. Chipeta, his aunt, wrung his hands and kissed his cheeks.

And then there was Shaylinn.

"Only five of you?" Mason asked.

"Jemma is still in the RC. Mia went to watch the liberation with Rand at some fancy party. She said we were *dim* for trying to escape again and that she didn't want an X. And Jennifer refused to leave without Mia." Shaylinn still couldn't believe she'd considered Mia a friend, even for a brief time.

"Get in," Mason said. "We have to keep moving."

Shaylinn climbed up the steps and sat in the first row of seats across from Aunt Mary. Mason got into the driver's seat and started the transport.

"So Mia wants to stay here?" Mason said. "Really?"

"Oh!" Shaylinn clapped her hand over her mouth. She'd forgotten Mia and Mason were supposed to get married.

"I'm sorry, Mason," Chipeta said. "We couldn't keep hold of her. The draw of so much glamour ... She never looked back."

"Mia chooses the gilded cage," Mason mumbled. "Fascinating." He steered out onto the main road, and the transport started to pick up speed. Shaylinn looked out the window and could barely see the harem shrinking away in the moonlight. Good riddance.

"What about the children?" Eliza asked.

"We can't leave the children here," Aunt Mary said.

"What happened to Kendall?" Shaylinn asked. "Where is the RC? Are we going to rescue Jemma?"

"I'm taking you to meet Jordan, who'll lead you to a safe location," Mason said. "Levi will meet us there, and you'll all make plans to free the children." He swerved over the yellow line and back. "Sorry. I'm not the best driver."

"What about you?" Naomi asked. "You're not coming with us?"

"I'm going to stay in the Highlands, so I can have access to the children."

Shaylinn looked at Mason with a new appreciation; she hoped his bravery wouldn't be a mistake. "But won't they know you helped us?"

"Not as long as we hurry so I can get back," Mason said.

"Bless you, Mason," Chipeta said. "You're a good boy."

Mason drove over to the Grand Lodge and parked beside a large truck. "I've got to do a little surgery on each of you before we go farther." He got up, turned on a flashlight, and removed a first aid kit from under the dashboard.

"Surgery for what?" Eliza said.

"SimTags. The computer chips they put in your hands. Scoot over, Shaylinn."

Shaylinn obeyed, and Mason sat beside her on her seat.

"I won't lie to you. It's going to hurt. I'll be as careful as I can, but I also need to be quick. We don't know how long the power will be out." He held up his flashlight. "Can someone hold this?"

"I will." Chipeta grabbed the light and held it aloft.

Mason took Shaylinn's right hand and set it on his lap. He tore open a little package and rubbed something cool over the side of her hand. Her heart skipped a little as he removed the lid from what looked like a pen but turned out to be a little knife. He wiped the blade off and looked into Shaylinn's eyes.

"Ready?" he asked.

She nodded. Mason twisted her arm so that the side of her hand faced up, which felt awkward. He squeezed and pressed the knife into her flesh. Shaylinn gasped at the sting and jerked her hand, but Mason held tight while she looked away and gritted her teeth.

"Got it," Mason said. "Can you hold this?"

Shaylinn looked back. Mason held up his finger, and on the top sat a tiny metal tube, covered in blood. Shaylinn pinched it off his finger, then Mason bandaged her hand.

"Don't lose that," he said. "Who's next?"

Mason worked fast, and soon had removed the SimTags from each of them.

"Don't tell Jordan I cut you," he said to Naomi; she smiled.

Mason collected all five SimTags in his hand and took them out of the transport. Then they were off again, moving through the dark city. He had to slow at intersections, as the cars that were out were having trouble deciding who would go first. In some places, enforcers waved traffic through, and each time their vehicle passed, Shaylinn found it hard to breathe.

Finally, Mason stopped again and got up. "Wait here." He opened the door and descended the steps. "I thought I saw a pair of eagle eyes," he said to the bushes.

"Just a stampede," Jordan's voice answered.

Naomi squealed and moved to the front of the bus.

Mason lunged back up the bus steps. "Okay, quickly now. Let's go!"

Naomi burst out the doors, with the other women close behind.

"Naomi!" Jordan jumped out of the bush. He looked his wife up and down and set his hands on her belly. "You're both okay?"

"We're fine," she said, though tears coated her cheeks.

Jordan clutched handfuls of Naomi's hair, kissed her, and said, "Omi, omi, omi," between kisses. Naomi laughed and cried at the same time.

Shaylinn looked away, embarrassed. Finally, Jordan and Mason led them around the bushes to an open manhole in a paved clearing at the back of the building. Jordan climbed down first, then Mason helped Chipeta onto the ladder.

Once Chipeta was down, Naomi peered down the dark hole. "I don't think I can bend over far enough to even get my feet on those rungs."

Jordan called up to her. "I'll help you down, baby."

Mason helped Naomi get positioned, then held her hand as he had for his aunt while she descended. "I doubt he'll ever let you out of his sight again," he said.

"Give him time," Naomi said, wincing as she slid her protruding belly past the lip of the hole. "He'll be desperate for a hunt."

"Not much to hunt in the Safe Lands," Mason said.

"True, but we won't be here much longer."

Mason waved Eliza forward, then Aunt Mary.

Shaylinn was the last to go. She sat down and put her feet through the hole.

Mason crouched beside her. "Shaylinn," he said, "thank you for your help and your courage. Is there anything I can do for you?"

There was only one question Mason might be able to answer. And while it embarrassed her to voice it, she forced out the words. "I'd like to know who the father is."

Mason's face paled a bit, then he smiled. "Fair enough. I'll find out."

CHAPTER 38

Once the women had cleared the storm drain, Mason pulled the cover over the opening, which proved to be nearly impossible for one man. Or maybe he was simply a weakling. He finally managed to push it into place, then ran around to the front of the bakery.

The door was unlocked, but when he went in, someone yelled, "We're closed!"

"I need a couple cupcakes," Mason said, inching through the darkness toward a glowing handheld Wyndo. He reached the counter, and his eyes adjusted to the low light.

A tiny man sat on a stool behind the glass case, Wyndo in hand. "Power's out. Can't process your ID."

"I'm a medic. My credit's good," Mason said. "Take down my number and process it when the power comes back on. Please? I've got a girl with a sweet tooth who I don't want to cross."

"What if I run your ID and it's empty?"

"Then you can turn me into the enforcers."

The man grunted. "I suppose. How many cupcakes you want?"

Mason set his hands on the glass case. "A half-dozen okay? You have spice cake?"

"Yeah, I've got spice cake."

"How about three spice cake and three chocolate?"

"What kind of frosting?"

"Surprise me."

The clerk boxed the cupcakes and wrote down Mason's ID number.

"Thanks!" Mason ran back to the transport and called Levi from the road. "Jackrabbit, this is Eagle Eyes. Come in."

"Got good news, Eagle Eyes? Over."

"The cargo has reached the promised land. Over."

"Any sign of Buttercup?"

"Sorry, Jackrabbit. No sign." Mason dropped the radio into his lap and used both hands to turn the transport onto Gothic Road. He picked up the radio and said, "You copy?"

"Yeah, I got that, Eagle Eyes."

"How's the leg?" Mason wished there was a way for him to be of more help. "Over."

"He's still breathing, Eagle Eyes. Over and out."

Mason said a prayer for Levi's friend and for Jemma, and for Levi not to lose his mind wondering where Jemma was. The lights were still out when he got back to the Westwall. He parked the transport and walked inside the building, carefully making his way up the stairs to Ciddah's floor. He raised his fist to knock on her door, but before he could, the door swung in.

Ciddah stood in the doorway, white-faced and red-eyed. She grabbed him in a hug that froze his breath. "Thank Fortune! I thought something had happened to you!"

"The power is out," he said, inhaling the vanilla-cinnamon smell of her hair to get his lungs working again.

"I know that!" She pulled him inside. Ciddah tugged him past the kitchen, where a bright beam momentarily blinded him.

"What is that?" Mason asked.

"A flashlight I set on the counter. What took you so long?"

"It's kind of hard to order cupcakes when the power is out. I had to convince the clerk it was an emergency." A clerk who would hopefully be Mason's alibi should anyone ask.

Standing in his shadow, Ciddah looked up into his face, her eyes like two crystals. "A cupcake emergency? Did she believe you?"

"He. And yes." Mason held up the box.

Ciddah grinned. She took the box and sat on the sofa. He sat beside her and closed his eyes, thankful the women were free — or at least in hiding. They'd actually done it.

A gasp from Ciddah caused his eyes to flash open. "You got spice cake."

"You said you liked it."

"And you listened."

He grinned. "Is that so foreign?"

"A man who listens?" Her expression darkened. "You'd be surprised."

Mason stretched his left arm along the back of the sofa and turned his body a bit, so he could see her face. "Okay, surprise me."

She cast her gaze to the box of cupcakes. "Mason, most men who live here ... are not like you."

"They're women, then?"

"No." She chuckled. "They're ... selfish."

"Not your father."

"In a way, he is. When I told him I was going to be a medic, he worried they'd use me."

"Worrying about your daughter isn't selfish. It's a father's duty."

"Fine. I said *most* men."

He wanted to ask about Lawten, but something held him back. "You knew many men who bought you the wrong kind of cupcakes?"

"One did. He always ordered my food. And when I said, 'I don't like my steak rare,' he'd say, 'Yes you do, shimmer.'"

"He called you 'shimmer'?"

"That's a word men use for beautiful here. He called me shimmer all the time, but he never made me feel beautiful. He'd say things like,

'You're going to wear that?' or 'Shimmer, you should probably skip dessert. Walls, skip breakfast tomorrow too. I like my women slim.' "

"He sounds like a jerk."

"He was. But I ..." She ran her finger through the frosting on one of the spiced cupcakes and licked the end of her finger.

Mason didn't know how to respond. He wanted to ask why she spent time with a cruel man, but he could tell from her pinched brow that it hadn't been that simple. And he'd been set up to marry Mia, so clearly he wasn't one to judge the inner workings of relationships.

"Omar betrayed my people," Mason said. "He's responsible for my father's death and the death of countless others. But he's still my brother. I hate what he did and the choices he's making now, but ... I love that kid. I always will. Sometimes relationships are complicated."

Ciddah turned those crystal orbs on Mason. The low lighting made her skin, and even her hair, appear bone white. She blinked, and when her eyes reopened, she was looking at his lips.

Heat crept over him. He wanted to kiss her. Instead, he removed his arm from the back of the couch and gestured to the box on her lap. "Are you going to share?"

She jolted a bit, as if coming back from someplace far away. She glanced into the box. "You like chocolate, I see."

"Doesn't everyone?" Mason said.

"I prefer spice cake." She handed Mason a chocolate cupcake with rainbow sprinkles. "Thanks for being my friend, Mason."

He let his gaze travel her face. The part in her hair ... her tiny nose ... those thick, impossible eyelashes ... the soft fuzz of her pale eyebrows ... the curve of her lips. "I like being your friend."

"But nothing more?"

Her words made him study the sprinkles on the top of his cupcake. Here was the moment he'd been dreading. And how should he answer? Win her love? Lose her friendship?

Ciddah's voice came cold and detached. "Forget I said that, okay?"

"Ciddah ..." *Do something! Don't let her think you don't care.*

"Mason, I didn't mean it. I mean, I did, but ..." Ciddah lowered her voice. "I just didn't mean to say it."

He stood and set the cupcake back in the box. And now he was Omar, running away. "I should probably go." *No! Stay, you fool!* What was the matter with him?

She popped up beside him. "Can't you wait until the lights come back on?"

"It might be hours — or days."

She stepped close, gaze focused on his shirt. "You could sleep on my couch." She touched one of the buttons on the front of his shirt. "Please?"

He *could*. But he didn't think she meant sleep. "Ciddah ... It wouldn't be right."

She looked up, brow pinched. "Your prudishness drives me crazy, do you know that?"

If she only knew what he was thinking. "It's not prudishness so much as propriety."

She reached up and touched his cheek, then brushed her thumb over his lips. "Your innocence is so stimming attractive."

He frowned at her flawed logic. "And so you want to take it? Then that which attracts you to me would be gone. And I would be at a disadvantage."

"Mason, what you hold as conventional standards of behavior are foreign in this place. Safe Lands propriety would dictate that you stay the night, because you want to spend more time with me and would find it enjoyable. That is, if you would ... like to, I mean."

"I would." He closed his eyes, not at all comfortable with the impulses welling up within him, seeking to take control. "I do."

"Then stay!"

He shook his head then opened his eyes. "What has Safe Lands propriety gained you, Ciddah? You said it yourself. Your men are mean. They lack self-control. They play, but they suffer no consequences for their actions. All in good fun, no matter who gets infected or hurt or heartbroken, correct? And that's what you want from me? Just another good time?"

She looked deep into his eyes and whispered, "I want someone who cares and won't leave."

Oh, how her words tempted him. But he dug down deep. "Believe it or not, Ciddah, my leaving right now is proof that I care for you a great deal."

CHAPTER 39

Levi shined his light over the ridged pipe until he spotted the purple number two he'd written with the makeup crayon. "One more." He shone the flashlight at his feet and took careful steps, holding Zane's waist with his other arm, half carrying him. They were almost back.

"Lonn will help you go after your girl," Zane said. "Now that he's free."

Maybe, but it wouldn't be easy. "If Bender knew how to break someone out of the RC, he'd have gotten Lonn out long ago." Levi moved the light away from the dirty water and over the pipe until he saw his number one. "This is it." He helped Zane stand beside the ladder. "Think you can climb up?"

"If I use my right leg and drag my left."

"I'll go up and move the sign. If you need help, I'll come back down." Levi put the end of the flashlight into his mouth and climbed. When he reached the top, he slid away the sign, hoping no one was near enough to hear it scrape over the concrete. Once the space above him was free, he climbed another rung and peeked out. The dead-end alley was vacant.

"How you doing?" he called down to Zane.

"I got this," Zane said.

Good. Levi climbed out and carried the sign toward the grass where they'd left the manhole cover. The wind blew his wet clothes against his skin, chilling him through.

When Zane's head appeared above the roadline, Levi pulled him up and helped him sit in the grass. Then Levi inserted the manhole hook into the cover to pull it.

"Need some help with that?" a voice from behind him said.

Levi spun around. Three men in civilian clothes blocked the alley's exit. Omar with his two enforcer friends.

"Hay-o, brother." Omar pointed a gun at Levi. "Guess this will be three marks for you."

"If you say so," Levi said as he reached for his rifle.

"Don't bother." To Levi's shock, Omar shot first.

For the third time, enforcers led Levi into the Rehabilitation Center and down the narrow pathway between the cells. People shouted at him, but the enforcers dragged him all the way to the end and put him in a cell on the right.

"Looks like you're here for the last time," the enforcer said and closed Levi's door.

Levi fell onto his mattress, face first, and lay there exhausted, trying not to think. But so many thoughts filled his mind. Omar had betrayed him again. Would they liberate him immediately? Would it be on the ColorCast? At least he'd freed the Glenrock women. All but Jemma.

He could hear her voice calling for help. He closed his eyes, overwhelmed at how he'd failed her. What if Levi never saw his love again? What if she were forced to live here forever? The thought made him sick.

"Levi of Elias."

He sat up and looked into the adjacent cell. A toothless man pointed away, across the corridor. Levi followed his direction to the cell directly opposite from his.

Kneeling at the door, face pressed between the two bars that she clutched with her fists, was Jemma. She smiled. "I thought maybe they'd given you a sedative."

"Jem!"

He practically flew across his cell to the door and reached out. Jemma reached as well, stretching until their fingertips brushed. Levi twisted so that his shoulder slipped between the bars. Jemma mirrored him, and their palms pressed together.

Levi bent his fingers around her hand and squeezed. She had an X by the number four on her cheek. "Are you okay? Did they hurt you?"

"I'm fine. But I don't know what happened to Shaylinn and Naomi and Kendall."

"Kendall had her baby, and they took it from her. Shaylinn and the others ..." He paused, not convinced the walls didn't have ears. "They're safe."

Jemma started to cry. "What about the children?"

"Still working on that."

"But what about you? You have three Xs. Arc they going to execute you?"

The look on her face, as if he were dying in her arms, was too much. He couldn't let her worry. "Maybe. But don't worry, Buttercup. Death cannot stop true love. All it can do is delay it for a while."

Jemma's face lit up. "I will never doubt again."

"There will never be a need."

CHAPTER 40

Omar sat on the soft red chair in the task director general's office, giddy with the knowledge that Renzor again owed him. As usual, Kruse stood beside the desk, holding his Wyndo and looking too busy to bother with Omar. Wait until the task director rewarded him — then Kruse would pay attention.

The task director leaned back in his chair. "Mr. Strong, what *shall* I do with you? You must know I'm not a fool."

"Of course not, sir," Omar said, distressed by the tone of the man's voice. A tone void of gratitude.

"How do I know you didn't help them? You never turned in your enforcer uniform."

Because he'd forgotten. And he'd been holding out hope. "I *didn't* help them. I stopped them."

Those vulture eyes watched him. "How did you know to listen to the radios?"

"I told you. I know my brother. And when I heard that someone in a DPT uniform was shooting, I figured it was Levi, since he tasks in maintenance and is still a scavenger at heart. He would've stolen radios from someplace. Why not from where he tasks?"

"But where did he get the gun? And how did he know where and when to shoot? These are things an enforcer has the resources to learn."

Cold despair threatened to bring tears. Anything but tears. Omar composed himself, fought to control his emotions. "But I caught him. I brought him to you."

"And I grow tired of seeing your face. You'll report to the Registration Department — "

"I don't believe this!" How could the task director think he'd helped Levi?

" — for task reassignment — "

"That's not fair! I helped you!"

" — and receive new lodgings in the Midlands."

Omar breathed slowly through his nose, glanced at Kruse, who stood like a tree shading the task director. A tree oblivious that Omar was even there. "That's my only option?"

"Unless you'd rather join your brother in the Rehabilitation Center."

"Gee, let me think it over, will you?"

"Your attitude does not bode well for your future here."

"So sorry, *sir.* If you ever got up out of that chair, maybe I'd do a better job at kissing your — "

"Good day, Mr. Strong."

Omar pushed off his chair, set both hands on the edge of the task director's desk, and leaned forward. "May you be liberated soon, you flaking zombie." That was finally enough to get Kruse's attention. The pink-painted assistant threw Omar out of the office.

Omar took the stairwell to the Registration Department, trembling so badly he had to sit on a step and vape just to calm down. This was *all* his brother's fault. Levi, who just had to be a hero. And now Levi was going to be liberated. Another death for Omar to feel responsible for.

Because liberation had to be death, and Bliss some twisted idea of heaven. Right? But Omar couldn't imagine people looking forward to death, even with the belief of returning as someone else. He also didn't put it past the Guild to lie.

Where else would the people go, though? Helicopters and planes came and went from the area every so often. Maybe they took the liberated to some city called Bliss? No, that was just desperate thinking.

Why didn't the Safe Lands nationals question any of it? They all longed for liberation as if it were a puff of brown sugar. Couldn't these people think for themselves? Why did they scarf down everything the ColorCast fed them?

After a quick visit with Dallin, Omar walked across the street to the Snowcrest, stewing over his situation. Living in the Midlands would make visiting the clubs in the Highlands more difficult. He hoped Skottie would come get him. The only positive thing to come out of this situation was that his reassignment meant he would be tasking as a SimArt designer. Dallin told him to report to a place called Sim Slingers.

Omar pushed up his sleeve and studied the black lines that wrapped around his arm. Maybe now he could do his owl.

Back in his apartment, he packed up his clothes, his art supplies, a few paintings, and several vials of juice. He was up to a brown sugar three now and a ten with grass. In the back of his mind, he wanted to cut back, but every time he went to buy more, his willpower betrayed him.

He went into his bathroom to grab his shaving tools and studied his reflection in his bathroom mirror. He didn't look sick. How long until his skin started to flake? How long until his veins started to show?

Belbeline.

Her name made him ache. Memories of her laugh, her touch, her eyes. Why couldn't he forget her? Brush her off like Skottie did with women? It was pathetic that he couldn't.

What if he simply filled his PV with a brown sugar ten? That would end this for good. Then he'd know if liberation was a load of dung.

But whatever remained of the old Omar insisted he should leave before he did any more damage to himself. Get out of the city. Go to Jack's Peak or Wyoming.

Jemma's face came to mind suddenly, surprising him at the powerful emotions she stirred within him. He'd heard on Charlz's scanner that she was in the RC. Jemma was one of the few people who'd always been nice to him, treated him kindly, and stuck up for him when his Father treated him like a cowardly animal.

Omar hated her. But the thought made him laugh. He *wanted* to hate her. But who could hate such light and beauty? Such goodness. No one. Especially not Omar.

Perhaps, if he was careful, he could find a way to help her.

The buzz of his doorbell made him jump. *Belbeline?* His heart swelled within him. Maybe she'd changed her mind. Wanted him back. He ran to the door and pulled it open.

Instead, Skottie stood on his doorstep, Charlz leaning beside him. "It's about time, peer," Skottie said. "Don't you answer your transmitter?"

As Skottie brushed past on his way into the apartment, Omar gazed down the hallway hoping for a glimpse of a red-haired beauty. But the hallway was vacant, filled only with memories. He closed the door.

"You listening to me, Omar?" Skottie said. "Just look at him!"

Omar turned then and saw that Skottie was supporting Charlz's weight, that Charlz was bloody and dazed. "What happened?"

"*Now* you're home," Skottie said. "You been vaping the sweet stuff today?"

"A little."

"Well, help me get him to the couch. He weighs a ton."

Omar moved to Charlz's right, and together he and Skottie hefted their friend to the couch. "Who did this?"

"Otley," Skottie said. "Turns out Janique is one of Otley's claims. When she heard Charlz was in the RC, she came to find out what happened. Otley didn't like that. Had Charlz worked over. They interrogated me too, asked a lot of questions about you and your outsider brother, like we know anything about that prude. But they didn't hit me. Just Charlz."

For the first time, Omar noticed that Skottie and Charlz both had an X by the numbers on their faces. "They Xed you guys?"

"Yeah, and kicked us out of the enforcers. Guess where I get to task now? Stimming taxi driver. And I've got to move to the Midlands. I've never been so fried in all my life."

Charlz spoke, slurred and soft. "I gotta clean poop."

"Sewage cleaner," Skottie said. "They made us both retake the test. Charlz was too out of it to really read the questions. He botched it bad."

Omar sank onto the couch beside Charlz. "This is my fault. I shouldn't have tried to catch Levi. And I definitely shouldn't have dragged you guys with me. Maybe my father was right, maybe — "

"Stim down," Skottie said. "Charlz and I aren't minors, you know. We make our own choices. Frankly, I don't blame those rebels for trying to get their peers away from Otley. Wish I had some way to burn that overgrown, hairy downer. Make him regret he ever saw me."

"Wait. You think my brother was right to shoot out the power?"

"I don't know. Maybe. Now that I'm banned from enforcement, the law just doesn't matter. Not like it used to."

"Wish I could liberate Otley," Charlz said.

Omar's mind felt like it was working clearly for the first time since he'd arrived in the Safe Lands. Skottie knew that Camella woman in Surveillance. They'd all done their tour of the RC in class. And Charlz had a collection of stunners. "I have an idea that could make the enforcers wish they'd never demoted us. But you need to help me get my brother and his girl out of the RC."

"Serious? Now you want to help him?" Skottie said.

"I'll help you do anything that'll make Otley mad," Charlz mumbled.

Omar raised his eyebrows at Skottie.

"Fine," Skottie said. "But you better have a plan, 'cause I don't want a premie lib."

"Did you guys turn in your enforcer IDs yet?" Omar asked.

Skottie shook his head.

Charlz said, "No."

"Me either. Skottie, tap that girl up in Surveillance and see if you can stop by. Charlz, I'll need you to help me get past the front desk and take out the enforcers at the RC, then keep watch. How are you feeling?"

"I'll be fine. Just need to clean up."

"Good." A rebellious thrill surged over Omar, making him feel powerful, strong.

"How we know Skottie's up there?" Charlz asked as they walked up to the front doors of the RC sometime after three in the morning. The sky was like a canvas coated in midnight paint flicked with glitter and illuminated by an oblong half moon.

"We don't," Omar said, bringing his gaze back to earth. "We just have to hope he is."

"And you're sure she can override the Authorization System once we get to the cells?"

"According to Skottie, she can log us in as anyone she wants."

Thanks to Charlz's connections with several female receptionists, they faced minimum questioning as they entered the RC, passed the front desk, and called the elevator. When the door finally slid open, Omar was relieved to find it empty inside.

He'd been smart to come at night. Fewer enforcers tasking at this hour. Fewer witnesses and possible fights. Omar wasn't looking forward to having to punch someone.

As soon as the elevator doors opened, Charlz slid in and covered the yellow camera lens as Omar put on a creepy Luella Flynn mask Charlz had grabbed from his apartment on the way over. It smelled like chemicals. Omar had wanted to wear the Finley one, but Charlz had insisted on first pick. Omar would never get why anyone would pay credits for stupid masks like these, though he was glad Charlz had them. His friend's odd quirks were finally coming in handy.

The elevator opened. Charlz stuck his boot against the door and peeked into the guards' chamber. "I see one. He's mine." He drew his stunner and ran out of the elevator.

Omar drew his own stunner and followed, but by the time he reached Charlz's back, the clicking of Charlz's weapon had stopped and an enforcer lay on his side, moaning. Omar took the man's weapons and handcuffs, which he used to secure the enforcer's arms behind his back, then dragged the man into the bathroom and ripped off his shoulder radio. Omar attached the radio to his shoulder and returned to the guards' chamber.

Charlz was sitting at the front desk still wearing his Finley mask. "I'm Finley Gray, coming to you live from the RC. Find pleasure in life."

Omar glanced up at the camera and hoped Skottie had it covered. "Only one guard?"

"It's three in the morning, peer."

Omar looked at the computer screen, though the information meant little to him. "You find them?"

"Cell thirty-nine and forty. Should be all the way to the end."

A man's yell drew their attention to the bathroom. The guard.

"I'll take care of him." Charlz said. "Get your people."

Omar held his stunner ready in case there were guards inside, and, with a long breath, he opened the door.

The cell block was dark but for three lights evenly spaced along the ceiling. Omar knew from his training tour that they shut down most of the lights at ten o'clock each night. No sign of enforcers. He strode down the aisle, his breath a steady hiss against the rubber mask.

His gaze darted back and forth across the aisle, checking the cell numbers. *Ten, eleven ... sixteen, seventeen ... Halfway there.* He glanced up at a yellow surveillance camera and really hoped Skottie had been able to get his girl to help.

When he reached the end, he nearly stepped on Levi and Jemma's arms, which were stretched out into the corridor, fingers intertwined.

The way they were both lying on the floor against the bars, he couldn't open either cell without waking them.

He stood there, frustrated, trying to decide which to open first. An image of Levi choking him to death popped into his mind. He spoke into the enforcer's shoulder radio. "E112 to Highland Gatekeeper, requesting entry to prison cell forty."

"Please verify identification," a woman's voice replied.

Omar set his fist against the black pad on the cell door and held his breath. Come on, Skottie. His girl better come through.

"Identification verified," the woman said.

Omar blew out his relief and nudged the door open. Jemma sighed dreamily, released Levi's hand, and rolled over enough that Omar was able to squeeze inside. He crouched, reached for Jemma's shoulder and—

"What are you doing?" Levi's voice made Omar jump. "Get away from her!"

Omar turned to see Levi standing at the door of his cell, gripping the bars and glaring.

"It's me, brother," Omar said, remembering his mask. He spoke into the radio again. "E112 to Highland Gatekeeper, requesting entry to prison cell thirty-nine."

"Please verify identification."

Omar slipped out of Jemma's cell and set his fist against the pad on Levi's door. "Keep your voice down, or you'll wake everyone," he said to Levi.

"You betrayed me again, Omar. What's your angle this time?" Levi asked.

"Identification verified," the woman said.

Omar pushed in the door. "To get you and Jemma out of here."

Levi glanced at the stunner in Omar's hand. "You going to shoot me with that?"

"No! Look, I'm sorry about before. I'm trying to make it right. But we don't have much time, so come on!" Omar ran back into Jemma's cell and grabbed her arm. "Jemma! Wake up!"

Levi tackled him from behind, and Omar felt all air leave his body. Levi smashed Omar's face against the concrete, and though Omar tucked his chin to protect his nose, his right temple slammed into the ground. Blinding pain shot all the way down his neck. The mask was little cushion.

"Stop it!" Jemma said. "Levi, don't!"

The weight vanished from Omar's back. It took a moment to straighten the mask, and when his eyes looked out through the holes, the cell was empty. He pushed up to his feet and saw Levi and Jemma halfway down the aisle, standing at another cell. Levi shook the door.

"Who's in there?" Omar asked, jogging to catch up. "One of ours?"

"None of your business," Levi said.

"E112 to Highland Gatekeeper requesting entry to prison cell ..." Omar glanced up. "Eighteen."

"Please verify identification."

Omar pressed his fist to the pad on the door just as Levi slammed his shoulder into Omar, knocking him out of the way. Omar stumbled to the side and barely caught himself on the bars.

"Levi, stop!" Jemma said.

But Levi pushed past her and grabbed Omar's shirtfront. "Stay away from me." He slammed Omar against the cell grate. The back of Omar's head struck—

" ... now, Omar? Huh?"

Omar blinked. Two bars pressed into his back. He squinted. What had Levi asked? "Uh ... I'm trying to ..." Omar said, struggling to breathe over the pain throbbing in his temple and the back of his head, straining to remember. "Make it right. That's all. Know I can't, but ..." He choked back a sob. "Just trying, okay? Should ... hurry."

"Identification verified." The woman's voice came through the speaker on his arm.

The door clicked open. Levi elbowed past, knocking Omar to the ground again. A wave of dizziness swept over him. He stumbled into bars on his right and took a deep breath, watching as Levi and Jemma helped a man with a bandaged leg out of cell eighteen. Omar grabbed the nearest bars and stepped toward them, but his leg gave out. He fell, nausea gripped him, and he threw up.

"Omar!" Jemma appeared at his side. "Levi, help!"

"I'm helping Zane!"

Jemma's face swam before Omar's, a haze of beauty and concern. He opened his mouth to tell her how pretty she was, how he missed looking at his drawing that used to hang above his bed. But her face went away, and Levi was there, scowling like always.

"You never ... smile," Omar said. "Why you ... hate me, brother?"

The scowl faded to a look of shock. Levi heaved Omar up to a standing position, but Omar's legs still weren't working. Omar slumped in Levi's arms.

"Wasn't supposed to happen," Omar whispered. "Forgive me."

Levi crouched and bent Omar's body over his shoulder.

The rest was a blur. Omar floated. Charlz spoke. Stairs. Screaming. Clicking stunners. Levi's voice. A yelling woman — not Jemma. Cool night air on his face. No mask. Sleep...

When Omar opened his eyes, his head was in Jemma's lap, her fingertips brushing through his hair. He wanted to stay in this place forever. But then the pain came, swelling from within, crushing his skull.

"He tried to set things right, Levi, and you could have killed him," Jemma said. "He asked forgiveness. You should respect that."

"Are you hearing yourself, Jem? He may as well have killed eighteen people with his own hand. Not to mention whatever happened to your mother and mine. How can I respect that?"

"And are you hearing yourself? He asked forgiveness. End of story."

"Jem — "

"Anyone who knows the good he ought to do and doesn't do it, sins." Jemma looked down on Omar then, met his gaze, and said softly, "I forgive you, Omar."

CHAPTER 41

Omar's friend Charlz drove Levi and the others to the back of the Bradbury—the place Jordan had taken the women underground the night of Lonn's liberation. Zane cut out Omar and Jemma's SimTags. He put Omar's in a pair of gloves, but destroyed Jemma's. He didn't think he could handle another trek through the storm drains on his leg, so Zane asked Charlz to drive him to the Highlands Public Task department, likely to see Dayle. He took Omar's gloves with him, promising to lead the enforcers on a pointless chase until Omar decided what to do next.

Levi, Jemma, and Omar traveled the storm drains until morning, making their way to the underground bunker. Evidently, Jordan had removed all Levi's purple crayon marks—smart thinking—to erase their trail, but it made it difficult for Levi to find the way.

When he finally located their destination, he made Omar stand back in the darkness of the tunnel. "Until I can talk to Jordan," Levi said. He stepped into the alcove that held the bunker door, took hold of Jemma's hand, and gave the secret knock.

The door swung in and revealed Jordan's smiling face. "What took you so long? I've been waiting all—*Jemma!*" He hugged her, kissed the top of her head, and rocked back on his heels, lifting her feet off the ground. "So glad to see you, sister."

"Everyone's here?" Jemma asked. "Everyone's okay? Shaylinn? Mama?"

Jordan's brows drew together. "We've got the women from the harem, all but Mia and Jennifer, who wouldn't come. But the liberation thing ... It didn't work out."

Levi stiffened. "What do you mean?"

"When Bender got there, no one was there. Turns out the liberations are recorded in advance."

"Why would that be?" Levi asked.

"We learned about this when we were in the harem," Jemma said. "It's so they can edit them. If they film in advance, they can make sure the people see only what the directors want them to see."

"Yeah" — Jordan shrugged — "that's pretty much what that Bender guy said too."

So ... Levi's mother was already dead? Or was liberation something else? He couldn't have lost his mother too. "What about the children? You come up with a plan to rescue them?"

Jordan snorted. "You kidding? Most of the women are paranoid because Mason didn't cut the SimTags out of their faces, and every mother here has a different plan for how to get her children back. I'm not cut out to be Elder of dung. I'm so glad you're here to take over."

Levi doubted he could handle the tension any better. First things first: He had to fix this mess with Omar. "I need a favor, Jordan. And you must promise not to hurt him."

Jordan's brow wrinkled low over his eyes. "Who?"

"Promise me."

"Yeah, if you say so. I promise."

Levi stepped back, reached around the corner, and pulled Omar out by the arm.

Jordan eyes flashed. He tried to push past Levi, but Levi held him back. Before Levi could react further, Jordan spun the other way, knocked past Jemma, and slid to his knees on the storm drain, splashing into the shallow water. He grabbed Omar by the legs and yanked him onto his rear. "You rabid, dung-licking ..." Jordan pushed Omar's head into the water.

"Jordan, no!" Jemma yelled.

Omar squeezed his eyes shut and pressed his lips together, though the water only reached his ears. He tried to squirm free. "I'm sorry! Don't hurt me!"

"Yeah, beg, you poor excuse for a maggot." Jordan scooped water over Omar's face.

Levi grabbed Jordan's waist and pulled him back. "You promised me!"

"Get off, Levi. This needs to be done."

"You want me to be the elder? You've got to respect my word. And I say stop it, now!"

Jordan elbowed Levi and crawled to standing. "Yeah, okay, *Elder Levi.* But you've got to convince me why I can't kill him. Can you do that, huh?"

"Yes. But I need you to keep him safe until I can prepare the women for his arrival. Can you hide him somewhere without anyone seeing him?"

Jordan growled. "Yeah, I can do that."

"Without hurting him?"

"I said yeah."

"Do it then." Levi helped Omar stand, and they all followed Jordan inside. Jordan secured the door and led them down a short tunnel. It smelled stale, as if it had been ignored for years.

"The big room with the kitchen and TV is to the right," Jordan said. "The bedrooms and bathroom are to the left. I'm gonna take your swine-stinking brother to my room."

"Actually," Levi said, "now that I've seen the layout, just hold him right here. I'll only need a minute. I'll call you in."

"You're the elder, *Elder.*"

Levi ignored Jordan's snark, knowing how hard it must be for Jordan not to pound Omar into flatbread. A few yards ahead, the hallway ended in a rotted wooden door. Levi and Jemma pushed it open. The "big room" wasn't all that big. It had a one-wall kitchen on the end, three round tables with chairs in the center, some ratty couches, and an Old TV.

"Jemma!" Shaylinn ran to the door and hugged her sister. "They found you."

The next half hour was a mix of mourning and celebration in the bunker under the Midlands. Levi didn't know which to feel, as he still had Omar to deal with. He finally brought his fingers to his mouth and whistled. "Listen up, everyone. We should make a plan to get you all out of here. I'd like to take you to Jack's Peak, where you'll have some protection until I can figure out how to get to the kids."

"What about the children?" Eliza asked. "We need to get them out of here."

"They're all alone ..." Mary's words disintegrated into sobs.

Aunt Chipeta smiled at Levi. "We appreciate your wanting to protect us, but none of us could live with ourselves if we simply left. That you got us out of the harem has given everyone hope we will see our children again."

Perhaps there was some way they could all help. "I don't know what they do with liberated people. I hope they're not ... Well, we need to find out. But Mason says the kids are in the boarding school or the caretaking facilities. The enforcers are going to be watching both closely for a while. So we need to be patient. And forgiving. I know this is really stressful on everyone, but we need to stand together. Love each other. Do you trust me?"

"Of course," Aunt Chipeta said.

"What's your plan, Levi?" Eliza asked.

Here goes. "First ... I ask you all to hold your tongues and open your minds and hearts at what you're about to see. Jordan!"

The door opened, and Omar stepped into the room with Jordan behind him, broad-shouldered and menacing.

"Oh!" Shaylinn clapped her hand over her mouth.

"What's *he* doing here?" Mary asked.

"Did you capture him?" Eliza asked.

Levi smiled at Omar, hoping it didn't look forced. "He freed me and Jemma from the RC."

"Omar rescued us," Jemma said.

Eliza narrowed her eyes. "Why?"

"Let's see what Omar has to say?" Levi sat down so that Omar would have the floor. His little brother, at only sixteen, looked hunched and frail. His skin was pale, his eyes bloodshot and creased with heavy circles, and the black tattoo that peeked out from his sleeve made him look wild. A true "shell" if Levi had ever seen one.

"I didn't mean for anyone to die," Omar blurted out. "I just wanted to do something my father would be proud of. Show I was good enough." He rubbed the scar between his eyes. "But I'm not. And the task director lied to me." Omar heaved in a deep breath. "I don't know if I can ever make up for what I did, but — "

"You can't," Jordan said.

Omar looked at his hands and threaded his fingers together. "You're right." He glanced up, then back at his hands, then up again. "I know you're right."

"What do you want?" Eliza's voice was low.

"To say I'm sorry."

"Sorry doesn't undo anything, Omar," Eliza said. "It doesn't bring Mark back."

"Why did you do it, really?" Jordan asked. "Your father wouldn't have been proud to see you in an enforcer's uniform." Levi didn't understand Omar's logic either.

"So he could prove his dad was wrong about him," Shaylinn said. "That he had worth. Elder Justin was so mean to him. He was mean to me too."

"My father was honest," Levi said. "He never meant to hurt anyone."

"But he did." Shaylinn folded her arms. "And he never apologized. I don't mean to speak ill of your father, it's just . . . we've all hurt people without meaning to. Isn't that right, Omar?"

Omar nodded at Shaylinn. "I never wanted any of these horrible things to happen."

"Fine," Eliza said. "Then why didn't you move to the Safe Lands and leave us be?"

Omar's forehead wrinkled. "Do any of you remember when Papa Eli told my father to take me hunting with him and Elsu? And how my father reacted?"

Levi hung his head in memory of that awkward moment. Father *had* been cruel.

"The next day I took a rig to Crested Butte," Omar said, "hoping to scavenge something that would prove to my father that I wasn't a useless mouth to feed. Instead, I ran into some enforcers. They asked if I wanted to see the city and took me to meet the task director general. The city was amazing, and I wondered what it might be like to live there. The task director said I could, that he'd send some men to Glenrock to see if you all wanted to give the city a try as well."

Omar had walked right into the lions' den. If only Levi had reached out to him sooner.

"I told them to come while Father was in Denver City," Omar said. "I figured that when he returned and found me gone, he'd be relieved to finally be free of me."

"*Omar* ..." Aunt Chipeta said.

His words were a fist to Levi's gut. Omar must have thought their father hated him.

"It's true, and you all know it," Omar said, matter of fact. "No one was supposed to get hurt. I didn't really understand what they wanted. I was stupid, like always." He heaved a deep sigh. "Anyway, I just wanted to explain to you and to say I'm sorry. Because I am. And now I'll leave, and none of you will ever have to see me again." He walked toward the exit.

What? He's just going to leave? Levi started across the room to stop him.

But Jordan was already blocking the exit.

"One of the things that drove Elder Justin nuts about you was how you always run," Jordan said. "So prove your father wrong now, Omar. Saying sorry isn't good enough. You need to stay and work, to help put things right."

"I got Levi and Jemma out of the RC," Omar said.

"That's a start. But this ain't over 'til we're home. All of us. And this place ain't home."

Omar rubbed the scar on the bridge of his nose. "What else do you want me to do?"

"Sit down, and let Elder Levi talk." Jordan pushed Omar into a chair and went to sit beside Naomi.

A swell of pride filled Levi at Jordan's words. He looked around the room and said, "I'm not the elder unless that's what everyone wants."

"But you're next in line," Naomi said.

"That may be, but Aunt Chipeta is the eldest." Levi nodded to where his aunt sat beside Jemma. "Then Mary, then Eliza, then Jordan, *then* me."

"Age doesn't matter," Aunt Chipeta said. "You're Elder Elias's heir. You're meant to be patriarch."

Levi agreed, but he didn't want to do this alone. "Papa Eli had an elder council to help him. I'd like one too."

So they formed an elder council: Mary, Aunt Chipeta, Eliza, Jordan, Levi, and Mason once he escaped as well. The five present council members crowded around one table to have their first official meeting. Jemma, Shaylinn, and Naomi went into the kitchen to make lunch. Omar sat alone on the sofa.

The council's first decree was that no one would leave the Safe Lands until every possible member of Glenrock had been rescued. They also discussed whether they should send a message to Jennifer and Mia and if they could be trusted, and ways they might try to free the children. Levi said that their efforts largely depended on Mason and Bender now.

Jemma approached the table and circled to stand behind Levi. She put her hands on his shoulders and squeezed. "The food is ready."

Levi turned to look up at her. He caught sight of the gold chain disappearing into the neckline of her dress and jumped up. "Elder Jordan!" He took Jemma by the hand and pulled her to Jordan's side of the table. "Will you marry us?"

Jemma gasped. Naomi hurried toward them from the kitchen.

"Oh, yes! Please do, Jordan," Aunt Chipeta said. "They should've been married days ago."

Jordan pushed up from his chair. "Really? Can I do that?"

Levi's heart raced. This was finally going to happen. His wedding to this beautiful woman. He removed the necklace from Jemma's neck and handed it to Jordan. "Only an elder can. And we are elders now."

"I'll do my best then." Jordan raised his voice. "Gather round, witnesses. We need your eyes. This man and woman wish — "

With a shout of protest, Aunt Chipeta, Mary, and Eliza all stood at once.

"Not right this moment, Jordan," Aunt Chipeta said.

"While this is far from the ideal circumstance, a bride deserves some time to prepare, both physically and spiritually," Eliza said.

The women whisked Jemma away to one of the bedrooms, leaving Levi speechless.

"But what about lunch?" Jordan called after them.

"Eat it," Naomi yelled. "We'll get some later."

And the boys were left alone.

Jordan walked toward the kitchen. "Guess I'll help myself then."

Omar's laugh pulled Levi's gaze to where his brother sat on the couch.

Levi went and sat beside him. "What's so funny?"

"Did you really think the women were going to let Jordan say, 'I declare you married' and be done with it?"

Levi fell back against the stale couch cushions. "That would have been nice."

They sat together. Omar had been watching a show called *Easy Bake*, in which a woman was teaching how to make something called boule bread, which reminded Levi of Kosowe, a woman he didn't want to be thinking about just before his wedding.

Maybe this was the time to do something hard. To try and dismantle this unspoken wall between him and his youngest brother. "Omar," Levi took a deep breath. "Do you remember a couple years ago? When we stayed the night in Jack's Peak?"

Omar raised one eyebrow and smirked. "I remember."

Levi wished he hadn't. He forced himself to speak. "I'm hoping you'll ... I don't think Jemma needs to, you know, know. I thought of telling her but ... I was wrong even to — "

"You weren't engaged to Jemma then," Omar said. "And you didn't really do anything to be ashamed of."

Levi sat up straight. "I didn't?"

"You don't remember?"

"Only waking up in Kosowe's teepee." And seeing Omar's face.

"You kissed her. A lot. But that was it. All five of us slept in there. Beshup and Tsana got up at a decent hour, but you and Kosowe were dead to the world. I got bored and woke you up so we could go home."

Levi had jumped to the worst possible conclusion. And Kosowe had let him. All this time the guilt had been for nothing. He looked at his brother in a new light. "Thank you, Omar."

Omar shrugged and looked back to the TV. "Glad to help clear your conscience."

Levi took a deep breath. Suddenly, he was trembling. "Omar ... would you ... That is, will you stand up with me? For the wedding?"

Omar turned his bloodshot eyes back to Levi and broke into a smile. "Sure."

The women bustled about all afternoon, making food and decorating the underground home with all manner of oddities. When Levi discreetly asked Aunt Chipeta about the fuss, she looked at him more seriously than he was prepared for. "I want to make sure Jemma has a wedding she deserves." She nodded toward Eliza and Naomi, who were making a bouquet out of pink and white tissues. "I think even the trivial things have a greater meaning right now. Plus, doing this for Jemma is a welcome distraction."

"I guess I didn't look at it that way. I just wanted to marry Jemma this minute."

Aunt Chipeta laughed. "As soon as Shaylinn and Mary finish putting together Jemma's dress, we should be ready. But while you're waiting, I suggest you take a shower. You look like you've been wearing the same thing for three days. I saw a shirt and a pair of pants in one of the bedrooms — don't come back until you've changed."

Levi did as he was told, though he discovered both the dark green long-sleeved button-up shirt and the dark blue pleated pants were way too big. When he returned to the main room and Mary saw him fisting the waistband, she threaded a black silk scarf through the belt loops.

Jordan and Omar laughed, so Mary put them to work moving the tables and setting up the chairs, which made an aisle that faced the shower curtain backdrop Aunt Chipeta had put up.

And then it was time.

Jemma stepped into the doorway, a princess in white. The other ladies stood and started to sing.

Here comes the bride dressed all in light,
Radiant and lovely she shines in his sight.
Gently she glides graceful as a dove,
Meeting her bridegroom her eyes full of love.

Jemma walked toward Levi. She wore a sleeveless white dress with a short flowing skirt that showed off her legs. Her hair was long and loose, clipped back above one ear by a single tissue flower. A layer of sheer white fabric poofed over her hair, barely covering her face. The world's shortest veil.

Levi took hold of her hand, thinking he'd never let go.

"Witnesses," Jordan said. "This man and woman wish to become one. Let us hear their pledge and hold them to it." He looked at Levi. "Levi of Elias, you bring a request to the elders of Glenrock?"

"I want to marry Jemma of Zachary," Levi said.

Jordan turned to Jemma. "Jemma of Zachary, your favor has been petitioned. What's your response?"

"I accept the offer."

Jordan leaned close to his sister. "Even though he snores?"

She smiled and tugged on Levi's hand. "Yes."

Jordan straightened and looked at the other faces in the room. "Does anyone have reason to speak against this union?" When no one spoke, he asked, "What elder will speak for this couple's commitment to one another?"

Aunt Chipeta stood up. "I will."

"People of Glenrock, you have witnessed an offer of marriage, an acceptance, and an endorsement by a village elder." Jordan's face blanked, as if he'd forgotten what came next.

Levi held up the rings.

"Right." Jordan took the rings from Levi and held them on his palm. "Exchange these rings as a token of your promise to one another."

Levi and Jemma took a ring and slid it onto each other's fingers.

"All right then," Jordan said. "She's yours! Take her in your arms and — "

"Don't forget the Father!" Naomi said.

"Of course!" Jordan clapped his hands. "My wife is wiser than me. Will you both serve our Father, the God in heaven, better together than you could on your own?"

"We will," Levi and Jemma said together.

"Then I declare you married! Be fruitful and multiply, and stay true to the ways of our elders. Kiss her, Levi, and keep her 'til God takes you home."

The little remnant from Glenrock cheered.

Levi wrapped his arms around Jemma's waist and looked down into her eyes. "You know, since the invention of the kiss, there have only been *six* kisses that were rated the most passionate, the most pure. *This one* will leave them all behind."

And it did.

CHAPTER 42

The Safe Lands Guild had summoned Mason to appear before them in regard to the escape of the harem women. He'd heard rumors they'd summoned Omar as well, after Jemma and Levi disappeared from the RC, but so far no one had been able to locate him. He hoped his brother was somewhere safe.

An hour and a half before the scheduled meeting, Mason dressed in the new outfit he'd bought, thinking it better not to appear before the Guild in scrubs. He came into his kitchen and glanced at the clock in the glass of the oven door. Time to go.

As he walked toward the door, he noticed the framed picture that hung over his couch was crooked. He crossed the room — stalling, he knew — and pushed up one corner of the picture until it was even.

Something fell off the top of the frame and landed with a soft *thwup* on the back of the couch. Mason picked up a small black rectangle and stared at the tiny words *MiniComm* that were engraved just over an on-off switch. The device was turned on.

He'd seen these before. On Ciddah's desk at the SC and on top of her Wyndo screen the night of Lonn's liberation. She had to have put it there. Ciddah was helping Lawten spy on him.

Mason's throat swelled, making it hard to swallow. He blew out a shaky breath and sat down on the couch. She'd no doubt left this device in his home the night Kendall had given birth, which meant that whoever was listening should have heard all his radio conversations with Levi. And now Mason had been summoned. No excuse he could give would stand against his own voice making subversive plans. Should he ignore the summons and try to find his brothers?

But if the Guild knew what he'd been doing, why hadn't he experienced opposition when he'd helped the women escape?

He thought back to when Ciddah had gotten up and gone over to the Wyndo the night of Lonn's liberation. Had she turned off the device? Changed her mind about helping Lawten? Or maybe she wasn't working for Lawten, but gathering information instead. But for what or whom?

Still feeling like his heart was lodged in his throat, he placed the MiniComm in the exact location where Ciddah had left it on top of the picture.

He'd been nervous about the summons before, but now ... Lord, help him. Suddenly, he felt very alone in this city. He should've left with the others.

But the children ...

Without recordings of him and Levi plotting, he didn't believe they could prove he'd had anything to do with the escapes. There'd been no cameras that night, not with the power out, so there should be no images of him driving the women across the Safe Lands. And he had the clerk from BabyKakes as a witness — and supposedly Ciddah.

She'd become the one person he'd thought he could trust in this place.

Clearly, he couldn't trust anyone.

Discussion Questions

1. If you were taken from your home and thrust into a culture different from your own, how do you think you'd react?

2. Have you heard of the saying, "The grass is always greener on the other side of the fence"? Omar was unhappy at home and believed that life would be better in the Safe Lands. Have you ever thought life would be better if you lived in another place?

3. Levi had a great relationship with his father; Omar had a poor one; Mason was somewhere in between. Do you think parents ever intend to play favorites?

4. Many of the men in Glenrock don't appear to tolerate Mason's training to be a doctor. Is that fair? Why or why not?

5. Is it a woman's birthright to be attractive and charming? What pressures do women face to measure up to certain societal standards for beauty? What pressures have you seen firsthand?

6. Do you think a paradise can also be a prison? Name some examples, if possible, that prove your opinion.

7. Safe Landers don't believe in death. How does this affect the way they live?

8. Is Mason misguided in his hopes to find a cure for the Thin Plague? Why?

9. Why does Omar fall so easily once he enters the Safe Lands, while Mason remains steadfast? What details from their personalities come into play?

10. Levi doesn't want to forgive Omar, but Jemma does. Do you think forgiving someone means condoning what they did? Why?

Acknowledgments

Thanks to Beth Moore for her Daniel Bible study, which inspired this story. And to: Amanda Luedeke, Jacque Alberta, Jeff Gerke, Stephanie Morrill, Chris Kolmorgen, Gillian Adams, Steve Rzasa, John Otte, Bill Myers, Kara Christensen, Kayla Ousley, Susie May Warren, Andy Lusco, Angie Lusco, Greg Bremner, Greg Armstrong, Neil Bauer, Marge and Chuck Wright, Eric Wiggin, Robert Treskillard, Go Teen Writers, Melanie Dickerson, Shellie Neumier, Nicole O'Dell, Richard Williamson, and as always, Brad, Luke, and Kaitlyn Williamson.

REPLICATION
THE JASON EXPERIMENT
JILL WILLIAMSON

J:3:3

(CHAPTER ONE)

Martyr stared at the equation on the whiteboard and set his pencil down. He didn't feel like practicing math today. What did math matter when his expiration date was so near?

His wrist still throbbed from Fido's teeth. Martyr touched the strip of fabric he'd ripped from his bedsheet and tied around his wrist to stop the bleeding. He hoped the wound would heal before a doctor noticed it. A trip upstairs to mend it would be unpleasant, as the doctor would likely use the opportunity to perform tests. Martyr shuddered.

To distract himself, he glanced at the other boys. Every Jason in the classroom except Speedy and Hummer scribbled down the numbers from the whiteboard. Speedy sketched Dr. Max's profile, staring at the doctor with intense concentration. His hand darted over the paper, shading the dark face with a short, black beard.

Hummer—as always—hummed and rocked back and forth, hugging himself. Martyr never understood why the doctors made Hummer take classes instead of putting him in with the brokens. Perhaps it had to do with Hummer's being so much older than the other brokens, or the fact that he could walk and didn't need special medications.

Movement at the back of the room caught Martyr's attention, and he twisted around to get a better look. Dr. Kane stood outside the locked door, looking in through the square window. A stranger wearing glasses stood beside him, much shorter and a little rounder than Dr. Kane. The man's head was also shaven like Martyr's, but the way he carried himself next to Dr. Kane showed he was nothing like a clone. Martyr's pulse increased. There hadn't been a new doctor on the Farm in a long time.

Dr. Kane opened the door, and both men stepped inside. Martyr gasped. The new doctor wore color! A narrow strip of fabric ran from his neck to his waist. Martyr jumped up from his desk and headed for the stranger.

"J:3:3!" Dr. Max's tone slowed Martyr's steps. "One mark. Take your seat immediately."

Yes, but one mark was not so bad. Martyr quickened his pace. *If I could just touch the strip once ...*

Dr. Kane shooed the new doctor back into the hallway, pulling the door closed behind him. Desperate, and knowing the door would lock once it closed all the way, Martyr stepped into the shrinking exit. The door slammed against his bare foot, and a sharp pain shot through his ankle. He winced and wedged his torso into the crack.

He was met by Dr. Kane's hand pressing against his chest. "J:3:3, return to your seat this instant. Two marks."

But the color on the new doctor was too tempting.

Something indescribable stirred inside Martyr. "He has color,

Dr. Kane." He tried to remember the word—like carrots, like the caps on the doctors' needles, like the slide. "It's orange!"

Martyr pushed the rest of his body through the doorway, and Dr. Kane moved with him, keeping his imposing form between Martyr and the new doctor—the same way Martyr did when a Jason picked on Baby or another broken.

Chair legs scraped against the floor, and the Section Five math class rushed from their seats. With a quick glance that seemed to hint more marks were coming, Dr. Kane reached around Martyr and yanked the door shut before any other Jason could escape, leaving Martyr in the hall with the doctors.

Identical faces filled the square window, but Martyr could barely hear the Jasons inside. The silence in the hallway seemed to heighten the severity of Martyr's actions. He glanced from Dr. Kane's stern expression to the new doctor, to the strip of orange color.

The man stepped back, face pale, eyes wide and slightly magnified through his thick glasses. He clutched the orange fabric with both hands as if trying to hide it. "Wh-What does he want?"

Dr. Kane rubbed the back of his neck and sighed. "It's my fault, Dr. Goyer. It's been so long since I hired someone. Years ago we stopped allowing any adornments below level one. They were a danger to the doctor wearing them. Plus, the boys don't encounter much color down here. It causes problems, as you can see." Dr. Kane turned to Martyr with a tight smile. "J:3:3 is harmless, though."

Dr. Kane's casual tone emboldened Martyr to carry out his plan. He reached out for the orange color, exhaling a shaky breath when the doctor allowed him to touch the fabric. It was smooth, softer than his clothes or his sheets or the towels in the shower room. A napkin, perhaps? Maybe it hung there so the doctor could wipe his mouth after eating. "What's it for?"

The new doctor tugged the orange fabric from Martyr's grip. "It's a tie."

"Enough questions, J:3:3," Dr. Kane said.

Martyr cocked his head to the side. "A napkin tie?"

"Three marks, J:3:3. Back against the wall, or it'll be four," Dr. Kane's deep voice warned.

Martyr inched back and glanced down the hallway. Rolo jogged toward them, clutching his stick at his side, his large body bouncing with every step. Johnson, the other day guard, loped along behind.

Martyr fell to the ground and immediately wrapped himself into a ball, covering his head with his arms. His curiosity had gotten him in trouble again. Three marks meant three hours of lab time. All to touch the orange napkin tie.

It had been worth it.

"What's he doing?" the man named Dr. Goyer asked.

Rolo and Johnson's footsteps on the concrete floor drowned out Dr. Kane's answer.

Rolo jabbed the stick between Martyr's ribs. "What's up, Martyr?" Another jab. Rolo liked when the Jasons fought back. "Getting into mischief again?"

Johnson's familiar crushing grip pried Martyr's arm away from his face, despite Martyr's efforts to keep it there.

Rolo stopped poking long enough to whack Martyr on the head, sending a throbbing ache through his skull. "Get up, boy."

Martyr complied as best he could with the stick still poking his side. He hoped the stinger wouldn't engage.

Rolo grabbed Martyr's other arm, and Martyr bit back a groan as the guards dragged him up and pushed him against the wall.

Rolo slid his stick under Martyr's chin and pressed up, forcing Martyr to look at him. "See, now? We're not so awful, are we?" Rolo's eyes were clear and cold. Martyr knew it was best to nod.

Johnson smirked at Martyr over Rolo's shoulder. Johnson had thick brown hair, a bushy brown beard, and a mustache. The boys were not allowed beards or mustaches or hair. They visited the groomers once a week to be shaved—to keep from looking like Johnson.

"These are our day guards," Dr. Kane said. "Robert Lohan, known as Rolo to the boys, and Dale Johnson. Men, this is Dr. Goyer. He'll be starting next week."

"Was it necessary to strike him?" Dr. Goyer asked Rolo. "He wasn't being violent."

Martyr looked from Dr. Kane to Rolo, then to Rolo's stick. Rolo always used his stick. Most of the time it wasn't necessary.

Rolo snorted, like Dr. Max sometimes did when one of the boys asked an ignorant question. He tightened his grip on Martyr's wrists.

"The guards know how to keep the boys in order," Dr. Kane said. "I don't question their methods."

"But why sticks?" Dr. Goyer asked. "Why not something more effective? A taser?"

"We use tasers if things get too far." Johnson bent down and snagged up Martyr's pant leg, revealing the stinger ring on his ankle. "They're remote controlled, and each has its own code. Lee, up in surveillance can turn each one on manually or in a group. If the boys gang up on us and manage to swipe our weapons, the tasers knock 'em flat in a hurry."

Dr. Kane put his hand on Martyr's shoulder and squeezed. "But J:3:3 doesn't cause those kinds of problems. He sometimes gets a little excited, that's all. Take him up to Dr. Goyer's office, Robert." He turned to Dr. Goyer. "This will give you a chance to try our marks procedure and get to know one of our subjects."

Martyr eyed Dr. Goyer. Would the new doctor be angry that he had touched the orange napkin tie? Would the marks be miserably painful?

"What do I do with him?" Dr. Goyer asked.

The guards pushed Martyr toward the elevator, and he struggled to look over his shoulder at the new doctor.

Dr. Kane's answer made Martyr shiver. "Whatever you want."

Martyr lay strapped to the exam table in Dr. Goyer's office, which he'd discovered was the third door on the right. He twisted his head to the side and squinted. The lab-like office rooms were always so bright. The lights buzzed overhead and the smell of clean made him sick to his stomach, reminding him of the hundreds of times he had lain on a table in such a room while a doctor poked and prodded. All the labs looked the same: a desk for the doctor, an exam table, and a long counter stretching along one wall with cupboards above and below. It had been five years since Martyr had been in this particular lab, though. He would never forget the last time.

The third door on the right had belonged to *her*. To Dr. Woman.

Many years had passed since the incident. Martyr was certain Dr. Kane would never allow another woman to enter the Farm because of what had happened, and the thought made him feel lonely. Dr. Woman had been kinder than any other doctor.

But it had gone bad.

Martyr blamed himself.

The door opened and Dr. Goyer entered. The light glinted off the man's head as he looked down at a chart, and Martyr wondered why this doctor had to see the groomers when the other doctors were allowed to grow hair.

Dr. Goyer jumped back a step when he saw Martyr on the table and put a hand to his chest, but then moved about the lab as if he hadn't seen Martyr at all. Martyr waited and watched Dr. Goyer file some papers, wipe down his counter, and sit at his desk. He was no longer wearing the orange napkin tie, only a white coat over a white shirt and black pants. Martyr frowned. Dr. Goyer would probably never wear the orange napkin tie again.

He hoped Dr. Goyer wouldn't use pain today. Occasionally he got lucky with his marks and only needed to answer questions or try new foods. Dr. Goyer hadn't carried in a steamy sack full of food, though.

Dr. Goyer suddenly spoke. "What am I supposed to do with you?"

Martyr met the doctor's eyes. They were brown, like the eyes of every Jason on the Farm. Martyr knew the color brown well. "What do you *want* to do?"

The doctor rubbed a hand over his head. "I don't know ... I

don't know. They gave me a list of starter questions, but you've probably had all those by now."

Martyr had answered them often. "What's your number? Do you have a nickname? What's your purpose?"

Dr. Goyer smiled. "That's right. Can we just … talk?"

Martyr relaxed. Talking would likely be painless. "Yes, we can."

"Do you like living here?"

The question confused Martyr. Where else would he live? "What do you mean?"

"Do you enjoy it? Do you find it fun?"

"Some days."

"What makes a good day?"

"No marks. No fights. Food with color. Being with Baby. Especially a day where no one is trying to hurt Baby."

"Is Baby your friend?"

Martyr nodded. "He needs me."

"Why?"

"Baby is a Broken, so a lot of Jasons pick on him."

"Broken."

"Yeah, you know. Something went wrong when he was made. He's small and doesn't speak. The doctors think he's ignorant and can't learn, but they just don't know his language. He talks with his hands, so I'm the only one who understands him."

"Why did the guard call you Martyr?"

"It's my nickname. I got it because I help Baby and the other brokens."

Dr. Goyer paused for a second. "Tell me about a time you helped one of them."

Dealing with bullies wasn't Martyr's favorite thing to talk about, but it was better than being poked with needles. He didn't want the doctor to change his mind, so Martyr answered quickly. "A few days ago, Iron Man and Fido attacked Baby, and I called Johnson to stop them. Fido found me later and was angry."

"What happened?"

Martyr saw no harm in pointing out the wound since he was

already in a lab. He jerked his head to the strip of bedsheet tied around his wrist. "Rolo was close by, so Fido only bit me."

Dr. Goyer stood and walked toward the exam table. "And that's why they call him Fido?"

"Fido is a dog's name." Martyr knew this because Rolo said it almost every time he spoke to Fido. "Rolo says that Fido acts like a dog."

"Have you ever seen a dog?" Dr. Goyer released the strap holding Martyr's wrist to the table, loosened the sheet, and inspected the bite marks. Then he went to his counter and opened a cupboard.

"Only pictures we're shown in class. Have you seen a real one?" Martyr had heard dogs were small and hairy and drooled a lot. Sometimes Hummer drooled, but no one called him a dog. Baby drooled a lot when he cried, but no one called him a dog either. Apparently Fido's dog-ness was due to something else, because he certainly wasn't small or hairy.

Dr. Goyer closed the cupboard. "I've seen lots of dogs."

Martyr's eyes flickered around the lab while he waited. A thick, black coat was draped over the back of Dr. Goyer's chair. "You can go outside?"

"Of course." Dr. Goyer stepped back to Martyr's side and rubbed cool alcohol on his wrist.

It stung and Martyr stiffened. "You take the antidote?"

Dr. Goyer paused and looked away. His throat bobbed. "I, um … yes."

Martyr blew out a long breath. He couldn't even imagine what it must be like in the outside world. "I know I'll never see things like dogs, but someone has to stay underground so people and dogs can exist." Sometimes, the knowledge of his purpose was the only thing that made the Farm bearable. "You took off your napkin tie. Will you wear it again?"

"It's a necktie, not a napkin tie, and I'm not allowed to wear it. I'm sorry I broke the rules today. It was a mistake."

"I'm glad you did. Orange is very rare on the Farm. So is red. Red is my favorite. Where did you get the … necktie?"

Dr. Goyer peeled a bandage and stuck it to Martyr's wrist. "My daughter gave it to me for Christmas."

A tingle traveled down Martyr's arms. Daughter was woman. He lifted his head off the table. "You have a woman?"

Dr. Goyer's eyebrows crinkled over his eyes. "My daughter. She's seventeen."

"What does she look like?"

Dr. Goyer reached into his back pocket. He unfolded black fabric and showed Martyr a colored picture. The doctors sometimes showed them pictures, but never in color. Martyr had never seen so many colors in one place. He stared at the face and exhaled a long breath. The daughter had orange hair! And it was long, past her shoulders, and very curly, like spiral pasta. His eyes were the color of peas.

"He is very colorful." Martyr's eyes did not leave the picture when he asked, "What are the colors of peas?"

"Green."

Martyr stared at the daughter's eyes. "His eyes are green."

"Her eyes."

Martyr glanced at Dr. Goyer. "Her?"

"Women's belongings are *hers* instead of *his*. They're called *she* instead of *he*. Personal pronouns are gender specific."

Goose pimples broke out over Martyr's arms. This was why Dr. Woman had been called *Her*. Martyr wished he could remember more about Dr. Woman, but it had been so long ago, and he had been so young. "I would like to see a woman."

Dr. Goyer's eyebrows crinkled together again. He put the picture back into the black fabric and tucked it into his pocket.

"What's that you keep the picture in?"

"A wallet. It holds my money and credit cards, my driver's license."

Martyr shook his head slightly, confused by the strange terms. None of the other doctors ever showed him things like this. He wished he could see the picture again—wished he had his *own* picture—but Dr. Goyer had seemed upset when he put his wallet back into his pocket. Martyr hoped Dr. Goyer wouldn't stop showing him fascinating things in the future.

As the silence stretched on, Martyr tried to think of something to say so Dr. Goyer wouldn't get bored and decide to use needles. "What is Christmas?"

Dr. Goyer leaned against the wall by the door and folded his arms. "It's a holiday. You don't celebrate Christmas here?"

"What's *celebrate*?"

"Celebrate is ... being happy together." Dr. Goyer straightened and looked into Martyr's eyes. "What do the other doctors do when you have marks?"

Martyr swallowed, torn over how to answer. If he didn't tell Dr. Goyer the truth, the other doctors would, and Dr. Goyer would know Martyr had lied. Lying always made things worse. "Mostly they use needles to test the contents of different vials. Medicines for outside, I think. Sometimes the vials cause pain, sometimes they make us sleep. Other times the doctors put sticky wires on our bodies that buzz our insides. And occasionally they just ask questions."

"What kind of questions do they ask?"

"Questions about pain. Questions about math and science. Questions about Iron Man and Fido, or Rolo and Johnson."

"Who is Iron Man?"

"The doctors call him J:3:1. He's the oldest who is still living, which makes him the leader. But many of us choose not to follow him. He's cruel. He's cruel to Baby."

Dr. Goyer walked to his chair and sat down, glancing over the papers on his desk. He picked one up and read from it. "What's the most important rule here?"

It was the standard list of questions. "Obey the doctors."

"What is your purpose?"

Martyr swallowed and closed his eyes. "My purpose is to expire. To be a sacrifice for those who live outside." Martyr opened his eyes and met Dr. Goyer's. "Like you."

Dr. Goyer folded his arms and stared at his lap.

Did the doctor want a longer answer? "I expire in twenty-five days, when I turn eighteen. Then my purpose will be fulfilled."

Dr. Goyer looked up. "Does that scare you?"

No one had ever asked if he were scared. "I don't want to expire."

"Because you want to live?"

"Yes, but not for myself. I'm content to sacrifice my life to save thousands from the toxic air. But if I'm gone, who will take care of Baby? And if Baby doesn't live until he's eighteen, he'll fail to serve his purpose. That wouldn't be fair."

"It's important to you to serve your purpose?"

"It's why I'm alive."

Dr. Goyer rubbed his mouth with his hand. "Can I answer any questions for you, Martyr?"

Martyr thought about the orange necktie and the picture of the daughter. "How do you celebrate Christmas?"

"You give gifts to those you love."

Dr. Max had explained gifts once, when they talked about being nice to others. But the other word was new. "What is love?"

Dr. Goyer ran a hand over his head again. "Uh … it's when you have kind feelings for someone."

Dr. Goyer had been kind. He had given enjoyable marks and mended Martyr's wrist with no lecture. "Will you give me a gift?"

"Maybe someday."

"An orange necktie?"

Dr. Goyer pursed his lips as if fighting a smile. "Probably not."